AINGE

Don Jones
2175 Radcliffe Dr.
Westlake Ohio
44145

AINGE

Orson Scott Card

Photo Credits

World Wide Photos:
front cover

Mark A Philbrick, Brigham Young University:
back cover and interior shots

Family portrait courtesy of the Ainge family.

Orion is a division of Signature Books

ISBN 0-941214-02-8
Library of Congress Catalog Card No. 82-80316
Printed in the United States of America

To Bill, Russ, and Ar—
in memory of
a thousand games

Contents

1

Making Things Happen

The NCAA Basketball Tournament in 1981, Notre Dame vs. Brigham Young. With star player Kelly Tripucka, the Fighting Irish were expected to win fairly easily against a western school that, after all, only had to compete in the Conference. If there was anything unusual about the game, it was the head-to-head conflict between Catholic and Mormon universities, and that, of course, had nothing to do with the game. Oh, yes—Brigham Young University also had Danny Ainge, a pretty good guard from Eugene, Oregon, who had an NCAA record or two and had got a bit of press attention earlier in the tournament. Some sports writers and broadcasters were quite excited about him, and looked forward to seeing him play. He might add some vigor to an otherwise routine Notre Dame victory.

The game didn't go quite that way. The BYU team was a fair match for the Irish, and when it came down to the last twenty seconds, BYU was ahead by a single point. But Notre Dame had the ball, and the TV-watching Notre Dame fans (who sometimes seem to outnumber the population of Japan) knew that, as so many times before, Notre Dame would make the miracle play and the gallant Cougars would go home, comforted in their defeat because at least they had held their own against the Irish.

The ball came in, the Irish efficiently got it to Kelly Tripucka, and on a beautiful outside jump shot Notre Dame won the game.

Well, it was as good as over—there were only a few seconds on the clock and the basketball court might as well be a mile long for all the BYU players were going to be able to do against the Irish defense. BYU's only hope was to give the ball to Danny Ainge, and hope that he got fouled. Certainly he couldn't hope to actually make a field goal, not with the Notre Dame players keyed to him the way they certainly would be. He'd take the ball downcourt, and when he saw they weren't going to foul him, he'd give the ball to somebody else to make a hopeless shot. If there was time.

As expected, the Cougars got the ball to Ainge, and down the court he went. Around one player, and another, and another, threading his way through the Irish players, who were being *careful* not to foul him—Danny Ainge was 82 percent from the line. They were so careful, in fact, and Danny was so dazzling in his manipulation of the ball, that he was right under the basket sooner than anyone could have imagined, and instead of trying to make a tricky outside jumper he laid the ball gently up to the hoop and Kelly Tripucka's miracle finish was out-miracled.

Sure, the Irish put up a desperation shot at the buzzer from somewhere in Kansas, but that would have been one miracle too many. The game ended on Danny Ainge's spectacular play, and it was Ainge that the fans remembered when they went home or turned off their sets.

In South Bend, Indiana, the Notre Dame student body had lots of time to think about the game. The Irish had been too cautious with a one-point lead—they should have defensed Ainge better. This player or that coach had failed to do this or that. But a few fans knew the truth. It wasn't the Irish who gave the game away—it was Danny Ainge who took it from them. A teacher assigned an English class to write an essay on what person in the world they would assassinate, if they were to assassinate someone. The Ayatollah Khomeini was the top choice in those days, of course—but Danny Ainge picked up a few heartfelt nominations, too.

All-American on every team; the darling of Provo, Utah, and every other town where there were enough Mormons to strike up a conversation; the hero of all the fans who hate Notre Dame (and *they* sometimes seem to outnumber the population of China)—if Ainge wasn't one of the first five players taken in the NBA draft, it would be proof positive that the NBA was out of its collective mind.

Or else proof that their lawyers could read a contract. Because the summer before, Danny Ainge, miracle-finish basketball player, had signed a three-year contract to play baseball with the Toronto Blue Jays.

Danny Ainge was not a basketball player. He was a *player*, and basketball was just one of his games. As he came out of high school, he was recruited most heavily in football, where his height and speed and skill and team play made him stand out even more than in basketball, where Danny Ainge was, after all, kind of little. And the summer before his freshman year, he was picked up by the Blue Jays as a hot prospect for his skill and his hustle. A few years in the minors and he'd be a top outfielder or infielder or, well, anything they decided to have him play.

In those days, Danny's favorite sport was whatever sport he was playing at the moment. When the football recruiters came to town, Danny was playing basketball. Besides, it was crazy to play football in college. One bad hit and you could have a bad knee for the rest of your life, or a weak shoulder. The risk of injury was too great. Basketball was a much more sensible choice than football.

And baseball—well, it was the most sensible choice of all. Serious, career-ruining injuries were almost unheard of, and a lot more players played a lot more years and made a lot more money in baseball than in any other sport. If you're making a career choice, baseball was the most sensible choice of all.

Besides, the guys from the Blue Jays came around while Danny was playing baseball, and so it was his favorite sport.

It happened again the summer before Ainge's senior year. He had been playing basketball in the winter and baseball in the summer, but the seasons overlapped enough that he had consistently missed out on spring training. Even so, he was doing well enough for the Syracuse farm team that the Blue Jays had called him up to Toronto, and now he was in the majors. He wasn't hitting brilliantly—in the low .200s—but everyone knew that would change when he didn't have basketball distracting him during the off season.

Basketball—that was what worried the Blue Jays. Danny was too good at basketball. If the Blue Jays were going to be sure of having Ainge play with them, they had to get him locked up before the NBA draft. Before Danny was even *thinking* about the NBA draft.

So they offered him a contract with a generous guaranteed salary and a bonus of $300,000 for not playing basketball. It was a warm and friendly contract—numbers like that make any contract warm and friendly—and Danny didn't need a lawyer to tell him that it was a good deal. Here he was, still in college, and already getting the kind of contract you only hope will come your way on the free agent market after years of professional play. Baseball was the most sensible choice an athlete could make, if he had enough ability in different sports to *give* him a choice. He wasn't a great baseball player yet, but he had never had spring training, and it was obvious that the Blue Jays thought he had the ability. Danny knew he had the ability to make a good pro baseball player. And so he signed.

Then he went to BYU and began his senior year. Playing with his best friends, playing the game that he played for love, not for money. Setting national collegiate records every time he scored more than ten points in a game. And he realized that by signing his name on the last page of that baseball contract he had made a mistake. Baseball was so *sensible*. But when it came right down to it, basketball was Danny Ainge's best game.

And not just because he was playing it at the time. Basketball is the perfect game for a player like Danny Ainge. Not baseball. Baseball requires a patient player who can stand just standing around waiting for the ball to come his way, staying alert and inert for hours on end. Baseball requires a player who relishes the duel with the pitcher, who has an eye for the little white bullet and a heart that believes that succeeding a quarter of the time is good.

Basketball, on the other hand, hardly stops for a moment. No endless interludes on third base waiting for the ball. The ball can come at any moment, *does* come every few seconds, and when you don't have the basketball you are allowed to go and get it if you can. And the teams work differently. There's none of this duel between pitcher and batter. You face a whole team, but a small team. Five men working as one against you. And you yourself are not an individual. You are five people, and as you get your rhythm going during the game, you become one whole, one shape, one pattern moving along the floor, weaving through the other team.

Danny Ainge is a basketball player. In the long run, he could not have been exclusively anything else, not for years on end, not happily. Basketball requires the kind of play that he was born and raised for—relentless in pace, requiring and rewarding individual brilliance, and yet giving Danny the most important thing of all: a team that can, for the time he is on the floor, become himself. When Danny is off the floor, if you ask him who he is, he'll point to the six-foot four-and-a-half- inch man in front of you. But on the court, Danny Ainge becomes five men moving together. He is not a would-be star, aching to get the ball so he can do his individual stunt and stand out from his team. All through his life as a player he has naturally done what all players are supposed to do but few ever can: he has sensed the shape of the game, the way the teams fit together, and he has acted for the benefit of the team as a whole. If another teammate is hot that game, he'll find Danny hitting him with the ball time after time, until the other team catches on and the shape of the game changes again. If there's a weak link in the other team, Danny will exploit it. If Danny isn't shooting well in a game, instead of panicking and shooting desperately—or refusing to shoot at all—he concentrates on getting the ball away from the other team, getting the ball to the players who are shooting, and methodically taking his own best shots as he normally would.

During basketball season in Eugene, Oregon, where high school sports are taken very seriously, a reader wrote in to complain. "Why do you always print pictures of one of those Ainge boys? How many Ainges *are* there? Doesn't anybody else play basketball in this city?" The photographer had never thought of it that way. "I just follow the ball and take pictures when things get exciting. I can't help it if there's always an Ainge where the ball is."

Sports writers who have watched Danny play have often commented on the way he seems to direct traffic on the court. He has been called an on-floor coach. This is not because he's always telling his teammates what to do. It is because, through many games together, they have learned that Danny not only sees what he's looking at, but also sees what he isn't looking at. Like a video-game wizard who can keep track of all the asteroids coming at him at once, Danny has that inborn ability that is part of what we try to measure with the IQ test: the ability to conceive the whole of something and respond to it well.

He is an on-court coach, not because he likes telling other people what to do, but because other players know that they can trust him to act, not for his own good, not for their individual good, but for the good of the team. Not that he does it consciously. Not that the other players are particularly aware that that's what is going on when they play. Because of who he is, because of his abilities, because of his nearly perfect sense of the shapes that people make in the game, and above all because what he does *works*, he can easily become the heart and mind of a good team, if the game allows it. Baseball doesn't allow it. Football does. Basketball requires it, and so basketball is Danny Ainge's game.

Daniel Ray Ainge was born 17 March 1959. When he played his first professional basketball game with the Boston Celtics he was twenty-two years old. He hasn't lived enough life yet for anyone to write a biography of him. Who knows what his life will be? He may be a brilliant pro basketball player, and he may not. Even if he is one of the all-time great players—which is possible—he'll still be a young man with most of his life ahead of him when his athletic career is finished. Anyone who thinks that Ainge will then sit back and be a former star player for the rest of his life doesn't know Danny Ainge. There are other games besides athletic ones, and Danny will choose one that he can love playing and he will do well at it, because he is that kind of player. It will be a long time before anyone can write the story of Danny Ainge's life.

At best, then, this whole book is Chapter One: the story of how a serious-faced little boy grew up into Danny Ainge, the story of how a child became a player. The story of why life is played out in games for Danny Ainge, and why games have become the structure of his life.

For he does live as he plays: by the rules, playing fair, doing his part and expecting others to do theirs. Oh, he'll argue a bad call with the referee, but he counts on the ref to keep things fair. When he realized during his senior year at BYU that his baseball contract had been a mistake, he took no action at all. He had signed his name to a contract, and he would live by it. Those were the rules. It would only be three years. At the end of that time, if he kept in practice, he could still try to make it in the NBA.

The basketball season ended. Danny went to Toronto and began to play baseball. Once again he started without spring training, without the winter practicing in which a batter tries a hundred variations in his stance, in his swing. The regular season is not the time to be learning new approaches to the game—by then your new, improved stance ought to be second nature.

Danny had faced such obstacles before, of course, in his previous baseball seasons, and he had done well enough to have been offered that contract in the first place. But this year was different. This year he saw baseball, not as a summer of getting paid for playing a game he loved, but as the first of three years of drudgery. He had read the fine print in his contract now, had read it and understood what it really meant. Now that the last season of college play was over for him, Danny's contract forbade him to play basketball at all. Not in any organized game, not even in a pick-up game at the YMCA. He had signed his name to a paper that forbade him to play with any team at all. He was cut off from what he knew and loved best.

It had to affect his baseball playing. Not consciously, of course. Ainge was not the sort of player who would deliberately slack off. In fact, the more unhappy he became, the harder he played, the more he concentrated. But he wasn't concentrating on baseball—he was concentrating on concentrating, which is something else entirely. He didn't come to the batter's box with the same genuine love of the contest that he had always had before. He saw his low batting average flashed on the scoreboard and then watched it get worse over the season, game after game. In a way, he knew that the sometimes cruel things being said about him by sportswriters and fans who love to cut down a big-money athlete were not true, that it wasn't ability that he lacked. He knew that with a good winter's practice he would improve markedly, that next season would be much better. But that didn't help him love what he was doing. And no matter how serious he is about a game, no matter how determined he is to do well, if a player doesn't love the game, he is never going to do his best.

So the fans watched him do what a player can *consciously* do, and he did it well. If the ball came anywhere near him, he was there for it. He made a few mistakes as a third baseman, but they were the kind of mistakes that new players can't help but make—by and large, he was a good third baseman, and he never stopped trying. Even after the legal squabbles began, Danny would throw himself into the fence chasing a foul ball, would stretch himself out to snare a ball hit or thrown just out of his reach. He never stopped trying until the end of his baseball career.

By the end, both he and the Blue Jays knew the truth.

Despite his considerable talent for the game, Danny Ainge would never be a baseball player now. He had made his real choice without meaning to. All those papers with lists of "pro" and "con" meant nothing. Baseball had everything going for it, except Danny's heart. And the fans and the coaches and the owners and Danny himself could see that the things a player does *un*consciously, Danny was not doing well. The instant judgments the batter has to make to hit the ball, the infinitesimal adjustments—in spite of his best intentions, he was not making them. When the other players came back from their season-splitting strike, Danny thought he was coming with them—but in spite of himself, the best of himself was still on strike. Danny Ainge could do almost anything, in almost any sport, but one thing he could not do was play brilliantly when he didn't really care.

The Boston Celtics didn't help. They expended a second-round draft choice on him, even though the Blue Jays had sent letters to all the NBA teams, informing them of the terms of Danny's contract and warning that they'd be in court if they tried to get him to play basketball.

The Blue Jays themselves didn't help. The team had a knack for losing games that they could have and should have won, and when a team is perennially in the cellar it takes its toll. If Danny had been with a team that believed in and trusted each other, a team he could have happily become a part of, he might have found he liked baseball better after all. But instead there were silent and not-so-silent recriminations throughout the team, as players fought back against their self-doubt by doubting each other. It wasn't fun to play with the Toronto Blue Jays in 1981.

Sportswriters weren't much help. Danny Ainge was so *good* at basketball—why was he wasting his time playing baseball? Look at his batting average—ridiculous, the lowest in the league! Danny paid no attention to the writers—he knew they were filling up columns, that they had no idea of what he could do if, just once, he had a decent preparation for a baseball season. Yet even though he didn't believe them, the writers were there, putting into words his worst fears. In some ways, sportswriters have more power than even they suppose. For good or ill, they determine the way that most fans receive the game. The sportscasters' patter during the games, the writers' accounts after the games—those are the stories that the fans hear, that the players themselves hear. To one degree or another, though the writers don't determine what *happens* in the games, they do determine what most people will think that it *means.* And they wrote, again and again, with amazingly shallow reasoning, that the events of the 1981 season were somehow "proving" that Danny Ainge couldn't play pro baseball.

He told a *Sports Illustrated* writer, "I've failed at things before. I think I've failed at baseball the last three years. I've set goals for myself, and I haven't come close to them. If I keep failing for a certain period of time, I'll definitely try something else. Basketball? Probably."* That was before the baseball season began, before he was drafted by the Celtics. By early June, unhappy and frustrated, Danny went to the Blue Jays' management and told them that he wanted out. He'd be glad to pay back the $300,000 bonus he had been given for not playing basketball. He could have done it, too—almost all of his income as a ballplayer has been invested, and by liquidating the investments he could have raised the cash. "You have to do what you have to do," he was told. "No contract could make a man do what he doesn't want to do." To Danny, that sounded like permission. To the Blue Jays, it was the beginning of a battle.

The question decided in court was whether or not the Blue Jays had let Danny out of his contract. Of course they hadn't—the courts will always prefer a written document over spoken words, especially when the words could be interpreted to mean almost anything.

The real question, however, was whether the Celtics would come up with the Blue Jays' million-dollar ransom before the

*"The Courting of Danny Ainge," *Sports Illustrated* (19 October 1981) p. 72. All the quotations in this paragraph are from that article.

Blue Jays decided to let Danny go for less. It was a classic businessman's battle between stinginess and greed, and that was a game with few rules and no sportsmanship, and Danny Ainge couldn't play it.

Feeling he had been lied to by the Blue Jays, knowing that his future as a professional ballplayer was no longer in his control, Danny went home to Provo, Utah, and began coaching the BYU junior varsity team. Some of the luster of professional sports was gone forever now, for Danny. The people who made the decisions for the pro teams weren't players, not in the sense that Danny Ainge was a player; or if they were, he certainly didn't like their game. It was all a matter of waiting, anyway. When the Blue Jays realized that Danny would never play for them again, no matter what, they'd no doubt come down in price—better to make a profit on the deal than to wind up without a player *and* without their money.

In the meantime, Danny would do just fine. In a way, he was just following in his family's pattern. His father and his older brothers had promising athletic careers that were cut off for reasons that were really out of their control. And they were good, happy people. He would do well in his life even without professional sports—that was part of what it meant to be an Ainge.

I met Danny Ainge and most of his family during those weeks when the Celtics and Blue Jays were haggling over the price of his future. And I realized that however they juggled the money, the transaction was not what they might have thought. For no matter how much they paid him, Danny Ainge would always be an amateur, playing for love of the game. He'd take whatever money they'd give, of course, and husband it carefully to provide for his family. But he wasn't playing for money; he wasn't playing for fame or for glory; he wasn't playing for the record books or to please his family or friends or teammates; he certainly wasn't playing because he didn't know how to do anything else.

Danny Ainge plays because he *is* a player. He still plays like a nine-year-old child, for the delight of the game itself. He strives to win, not because he cannot bear defeat, but because the game is only fun if you play it seriously. And even though the Celtics, who finally bought him from the Blue Jays, are now paying him a bit more than minimum wage, the truth is that the most valuable thing they are giving Danny Ainge is a court and a team and a game. And in return they won't get Danny Ainge the Shooter, or Danny Ainge the Ball Handler—they've got Danny Ainge the Player.

How will Danny Ainge work out in Boston? That is impossible to say. He has a lot of talent, but so do many other players, and as Danny is quite aware, he may turn out to be only an average guard in pro basketball. He isn't the only college star ever to reach the pros, and no college player is so good that he is guaranteed success in the National Basketball Association. I suspect that a team will get the best that Danny Ainge has to offer only when they realize that you don't "play" Danny Ainge like a piece in a game of chess. He is never a piece in someone else's game. He is a *player*, and when he feels like the team is himself and the game is his own, he is a fair match for any master.

2

The Littlest Ainge

Whenever the ten- or eleven-year-old boys in that neighborhood got up a football game, Doug Ainge was one of the team captains. And Doug's first choice for his team was always his little brother Dave, one year younger but a match for any of the other kids. That Ainge combination was always hard to beat, so his opponents were glad when one day Doug wasted one of his last choices on his skinny little second-grade brother, Danny. If Doug Ainge wants to cripple his team by putting a seven-year-old on it, let him.

The game got underway, and when Doug's team got possession he sent little Danny out as a receiver. After all, that's the best way to keep a little kid from getting hurt by the bigger boys. The other team didn't even bother to defend against him.

After a few plays, Doug dropped back and passed. The ball didn't go to Dave. It didn't go to any other fifth- or sixth- grader. It went to little Danny, who caught the ball perfectly and took it into the end zone all alone.

From then on Danny had a defender assigned to him. It might be embarrassing for a ten-year-old to have to cover a seven-year- old, but the kid was *good.* Put your hand in his face and he catches the ball anyway. If he gets one clear look at an overthrown ball he'll run under it and catch it over his shoulder without looking back again, his arms outstretched for the ball, his feet never breaking stride, just the way they do it in the pros. Underthrow him, and he'll run back and get it. And if you hit him right after he catches the ball, he hangs right on. Seven years old. Takes all the fun out of the game when you can't beat a *seven-year-old.*

Danny Ainge was his brothers' secret weapon for a while, but after a few games it wasn't a secret anymore. People were used to the Ainge boys being the best in the neighborhood, but Danny was a prodigy. Well, why shouldn't he be? From the time he was old enough to move under his own power, his brothers competed with him like an equal. He was little, he was skinny, but they didn't hold back. If he needed tackling in a football game on the beach or in the back yard, his brothers tackled him. If he was shooting at the basket, his brothers would use every inch of their height to block him, every inch of their reach to try and steal the ball. Whatever the sport, his brothers demanded that he play with them as an equal. And so he did.

They adored him. When he was small his brothers would dress him up in his parents' clothes. He would clomp around the house in high heeled shoes, looking so serious that the rest of the family laughed until they cried. Doug and Dave taught him everything they knew, included him in family games, and taught him what it meant to be an Ainge. Ainges might not always win, but they always played well, and when they lost they made no excuses. So what if Danny was smaller than his brothers? He just had to work harder at it if he was going to win. He had to scramble better, handle the ball better, get around his brothers so he could get a clear shot at the basket. He had to make heroic catches in football, because if the ball was thrown right at his chest it would be in easy reach of the defender. If his legs were short, he just had to run all the faster to get to first base before the ball.

If the pressure had been too much for Danny, if he had always failed and begun to hate the game, his parents would have changed the rules and made sure he had a break. As it was, whenever they had a family contest in things like footracing or basket shooting, Danny and his little sister Laurie would always get the benefit of a little strategic handicapping. But even when Danny played with his brothers, without any allowances for his size, he held his own.

At first, when he was just learning, his brothers beat him every time. Yet not by *that* much. If he couldn't score against them as often as he'd like, he could still score sometimes. If they kept him down for most of a game, they couldn't keep him down for all of it.

It wasn't long before he was a legitimate competitor. And anybody who could compete with Doug or Dave Ainge was going to be one of the best players in that age group in town. That was to be expected. Their father, Don Ainge, coached a kids' team for the Eugene Boys Athletic Association in practically every sport, and his teams were always winners. He wasn't one of those win-at-any-cost coaches, though. He met with the parents of the team members at the beginning of every season and told them, "The game lasts twenty minutes. Every kid on the team will play at least five minutes in each game. No kid on the team will play more than eighteen minutes in a game. All the kids will be part of the team, and when we win, all the kids will be part of the win."

Within those limits, Don Ainge put together teams that usually won. If his own boy played more than most of the other kids, no one could complain, because his own boy always was obviously one of the best players on the team. Partly—or mostly—because of the Ainge boys, the teams won. And all the kids knew they had played on a winning team.

In a way, the Eugene Boys Athletic Association was a farm club system for North Eugene High School. North Eugene coach

Barney would meet with the coaches of the junior high and grade school boys, and teach them how to teach the basics of the game to their teams. Barney did demonstrations for the young boys, showing them how easy basketball really was. "Look," he'd say, "you don't have to beat the ball to dribble it. It bounces back up to meet your hand." He'd show them that the hoop wasn't as little as it looked—you could put two balls through it at the same time.

Don Ainge put his teams—and his sons—through exercises of his own. He'd make them wear goggles with pieces of paper fastened under them so they couldn't see the ground—then he'd make them practice dribbling the ball. They soon got adept at dribbling well without watching the ball.

He had his teams practice scrimmaging without the ball. When no one had a ball, the kids couldn't stand around waiting for the ball to come to them. They learned to move *without* the ball, to get into position and maneuver for advantage constantly.

All his team members benefited from the training Don Ainge gave them, but his sons also inherited his natural athletic ability, and so they were able to use that training to the best advantage. By the time they got to junior high they had habits that most high school seniors don't yet have. When Doug or Dave or Danny went up for a rebound, he already knew where he was going to throw the ball when he got it; it was second nature for all three of them to fire off quick outlet passes before their feet hit the ground from a rebound. That isn't the kind of thing you can think about. You just have to do it, and Don Ainge's kids did it. He didn't work with them on shooting until they had made a lot of progress in the other areas. Shooting is the easiest thing, he believed—it's the unspectacular things that decided who got and kept the ball in order to make those shots.

These skills weren't beaten into the boys or frightened into them, though. Don Ainge was dealing with children, and he knew that if a kid stopped having fun, he'd stop playing. So everything became a game, even drills and practices. And when his own sons got so good at the game that other boys became discouraged, Don had a way of handling that, too. Danny was getting twenty points a game in only fifteen minutes of play—and this was in a league and an age group where the other teams were likely to get sixteen points total. If all the kids had to look at after a game was scoring, they'd begin to wonder why anybody but Danny even bothered to play. So Don kept statistics on everything. Passing. Rebounding. Guarding. Sometimes he'd even make up some of the stats. "You didn't score any points, but I saw you set two of the greatest screens I ever saw." And the kid would put his heart into setting screens, because he was good at it, because he knew that the winningest coach in the Eugene Boys Athletic Association had *noticed* that he was good at it. The game was still fun.

Don's sons inherited his talent and he taught them how to play, but that was only a part of what they learned from him. Sports were not just something they did during games and practices. The game was at the center of their lives. From the time that Doug and Dave were little, they were attending their father's amateur games. More than once, a game couldn't resume after halftime or a time-out because Don's sons were out on the court trying to dribble or shoot. "Ainge, will you get your kids back in their seats so we can *play*?"

Games were the way the Ainge boys related with other people. The Ainges had the "neighborhood basket," with a lighted playing area so the games could go on after dark. The kids would be out there, day after day, playing even in the rain. As Danny grew up, almost all his associations with other people were through games and sports. It was only natural. A good team requires its members to depend on each other as closely as the best of friends, so that they feel like one person. The team members often became his closest friends. And if Danny wasn't practicing or playing with the team, he'd be playing some other game, and he always wanted to play with someone who was good at it. He picked up new games and sports too quickly—someone who was clumsy at it just wouldn't be able to keep up.

One reason why games became the basis for the boys' outside friendships was that games were at the heart of almost everything they did at home. Everything became a game, and every game had to have a winner. They'd play games to pass the time in the car on long trips, play games to occupy their time in the house. In order to keep the kids relatively still, Don and his wife, Kay, would sometimes get them to play "I Spy," in which a parent hid something in plain sight and the kids had to remain seated on the couch and spot it just by looking. This was a game that Laurie, the youngest, would usually win, because the boys spent most of their time trying to catch each other cheating. "You stood up!" "I did not!" Their father sometimes hid the object where they couldn't possibly see it—it kept them in their chairs longer, and sometimes there was no other way to get them calmed down after a day's activity.

There was a time when Dave and Danny could never finish a one-on-one basketball game. They'd get close to the end of the game and one would accuse the other of fouling or stepping out of bounds and the other would deny it. It would become a heated argument and one of them would storm off the court. Their parents remember that they "quickly forgot" these quarrels, and in the sense that by the next day they would be back outside playing again, it was true. But in another sense, they both remembered those battles and probably always will. They were the outward shape of the rivalry that naturally grows up between brothers; they merely played it out in the game, and so kept it under control.

Outsiders saw the three Ainge boys as being very much the same. They were all good athletes, weren't they? They all looked alike. They all seemed to play alike. Their names even sounded alike.

But the boys were not the same. If outsiders couldn't see the difference, the brothers saw the differences all too well. Some of the differences were athletic. It became plain to them all fairly early that Dave was not as skillful an athlete as his older brother, Doug. He didn't have the same eye-hand coordination. But the story that they told themselves about this difference between them was that while Doug had natural ability, Dave had hustle. Dave would go into games and make things happen, while Doug simply finessed his opponents to death. It was a way for the boys to cope with the difference between them, and still feel equal. And, like so many of the stories we tell ourselves, it became true. Dave still hustles, still makes things happen. Those who play occasionally with Dave know that even today in an unrefereed game it's impossible to convince Dave that he committed a foul; you may become intimately acquainted with his elbows, but Dave *will* get the ball.

Yet the differences cannot be named and dismissed so easily. Doug grew up in his father's shadow; Dave grew up in Doug's. With the curious ambivalence of childhood, the younger in each pair was both drawn to and resentful of the older. When Doug first started getting written about in the Eugene papers, the sportswriters remembered his father well, not just as a boys' team coach, but also as a high school and amateur league player. Doug resented always being called Don Ainge's son. He wasn't Don Ainge's son, he was *Doug Ainge.* And yet he relentlessly pursued his father's athletic achievements and matched and surpassed them.

Dave, in turn, followed his older brother. Only a year apart in age, they were inseparable through their early childhood. Inevitably, however, when Doug reached his teens he wanted to play with older boys. He was getting taller. He could play in what he saw as "real" games rather than kid games. But if older guys were going to take him seriously and let him play, he certainly couldn't have his little brother along. Dave was deeply hurt when Doug suddenly started telling him to leave him alone, to stop tagging along.

One time he looked out the window and saw Doug in a fight with one of his friends, and not getting the best of it, either. Dave charged outside and plunged right in. Dave was often a better fighter than Doug—his grim determination to ignore his own pain while slaughtering his opponent made him formidable. But instead of Doug being grateful that Dave was saving him, Doug turned around and joined his friend in beating up Dave. Dave couldn't even fight then. The betrayal broke his heart.

Dave understands now, of course—it was Doug's best friend, and if Doug's little brother had beaten him up, that would have been the end of the friendship. Dave didn't understand then, however. He felt that his older brother no longer thought that he was any good. If his brother didn't think he was good enough to play with anymore, Dave didn't have the confidence in himself to disagree.

Both Doug and Dave had strong forces pulling them toward athletics; both also had strong reasons to reject the game. Doug's high school teams had a way of getting into the playoffs as a favored team, and then losing in the clutch. It would be absurd to blame this on Doug—he consciously did his best whenever he played. But it is not meaningless to note that when Doug got into major college basketball, he stayed only four months. Not because he wasn't good enough—He went on to be a top NAIA small-college player. To an outsider, it looked as though Doug wanted to cut down on the pressure of the game. Perhaps it is only coincidence, but Doug lasted almost exactly as long in career-oriented sports as his father had.

Dave, of all the Ainge boys, had the most cause to give up competitive sports. He had a strong interest in nonathletic things. From earliest childhood, he was the curious one, turning over rocks, searching for arrowheads, simply wandering around, observing. His mother noticed it, wanted to encourage this tendency in him, but hadn't the strength to overcome the other influences in the family.

Dave was also hampered by his relative lack of eye-hand coordination. With Don Ainge's forthright coaching style, Dave knew from fairly early in his athletic career that he was not as coordinated as his brothers. There was no point in denying it—he could see it for himself. With the finely tuned exercises the boys were going through, even subtle differences in ability were bound to show up, and Dave had clear evidence that he couldn't do many things as well as Doug. He could not shoot or catch as accurately, was never as sure to be on the mark as his brother.

Only later did his parents realize a possible reason for this.

When Danny came along, they noticed a curious thing about him. He ate and wrote left-handed, but shot at the basket from a right-handed stance, pitched and batted right-handed, threw the football right-handed. He could dribble equally well with either hand. He has been called ambidextrous, but it is more correct to say that for some tasks he is right-handed, for some he is left-handed, and for some he can use either hand equally well. It caused him problems sometimes—in fifth and sixth grades, he had to wear a string on one finger because he had a tendency in football games to call left and go right. But much of Danny's extraordinary athletic ability may be due to this right-left crossover. Many of the best hitters in baseball have been discovered to be right-handed and left-eyed; some athletic tasks reward a player who has unusual but useful physical arrangements.

Only after seeing this crossover in Danny did the Ainges realize that Dave also had the same crossover, only in reverse. Dave ate and wrote *right-handed*, but his natural stance as he was learning to golf was left-handed. When he was learning basketball and football and baseball, however, years earlier, he had consistently adopted a right-handed pattern, which, if he was like Danny, only reversed, would have been wrong for him. This might go a long way toward explaining his seeming lack of eye-hand coordination.

This is not to say that he was not as good an athlete as his brothers—simply that his abilities were not the ones that were most likely to make him a star in team sports. Dave's strongest ability was one that did not require team play: he was a runner. The first time a school coach put Dave in a race, he started out sprinting. Dave's father laughed a little—he'd never last the whole race, not at that level. But Dave finished as he had begun, with the next kid four hundred yards behind. At the age of twelve, Dave was running the mile in 4:59; in eighth grade he ran the half-mile in just over two minutes. It looked as though track was an area of competition where Dave would surpass everyone in his family.

Yet in ninth grade Dave gave up running competitively. It was boring. He was too alone. Here was a boy who loved solitude, and running was too solitary for him.

With his natural curiosity, his interest in nature, his need sometimes for solitude, and his seeming deficiencies in team sports, why didn't Dave take a different course from his older and younger brothers? He had ample personal reasons to go his own way. His parents tried to encourage him in these other activities. We cannot even point to the influence of his athlete father and say that David was trying to become like his Dad. The old saw, "Like father, like son"—or, translated into more fashionable terms, the idea that a child cannot resist a powerful role model—cannot explain it all. Dave's father was an athlete, but he was not *just* an athlete, as we will see later. In fact, it has been possible for all of Don Ainge's sons to grow up very much like him without being all that much like each other—Don Ainge never intended his children to center their lives wholly in athletics, and in some ways was a little disappointed when they did.

Why, then, did Dave stay so closely bound to team sports? Part of the answer is his brother Doug. Doug never thought of himself as a natural leader—as far as he knew, he was just one of the gang. It did not occur to him that when he and his friends—or he and his brother—went to do something, the others were following him. If he had been conscious of his power over others, he might have controlled it, used it better. Instead, he assumed that the others were always acting for the same reason he acted—because they wanted to. It is the dilemma of all human beings: the only person whose intentions we ever really know is ourself, and if others never tell us otherwise, we haven't a chance in the world of finding out what they really think they want.

For years Kay Ainge remembers that her son Dave was spanked repeatedly for one particular prank—opening a loaf of bread, eating the center out of the whole loaf, and then closing up the bread again so that only when Kay went to make sandwiches or toast would she discover that there wasn't a whole slice of bread from crust to crust. Why didn't Dave learn to stop doing something that inevitably got him in trouble? At last she got the answer when she happened to overhear what was going on in the kitchen: Doug was putting Dave up to doing it. In fact, they were doing it together. And yet as many times as Dave was punished, he never even hinted that Doug was involved in the prank at all.

Doug, with his powerful personality, always sure of what he wanted to do, had a perfect disciple in his little brother Dave. It was not Doug's fault, by any means. There were many times he wished his little brother wouldn't always hang around and try to do everything he did. Doug was busy trying to live up to the impossible standard his father had set for him, unaware that his little brother was trying to match him stride for stride—and failing where Doug succeeded.

That is why Dave could not pursue track. Of course he could do better at track than Doug—but Doug was not interested in track, did not care about running. If it didn't matter to Doug, it couldn't matter to Dave. If Dave was ever going to be worth anything in Doug's eyes, he was going to have to excel in the sports where Doug excelled.

Dave's adoration of Doug went further. No one ever compelled Dave to shoot right-handed instead of left. But Dave was not just learning to shoot a basketball: he was learning to do what Doug did, and what Doug did was take a right-handed stance. Doug threw right-handed, and so Dave learned to throw the same way. It was never a conscious choice. Dave just hated being different from Doug. He had inherited his mother's skin coloring—she and Dave both tanned easily, turned nut-brown in summer. The others, like their father, were more likely to burn and keep a fair complexion. The rest of the world might glorify the Coppertone tan, but not Dave. He hated being different from his brother, wished for the same painfully light skin. It was the consistent pattern of Dave's childhood.

Except for a few incidents. Dave detested hand-me-downs. He listened to his parents' explanations that they couldn't afford to buy new pants for Dave when there were perfectly good trousers with lots of wear left in them. Dave listened, took the pants—but instead of wearing them, he buried them in the back yard. His parents got the message—Dave was not going to wear clothes that Doug had worn.

And Dave found that following behind Doug meant competing with *himself*. Doug did not enjoy writing poetry. When he had to write some poems for an English class, he despaired of writing anything that was worth turning in. But he knew his brother Dave was already a frequent and talented poet. What one Ainge had done belonged to all Ainges, didn't it? So Doug liberated some poems from Dave's drawer, copied them over, and turned them in. He got an *A* in the class. The next year, Dave had the same teacher—and turned in some of the same poems. Gravely the teacher called him in and informed him that she knew that he had copied from his brother's poetry. The point, she said, was for him to do his *own* work. It took a bit of investigation before matters were straightened out. Dave forgave his brother, however. He could forgive Doug anything; but no one in the family can forget anything.

When Dave got to college, he was not a scholarship athlete. Oh, he had been recruited by a few schools, but he never once considered going anywhere but BYU. After all, his brother Doug had gone to BYU to play basketball. Doug had played in twelve games as a freshman. So Dave, unrecruited, would also go there and try out for the team.

He almost made it, too. If Ainges are anything, they are honest with themselves about their own limitations. When any of them does badly, he knows it, and says so. Dave did not do badly in his tryout for the BYU basketball team. He played well, perhaps better than some who made it onto the team. Why wasn't he picked? There are several possible reasons, the most obvious one being that he was Doug Ainge's little brother. Doug Ainge had played for BYU as a freshman the year before, but during the season he had been given the choice between resigning from the team and being dropped from it. It was for an infraction that at any other school would have resulted in a short suspension from the team—but BYU was a Mormon school, and in the early seventies it was more insecure about its students' reputation for perfect rectitude. Doug Ainge had caused problems for the team, they remembered, and now here was his little brother. It was no doubt easier to notice weaknesses in Dave's play, knowing that he was Doug Ainge's brother. And Dave admits, freely, that there were always weaknesses in his play.

When he was rejected by the team that first year, Dave might have gone back and tried again the next. He was a good player, and he knew as he watched the games that with his speed, his hustle, he could do things for a lackluster team. But he did not go back and try again. He did not believe he'd ever make it. He lacked the confidence in himself. Also, there was that perfect symmetry: Doug had come to BYU, had played his best, and then had been forced from the team in circumstances that were at best a bit less than fair. Dave had now done the same. Dave had followed his brother's pattern, and it was complete, at least in the major outline.

There were some satisfactions for Dave. Doug had had a brilliant high school sports career. His basketball team had gone to the state championships repeatedly, and never did better than third. Dave had only one year of high school play without having Doug ahead of him on the team. And in that year, though the team was admittedly less talented, they took state. Dave had not done a bad job of following in his brother's footsteps.

Dave was always interested in other things besides the game. He remembers feeling through his childhood that he was never so single-minded about athletics as Danny and Doug seemed to be. Yet he did not follow his own inclinations—he followed theirs. Dave couldn't find any other way to be a real Ainge except in the game. Ainges play; Ainges win; when I do not play and do not win, I am not an Ainge. If these words had ever been spoken aloud, Don and Kay would have taken immediate steps to change their family patterns, for neither of them wanted the children to feel that the game was necessary for them to belong, to be loved. But the words were never spoken because they never needed to be said: to Dave, at least, it was simply the way of the world. To belong to a family, you play the same games. Didn't he hear outsiders say it almost from the start? Those Ainges, they're super athletes, all of them. So Doug and Dave were both caught up in patterns that did not satisfy them, patterns which they eventually bent to fit the man each really is.

Danny's situation was different. He was told from the beginning that he was something special. "You have Doug's natural ability, and you have Dave's hustle," his father told him. "Watch both your brothers and learn from them." An attitude that might have begun as consolation or encouragement to an undersized kid with big ears and a too-serious expression turned into prophecy. Danny became the compleat Ainge. Where the other boys found an end to their playing, Danny could not. All the other Ainges—Don, Doug, and Dave—had come close, but finally missed the mark. Danny would not. After a brilliant high school career, he would have a brilliant college career. After that, the pros. Danny is the fulfilment of all his family's dreams.

He did not begin as a competitor. Kay Ainge remembers that her three sons were very different as toddlers. Doug was always social, insisted on staying with his parents, with other people. Dave would go off by himself, spend hours alone. Danny, on the other hand, never really had much choice—his brothers wouldn't leave him alone if he wanted to be. They played with him as if he were the best toy they had ever been given; they loved him, were like little fathers to him. But this also meant that Danny never had much choice about whether he would be with other people or not. With his family, he was always onstage, always expected to perform. He performed brilliantly and loved how they loved him for it. But he also learned to be reticent. His mother doesn't remember him ever crying in public. He was always an inward person, unwilling to tell his feelings. Telling feelings didn't accomplish much anyway. It was almost always better to let time pass to heal a hurt, or to joke and smooth it over. Talking about problems just wasn't Danny's way with his family.

Still, Kay remembers that little Danny would sometimes come to her, needing a quiet time away from the constant, frantic, competitive play of his brothers. He would crawl up on her lap and just sit there and wordlessly cuddle with her. Or maybe it wasn't his own need he was answering—maybe he sensed that Kay needed a son who would need her that way, maybe he knew that she sometimes felt lost among a houseful of manly boys. Danny was a genius at discovering what people needed and giving it to them. It is one reason why you could search and search among the people who know Danny at all well without finding one who feels anything but love for him. Without planning it, from infancy on he gave to each person who touched him what that person needed most. Danny was born to satisfy everyone's dreams.

As anyone would expect, there were teammates who resented Danny Ainge. It's hard for a guy who knows he has talent to practice and practice and come out on the floor and give it his best shot, only to have Danny Ainge come along and do it three times better, and with ten times the style, all without seeming to try. Danny could sense it, too, when a teammate felt bad toward him, just as Danny could sense weaknesses in the team during a game and work to fill holes that other people never even knew were there. A jealous player is not a good player—a team with enemies on it is no team at all. So Danny would make a conscious effort to win that player's trust, to help him understand that just because Danny played well didn't mean that other players were not valuable.

Danny did not take such players aside and talk to them, of course. As always, he spoke symbolically within the game. It means nothing to say, "We need you and trust you on this team." It means everything, though, when the star player repeatedly passes you the ball, silently insisting that *you* take the risk of putting up a shot. In his career there are hundreds, thousands of shots that Danny Ainge might have taken, might have made—but instead he passed the ball off to someone else, because the pleasure of the game was in the teamwork.

It is no coincidence that BYU's basketball team was never overwhelmingly Danny Ainge. Ainge was high-scorer in more than half the games they played, but usually three or four other players were also in double figures. Other teams soon found, to their dismay, that shutting down Danny Ainge did not shut down BYU's offense. The other players were used to getting the ball and shooting; they didn't panic when Ainge wasn't getting his points. But there was never any question in their minds about the fact that Danny was at the heart of the team's success. The scoring stats were almost meaningless. Danny had a way of knowing who was open before he got open, a way of knowing where the ball needed to be in two seconds and getting it there. He was the best player on his team and knew it; he was expected to be the gunner, firing off the shots and racking up the points. But that wouldn't have been fun, to do just *that*. Being a solo player was not his style. He would drive to the basket so someone else's man would pick him up. Danny would let *him* get the basket, even when he could have forced the shot himself. Danny didn't give the ball to the other players just to be nice—he gave it to them because that's where the ball ought to be for the points to be made, for the game to be won, for the game to be *fun*. There were times when he knew he should shoot more himself in order to be sure of winning—but winning really wasn't everything.

Danny Ainge plays for fun. He was never at his best when he was playing intensely. Instead of concentrating on an upcoming game, he'd go out and play eighteen holes of golf. When he was a freshman at BYU, the team had a quiet room where they would go and relax before the game. It just wasn't Danny's style to lie there trying to relax while getting more and more intense about the struggle ahead. Instead of lying there he'd start pillow fights. He'd watch TV. He started having fun, enjoying himself. "They all thought I was crazy at first," he remembers, "but then they did it, too."

In a way, though, his love for other people pulled him away from his family. The more he became the emblem of the Ainge family, the less he was a member of the family. They loved each other intensely—that was never in question—but Danny was getting all the pleasure in his life from the people he played with.

He was rarely home once he got into school sports. He went to church with his family—his high school coach learned to schedule practices around Mormon meeting schedules—but much of the rest of Sunday would be spent with the team. When he relaxed, he relaxed at another sport. Besides his teammates, he had tennis friends and water-skiing friends. He talked to other people, but always within the framework of a game. It was the structure of his life, getting ready for a game, playing a game, thinking about the game just past. And as his brothers went off to college, there he was at home with a father increasingly into church work, a mother who did not participate in sports, and a sister who just wasn't involved in games the same way as her brothers. His family watched excitedly everything that Danny did; they encouraged him, they praised him, they adored him. They helped him all they could. But as the years went by, they knew him less and less. They were not participants in the most powerful events of his life. That made them, too, outsiders.

No one felt this more keenly than Laurie, who was in some ways an outsider in her own family almost from birth. They included her in everything—in their family football games she hiked the ball; she raced with them; she even got a good start on her own athletic career, though a minor injury kept her out of girls' basketball in high school. But girls simply did not play on the same teams as boys. She was not to be coached by Coach Barney. She would never have a pro career in a team sport.

So she watched her brothers, worshipping them as they excelled, but discovering as years went by that, while Danny was the compleat Ainge, she was in some ways not an Ainge at all. Again, if she had said anything about it there would have been changes made in the way the family did things. But she said nothing. She accepted her role as idolater of her brothers, as family cheerleader.

And then married a man as unlike her brothers as she could possibly find. David Fletcher is a bafflement to the Ainge boys, or was at first. They knew him in high school; they even *liked* him. But he was not a friend, particularly, because he wasn't into team sports. He's an English major in college, for heaven's sake, and takes it seriously.

Yet he does play—but a different sort of game, one that does not have to have a loser in order to have a winner. Laurie's mother was visiting with them not long after their wedding, and while they were both out of the house she did some routine cleaning up—clearing the table, doing dishes, that sort of thing. During the clean-up she found a leaf on the table. She threw it out, of course.

Then Laurie's new husband came home. After a few minutes David came into the kitchen and sheepishly asked Kay, "Did you, uh, see a leaf on the table?" She told him where it was. He fished it out of the garbage. When Laurie got home he walked up to her, handed her the leaf, and said, "Boy got Girl a leaf." Kay watched in delight as Boy and Girl danced around the table, celebrating; but she suspected that Laurie's brothers wouldn't understand.

Her brothers loved her and cared about her, and she was devoted to them. Doug and Dave were hard on Danny because they loved him; because they loved Laurie, they were usually gentle with her. This was back in the days when the word *sexism* was yet uncoined, and little boys had less to feel guilty about if they didn't pick their sister for their teams. Laurie learned to be realistic at an early age. Her brothers were going to have the limelight; she could come along if she liked. She would always be included, but never be the star. Her mother was actually a little relieved when the baseball strike ended in the summer of 1981 just before Laurie's wedding. It meant that Danny wouldn't be able to come to the wedding, which disappointed Laurie and Danny both; but it also meant that none of the guests at Laurie's wedding would give more attention to Danny than to the bride and groom. For one day Laurie was *the* Ainge.

Yet Laurie never complained. It was the only family situation that she knew. She grew up on the fringes of the main activity; it did not occur to her that she should be anywhere else.

In fact, the family pattern of athletics was never chosen by anyone. Don and Kay didn't get married in order to produce a family of super athletes. It just happened. Each child, in turn, saw everyone else as the reason why the game was at the center of family life. Each child was sure that he or she was just going along with what the others wanted. Doug and Danny had no way of knowing that Dave and Laurie would really rather be doing something else. Dave and Laurie didn't say anything. And so it never occurred to anyone to change.

Why should they have changed, anyway? On the whole, they were all happy. Whatever its drawbacks, having athletics as the center of family life provided the Ainges with something that too many families never find: stability, rules, roles that each could fulfil. From the first moments of life, each of the Ainges knew what it meant to be an Ainge, and what it meant to be this particular Ainge. They all learned precisely what things they did alike; and, sometimes openly, sometimes secretly, they all knew what things made them different from the rest of the family, what things made them not really an Ainge at all. That's the problem with all names. They don't just tell what a person is. They also tell what a person is not.

3

The Game of Survival

Don Ainge's father, Everett Charles Ainge, was a professional gambler. Gambling was legal in those days in Venice and Ocean Park, California. Don's father was pretty good at it. He even had a chance to go to Reno for Harrah's, to supervise some of the gambling there. Don spent much of his childhood at race tracks. He loved the excitement of the race. He didn't see anything bad about it—it was what his dad did, and his dad was great. Don also saw his father play professional golf, and knew that he had been a good athlete in school.

He loved his father and his mother, Kathleen Rankin Ainge. Sure, he knew there were problems, but then his parents had always had problems. He figured that was just the way things were with grown-ups. It took him completely by surprise when they got divorced.

Don was thirteen. His brother, Ray, was ten. The divorce was not exactly cheerful. The boys were forced at first to choose between their parents. Later, however, things changed. It was the parents who decided which of them had to put up with the boys. Don remembers staying with one parent until he got into too much trouble, then getting sent to the other until he got into trouble there. Both Don and Ray were on their way to serious problems, when Don's mother remarried and the new stepfather moved them to Oregon.

In Eugene, Don got involved in high school athletics. He had been an athlete in California, too, but here it was better. He really stood out; the local papers made much of him; perhaps most important, he did not have to notice anymore that his father never, never came to watch him play. Don was no longer a troublemaker. When his mom and stepfather moved back to California, Don stayed in Eugene for his senior year of high school, living with the families of two friends, the Rasors and the Hills.

Don worked at Wyatt's tires and pumped gas to support himself, but it was on the teams that he really came alive. He played passionately, and the local fans responded in kind. They loved Don Ainge so much that when his sons came along a generation later, they still remembered him.

He had just broken up with a girl named Tish, when one of his friends pointed to a pretty girl who had just moved to Eugene. "Hey, Don, that girl looks like Tish!" the friend shouted.

"She's better-looking than Tish," said Don. He had said it—then he thought about it and decided to ask her out. He called the next night at eight-thirty. Kay Ballantyne was in bed.

"What's wrong, is she sick?"

But no, she always went to bed early. The next day she looked for Don. "You called last night?"

He asked her to a dance. She already had a date. She didn't realize that Don didn't take things like that very seriously when he liked a girl. She went to the dance with her date—but Don Ainge took her home afterward. They got married too young, they both realized later, but at the time it seemed silly to wait. Don had been on his own for a year already, and eighteen and seventeen seemed old enough for anything.

Kay was feeling rebellious, too. She had not wanted to move to Eugene. She never said anything about it, though. If her mother had known that Kay didn't want to move, she would have been deeply hurt. Eva was so hopeful about her new husband. Kay couldn't bear the thought of worrying her. Yet her anger at being moved against her will showed in other ways. At first she skipped school fairly often. And then she got married, the ultimate refusal of parental authority. She didn't marry foolishly—Don was far readier for marriage than the average eighteen-year-old—but the marriage wasn't wise, either. She had not yet learned that her mother's way of being a wife was not the only way.

She finished high school, but then children started coming. Don made a start at the University of Oregon, but when athletics didn't work out, he didn't stick around. He had to support a family.

Kay was a perfect wife, as perfect wives were viewed then. She was loyal and supportive, and focused her entire life around Don's interests. If she didn't like the way things were going, she just kept still about it. She had learned long ago that that's what a good woman does.

Her father, Douglas Ballantyne, was dying all her life—Kay can't remember a time before he knew that his illness, Hodgkin's disease, was terminal. But he lingered for years, and because he was disabled and knew his life was nearly over, he drank. It wasn't like drinking with the boys after a day at the mill in Bend, Oregon. He was a pretty serious alcoholic.

All through those hard years, Kay watched her mother. Eva Rollins Ballantyne worked every day at Pacific Power and Light in Bend. Then she came home to Prineville and did all the housework, and helped her husband endure the end of his life for years before it ended—and through it all, Eva never complained. Never so much as got a little angry, at least so far as Kay noticed. If Kay learned one lesson from her mother, that was it: a good woman, a heroic woman, is one who never bemoans her fate. She struggles, she survives. That was the only rule of the game.

Her mother remarried and her stepfather took them to Eugene. When Kay met Don Ainge, she was attracted to him at once. After all, he was all-state in three sports and popular with everybody in school. And despite the fact that they married so young, despite the hard times they've been through, she has never regretted choosing him. She knew what marriage meant—total, perfect commitment to a man, regardless of sickness or health, kindness or anger, security or poverty.

Their first home together was a strange little apartment above a general store. Their sleeping rooms were across the hall from their living room and kitchen—a hall shared by the other six rental units. From there they moved to a small vacation trailer owned by the parents of one of Don's teammates in high school football, baseball, and basketball, Norm Willoughby. By the time Doug was born, they were living in a rental apartment in Kay's parents' house. But Kay complained about none of this. She had nothing to complain about, she knew—her mother had endured far worse than strange living quarters.

They had high hopes that first year. Don was going to the University of Oregon on an athletic scholarship. They had recruited him to play basketball, and that's all he wanted to play—football was too dangerous, careers could be wiped out in a moment, and such moments happened to player after player every season. Because he was a local boy, however, the basketball coach felt safe in giving his limited number of scholarships to other boys. Don was given his scholarship by the football program. As Don understood it, he would be listed as a football player, but he would play basketball. That was fine with him. He didn't care what it said on the paper, as long as he got to play.

That first term he was with the basketball team, practicing, getting ready for the upcoming season, when he got the word that the football coach was angry. If he didn't get out to practice *now*, he was out of a scholarship.

Football practice? In vain Don reminded people of the promises that had been made to him. In answer they just pointed to their rosters. Don was getting a free education as a football player. No football, no free education.

So Don played football, and within weeks he was out with an injured knee. It wasn't just a week-or-two-and-you-play-again injury. It was the end of his serious athletic career. He had a year left on his scholarship, but he had lost heart for college. He quit school and went to work as a meat cutter.

He hadn't exactly dreamed all his life of being a meat cutter. Just as he had gone to college in order to play ball, so he cut meat in order to play for the McKay's Market team in the Amateur Athletic Union games. He had knee enough for that, and he distinguished himself as a player. In the meantime, cutting meat paid the bills as Doug and Dave came along. Basketball helped, too—the AAU was semi-pro ball, and McKay's Market paid him $75 a week for playing.

Without either Don or Kay planning it, ball games were determining the shape of their life together. Don didn't think of himself as nothing but an athlete—he knew that he had a lot of other interests. He wrote poetry, he read books, he was interested in other people. But ever since sports pulled him out of the morass of his teenage years, he had learned that he could win respect as a player. Not just the respect of other people, but self-respect, too. He enjoyed playing.

Kay might have pulled him away from his intense athletic interest then, and given her family a different life. She didn't understand her own strength in her home. She was like an anchor for Don. He would go out and play, then come home to a stable center, where Kay had things under control, going smoothly. He could work a full-time job, play a heavy athletic schedule, and his family would still function, still adore him. Kay never complained, never tried to tone down his interest in athletics. Don thought it was because she didn't mind. After all, she had been a gymnast in high school, she loved sports, why should she mind that her athletic husband kept his hand in?

And she didn't really mind that much at first. The children were hers, after all, in those early years. Doug and Dave toddled around one rental house after another, romping with their father when he was there, but the rest of the time living life pretty much as she shaped it.

Only as the boys grew older did she realize that things were getting out of hand. They were always going to some game or another. All Doug and Dave wanted to do was play. And as Danny came along, he fell into the same pattern. With the demands of housework, the tensions of an uncomplaining life, Kay began to be less and less involved in the games the children played with their father. She began to get out of condition physically. She became a watcher on the sidelines as her family swept along through the seasons of the year—football season, basketball season, baseball season. After all, they had little money to spare, and it was a good thing the boys loved sports so much—a membership in the local recreation center used up their meager entertainment budget, but the kids never minded.

Where Don's frenetic schedule had once taken him away from the family and left the boys to her, now the boys went along with Don and kept a schedule even more frantic than his. Kay was delighted at how good a father he was, how his sons loved him. Don was the opposite of his own father in many ways. His children were the most important things in his life. He didn't manipulate them, he just enjoyed them, whatever they did. He went to every game they played, if he possibly could. He even began coaching boys' teams. All of this was wonderful—Kay knew that Don was the consistent father that neither Don nor Kay had had while growing up. But Kay also began to feel, just now and then, like a tag-along with her own family.

Then her headaches began. Began and did not relent for fifteen years. The doctors were baffled. After a few tests they decided that Kay's migraines must have a psychological cause. She was too tense. She had to lie down and rest. She had to take valium. Anything to relax.

That was when her life slipped out of her own control. The valium did almost nothing to relieve the headaches. The pain was so bad that sometimes she could only crawl to the bathroom and vomit, then struggle back to bed until she had to throw up again or until, blissfully, sleep brought her some relief. Housework was out of the question during these times. It was all she could do to keep meals on the table. Yet through it all she never explained to her children about the pain she was going through. A good mother simply didn't complain. Besides, even if she had tried, it is unlikely her healthy, active, dare-all sons would have understood a pain that didn't bleed or bruise, that didn't heal up in a few days.

She became adept at hiding her pain. As often as not, when she sat on the sidelines watching the rest of her family play she would rather have been taking part, but she was hiding an excruciating headache, and had to follow the doctors' advice and rest. But she couldn't say, "Mommy can't play because Mommy's head feels like it's getting ready to shrivel up into a raisin." Instead she said, "Oh, you go ahead and play, I'd rather watch."

Children are wise and perceptive. You can't hide everything from them. But you can hide some things from them. They saw that their mother didn't take part in family activities, that she let the house get messed up and just lay in the bedroom with the curtains drawn for hours and hours. Once she overheard one of her kids explaining to another, "Mom's just lazy." It hurt her deeply, but she responded even to this pain as heroically as her mother had done: she said nothing, she bore her suffering.

It was only after her children were all grown up, the youngest a teenager, when a doctor in California finally found the cause of her headaches. Kay had quit taking valium herself, despite the dependence the drug imposed. She had decided one day that the drug wasn't doing any good anyway, and it wiped her out too much for her to enjoy life. So she cut down her dosage gradually until she wasn't taking anything at all. It was a struggle, but she won it. Her sons don't get all their tenacity from their father.

Then a doctor examined her and informed her that she had problems with her spine. The nerves were getting pinched, causing agonizing headaches. Back in high school, when she was in gymnastics, her body in perfect shape, the muscles of her neck and spine had kept her spine in position, And now that was still the only real cure—exercise and activity. What about the rest and relaxation that had been prescribed for her for all those years, in order to reduce tension? Her headaches had nothing to do with tension at all. The cause was purely physical. If she had been athletic all those years, she wouldn't have had those headaches. And as for rest and relaxation—that was the worst possible thing she could have done.

Now the headaches are very nearly gone. But so are all the years when she sat on the sidelines and watched, all the years when her children saw her retire to the bedroom and leave the mother's place, as they saw it, empty. It certainly didn't cripple her children—they are all happy, good people. Besides, no one thing that a parent does will have an overwhelming effect on a child's life unless the child wants it to. But it is tempting to speculate on what the Ainge family might have been like if Mom had played right along with Dad, if Laurie had grown up seeing her mother as a participant instead of an onlooker. Kay's influence with all the children might have been stronger.

As it was, however, her influence was not negligible. Laurie, in her turn, had learned about uncomplaining endurance, though, unlike her mother, she has learned that there are times when a little complaint, a little open rebellion can stir things up and make them come out better in the end. The boys had fun with their Dad, tried as hard as they could to be like him. But home was Mom. Always there, she was the one steady thing in their ever-changing days.

22
12
40
EXIT

BRIGHAM
22
YOUNG

22
YOUNG

BRIGHAM
22
young

BRIG
44
YOUNG
22
YOUNG
5

BRIGHAM
22
YOUNG
34

4

The Whole Man

Wendell Rasor, one of Don's closest friends in high school, invited him one day to play basketball with his team. It was a church team. Wendy had joined the Mormon Church, and Don knew perfectly well that Mormons tried to baptize everybody who held still for more than fifteen minutes. The missionaries had already annoyed him a couple of times. So Don agreed to play—on the condition that nobody bugged him about becoming a Mormon. Fine, he was told—but he couldn't be eligible to play unless he attended at least two sacrament meetings a month. Don didn't mind that. He was willing to listen to sermons. He thought a lot about religious questions along with a lot of other things. So he started playing for the Mormon team and attending the Mormon meetings.

It wasn't long before Don got interested in what was going on at the meetings. He liked a lot of things about the Mormons. He liked the fact that the regular members of the church did most of the preaching. He liked the way that the church stressed family life, how important it was for parents to create a good, happy home for their children. Don knew how important it was—his own childhood had left scars enough that he had no trouble remembering the price children pay for their parents' misery. Without really planning it, Don slipped from curiosity to admiration, from admiration to belief.

A member of the ward (parish), John Riggs, began coming to his home to teach Don about the Mormon gospel. Don listened avidly. Kay, however, was not so easily won over. She wasn't playing basketball with the Mormons. She wasn't all that interested in what was going on. And she didn't believe their doctrine. Brother Riggs saw that, and didn't push. Let Don's wife get used to the idea. No point in forcing the issue and turning her against the church.

So the months went on, and Don got more and more actively involved with the Mormons. He noticed that while the guys at the market never talked about Don's family with him, the Mormons knew all his kids' names and remembered them. He got sick once, and the only friends who came to visit him were the Mormons. They really cared about him as an individual, more than most of his friends, even the ones he had known for years. Before long, Don thought of himself as a Mormon. The Mormons were his kind of people.

But he hadn't been baptized, which to Mormons is the essential sign of permanent commitment to the church. Kay, after all, wasn't convinced. It might have gone on that way for a long time, except that two young Mormon missionaries, barely twenty years old, found out that Don Ainge wasn't exactly a member yet. McClure and Meadows, the two "elders," came and talked to him on April 6, 1962.

"I understand you-all've taken the discussions," said McClure.

Don laughed. He knew that there were only six discussions in the Mormon system of teaching prospective Saints, and he had heard them all several times. "I guess I've had about twenty-two of them," he said.

"Well, why aren't you baptized?"

Don shrugged. "I guess nobody asked."

So the missionaries took him through a review of the discussions all over again, and at the end of an hour they put it to him point-blank. Do you believe in the gospel? Yes. Do you want to be a Mormon? Yes. Will you be baptized?

Kay knew her husband's answer before he gave it. Yes. Well, she thought, it's the duty of a wife to go along with her husband. She would endure this. At least the Mormons were against drinking.

"We're having a baptismal service tonight," they said. "Why wait?" They only bent the truth a little. The truth was, they were only having a baptismal service if Don got baptized.

The baptismal service went off on schedule.

A funny thing happened then. Don's non-Mormon friends had never mentioned religion to him—it was something they just didn't discuss. What difference did it make if a guy was Lutheran or Baptist or Methodist or uninterested? But apparently it made a difference if he was Mormon. His friends started telling him terrible things about the Mormons. They didn't realize they were already too late to save Don from the Saints. And the more they said against the church, the more Don realized that his Mormon friends were his best friends, and the Mormon way of life his way of life.

From that time forward, Don was as obsessed with Mormonism as he had been with athletics. That made him pretty much a normal Mormon—the church expects all its members to be "active." Being active means going to all the meetings—and there were hours and hours of meetings. It means doing volunteer church work that can sometimes be as demanding as a full-time job.

Don was hardly in the church when they put him in the Sunday school superintendency, helping manage an organization that taught two dozen weekly classes to every age group from three-year-olds to adults. Then he was made priests quorum adviser, teaching sixteen- and seventeen-year-old boys. He brought to all these assignments the same vigor and devotion that he had previously given only to sports and to his family. And as a result, he quickly rose within the Mormon lay hierarchy. After only a few years he was in a stake presidency, and after only a few more years he was a bishop, which is the most demanding position in the Mormon Church.

Gradually, as Don got more involved in Mormonism, Kay did too. Women are even more involved in the church, on the average, than men are, and as Kay supported her husband in his new obsession, she gradually found what he had found before her—that the Mormons were good people, good friends. And without particularly noticing when it happened, Kay found that she, too, was a believer. She didn't become a Mormon because she believed. She believed because she had become a Mormon.

It is difficult for non-Mormons to understand the powerful influence the church has on all its members, from infancy on. But it is impossible to understand the Ainges without realizing that almost from the start, Mormonism provided the only structure that competed with athletics for the family's hearts.

The children grew up attending Sunday school and sacrament meeting on Sundays, other meetings during the week, seminary classes before school every day during their high school years. They went to church dances, played on church teams when they weren't too tied up with school athletics. They gave short talks in church as soon as they were old enough to memorize; they were expected to compose their own sermons and deliver them to the entire congregation by the time they were in their teens. The church put on plays, and the kids acted in them.

At the age of twelve, Mormon boys are given the priesthood, and so Doug and Dave and Danny, each in turn, helped administer communion to the congregation, and visited members' homes as teachers or to collect offerings. They knew that as Mormons they didn't smoke or drink even when their friends did. It is almost impossible for a Mormon boy to forget for a single hour that he's a Latter-day Saint. There is always something that he must do, or that he can't do, to remind him.

Like most children, they undoubtedly got bored and restless at times, but they took part, and along with their understanding that being an Ainge meant being an athlete, they also learned that being an Ainge meant being a Mormon.

Danny's earliest memory is not of playing ball. His earliest memory is of the trip his family took to Salt Lake City to be "sealed," a rite in which worthy Mormon families bind themselves to each other as a family to continue even after death. He wasn't four years old yet, riding on the bus hundreds of miles with his parents and brothers and sister, but he doesn't remember the bus ride. What he remembers is the nursery in the Salt Lake Temple, where the little children were kept until the time came for them to be sealed to their parents. He remembers wearing the white clothing they gave him. He escaped from the room for some reason, and wandered through the forbidden corridors of the temple until he pushed open a big door that led to a large room filled with people. There were people kneeling around an altar. Only when he went to the temple as an adult did he understand that his earliest memory is of the most sacred rites of the temple.

His parents have another memory from that trip. They remember that on the bus, some comment was made about a certain young man who looked more like Danny than Danny's own father did. The same jug ears, the same cockeyed smile. Danny heard and understood more than they thought. When the bus stopped, Danny announced, "I want to go with my Daddy." Then he set off after this young man, who was quite innocently heading for the bus station restroom. Don and Kay followed him, embarrassed that he should suddenly decide that this stranger was really his father. Then, in front of the bus depot, Danny suddenly stopped and virtually fell apart laughing. It was all a joke. His parents remember this because it was another sign of how precocious Danny was. Perhaps they also remember it because it was disturbing. Even then, Danny knew that he could shake up his whole world just by changing the pattern here and there. He was in charge of his life from the beginning.

That's one of the things that is easy to forget, when we watch each of the Ainge children become so much like their parents, so much like each other. The family could determine what game each child would play, but each child, in turn, changed the rules of the game for the others. If they focused tightly on athletics, it was not because nothing else was available. They devoted themselves to games because they liked the games, because they got what they wanted most from the games—at least to a point.

But there were other things going on in the family from the start. Don Ainge had not majored in physical education during his short tenure as a student at the University of Oregon. His major was journalism. He wanted to be a writer. And even after it became plain that he would never get back to college, he refused to let himself become an aging basketball player who cut meat for a living. He insisted on being whatever he felt like being. He felt like being a Mormon, and soon he was an outstanding one. He decided to be a coach, and so he was the best coach in the boys league.

He also decided that he was through cutting meat. It was a good job, but when he was through with one side of beef, there was another; it never ended, there was no challenge. Don first began a freelance recording business on the side. He and a partner took recording equipment to high schools and junior highs and recorded the school choruses, then sold the records to the students and their parents. It meant huge chunks out of his already busy schedule as he drove miles and miles, getting home sometimes at one in the morning.

In the meantime, Don found that there was a market for his poetry and music. He had always written poems, ranging from clever doggerel to unusually moving verse. It was the kind of poetry that works best in the context of an existing relationship. If it is given to someone by the right person, it can be powerful, unforgettable; if it is handed to strangers, it can sound hackneyed or sentimental. Like most of the poetry of E.E. Cummings, it cannot create its own context. But Don already had a milieu at home: his wife and children loved what he wrote, and still do. To his surprise, however, when friends found out he wrote poetry they didn't sneer—they simply commissioned him to write poems for *them.* Love poems for their wives' birthdays or anniversaries, occasional verse for special events. Don got ten dollars a poem, which is above average for American poets.

Don also loved music, and wrote songs. Here again he found there was a market: Nalley's Corn Chips paid him a nice sum for a radio jingle, and other advertisers took advantage of his talents. But neither his poetry nor his music made enough money consistently enough that he could even dream of them as a full-time career. It was still the meat market, day after day.

Until a friend from the church let him know about a new insurance company that was starting up in the area. The company needed salesmen, not only to sell insurance policies but also to sell stock. Don and Kay looked at the family's financial situation. They were far from rich, but they had paid off all their bills and had money in the bank. Their kids were still young. If they were ever going to have a chance to make good money, to succeed financially, now was the time to do it. And not part time, not on weekends and at night. If Don was going to sell insurance, he was going to be an insurance salesman. He quit his job at the market and began selling stock.

Sales were slow and commissions were small. Don worked with his customary vigor. He believed in the company, believed in what he was selling, and believed in himself—but he was not making enough to break even. He found that he had to cut meat at night for some extra income. His recording business, Century Records, became more and more important—but he and his partner soon discovered that when it was going at top volume, the company only made enough to support one family, not two. And now the poems and jingles meant, not extra cash, but food on the table.

Savings ran out. Bills piled up. Neither Don nor Kay had grown up with money, but they hadn't grown up without any, either. Don had given selling insurance his best shot. He gave everything his best shot. Even though they had scarcely enough to get by, he still donated ten percent of everything he earned to the Mormon Church, as faithful Mormons all do. He and Kay would sometimes laugh—Don was his company's leading salesman. How was the number two guy staying alive?

The kids never knew the family was having hard times. Kay wasn't a complainer, of course, and Don never lost his excitement about life for a moment. So what if the kids never got to see a movie? They all had passes to the rec center for the summer, they all had friends and each other and balls and bats and a basketball hoop. They were having as much fun as anybody—more fun than most. Television was boring anyway. Like their father, the boys had no time in their lives for moping about what they didn't have. They didn't even notice that they were deprived of anything. They had games, didn't they? As long as they had games, they were fine.

Don was out one day with Jack Buck. Jack worked with Don in the church's local mission, teaching other people the gospel so they'd get converted and join the church. Jack was also a salesman for the same insurance company. Like most Mormons, they didn't bother drawing a line between business and religion. They were both starving as they drove around in a Volkswagen; they were both excited about the gospel and talked religion the whole time they were together.

They had gone into the office and complained to Glen Pinegar, the office manager, "There's nobody else to see. Nobody wants to buy." Pinegar—also a Mormon—said, "You go out and find somebody raking leaves—but find somebody." It was just a figure of speech, of course. You don't sell stock door to door.

But since they weren't selling anything today, Don and Jack decided they might as well try to teach somebody about the gospel. They saw an eighty-year-old man out in his yard raking leaves. Old guys always like to talk, they figured. So they stopped the car, got out, and struck up a conversation. And because they knew it turned people off to know you were trying to preach to them, they started the conversation by telling him they were out selling stock in an insurance company.

They didn't get much beyond that in the discussion. The old

fellow's name was Bairsto. He was head of Bairsto Brothers Auto Company. He bought a thousand dollars worth of stock and gave Don and Jack a list of ten people to go see.

The Bairstos, it turned out, were one of the oldest families in that part of Oregon. They had family and business connections with other families—Ayres, James, Cox, all early pioneer families, all loaded with old money and delighted to invest in a new company—and in these two eager young men. They sold $160,000 worth of stock to the older generation, then sold even more to their grandchildren.

This put the company on a firm footing—it wouldn't go out of business now. And the commissions helped the Ainges stay afloat awhile longer.

The time soon came, however, that they just couldn't go on. Kay had taken as much money pressure as she could bear. Her children were going without necessities. They were so deeply in debt that she didn't see how they could recover. Don realized she was right, but he couldn't bear to quit without winning. "Just hang on one more month," Don said. "I'm sure something's going to happen."

It happened. Don's bishop in those days was Dale Brunken. Dale worked for another insurance firm, writing employee benefits programs for client companies. Dale got an offer from a Midwestern insurance company, an offer so good that he couldn't turn it down. When he left, several things would be vacant: his job as bishop, his insurance position, his house, his lease car.

Don had no experience with group insurance beyond selling one program. But Dale knew that Don would pick it up quickly, knew that Don would do well with it. Besides, it was a steady income, and a good one, and as bishop Dale knew that Don was the kind of man who would pay his tithing even when his family didn't have enough to eat. That kind of dependability counted for more than expertise. So Dale recommended Don for his group insurance desk. And Don got the job.

Since Don now had a steady income, he could afford to

make payments on a good house. Dale just happened to have a house that was just going on the market. Don didn't really have the down payment, but Dale gave him very favorable terms, extended credit to him—and so the Ainges would move in as the Brunkens pulled out. Dale's lease car replaced Don's Volkswagen. It was almost a foregone conclusion that Don would be made bishop, too. Dale joked about it. "I'd better get out of town before you take my wife."

Ironically the insurance company Dale went to was lagging in sales; Dale boosted sales dramatically, but ran into controversy, and he and his new company agreed to a parting of ways. Don immediately invited Dale to come back to Eugene and have his old job back—and his house, and his car. Dale, though, had fire in his eyes. He went to California and launched a company in direct, head-to-head competitipn with the one he had just saved. He did well with it, too.

It seems only appropriate that after theis kids were all grown up, Don and Kay left Eugene and moved to San Jose, California—for Don to work with Dale Brunken again in his group insurance business.

Now, however, in Eugene, Dale Brunken had given the Ainges security. No more fear, no more scrambling to make ends meet. Don Ainge was a free man. He could live as he wanted to now—and how he wanted to live was as the best father, the best bishop, the best insurance man, and the best coach he could possibly be—in that order.

Being a Mormon bishop is a full-time, unpaid job. The bishop heads an organization of hundreds of members, almost all of whom have one or more church callings. The bishop has to put the right person in each calling, satisfy the needs of all the competing auxiliary organizations, make sure that the weekly sacrament meeting is inspiring and interesting—and his work has only just begun.

The Mormon bishop is also the father of his ward. Don found out quickly that this was the hardest and most important part of his calling. Saints who have sinned come to the bishop to confess and receive counseling, church discipline, and forgiveness. Don had to judge the hearts of the penitent and the rebellious. He remembered back to his own years as a rebellious child in California, when he had committed a few pretty serious errors himself. He found it easy to be compassionate, hard to be stern. Above all, though, he kept confidence. He never spoke of the private griefs and failings of those who confessed to him—he would not tell even Kay. It was a burden he had to bear alone.

He was also responsible for the local welfare program, helping people with financial problems make it through. He could provide food, clothing, and sometimes even money to meet the emergency needs of the Saints. Sometimes he found himself in the ironic position of giving welfare assistance to families that were making twice as much money as he had made without ever getting welfare help at all. "There *are* people getting by on less than you're making," he'd say, and then help them make a budget and stick to it. He had always regarded welfare as something you turned to when your children had to go without two meals in a row. But he was patient with people who did not have the same idea of self-reliance that he had.

His ward members loved him, as good bishops are always loved. His children missed none of this. Being the bishop's children put a burden on them, too. It did not give them special prestige, but it did mean constant reminders that they had to set an example. It would undermine their father's credibility as spiritual leader of the congregation if they were wild or rebellious. So they weren't.

In fact, to varying degrees the children responded strongly to the gospel. Doug and Laurie in particular were engrossed in the doctrine, and would talk to their father about questions of theology on a level that would be unthinkable to most kids their age. Later, both Doug and Laurie would be forced to learn that not all bishops are as compassionate or trustworthy as their father, and those hurts have not all healed. But from their father they learned the ideal, what a Mormon ought to be.

Of all the Ainge children, Dave eventually became the most

deeply involved in the Church. He attempted to serve a full-time mission when he was nineteen, but had to come home for an operation on an injured knee. Today he is a leader in his ward, trying to measure up to the standard his father set for him.

With his playing schedule, Danny has never been in a ward regularly enough to have a calling as an adult. When it came time for Danny to serve a full-time mission—something all Mormon young men are expected to do at the age of nineteen—he was well into a brilliant college basketball career, not to mention a professional baseball contract. At BYU, provision is made for athletes to leave school to serve missions for two years, then return without any loss of scholarship or eligibility. But Danny wanted to play, and BYU wanted to win. Danny was dating Michelle Toolson at the time. Michelle knew that a Mormon man worth his salt went on a mission—she didn't want to marry him if he hadn't fulfilled that obligation. So Danny asked the advice of an apostle of the Mormon Church, who told him that sometimes a person who was blessed with unusual fame could serve the Church more by being an example in the public eye as by proselyting actively for two years. The message was clear: if Danny stayed home and won games for BYU instead of serving a mission, the Church wouldn't mind. Danny stayed; BYU won. And Michelle Toolson must have forgiven him for not going on a mission, since she goes by the name of Ainge now.

Though the Ainge children were never involved in any activity as deeply as they were in athletics, they grew up seeing their father, not just as an athlete or coach, but as the leading figure in the local church, as a poet, as a businessman, as a musician. Don Ainge was always a well-rounded man, always interested in everything going on around him. Don and Kay tried to instill that goal in their children, telling them, "Be a well-rounded person. Sports aren't everything." But the kids were born participants and impatient observers. They could *watch* their father being a bishop, but never take part in his work. Poetry was too difficult when they were young. Only on the court, the diamond, or the field could they do something on a level with what their father had achieved.

Still, despite the family obsession with athletics, there was never a time that any of the children was fooled into thinking that the game was anything but a game. They were born competitors and never played to do anything less than win, but they did other things, too, and took them seriously. They loved their father's poetry, and they knew that when he wrote something tender or powerful, it was more real, more important than when they played golf and made bets on each hole. Danny and Dave both write poetry today. They both recognize that their poetry, like their father's, works best within the context in which it was written. Danny and Dave show their poetry to no one but family members, not because they are ashamed of it, but because it is private. Their father, more practiced and perhaps more introspective, writes with a surer hand:

If I must fall away, I pray to God,
That I will do it quietly. One night
As I stretch out and grope for stars, the light
Will dim, the wind will blow. Like goldenrod
The breeze will gather me without a trace
And redistribute all my flaws and pain.
Maybe weave them twixt the clouds and rain,
An incidental tapestry in space.
I know I must not whine nor weep, but still
As I suppress the crying (midst the hush),
I feel like oil washed from master's brush,
Waiting now, on cosmos canvas unfulfilled. . . .

Danny and Dave are still more closely tied to the feeling of the moment, and yet have a gift for finding apt and telling words, as in this poem of Dave's:

Some days up ahead
    will come down empty
And some years
    fuller than
The fullest ones
    we've known before.

But today
has been the best day
yet for me.
I thought you ought to
know that
Because
it's because
of you.

When Laurie married a writer instead of an athlete, she was not really turning away from all that her father and brothers stood for. In a way she was affirming perhaps the most fragile aspect of the tough, resilient males who had surrounded her all her life.

Each of Danny's siblings has come to the end of playing as the center of their lives. None of them can move very far from the game. Doug is a high school coach in Oregon, where he has taken a regular loser into serious competition—he has his father's gift for teaching young people to love the game and perform at their best. Dave, too, coaches, though not for a living: he works with boys' teams on a volunteer basis, as his father did. Both Dave and Doug faced painful times when the game seemed to be taken away from them unfairly. Both went through a time of resentment. But when the game was over for them, when other people were getting the headlines and making the baskets in front of thousands of fans, they did not find themselves empty. They had resources they had perhaps not expected. Even though they had long regarded "being well-rounded" as an onerous duty imposed by their parents, when the obsession of their childhood ended, they did not come down empty.

Danny, too, faced something similar during the agonizingly long time between quitting the Blue Jays and joining the Celtics, when he had no way of knowing whether he would ever play professional basketball again—or any kind of basketball for the next two years. After watching the Blue Jays' management show him one attitude in private and quite another attitude in court and before the media, Danny did not doubt that they might just be vindictive enough to keep him from playing anything at all for as long as possible. It was a grim prospect. For of all the Ainge boys, Danny had probably the least preparation for a life without sports. Financially he would do just fine—almost all his money from the Blue Jays was wisely invested, and he would have no trouble finding a job and doing well at it. Frank Arnold, at the head of BYU's basketball program also knew how valuable Danny would be at coaching, though it would take some transition before Danny learned to be a non-playing coach, to see things clearly without being able to do anything with his own hands.

Danny wasn't all that excited about coaching. He was still an assistant to coach Arnold in getting the varsity team ready to play. He enjoyed working with Coach Arnold, but it wasn't like playing. In a few days, once the season opened, he would have the junior varsity team, and instead of being an assistant he would have the authority and responsibility himself. He was looking forward to that—Danny wasn't used to having to submit all his ideas for approval before he could do anything about them.

But he didn't know if coaching was what he wanted to do with his life. If he couldn't *play*, the game wasn't quite as fun. Perhaps if he had had a more definite sense that his career was over, he might have been able to discover what he really wanted to do with his life after basketball.

Unlike his father' however, he had no injury; unlike Dave, he had no lack of faith in his own ability to perform. His situation was more like Doug's, in that people whom he had naively trusted had turned out not to measure up to his standard of what sincere, honest dealing was—and they had put him in the position of looking like a man who doesn't honor contracts, which is not an accurate picture of Danny Ainge. In a like situation, Doug, disillusioned, made his choice and left.

Danny watched the Celtics and the Blue Jays bargaining over his life and he, too, wondered if he really liked pro sports. They weren't in it for fun, and if it wasn't fun, Danny didn't want to play.

Yet as he lingered, uncertain of what his future would be, he found that it didn't matter to him as much as some people might have thought. He was not being torn apart. In fact, he was enjoying the fact that for the first time in his married life, he was able to be with his wife and children.

His daughter Ashlee was born 20 December 1979. All during the summer when she was really coming alive, becoming a person, Danny was either with Syracuse or Toronto, off to games for days, weeks at a time. That fall and winter, when she learned to walk and said her first words, Danny was playing for BYU, constantly away for games and practices. And then baseball again. Sometimes Ashlee wouldn't recognize him; sometimes she wept bitterly when he left her again. He had learned how to be a father from Don Ainge—he knew that a good father spends time with his children. It was the cruelest blow of all that he had to be in court about the dispute with Toronto when Michelle gave birth to Austin Daniel Ainge, 29 September 1981. Now, however, for a little while at least, he was with his wife and children.

Ainge children are definitely *not* "seen and not heard." They grow up with the confidence that comes from being treated with respect from childhood on. There was nothing that Danny or Michelle—or any of the adult Ainges—was doing that was so important that it couldn't be interrupted when Ashlee, or Dave's daughter, Briawna, had something to say or ask. Sometimes the girls just wanted to play, and that, too, was important. Kay Ainge watched her grandchildren and wondered, "Do we spoil these children?" She shrugged. The children had rules to follow, but none of the rules ever taught them that their desires were less important just because they were children. That wasn't spoiling them.

Danny, usually quiet with strangers around, was not shy when Ashlee wanted him to play. It is as if he learned from his parents that children are a special case at all times. You can be as shy as you like, but if your child wants you to romp and laugh and shout, then the stranger who is watching you doesn't matter—you romp and laugh and shout until Ashlee is too tired to play anymore.

What if Danny's son isn't interested in athletics? It wouldn't matter, Danny said at first. Then, upon reflection, he said, "I can't believe he wouldn't at least like to *watch* the games." If he has even a modicum of Ainge traits in him, of course, he won't be content to watch anything. But Michelle is small and fragile-looking, and Danny's son may not be as tall as he is. And if his son is no huskier, his choice of sports is going to be limited, since Danny himself is skinny enough that when he ran out on the floor in that high school tournament in Florida, someone in the crowd got a laugh by shouting, "Hey, kid! Who locked you out of the weight room!"

Whether Danny's children are athletes or not, however, probably won't make much difference in their lives. Professional playing careers are short; even if he plays longer than most, Danny will probably be out of the game in his thirties. It is inconceivable that he'd sit out the rest of his life, or try to live his life through his children. Like his father, like his brothers, Danny is no observer. Even if he can't do what he loves most, he'll love doing what he can still do. And like his parents, Danny is already more interested in discovering who his children are than in trying to make them into what he wants them to be.

Perhaps that's what it means to be a whole man: Danny Ainge has known all along that even though he loves the game, it's a game. After an embarrassing loss to the University of Utah, in which Danny had a streak of missed shots that left him four for nineteen in field goals, it was no sham when he shrugged off the loss. He wanted to win, but he wasn't going to flagellate himself for a bad night. He knew he'd be better the next time. While he was playing, he cared, perhaps more than anyone else on the floor, whether the team won or lost. But now the game was over. It didn't matter anymore.

When the game is over, it won't matter anymore. When younger guys start getting down the floor before him, when the ball just won't drop anymore, when his hands don't fly out and steal the ball without his even having to think about it, Danny

Ainge's life won't be over—just the game. He won't have to live on memories. Because there are things he loves better than basketball.

5

Rules and Referees

The game is not just a contest. It is also a story, a little morality play that is enacted before an audience. To one degree or another the audience believes or disbelieves it: the audience can be emotionally detached or involved as they need. But the good player has to believe the story of the game with his whole heart.

What is it that Danny Ainge and, perhaps, most players of the game have learned to expect from the game? Not that life will always be fair. There are breaks in the game, and they won't always go your way. The referee won't see something; the referee will see something that didn't happen. But there's always a referee. There's always someone who will make the decision, and the referee will always call it honestly, and the referee always knows the rules. It's the one thing a player learns to count on. You can yell, you can argue—but the referee needs to be there.

By the semifinals of that high school tournament in Florida, Danny and his miraculous team of middle-class high school kids from Oregon had captured the imagination of the sportswriters. It was going to be a battle between kids from suburbia and inner city blacks—a team from Maryland led by Albert King, Bernard King's little brother, an all-American player who was regarded as one of the hottest prospects coming out of high school. If Danny's team won, they would face Irwin "Magic" Johnson in the finals.

The game was played by Olympic rules. There were four ten-minute quarters, a thirty-second shot clock, and no center line. The referee didn't handle the ball on violations, so the game moved faster; there were no free throws except on shooting violations until the last two minutes of each half. The differences in the rules were important. The teams studied them carefully and practiced to take every possible advantage of them.

The game was close. But it looked like the Oregon team had made it. The clock had seven seconds left till the end of the game, the score was 109-108 in Oregon's favor, and Oregon had the ball out of bounds.

Johnny Parriseau threw the ball in to one of his teammates, and Danny's team was all set to run out the clock or take a couple of foul shots—when the referee blew the whistle. What possible violation could he call? Parriseau had thrown the ball into back court, said the referee. Well, yes—but there *was* no backcourt violation possible under Olympic rules. Didn't the ref know that? Apparently he hadn't done his homework the way the players had. He did not listen to arguments—he gave the ball to the Maryland team. They scored, and the game ended 110-109.

The referee was plain wrong. Danny's team would almost certainly have won the game, yet it was taken away from them because the one person who should have known all the rules broke them. It's something that shouldn't happen in the game. If the referee doesn't know the rules, then there are no rules, and if there are no rules, there is no game. It's the worst thing that can happen to a player, because it undermines his faith in the game.

Danny was able to take it in stride. It was disappointing; he and his family never forgot it. Still, he was signing a pro baseball contract that summer and going off to play basketball at BYU. The Florida tournament really meant nothing, in the long run. Yet he had lost something.

The possibility of disillusionment always remains for a player who believes. If the ref doesn't follow the rules, the game is over. It happens rarely in sports—but it happens all too often in life. Still, the Ainges always insisted on fair play.

In the Ainges' neighborhood there was a vacant lot where the kids played. The games had a way, though, of spilling into other yards—balls don't always go where they're meant to go. One neighbor lady became irate at balls flying into her immaculate yard. Getting angry at kids is the surest, most irresistible invitation for pranks, and soon the lady found dirt clods on her neatly clipped lawn. Kay Ainge listened to her complaints, apologized for her kids' involvement in the incident, but was, in fact, unsympathetic. "Your yard can stay perfect only because your kids can always go over to the vacant lot and play, or come over to our house and shoot baskets. Since your kids use the rest of the neighborhood, is it really fair for you to object to balls in your yard?" Those who believe in fairness have a hard time understanding that there are many others who have never learned to subordinate their own desires to the good of a team, for the sake of the game.

Fair play is fair play. Equity, balance, everything coming out even in the end. If things don't come out right *naturally,* then the referee will step in and make sure things get straightened out.

If the game harmed the Ainges, it was because it left them unready for incompetent referees. One sight that fans in Provo, Utah, and Eugene, Oregon, have gotten used to over the years is Danny Ainge arguing with the referee after a call that went against him. Danny does not swear, does not abuse the referees. Yet he has been hit with technical after technical because of these arguments. Part of the reason that referees react so strongly to Danny's arguing is that Danny has such presence, such dominance on the court that the referees feel intimidated. Most of the reason, however, is probably that Danny does not have to use foul language to have the same effect. Danny can put the same passion and outrage into standard English, so the referee feels attacked with the same force.

When Danny argues a call it is not a show, not a strategy—what kind of strategy is it to get technical fouls at key moments of the game? Danny argues the call because he believes the call was wrong, unfair, and the referee is supposed to be *right*. Danny has played without referees, in those truncated contests with his brother Dave. Without a referee to decide right from wrong, Danny and Dave could start, could play, but could not finish.

The Ainges' expectation of fairness was partly an outgrowth of their Mormonness. The kids had grown up knowing that in life, the Mormon bishop was a referee. If you broke a rule, he helped you set it straight. He always played fair, he always kept confidence. The kids learned what a bishop was from the same man who taught them every game they knew—their father. But not every bishop measured up to Don Ainge, any more than every coach did.

Doug found that out when a bishop relayed to a BYU basketball coach a confidence about an offense that at any other school would have been considered minor—it helped end Doug's athletic career at BYU. Laurie, too, had a time when she needed a compassionate bishop, a man like her father had been. But different people do their best in different ways. At one point in her counseling with her bishop, when it seemed Laurie wasn't accomplishing all she ought, her mother said, "Maybe you just shouldn't waste the bishop's time."

Like the rest of the family, Laurie expected equity. "My dad gave so much time to other people when I was growing up, I don't have to worry how much time I take now!"

But fair play just doesn't happen that often in the real world.

However, the lessons of the game can be unlearned, too. Like his brothers and sister, Danny has gradually been learning the difference between the two halves of his name. He is an Ainge, yes, and in many ways *the* Ainge. From infancy he has been at the center of his family, the emblem of all that being an Ainge meant.

It wasn't an easy role to play; nor is it an easy one to give up. But gradually he is finding out what it means to be, not just Ainge, but *Danny*.

Danny's father and both his brothers were thwarted during their freshman year of intercollegiate athletics; Laurie gave up athletics before the end of high school. Danny, however, was unplagued by injury or self-doubt, and he had already lost some of his illusions about the game. From that time forward, he was charting new territory. There were no stories in the Ainge family to tell him what happened now, who he ought to be. At the precise time when everyone else in the family had detached from the game, Danny was finally getting started. It meant a subtle change. Dave remembered that even when he didn't like playing games all the time, he kept playing "I guess because I'd feel like I was ruining the fun for everyone." Now, in college basketball and pro baseball, Danny was moving into the game as a career, not just for fun. He was making money from the game.

Anytime you start making a living from what you used to do for play, you have to make some changes in who you think you are. Either you start to accept the money you get as an evaluation of your worth as a person, or you have to find ways to name yourself apart from your career. All through high school, Danny could name himself through games alone, because he could always believe that his potential was infinite, because he could always remind himself that it was just a game. Now a cash value—and not a low one—was being placed on his play, and that meant someone else had the power to say what his playing was worth. Too many athletes have accepted that valuation of their souls, and it has destroyed them, either by making them think themselves far more important human beings than they were, or by making them think that because they aren't good enough for a pro team, they aren't good.

Danny didn't think all this through and calculate his next step, of course—this kind of thing can't be handled consciously at all. But he seemed to know, instinctively, that his family was no longer adequate to tell him who he was. They were believing too much of the outside world's valuation of Danny Ainge. They were too impressed with him. Danny's father went into partnership with him, guiding his baseball income so that he could make the most possible money from it. Danny's mother did what she had never done for her other children—packed his clothes for him whenever he had to change residence for a different playing season, all because he was too busy with "important" things to do this for himself. He accepted the help they offered because it was help, and because he knew it was an expression of his parents' love. It did free him to concentrate on the game. But it also tied his relationship with his parents too closely to the game itself. In high school, his parents were excited about his playing, the way all parents are excited about what their kids do. Now that playing was Danny's career, however, their helpfulness had changed meaning, though none of them saw it at the time.

Without being aware of it, however, Danny knew when he arrived at BYU that he needed someone else now. Someone who was not tied to the game at all. For the first time in memory, at BYU he would be meeting people who had never heard of Danny Ainge, to whom the name Ainge meant nothing at all—both of Danny's brothers had married Oregon girls who had practically been weaned on the Ainge mystique. They could be happy that way, since they were no longer playing as a career. Danny could not. His parents had slipped at least partly into the role of worshippers: Danny needed someone who could help him discover the difference between Danny Ainge the pro ballplayer and Danny Ainge the human being.

Michelle Toolson was just a girl in Danny's health class. The BYU campus abounds with girls who look like Michelle: clean, attractive in a way that can only be described as cute, at once frail and tough, yielding and dominant. It's a breed of woman that seems to thrive in the Mormon climate—they are able to adapt to social structures that seem to put all power in the hands of men, and still retain control of their own lives and identities without any overt rebellion.

Danny, like all BYU freshmen, was required to take health. He came into the classroom, saw her, walked straight to the chair beside hers, and struck up a conversation. It sounds like the sort of thing any jock might do—but it was completely untypical of Danny Ainge. He was always shy when he wasn't playing, and when he started talking to Michelle he definitely wasn't playing. He was searching, and on the first try he had found precisely what he was looking for.

From the first conversation with Michelle, Danny talked to her as he talked to no one else in his life. There was his normal joking and camaraderie and gentle playing, yes—but he also talked to her about the things he wanted to make more important in his life than they had been. He wasn't an Ainge to Michelle—from the start he was Danny, the private person who had been masked behind a ballplayer all these years. At first she didn't know what to make of him. He was nice, she liked him, but he didn't even ask her out for a while. He'd just come over and visit her apartment, talk to her and her roommates, tease them all unmercifully. In health class it was a miracle they passed— they can't recall listening to anything the poor teacher said. Then, at Halloween, he gave her a card, and she discovered that he was a writer. What he had written to her was simple, but powerful—he made it plain that he was not just playing games. He really cared for her, and upon reflection she realized that she really cared for him. That much was settled before basketball season began and she discovered that she was in love with the best basketball player in BYU's history—and one of the best in the world.

It was a good thing she already loved him, because as soon as Danny started getting attention in Provo, she became "Danny Ainge's girlfriend." It was crazy of her not to like that, she knew—after all, the ideal Mormon wife *should* be submerged in her husband's career. But she didn't like it. She didn't like the way some people began to be friends with her only so that they could meet Danny. She learned to be suspicious of new friends, of friends who had no *reason* to be friendly. In fact, Danny's fame disrupted her life enough from the start that if she hadn't already known and needed Danny, she would never have put up with it. But she *did* need him, and was coming to know him better all the time. What worried her was that the better she got to know him, the more she realized that he was *not* what she had grown up expecting the proper Mormon husband to be.

Michelle grew up in San Diego, one of a large old-time Mormon family. She knew exactly what a Mormon man was supposed to be. He must be a fervent believer in the gospel, he must serve a two-year mission for the church, he must attend all his meetings, he must be the head of the household, he must make all his own decisions, handle his own money, be successful and dedicated to his career, and love his family. The list goes on, but that's the gist of it. In turn, Michelle knew that as the perfect Mormon woman she must be what she now calls a "good little wife"—keeping house and children in perfect order while Daddy is gone from eight to five; working hard in church callings; setting an example of Mormon life to nonmembers; nurturing children as a full-time job.

As she got to know Danny better and better, she had to face the fact that he was definitely *not* the perfect Mormon husband. He believed in the gospel, of course, but not *fervently*—he didn't seem to care much. He wasn't particularly planning on a mission, which disturbed her greatly. She had grown up knowing that every *good* Mormon man goes on a mission. He didn't worry about going to every available church meeting, either—there were too many meetings available at BYU. And though Danny was strong and good, and though he excelled in his field of work, he would never be the typical eight-to-five husband. Professional sports meant going where the team went; it meant weeks home and weeks away, a complete disruption of what Michelle thought was the proper order for a home.

Yet, even though he did not measure up to what she thought a fit husband *ought* to be, she soon realized that she could not possibly marry anyone else. It wasn't that he was a star athlete, for in some ways that was a drawback. Michelle is not the sort of person who could love someone for his fame—she's more likely to be put off by it. What drew her to Danny was something else. He was funny at times, he was sometimes unabashedly affectionate, but that was merely what made loving him easy. What made loving him essential was, perhaps, that seriousness that he was born with. She listened to Danny, talked to Danny, and discovered that he wasn't just a player. He was, as she calls him now, brilliant. He could be anything. He could think anything. He was interested in everything. She had never come to know anyone before who had quite such depth and breadth of soul. When he listened to her she felt understood and cared for; when she listened to him, she was at once fascinated and awed. He was the first man she had known that she could imagine living with forever and never being bored.

She did not realize that from the very moment that he spoke to her, Danny was changed. She had not known him before, of course, and so she was not aware for a long time that she was seeing a side of him that no one had seen since he was a little child. Nor did she realize, at first, that she was changing too. She had a certain stubbornness of character that she had always successfully pretended she didn't have. She thought she wanted to be the perfect Mormon wife. Now she realized that she'd rather be the perfect wife of Danny Ainge, which was something else again. She learned, as most people learn, that the myth of what she ought to be in marriage has little to do with the thousands of accommodations that are required for two people to live one life.

But all these accommodations took time. And Michelle saw, more clearly than Danny had seen, that his relationship with his family had to change before he could become a whole person—before he could be her husband. She was appalled to discover that Danny didn't even know how much money he made. Oh, he knew vaguely what was in the contract, but how the money was parceled out into taxes and investments—that was all handled by his father. Don Ainge was doing well with it, and Danny had an ample allowance—not for a moment did Michelle think Danny was being exploited. On the contrary, she thought that Danny's family was teaching him to exploit *them*. And when she discovered that Danny's mother actually flew to Provo to pack up his belongings so he didn't have to waste time between basketball season and baseball season, she was horrified. How could Danny be so reliant on other people? How could he be so *dependent*?

That was how Michelle discovered just how *in*dependent *she* was. She was not just going to take Danny Ainge, family and all. Before she'd marry him, there'd have to be some changes made.

The trouble was, Danny didn't *want* all those changes. He didn't want to have to worry about finances—if he didn't concentrate on the sport he was playing, pretty soon there wouldn't be enough money to manage. His family really *was* helping him, and he had no desire to complicate his life just to satisfy Michelle's idea of what a husband ought to be. Danny and Michelle didn't quarrel about it, though. As Michelle tells it, their lack of quarrels was not because she didn't *try*. She's a talker, a shouter sometimes, and she lets her views be known in clear, emphatic language. Danny, however, merely listens. Politely for a while, and then with amusement. "You're so funny when you're mad," he says. She is still a little annoyed at how easily he can tease her out of a quarrel. Things had a way of getting forgotten without being settled. The way Danny used to handle his fights with Dave.

That's why she went ahead and married him even when he wasn't everything she wanted him to be. Oh, she tried to end their relationship when he decided not to go on a mission—that was a vital point for her. "If you're not going on a mission," she said, "I'm not dating you." They even broke up, dated other people, but it never worked—they kept seeing each other anyway, and neither of them could possibly find someone to satisfy the needs they had taught each other to have. Whether she liked it or not, she was going to be Danny's wife. They would just have to work out what being husband and wife actually meant.

Danny didn't help matters when instead of going shopping for an engagement ring with Michelle, he let his mother go in his place. Michelle felt it rather spoiled the romance of it not to have

Danny there.

And once the wedding was over, almost immediately she found her life turned upside down. "Oh, give me the eight-to-five life," she sometimes laments. When I talked to her, she was relishing the hiatus between the Blue Jays and the Celtics—Danny was home, night after night, just like a real Daddy ought to be. Now, though, Michelle is accustomed to his disappearances on road trips; at first, it was maddening. She did not like Syracuse, where she had to live in his farm club days. There was nothing *wrong* with the town, except that sometimes she felt that she saw Danny less than she had seen him before they were married. It wasn't true, but it felt that way because in Syracuse she had nothing else to do but sit around and wish she weren't in Syracuse—or that Danny were.

But in some ways it was almost worse in Provo, during basketball season. Danny's parents called every day or so, to remind him that he needed to sign these papers or pay that payment or write another check. Danny's father still tried to come to as many of Danny's games as he could. Michelle thought it was admirable for a father to do that—for his children. But Danny was not a child, and he hardly needed his father in the stands so he would still feel loved. Things had changed—was it Danny who needed to have his dad watching, or Don who needed to see his most successful son play?

Michelle couldn't help but feel that his family was intruding on their lives. Bit by bit, sometimes subtly, sometimes with quite open anger, Michelle retrieved from Danny's family the decisions in his life that had to be made by Danny and her. At Michelle's insistence Danny became more involved in his own finances. They separated their funds from many of Danny's and Don's joint ventures—including, most importantly, buying out Don's half-interest in their condominium in Provo. Danny and Don had bought the condo when Danny first came to BYU, and his roommates had paid rent to him; now, however, it was essential to Michelle to have a home of her own.

At first there was some bitterness. Michelle could only see

Don and Kay meddling in their grown-up son's life; the Ainges could only see Michelle trying to cut them off from their son. As time passed, however, good sense prevailed. Michelle began to realize that Don and Kay had been genuinely helpful to Danny, and that what she had thought of as meddling was really the intense interest that this exceptionally close family always took in each other's lives. And Danny's parents, in turn, learned to withdraw from Danny's life. He might be the emblem of the Ainges, but he was also Danny, and he was making a life of his own. And out of the struggles of the first few months has come a pleasant, stable pattern. Good manners between the Ainges and their daughter-in-law have given way to real affection.

But the fact remains that Michelle Toolson did not become an Ainge when she married Danny; rather, she has made sure that Danny's family is something new. Doug's wife Diane and Dave's wife Stacy might have accomplished the same task more gently, but then, they knew what marrying an Ainge would mean long before they married one—and they were willing from the start to accept a closer involvement in the family than Michelle had ever expected.

There were also domestic adjustments they had to make. Danny's mother had firmly divided women's work from men's work in her family, and whatever was considered women's work Danny simply did not do. He did not know how to cook. He did not know how to clean. Michelle's father and brothers had been athletic, but they weren't utterly *useless* in the house, either. It has taken time, but Danny has learned to find a few implements in the kitchen drawer, and knows how to use them, too.

It isn't that Michelle has made Danny over into something else, however. It was no accident that he chose her—consciously or not, he wanted to become the sort of person who could be happily married to Michelle Toolson. And he came better prepared for some aspects of family life than most men. He knew, for instance, how to be a good, affectionate father. Watching him with Ashlee and Austin says more about Danny Ainge than anything that he could tell you himself, or that others could tell you about him. Like his parents, he is always willing to be interrupted by the children. He lights up, opens up when his children are there. It is a debt that Michelle and her children owe to Don Ainge—Danny's fatherhood means more to him than anything he can possibly be given by basketball, and he is, if anything, a better father than basketball player.

But unlike Kay Ainge, Michelle is not a silent sufferer. If something that matters is wrong, she makes Danny acquainted with the fact. When they were first married, she insisted that he had to write the checks to pay the bills himself, and though she now handles more of those chores then she used to, they do make the money decisions together. The result is that now she and Danny both know at all times exactly what condition their finances are in.

This matters more than most outsiders might think. Large numbers are bandied about in discussions of what Danny makes. What most people forget is that the "annual income" of an athlete is not an annual income at all. For every year that an athlete plays, there are three or four years ahead—or more—that he *won't* play, and therefore won't earn those astronomical sums. Like every other wise athlete, therefore, Danny is investing most of his money and living on a much more modest scale than his salary might suggest.

Furthermore, it's expensive being a professional athlete. The Ainges have had to maintain two homes, and pay for the family's travel back and forth. And there have been times—especially during the baseball strike and that period of agonizing uncertainty while Toronto and Boston decided what Danny's career would be—when they have had exactly the sort of financial worries that most people think a star athlete never has. Despite occasional financial woes, however, Danny and Michelle have never had to argue about money. They both fully understand what money is there; they agree on almost all their priorities about where the money should go.

Michelle and Danny have also found a way to accommodate their lives to the needs of the game. Michelle watches him play when she can, though because she must take care of the children she often can only watch on television. If he comes home from a game or from practice looking depressed, she has learned not to ask, "What's wrong?" During the time when his batting average and his desire to play baseball were both sinking rapidly, she never asked, "Why aren't you hitting more?" There is never a sense that he must account to her for his performance in a game. She does not have to keep utterly silent, however. When he had been sent back to Syracuse and was on a multi-game no-hitting streak, Michelle called him on the road and said, "You've got to start hitting or we'll never get out of Syracuse." Danny laughed. That was all right—that was a joke. She wasn't saying, "Why aren't you doing better?" She was saying, "We're in this together."

Because she has not set herself up as judge of his playing, Danny can talk to her about the game. There is none of the analysis that used to go on between Danny his and father after all Danny's games. Danny can ask her, excitedly, "Did you see what I did? My steal? That shot I made?" And Michelle, who knows her basketball, can say, truthfully, yes. She knows when he has done well, she knows when his work has been remarkable. She is not an expert, she cannot teach him how to play. But she is an intelligent audience for him. He knows that she knows when he has done well.

They also play together in that most cruel and direct of one-on-one sports, tennis. Michelle plays very well, and did before they met. Danny, who came late to the game, plays against her as intensely as ever. He gives no quarter, and he expects Michelle to be excellent. She does not disappoint him. Now, however, he is able to finish a one-on-one game. He can even cope with losing to her now and then.

There are some things about Danny that marriage will never change, however. He is an incorrigible tease, and if Michelle didn't know how to laugh she would have been reduced to mental rubble years ago. And when Danny has made up his mind, he will not be bullied. Even on petty things, like what he eats. He hates peas. Michelle thinks vegetables are good for him—that's part of being a good wife and mother, to make sure her menfolk eat all their vegetables. He looks at his plate and says to her, "It's nice of you to put these peas on my plate for decoration." The peas end up on the plate, untouched, after the meal, and Danny is moaning softly. "Oh, I'm sick, I'm sick, just the sight of those little green things—" Still, though he's a picky eater he isn't a fussy husband—dinner doesn't have to always be on time, and he doesn't throw a tantrum if the house isn't always spotless.

Danny is also always the prime sufferer in their family. If Michelle is in pain, Danny hurts worse. Her back aches? His back hurts, too, but he hardly notices it because of the pain in his shoulders and calves and neck. Michelle sums it up this way: "When he's in pain, I don't give him much sympathy—but I take care of him. When I'm in pain, he really sympathizes with me—but I pretty much have to take care of myself."

Michelle has had to revise some of her expectations because Danny will never fulfill them—but she has also learned to love things she never knew a wife could have from a husband. In Toronto, she and Danny were one of the four Mormon couples associated with the team. Being Mormons together, far from home, the four wives almost inevitably became friends. At church meetings people began calling them "the Blue Jay wives." Rebelliously, Michelle would insist, "We are not Blue Jay wives, we are Patty Iorg, Cindy Garvin, Stefnie Bonnell, and Michelle Ainge." But the name stuck anyway—and Michelle invariably refers to them as the "baseball wives." They were visiting in her Toronto apartment once, and happened to notice a card that Danny had given her on Mother's Day. In it he had written, as his father would have, a poem, a private statement that could never have been purchased for fifty cents from Hallmark. Though Danny hates to have anyone read his poems but the people he wrote them to, Michelle read the poem to them, still awed that her husband could not only feel these things about her, but say them, too. And they told her what she already knew—that it was an uncommon and precious thing to have a husband who is never content with prefabricated affection.

Another change in Danny was one that he had already begun before he met Michelle. He had had little time for church when he was growing up, but he knew that much of what he loved best about his father was that part of his father which was contained within Mormonism. Danny never had any illusions about Michelle and the church—she was willing, after much praying and agonizing and some guilt, to stay with him even though he did not serve a mission. But she could make that compromise only because she knew that he would still be a faithful Mormon. And over the years of their marriage, he has become more comfortable with his own role within the church.

Every Mormon man is expected to be a priest in his own home—a son of Don Ainge even more than most. And Danny has become that. It is an aspect of the man that jars with the conventional image of an athlete, to think of him privately administering religious rites that in most churches are performed only by members of a specially ordained group. But you do not understand Danny Ainge if you only think of him sinking those incredible outside shots. You must also think of him in the middle of the night, anointing his sick child with consecrated oil, laying his hands on her head, and blessing her in the name of Jesus Christ.

Danny does not regard himself as especially righteous—this is what most Mormon men do from time to time. Nor does Danny, still shy in public, try to make a big stir about his beliefs. But with Michelle's encouragement, her high expectations of him in religious matters, he has been able to fill that part of his life. His work still keeps him from heavy involvement with the daily workings of the ward he is in—there is no way he could function, for example, as a bishop. But on his first Sunday back in Provo after leaving the Blue Jays, this man with so much turmoil in his life could still rise to his feet spontaneously in a Mormon testimony meeting and quietly speak of his faith, his gratitude, his love of God.

Danny's life, his habits, his desires, have changed because of

Michelle. The changes are not radical—they are, many of them, changes that are normally associated with growing up. Danny's brothers have become no less independent than he, no less devoted fathers and husbands. What matters is, perhaps, that Danny was able to pass from childhood to manhood without breaking with the game; because he had Michelle, he could keep playing without being swallowed up.

That is why he no longer has to dread the fact that there are no referees. When his future was being decided by people who were not necessarily being governed by a sense of what was fair to Danny, he was not afraid. He no longer *needed* to believe in an impartial, fair referee. Instead he had put his trust in Michelle, in his children. They are definitely *not* fair and impartial. They are overwhelmingly biased in his favor, and that makes up for a lot of unfairness in the rest of the world. Things balance out after all, because of them.

I sat in Danny's living room, copying some documents by hand while Kay, Michelle, and Dave's wife Stacy conversed. Their talk turned to actresses, comparing the relative beauty of Jaclyn Smith and Brooke Shields. Then they started discussing Jaclyn Smith's performance in *Jacqueline Bouvier Kennedy*, which had aired on television a short time before. Michelle, herself the wife of a famous man whose life in many ways centers outside the home, said, "Jacqueline Kennedy suffered a lot—but she wanted it—wanted to be a senator's wife." This statement has struck me as revealing, not how much Michelle is like that, but how unlike it she is. She did not choose to be a pro ballplayer's wife. She chose to be Danny Ainge's wife. That has made all the difference to both of them.

6

The Stories of Danny Ainge

Whatever its drawbacks, having athletics as the center of family life provided the Ainges with something that too many families never find: stability, rules, roles that each could fulfil. From the first moments of life, each of the Ainges knew what it meant to be an Ainge, and what it meant to be this particular Ainge. They all learned precisely what things they did alike; and, sometimes openly, sometimes secretly, they all knew what things made them different from the rest of the family, what things made them not really an Ainge at all.

The Ainges didn't just play. They told each other stories about their games. They all have a phenomenal memory for games played, partly because they practiced noticing and remembering all that happened. After a game, even when their father wasn't their coach, the boys would talk through the game with him. In those conversations, Don Ainge helped them understand why things went the way they did in the game. He may not always have been right, and the boys may not always have learned the specific skill he was trying to help them improve. But they did learn this: things don't just happen, they happen for a reason. You only learn from a game by studying it and believing the lessons that you draw from it.

Dave still remembers a fifth-grade game in which he fouled out in two minutes. He recalls clearly that two calls were correct, but three of the calls against him weren't. The family remembers the story because to them it means that Dave has a bad temper when he plays. The fact that the story is still remembered means something, too.

The stories the family told about each other helped shape the picture the children had of themselves. Doug has finesse; Dave has hustle; Danny has both—that was a story they still believe. Was it true? Whether it started out true or not, it ended up true. Dave didn't believe he had the skill to make it, and even now refuses to take seriously the idea that his right- and left-handedness confusion might have hampered him when young. Danny, on the other hand, grew up believing he could do anything. It isn't true, of course. There are things he can't do as well as other players, and he knows it. Knows it intellectually. But when he gets out on the floor, his instinctive, unconscious belief is that nothing is going to stop him. Anyone who saw him weave through the whole Notre Dame team to score the winning points in the 1981 NCAA playoffs will find it fairly easy to agree with him.

Because the stories the family told each other, consciously or not, were sometimes downright wrong, the children struggled against them. When Don told his sons that Doug had skill and Dave had hustle, he thought he was telling them that each was as good as the other. In fact, Dave heard it as a comparison between him and Doug, and Doug was better. The seeds of self-doubt were planted. Dave grew up believing that Doug was better than he was, and that Danny was better still. He believed it so much that when he found a sport—running—where he was better than they were, he gave it up.

Doug, too, found the role he had been assigned in the family hard to bear. He did not play with Danny's joy or Dave's mad fanaticism. He used to get sick before games, he was so tense. He had not learned, as Danny did, that he would succeed at everything. Instead there was that constant comparison with his father. His story was that he was Don Ainge's son. The problem was that he didn't *like* doing all the things that Don Ainge did. If he lived up to that story, he was bound to be unhappy; but if he did not live up to that story, he would also be unhappy.

When he was still in his teens, Doug was called by the church to serve as president of the teen council of the stake. With all his athletic responsibilities, it was absurd to expect him to fulfil a high-powered church assignment, too, yet he was put in charge of an entire youth conference, a management responsibility that most adults aren't ready to handle. Doug took on the responsibility in part because he had learned from his father that you don't say no to church assignments. When Don and Kay heard about the calling, they were a little upset. For one thing, it was not proper to call a teenager to such an assignment without getting his parents' approval. But Doug seemed to be taking everything in stride. He knew what he was doing. He was Don Ainge's son, and if he was in charge of something, it would be done right.

The conference went smoothly. Doug had done a near perfect job. But the price was high. His mother congratulated him on his success, and Doug wept. "I'll never do it again," he said.

All the Ainge children, in their own way, have denied or refused some of the most important stories their game-playing family taught them. Yet the names given in childhood are not so easily shed.

It is ironic, at least, that Doug's college athletic career took a dramatic turn at almost exactly the same point as his father's, with broken trust and more than enough grounds for many years of bitterness. But like his father, he has learned, not bitterness or anger, but compassion.

As a high school coach he was faced with a tough situation, three players who simply weren't trying. They thought they had it made—they were seniors, they had been starters the year before.

Doug couldn't let them go on using a place on the team that could be given to students who really cared, who were willing to learn. And yet he knew how it felt to be removed from a team by the all-powerful coach, from whom, like God, there is no appeal. He called the boys in and told them they had to turn in their uniforms; he told them why. "But you're still on the team," he said. "You can earn these uniforms back."

Angry, two of the boys quit. But the third boy stuck with the team, worked hard, and got his uniform before the end of the season. Doug told his parents about it, saying, "I don't want to hurt any kids. I don't want to mess up their lives."

It is important, though, to notice that like his father, Doug was also using these events to tell these three boys a story about themselves. He was teaching them, not what choice they must make, but that the choices they made meant something about what kind of people they were.

I have been telling you a story, too. The story of Danny Ainge and how he became who he is. I listened carefully to all the stories that Danny and Michelle and some of Danny's family members told me. I heard what they thought their stories meant. And I have written here what *I* thought the stories meant, and have told other tales besides, ones that they did not realize they were telling. Which versions of these tales are "true?" None of them, including mine, are objectively, demonstrably true. All of them, however, are true in this important sense: they represent a way of making sense of the world.

Like the Ainge boys sprawling around the living room after a game, I think there are some things that happened to Danny and his family that do not belong just to their lives, but that are true for many people, perhaps even most people. I can imagine someone writing their story in horror at the way their lives were consumed by competition. I can also imagine someone writing in adulation, trying to discover the Ainges' secret for raising super-athletes, as if anyone would set out to do such a thing.

Both views, I think, miss the point. It does not matter that the family was intensely involved *in athletics*. What matters is that *the family* was intensely involved in athletics. That most potent of human associations used the game as a way of binding its members together, naming each of them, and shaping them in a way that made them, eventually, competent and happy adults. By that measure, the family was an unqualified success. But a family has no single mind—it exists in the tension among the competing desires of the family members. The family never chose to be athletic. Rather, the game was where the family repeatedly found satisfaction, and so the game was played repeatedly. If most family members had not been good at sports, a family obsession with athletics would have been impossible. If anyone had tried to force it, it would have been a wedge to drive them apart.

By the measure of how each member of a family turns out, I have called the Ainge family a success. But in fact that standard is impossible to apply. Because people change with time, no one ever "turns out" until he's dead. That's why most biographers are not so premature as I have been—they wait until their subject is safely under the ground, where he cannot possibly object to their conclusions. Unfortunately, however, a biographer writing about the dead is limited only to the most frail evidence, and cannot often learn the most important information of all—the stories that a man tells himself about himself, what he believes he was doing in all the acts of his life. And an autobiographer is limited to seeing only his own account of himself. For good or ill, this tale of Danny Ainge has neither of those limits. It has other limits: it is fragile and temporary. The Danny Ainge that I have shown you is only the Danny Ainge that I came to know during a certain time of his life. Much of what I have seen in him has always been and always will be true of him. Some of what I have seen, however, is doubtless already changing. And all of this story is colored by what I find valuable and interesting in a person.

Danny himself views his life more complacently than those around him. Through the conflict between Michelle and his parents, Danny did not see himself being changed. He knew that his parents were involved in his life, but it did not alarm him, because he had always felt that he made his own decisions. When his mother said, "Are you sure you want to get married?" he took it as he had taken it when, in high school, he heard her ask, "Are you sure you want to play football?" She worries, that's all. Moms are like that. It isn't meddling. You can just ignore it, and there's no problem.

When Michelle took these things much more seriously, Danny was patient with her, too. "There was about a year that I had to prove to Michelle that she was most important in my life," he says. "I always knew what great parents she had, but it took a while for her to see how great mine are." There was no great revolution in his life; he is who he always was. Before he got married, he would live off his BYU scholarship money, and send the money his roommates paid him as rent to his parents. He wasn't interested in money, that's all—he just wanted to play. When Michelle wanted him to take responsibility, that was fine, too. She was right—if he was going to be a husband and father, it was time that his parents stopped taking care of his finances. He couldn't understand why his parents and Michelle seemed to think it was all so *important*.

And yet through this time Danny was making radical changes in his life. He remembers that as a little child he would cuddle up with his mother on the couch and watch TV, but for years he was undemonstrative. It was hard for him to show affection for people, hard for him to open up and talk. He knew it was not like himself when he first started talking so freely with Michelle. For years he had remained detached from other people. If he did not hold grudges, he also did not allow himself to openly need anyone. Now he has cracked that emotional self-reliance, beginning with Michelle, but now reaching out to other people. The priorities of his life have been reordered.

But none of these changes came any sooner than Danny wanted them to come. So they don't feel like changes. They feel to Danny Ainge like the way things ought to be. That's pretty much how things felt to him a dozen years ago. Everything is as it ought to be. And that's about as good a definition of happiness as I've ever heard of.

Danny believes that he is in charge of his life, and because he believes it, it is largely true. If he is not in command of something, it is because he is uninterested in it. His coaches have discovered this streak of independence in him. During the very time when he was letting his parents handle his finances, Danny was handling his own development as an athlete—which was, after all, his most important financial asset. He liked working with Frank Arnold, his coach at BYU, but Danny admits ruefully that he must have annoyed Coach Arnold sometimes. For Danny could never just do what he was told. He had to think first. If he agreed, then fine, he'd do it and be glad of the advice. But if he disagreed, he just wouldn't do it.

No argument, mind you. Coach Arnold once told him he needed to get his elbow *in* when he shot. But Danny knew that his shot was already fine. He didn't miss shots because his elbow wasn't in, he missed shots only when he didn't do what he already knew how to do. But when Coach Arnold had told him to do it a couple of times, Danny didn't argue. He said yes, went out and shot a few baskets that way—and then proceeded to forget all about it. Danny doesn't make waves—but he doesn't get swept along in the current, either.

This is why Danny is sometimes marvelously teachable, sometimes infuriatingly stubborn. He is always cheerful, always eager to learn—but he won't take anybody's word as final. He must judge for himself if it works or if it doesn't.

When he first started practicing with the Celtics, he knew that it wouldn't be easy. The team had already been playing together for months, and everyone knew that because Danny had joined, someone else would have to go. If Danny had come in as a brash, arrogant rookie—or, just as bad, if he had come in utterly meek, willing to be pushed around—he would have been doomed from the start. The management can hire whomever they like, but it's the team that decides who really fits in with the team.

Danny did not make either mistake, however. He came in as quietly as ever, unimpressed with the publicity that had surrounded his arrival, and set out learning how to play pro basketball. He discovered right away that in the pros, there is no let up. Everybody on every team is good, and Danny couldn't just rely on what he had learned in college and high school and from his dad. Danny listened to everything, watched the other players, tried out new techniques, worked on skills that had always been good enough before, but weren't good enough now.

The results have been predictable, not stunning. Danny did not come onto the court in his first few games determined to make a splash. He came onto the court determined to be part of the team. It's what he always excelled at, and he excels at it still. He was not directing traffic—these men knew their way around the court better than he did in the professional game. But he was filling the role he had to fill, shooting when he should, and making it when he could. One or two field goals a game, at first. A few minutes of playing time at the most. And then, gradually, as he gained confidence, more minutes, more shots, more points. Within the first month of professional play, he was averaging ten minutes a game, and had scored as many as ten points in a game against Seattle. He has already shown that he can score in double figures as a pro, this man who holds the NCAA record for most consecutive games in double figures. It is plain that at the least Danny Ainge will be a good, dependable pro basketball player. It remains to be seen whether he will be a star. What makes me admire Danny Ainge as a man, and not just as an athlete, is that he *will* be happy whether he becomes a star or not. He is not in it for fame or money; he is in it because he loves to play. But playing is no longer what he loves best. And that makes all the difference.

7

Statistics

In addition to his NCAA record for scoring at least 10 points in the most consecutive games, Danny Ainge holds the following BYU records (records which he already held by the end of his junior year at BYU are marked *):

Single season records

* * Most points scored in a season (782, in 1980-81)
* Highest average points per game (24.4, in 1980-81)
* * Most field goals made in a season (309, in 1980-81)

Career records

* * Most points scored (2,467)
* Highest career average points per game (tied with John Fairchild at 20.9; Fairchild only played two seasons)
* Most field goals attempted (1,875)
* * Most field goals made (987)
* Most free throws attempted (604)
* Most free throws made (493)
* Best free throw percentage (81.6%)

Danny Ainge's BYU Statistics[1]

	1977-78	1978-79	1979-80	1980-81	Career
Games played	30	27	29	32	118
Field goals attempted	473	376	430	596	1875
Field goals made	243	206	229	309	987
Field goal percentage	51%	55%	53%	51.8%	52.6%
(Team average)	(49%)	(53%)	(54%)	(49.1%)	
Free throws attempted	169	112	124	199	604
Free throws made	146	86	97	164	493
Free throw percentage	86%	77%	78%	82.5%	81.6%
(Team average)	(71%)	(70%)	(71%)	(71.4%)	
Rebounds	173	102	114	152	541
Average rebounds per game	5.8	3.8	3.9	4.8	4.6
Total points	632	498	555	782	2467
Average points per game	21.1	18.4	19.1	24.4	20.9
Average minutes playing time	38	34.1	33.9	37.9	36
Games leading scorer for BYU[2]	21	13	15	26	74
Personal high score[3]	36	40	32	39	40

1 All statistics based on Brigham Young University Sports Information Office information.

2 In 1979-80, Danny Ainge tied for BYU leading scorer twice, once with Alan Taylor and once with Fred Roberts. In 1980-81, he tied once with Fred Roberts.

3 1977-78, against Idaho State; Idaho State won 94-87. 1978-79, against Oral Roberts; BYU won 120-104. 1979-80, against the University of North Carolina at Charlotte, game played at Portland, Oregon; BYU won 104-91. 1980-81, against Utah State University; BYU won 104-89.

Danny Ainge at BYU

In addition to his NCAA record for scoring at least 10 points in the most consecutive games, Danny Ainge holds the following BYU records (records which he already held by the end of his junior year at BYU are marked *):

Single season records

* *Most points scored in a season (782, in 1980-81)
* Highest average points per game (24.4, in 1980-81)
* *Most field goals made in a season (309, in 1980-81)

Career records

* *Most points scored (2,467)
* Highest career average points per game (tied with John Fairchild at 20.9; Fairchild only played two seasons)
* Most field goals attempted (1,875)
* *Most field goals made (987)
* Most free throws attempted (604)
* Most free throws made (493)
* Best free throw percentage (81.6%)

The Ainges. Back: David Fletcher, Dave, Kay, Don, Danny, Doug. Front: Laurie, Stacy and Briawna, Michelle and Ashlee, Diane.

GREEK
MADE EASY

A SIMPLIFIED METHOD OF INSTRUCTION IN MODERN GREEK
FOR SCHOOLS AND SELF STUDY

By GEORGE C. DIVRY

Author of New Divry's English-Greek and Greek-English Dictionary,
Simplified English-Greek Method, First English-Greek Readers,
Modern Greek School Readers, etc.

THIRD EDITION
REVISED AND ENLARGED

D. C. DIVRY, Inc., Publishers
NEW YORK
1950

THIRD EDITION—
PUBLISHERS' NOTE

Due to the demand for "GREEK MADE EASY" —a demand which gratifyingly exceeded the expectations of the publishers — a third edition has been found necessary. In this new volume the scope of the work has been broadened, the material amended to insure greater interest and value, the entire contents rearranged for convenience and carefully revised to meet the specific requirements of the earnest student. The publishers, realizing the difficulties of mastering any language, have aimed in this new edition to ease and smooth the student's effort in acquiring modern Greek.

Printed in the U. S. A.
By D. C. DIVRY, Inc.
293 Seventh Avenue
New York

PREFACE

The study of Greek among the English-speaking peoples has lately received new impetus, owing to the interest taken in everything Greek by the descendants, relatives or friends of the Greek settlers on the North American continent.

Modern Greek—an evolutionary form of ancient Greek—is much simpler than classical Greek. In fact, it can be acquired as easily as the most popular European languages of today. However, for lack of the proper means of instruction, its study has been greatly handicapped both in schools and homes.

This book is intended to fill a long existing need for a simple, methodical and attractive medium of instruction, enabling the student of average education and intelligence to master the elements of Modern Greek grammar and at the same time to acquire a working knowledge of everyday Greek.

Our method of instruction is the same as that used in all our English and Greek instruction books—a system of gradual progress from the simpler and more useful elements of speech and grammar to the essential grammatical rules and expressions required for advanced study.

We have taken minute care that the student meet with as little difficulty as possible in his studies. With this in view, we have marked the pronunciation of all Greek words in our Vocabularies with the phonetics used in American textbooks, and given the English equivalent for every Greek word or phrase introduced in this manual.

To further facilitate the work of the student, we have tried, as much as advisable, to have the English phraseology correspond with the Greek, for this purpose sacrificing the elegance of expression in certain cases. For the same reason, the style of speech in this manual, both Greek and English, is that used in everyday conversation by the average person in Greece and in America.

In presenting this book to the Philhellenes of Greek or other origin, we trust that it will assist them in their studies, and that it will contribute to the advancement of the language of the New Testament and of the greatest civilization of all times.

ABBREVIATIONS USED IN THIS MANUAL

mas. or m.	for masculine
fem. or f.	" feminine
neu. or n.	" neuter.
nom. or n.	" nominative case.
gen. or g.	" genitive case.
accus. or ac.	" accusative case.
voc.	" vocative case.
sing. or s.	" singular.
pl. or p.	" plural.
f. e. or for ex.	" for example.
col. or c.	" colloquial.
pur.	" puristic.

PRELIMINARY LESSON

MODERN GREEK

Modern Greek is a simplification of ancient Greek, which it resembles to a high degree. Literary, or written, Greek, in vocabulary and grammar, is almost identical with the Greek of the New Testament. In the spoken language (δημοτική) some words in common use have been borrowed from other languages, while others have undergone changes which seem to have carried it away from classical Greek. However, since the Greeks have gradually gained their independence, the purification of the language has been progressing steadily, and today the καθαρεύουσα—or purified—language, the language of the courts, the Parliament, the newspapers and educated Greeks, differs little from classic Greek.

The spoken, or colloquial, language (ὁμιλουμένη or δημοτική) is in general use in everyday conversation, even by well educated Greeks. In this manual we have used the language prevailing, avoiding vulgar or slang expressions as well as classic words not easily understood by the average Greek of today.

PRONUNCIATION

Greek pronunciation is very simple. As a rule, each letter has, invariably, the same phonetic sound. The exceptions are few and follow fixed rules. There are no variations in the pronunciation of the Greek letters as in English (rough, though; fat, fate), no silent characters, no long or short vowel sounds. The accented syllable is marked in each word.

To further facilitate the work of the student, we have given the pronunciation of each Greek word according to its nearest English equivalent. The beginner must have in mind that each phonetic sound always has the same value in quantity and quality. Even the accents indicate only the syllables stressed, but do not change the quality of the accented vowels. There are only two letters without English equivalents, γ and χ, the sounds of which must be heard from a Greek to be mastered.

THE ALPHABET

WRITTEN

PRINTED

		Represented in Phonetic Pronunciation by	Pronounced as
Α α — ἄλφα	(ȧl′fa)	ȧ	a in father
Β ϐ β — βῆτα	(vï′tȧ)	v	v " victory
Γ γ — γάμα	(γȧ′mȧ)	γ, y	y " yes or year*
Δ δ — δέλτα	(thĕl′ta)	th	th " they
Ε ε — ἒ ψιλὸν	(ĕ psĭlôn′)	ĕ	e " red
Ζ ζ — ζῆτα	(zï′tȧ)	z	z " zero
Η η — ἦτα	(ï′tȧ)	ï, ĭ	i " ill or machine**
Θ θ — θῆτα	(thï′tȧ)	th	th " thin
Ι ι — ἰῶτα	(ĭ ô′tȧ)	ï, ĭ	i " ill or machine**
Κ κ — κάππα	(kȧ′pȧ)	k	k " king
Λ λ — λάμϐδα	(lȧm′vthȧ)	l	l " lot
Μ μ — μῦ	(mï)	m	m " mother

* Asterisks refer to remarks accompanying each lesson.

			Represented by	Pronounced as
Ν ν	— νῦ	(nï)	n	n " now
Ξ ξ	— ξῖ	(ksï)	x, ks	x " extra
Ο ο	— ὂ μικρὸν	(ȯ mĭkrȯn′)	ȯ	o " corporal
Π π	— πῖ	(pï)	p	p " paper
Ρ ρ	— ρῶ	(rȯ)	r	r " red
Σ σ ς ***	— σῖγμα	(sïγ′mȧ)	s	s " sister
Τ τ	— ταῦ	(tȧf)	t	t " tin
Υ υ	— ὖ ψιλὸν	(ï psĭlȯn′)	ï, ĭ	i " ill or machine**
Φ φ	— φῖ	(fï)	f	f " fat
Χ χ	— χῖ	(hï)	h	h " hill, but heavily aspirated****
Ψ ψ	— ψῖ	(psï)	ps	ps " lips
Ω ω	— ὦ μέγα	(ȯ mĕ′γȧ)	ȯ	o " corporal

REMARKS

A, α.—The vowel α is pronounced as **a** in **father** or **artistic** (Continental a). It is neither short nor long. In our phonetic pronunciation it is marked " ȧ ". For example:

καλὰ kȧlȧ′ well θάλασσα thȧ′lȧsȧ sea

B, β.—This is always pronounced as **v** in **victory.** Examples:
βιβλίον vĭvlï′ȯn book ἔβαλα ĕ′vȧlȧ I put

* **Γ, γ.**—The sound of γ can be correctly learned only by listening to a Greek. It is a soft, guttural **g**, equivalent to the consonant sound of **y** in **year** or **yellow**, or the sound of **w** in **woman.** Before the vowels α, ο or ω and the diphthong ου, γ can be likened to the consonant sound of **y** in **yard** or **yoke**, with the vowel sound of **i** eliminated. It would not be correct to represent it in all cases with **y** or **w** or **g**, therefore in the phonetic pronunciation we have mostly retained its Greek character "γ":

γάτα γȧ′tȧ cat γεμᾶτος yĕmȧ′tȯs full

γγ and γκ are pronounced as **ng** in **longer** or **angry**:

ἔγγονος ĕng′gȯnȯs grandson ἀγκάλη ȧngȧ′lĭ bosom

γ before the consonants χ or ξ is pronounced as **ng** nasal, as in **song**:

συγχωρῶ sĭng**h**ȯrȯ′ I pardon πλάστιγξ plȧs′tĭngks scales

Δ, δ.—This is always pronounced as **th** in **they**. In our phonetic pronunciation it is represented by **"th"** in bold-face type:

δίδω	**th**ĭ'**th**ô	I give	δέμα	**th**ĕ'mȧ	package

Ε, ε.—It is always pronounced as **e** in **red** or **there.** It is neither long nor short, the same as the Continental **e.** In our phonetic pronunciation it is represented by "ĕ":

ἔλαβε	ĕ'lȧvĕ	he took	ἔπεσε	ĕ'pĕsĕ	he fell

Ζ, ζ.—This is always pronounced as **z** in **zero** and represented by "z":

ζώνη	zô'nĭ	belt	ζητῶ	zĭtô'	I ask

** **Η, η.**—This is pronounced as **i** in **ill** or **machine.** It is neither long nor short. In our phonetic pronunciation it is represented by "ĭ" or "ï".

Note. The vowels η, ι, υ, and the diphthongs ει, οι and υι are all pronounced alike, as the Continental **i.** When accented, they sound more like **i** in **police** and are represented in our phonetic pronunciation by 'ï'. If unaccented, they are represented by the short **i** (ĭ). Both (ï and ĭ) have the same phonetic quality of the Continental **i.**

ἥλιος	ï'lĭôs	sun	μήτηρ	mï'tĭr	mother

Θ, θ.—This is always pronounced as "th" in **thin.** It is represented in our phonetic pronunciation by "th" in regular-face type:

θέλω	thĕ'lô	I wish	θύρα	thï'rȧ	door

Ι, ι.—It is pronounced the same as η (which see) and represented by "ĭ" or "ï":

ἱστορία	ĭstôrï'ȧ	history	φιλία	fĭlï'ȧ	friendship

Κ, κ.—It is always pronounced as **k** in **king** and represented by "k":

κακὸς	kȧkôs'	bad	ἔκαμε	ĕ'kȧmĕ	he did

Λ, λ.—It is pronounced as **l** in **lot** and represented by "l" :

λαὸς	lȧ ôs'	people	λύπη	lï'pĭ	sorrow

Μ, μ.—Always pronounced as **m** in **meat** and represented by "m" :

Μαρία	mȧrï'ȧ	Mary	μόνος	mô'nôs	alone

Ν, ν.—Always pronounced as **n** in **nine** and represented by "n" :

νέος	nĕ'ôs	young	ἐννέα	ĕnĕ'ȧ	nine

Ξ, ξ.—It is always pronounced as **x** in **extra** or **ks** in **weeks** and represented in our phonetic pronunciation by "ks":

ξένος	ksĕ'nôs	stranger	ξύλα	ksï'lȧ	wood

Ο, ο.—This is pronounced as **o** in **corporal** (Continental **o**). It is neither long nor short. Represented in our phonetic pronunciation by "ô":

ὁμολογῶ	ômôlôyô′	I confess	ὄνομα	ô′nômȧ	name

Π, π.—It is pronounced as **p** in **paper** and represented by "p":

πάππος	pȧ′pôs	grandfather	πολὺ	pôlï′	much

Ρ, ρ.—This is pronounced as **r** in **red**, and is always heard clearly, whether before a vowel or a consonant or at the end of words. It is represented by "r" or "rr":

ρόδον	rô′**th**ôn	rose	ρήτωρ	rï′tôr	orator

*** **Σ, σ, ς.**—This is pronounced as **s** in **sister.** Before the consonants **β, γ, δ, λ, μ, ν** and **ρ** it takes the sound of z, which is considered more euphonious. In our phonetic pronunciation it is represented by "s" and "z".

σύστημα	sï′stĭmȧ	system	σανὶς	sȧnïs′	board
κόσμος	kôz′môs	world	ἄσβεστος	ȧz′vĕstôs	lime

*****Note.** ς is used only at the end of words; in all other cases the character σ is used. For example: πόλις—city; σωρός—pile. In capital letters the same character is used in all cases. For example: ΠΟΛΙΣ, ΣΩΡΟΣ.

Τ, τ.—This is pronounced as **t** in **tin** and represented by "t":

τύχη	tï′**h**ĭ	fortune	τακτικὸς	tȧktĭkôs′	regular

Υ, υ.—This is pronounced the same as ι or η (which see). It is represented in our phonetic pronunciation by "ĭ" or "ï":

ὕπνος	ïp′nôs	sleep	ὕλη	ï′lĭ	matter

Φ, φ.—This is pronounced as **f** in **fat** and represented by "f":

φέρω	fĕ′rô	I bring	φίλος	fï′lôs	friend

**** **Χ, χ.**—This is a guttural consonant pronounced as a heavily aspirated **h**. The correct sound of χ should be learned from a Greek. It has no equivalent in English. It is similar to the German **ch** in B**ach**. In our phonetic pronunciation it is represented by "**h**" in bold-face type:

χαρὰ	**h**ȧrȧ′	joy	ἔχω	ĕ′**h**ô	I have

Ψ, ψ.—This is pronounced as **ps** in **lips**. It is represented by "ps":

ψαλὶς	psȧlïs′	scissors	ἔρριψα	ĕ′rĭpsȧ	I threw

Ω, ω.—This is pronounced as **o** in **corporal** (Continental **o**), the same as **ο** (which see). It is also represented by "ô":

ὠφέλιμος	ôfĕ′lĭmôs	useful	ὥριμος	ô′rĭmôs	ripe

DIPHTHONGS (Two Vowels Pronounced As One)

αι is pronounced as ĕ: — αἷμα (ĕ′mȧ) blood.

ει, οι, υι are pronounced as ĭ or ï: — εἶναι (ï′nĕ) is; οἶνος (ï′nôs) wine; υἱός (ĭ ôs′) son.

ου is pronounced as oo: — οὐρανός (oorȧnôs′) sky.

αυ, ευ, ηυ. These diphthongs are pronounced as ȧv, ĕv, ĭv. But if followed by the consonants ϑ, κ, ξ, π, σ, τ, φ, χ, ψ, they are pronounced as ȧf, ĕf, ĭf. Examples:

αὐγή (ȧv γï′) dawn	ηὗρα (ïv′rȧ) I found
αὐτός (ȧf tôs′) he	ηὐχήθη (ĭf hï′thĭ) he wished
εὐήλιος (ĕvï′lĭôs) sunny	εὔκολος (ĕf′kôlôs) easy
εὐθύς (ĕf thïs′) immediately	Παῦλος (pȧv′lôs) Paul

From the above it will be seen that the vowels **ι, η, υ** and the diphthongs **ει, οι** and **υι** are all pronounced alike as **i** in **ill** or **police** and in our phonetic pronunciation they are all represented by the characters 'ĭ' or 'ï'. Also the vowels **ο** and **ω** have the same pronunciation of **o** in **corporal** (represented by 'ô'). Likewise, the vowel **ε** and the diphthong **αι** are pronounced alike as **e** in **red** or **there** (represented by 'ĕ').

ACCENTS, ASPIRATION AND PUNCTUATION MARKS

Three accents are used in the Greek language: The **acute—ὀξεῖα** (′), used on one of the last three syllables (for example: μέλισσα, κάμνω); the **grave—βαρεῖα** (`) used on the last syllable (f. e. καλὸς πατὴρ); and the **circumflex—περισπωμένη** (῀) used on either of the last two syllables of Greek words (for ex. μῆλον, ἀγαπῶ).

On words beginning with a vowel, the aspiration marks **ψιλή** (') and **δασεῖα** (ʽ) are used over this vowel. On words beginning with a diphthong (two vowels pronounced as one) the aspiration mark is placed over the second vowel. The aspiration marks are silent and do not in any way affect the pronunciation of the vowels and diphthongs.

Greek punctuation marks are the same as in English, except the semicolon which is represented by a high period (·) and the interrogation mark represented by a semicolon (;).

LESSON 1

ποῖος, *colloq.* ποιός	pï′ôs, pĭôs′	**who**
ἐγὼ	ĕγô′	**I**
σὺ	sï	**you**
ὁ πατέρας	ô pȧtĕ′rȧs	**the father ***
ἕνας πατέρας	ĕ′nȧs pȧtĕ′rȧs	**a father**
ἡ μητέρα	ĭ mĭtĕ′rȧ	**the mother**
μία μητέρα	mï′ȧ mĭtĕ′rȧ	**a mother**
τὸ παιδὶ	tô pĕ thï′	**the boy, the child**
ἕνα παιδὶ	ĕ′nȧ pĕthï′	**a boy, a child**
ἡ κόρη	kô′rĭ	**the girl**
τὸ ψωμὶ	tô psômï′	**the bread**
τὸ κρέας	tô krĕ′ȧs	**the meat**
τὸ τυρί	tô tĭrï′	**the cheese**
τὸ πιάτο· ἕνα πιάτο	tô pĭȧ′tô; ĕ′nȧ pιa′tô	**the plate; a plate**
ἕνα πιάτο κρέας	ĕ′nȧ pĭȧ′tô krĕ′ȧs	**a plate of meat**
ἔχω, ἐγὼ ἔχω	ĕ′hô, ĕγô′ ĕ′hô	**I have ****
ἔχεις, σὺ ἔχεις	ĕ′hĭs, sï ĕ′hĭs	**you have**
ἔχεις;	ĕ′hĭs?	**have you? *****
ἔχει	ĕ′hĭ	**he (she, it) has**
καὶ	kĕ	**and**

Elementary Grammar

Ποῖος ἔχει τὸ ψωμί;	Who has the bread?
Ὁ πατέρας ἔχει τὸ ψωμί.	The father has the bread.
Ἡ μητέρα ἔχει τὸ ψωμί.	The mother has the bread.
Μία μητέρα ἔχει τὸ ψωμί.	A mother has the bread.
Ποιὸς ἔχει τὸ τυρί;	Who has the cheese?
Τὸ παιδὶ ἔχει τὸ τυρί.	The child has the cheese.
Ἕνα παιδὶ ἔχει τὸ κρέας.	A child has the meat.
Ἕνα παιδὶ ἔχει τὸ κρέας καὶ τὸ τυρί.	A boy (*or* a child) has the meat and the cheese.
(Ἐγὼ) ἔχω ἕνα πιάτο κρέας.	I have a plate of meat.
(Σὺ) ἔχεις τὸ κρέας καὶ τὸ ψωμί.	You have the meat and the bread.
Ἔχεις τυρὶ καὶ ψωμί;	Have you cheese and bread?
Ἡ κόρη ἔχει τὸ τυρὶ καὶ τὸ ψωμί.	The girl has the cheese and the bread.

EXERCISES

* There are three genders in Greek: masculine, feminine and neuter. Inasmuch as there are no rules for distinguishing the gender, we denote it with the definite article before each noun introduced in this manual.

The definite article is **ὁ** for the masculine, **ἡ** for the feminine and **τὸ** for the neuter gender. For example:

ὁ πατέρας	the father
ἡ μητέρα	the mother
τὸ παιδὶ	the child

As indefinite articles serve the numerals ἕνας for the masculine, μία for the feminine and ἕνα for the neuter gender — meaning **one**:

ἕνας πατέρας	a father
μία μητέρα	a mother
ἕνα παιδὶ	a child

Both the definite and indefinite articles are declined or change form according to cases and numbers, as we shall learn later.

* * Greek verbs are not necessarily preceded or followed by personal pronouns as in English. The change of the last syllable indicates the person of the verb. For example:

Ἔχω	I have
Ἔχεις	You have
Ἔχει	He has she has, it has

—:—

*** In Greek the interrogation is indicated only by the tone of speech and the interrogation mark (;) placed at the end of the sentence. For example:

Ἔχω	I have	Ἔχω;	Have I?
Ἔχεις	You have	Ἔχεις;	Have you?
Ἔχει	He (she, it) has	Ἔχει;	Has he? Has she? Has it?

LESSON 2

τὸ νερὸ	tô nĕrô′	**the water**
τὸ κρασὶ	tô krási′	**the wine**
τὸ γάλα	tô γà′là	**the milk**
τὸ βούτυρο **	tô voo′tĭrô	**the butter**
τὸ ἅλας, τὸ ἁλάτι	tô à′làs, tô àlà′tĭ	**the salt**
τὸ πιπέρι	tô pĭpĕ′rĭ	**the pepper**
ἡμεῖς, *col.* ἐμεῖς *or* μεῖς	ïmïs′, ĕmïs′, mïs	**we**
σεῖς	sïs	**you (plural)**
ἕνα ποτῆρι	ĕ′nà potï′rĭ	**a glass**
ἔχομεν, ἔχομε **	ĕ′hômĕn, ĕ′homĕ	**we have**
ἔχετε	ĕ′hĕtĕ	**you have (plural)**
ἔχουν	ĕ′hoon	**they have**
δὲν ἔχω	**thĕn ĕ′hô**	**I have not ***
δὲν ἔχεις	**thĕn ĕ′hĭs**	**you have not (sing.)**
δὲν ἔχεις;	**thĕn ĕ′hĭs?**	**have you not? (sing.)**
δός μου	thôz moo, thôs moo	**give me**
παρακαλῶ	pàràkàlô′	**if you please, I beg you**
ναὶ	nĕ	**yes**
ὄχι	ô′hĭ	**no**

EXERCISES

Σὺ ἔχεις τὸ νερὸ καὶ τὸ κρασί.	You have the water and the wine.
Ἡ κόρη ἔχει τὸ πιπέρι καὶ τὸ ἁλάτι.	The girl has the pepper and the salt.
(Ἡμεῖς) ἔχομεν τὸ γάλα καὶ τὸ βούτυρον.	We have the milk and the butter.
Δὲν ἔχομεν κρέας.	We have no meat.
Ἔχετε κρέας καὶ τυρί;	Have you meat and cheese?
Τὸ παιδὶ καὶ ἡ κόρη ἔχουν τὸ γάλα καὶ τὸ νερό.	The boy and the girl have the milk and the water.
Δὲν ἔχουν τὸ ψωμί.	They haven't the bread.
Δὲν ἔχετε τὸ νερό;	Haven't you the water?
Ναί, ἔχομε τὸ νερὸ καὶ τὸ κρασί.	Yes, we have the water and the wine.
Ἔχετε σεῖς τὸ γάλα;	Have you the milk?
Ὄχι. Ἡμεῖς δὲν ἔχομε τὸ γάλα.	No. We haven't the milk.
Ἔχομε τὸ νερὸ καὶ τὸ γάλα. Ἔχομε τὸ πιάτο.	We have the water and the milk. We have the plate.
Δός μου τὸ ἁλάτι καὶ τὸ πιπέρι, παρακαλῶ.	Give me the salt and the pepper, please.
Παρακαλῶ, δός μου ἕνα ποτῆρι γάλα.	Please give me a glass of milk.

Elementary Grammar

* The negative form in verbs is expressed by the word δὲν preceding the verb. For example:

Ἔχω	I have
Δὲν ἔχω	I have not
Βλέπω	I see
Δὲν βλέπω	I do not see

** In colloquial Greek the final ν in nouns and adjectives is often omitted. Thus we may say:

βούτυρο	for	βούτυρον	butter
μῆλο	"	μῆλον	apple
καλό	"	καλόν	good (neu.)

Final ν may also be omitted in verb forms ending in εν. For example:

Ἔχομε	for	Ἔχομεν	We have
Κάμνομε	"	Κάμνομεν	We do

In this manual the full form of words is mostly used, leaving to the student the liberty of retaining or dropping the final ν.

LESSON 3

ποῦ	poo	**where**
ἐδῶ	ĕthô′	**here**
ἐκεῖ	ĕkï′	**there**
μέσα	mĕ′sȧ	**in, inside, within**
ἔξω	ĕx′ô	**out, outside**
ἐπάνω	ĕpȧ′nô	**up, upon, upstairs**
κάτω	kȧ′tô	**down,under,downstairs**
εἶμαι	ï′mĕ	**I am**
εἶσαι	ï′sĕ	**thou art, * you are**
εἶναι	ï′nĕ	**he (she, it) is**
εἴμεθα	ï′mĕthȧ	**we are**
εἶσθε	ïs′thĕ	**you are** (plural)
εἶναι	ï′nĕ	**they are**
ὁ ἄνθρωπος	ô ȧn′thrôpôs	**the man**
καλὸς ἄνθρωπος	kȧlôs′ ȧn′thrôpôs	**good man**
καλὴ γυναῖκα	kȧlï′ yĭnĕ′kȧ	**good woman**
καλὸ παιδὶ	kȧlô′ pĕthï′	**good boy, good child**
κακός, κακή	kȧkôs′, kȧkï′	**bad** (masc.), **bad** (*fem.*)
κακόν, *colloq.* κακό	kȧkôn′ *or* kȧkô′	**bad** (*neuter*)
ὁ ἀδελφός	ô ȧthĕlfôs′	**the brother**
ἡ ἀδελφή	ï ȧthĕlfï′	**the sister**

EXERCISES

Ποῦ εἶνε ὁ καλὸς ἄνθρωπος;	Where is the good man?
Ὁ καλὸς ἄνθρωπος εἶνε ἐδῶ.	The good man is here.
Ποῦ εἶνε ἡ κακὴ γυναῖκα;	Where is the bad woman?
Ἡ κακὴ γυναῖκα εἶνε ἐκεῖ.	The bad woman is there.
Ἐδῶ εἶνε ἡ καλὴ ἀδελφή.	Here is the good sister.
Τὸ κακὸ παιδὶ εἶνε ἔξω.	The bad boy is out.
Δὲν εἶνε μέσα.	He is not in.
Ποιὸς εἶνε ἐπάνω;	Who is upstairs?
Ὁ πατέρας εἶνε ἐπάνω.	The father is upstairs.
Μία γυναῖκα εἶνε κάτω.	A woman is downstairs.
Ποιὸς εἶνε μέσα;	Who is inside?
Ἡ μητέρα εἶνε μέσα.	The mother is inside.
Εἶνε μέσα ἡ ἀδελφή;	Is the sister inside?
Ὄχι. Ἡ ἀδελφὴ δὲν εἶνε μέσα.	No. The sister is not inside.
Ἡ ἀδελφὴ καὶ ὁ ἀδελφὸς εἶνε ἔξω.	The sister and the brother are outside.
Ἡμεῖς εἴμεθα ἐπάνω καὶ σεῖς εἶσθε κάτω.	We are upstairs and you are downstairs.
Εἶσαι καλὸς ἢ κακός;	Are you good or bad?
Εἶμαι καλός· δὲν εἶμαι κακός.	I am good; I am not bad.

Elementary Grammar

Adjectives in Greek change form according to the gender, case and number of the nouns they qualify.

Most adjectives end in **ος** for the masculine, **α** or **η** for the feminine and **ον** (or abbreviated **ο**) for the neuter gender. For example:

Ὁ καλὸς πατέρας	The good father
Ἡ καλὴ μητέρα	The good mother
Τὸ καλὸν παιδίον or col. Τὸ καλὸ παιδὶ	The good boy
Κακὸς ἄνθρωπος	Bad man
Κακὴ γυναῖκα	Bad woman
Κακὸν (c. κακὸ) πρᾶγμα	Bad thing

* **Note.**—In English verbs the second person singular has been replaced by the second person plural. In Greek, however, the second person singular is in constant use when speaking to persons with whom one is familiar. The second person plural is used only when politeness or formality is desired to be shown.

LESSON 4

ἔλα, ἐλᾶτε	ĕ′lȧ; ĕlȧ′tĕ	**come,** *sing.*; **come,** *plu.*
κάθησε	kȧ′thĭsĕ	**sit down,** *singular*
καθήσατε	kȧthĭ′sȧtĕ	**sit down,** *plural*
πῶς	pôs	**how**
καλά	kȧlȧ′	**well**
πολὺ	pôlĭ′	**much, very**
εὐχαριστῶ	ĕfhȧrĭstô′	**thank you**
πήγαινε	pĭ′γĕnĕ	**go**
ὁ Γιάννης *	ô yĭȧ′nĭs	**John**
ὀλίγον	ôlĭ′γôn	**a little**
ἄρρωστος	ȧ′rôstôs	**ill, sick**
αὐτὸς ὁ ἄνθρωπος	ȧftôs′ ô ȧn′thrôpôs	**this man**
αὐτὴ ἡ γυναῖκα	ȧftĭ′ ĭ γĭnĕ′kȧ	**this woman**
αὐτὸ τὸ παιδὶ	ȧftô′ tô pĕthĭ′	**this boy, this child**
αὐτοὶ οἱ ἄνθρωποι	ȧftĭ′ ĭ ȧn′thrôpĭ	**these men**
αὐταὶ αἱ γυναῖκες	ȧftĕ′ ĕ yĭnĕ′kĕs	**these women**
col. αὐτὲς ἡ γυναῖκες	ȧftĕs′ ĭ yĭnĕ′kĕs	**these women** (colloq.)
αὐτὰ τὰ παιδιὰ	ȧftȧ′ tȧ pĕthĭȧ′	**these children**
τὸ πρᾶγμα	tô prȧγ′mȧ	**the thing**
αὐτοὶ	ȧftĭ′	**they,** *masculine*
αὐταί, *colloq.* αὐτές	ȧftĕ′, ȧftĕs′	**they,** *feminine*
αὐτά	ȧftȧ′	**they,** *neuter*

EXERCISES

Ἔλα ἐδῶ, Γιάννη.	Come here, John.
Κάθησε κάτω.	Sit down.
Πῶς εἶσαι; Εἶσαι καλά;	How are you? Are you well?
Ναί· εἶμαι πολὺ καλά. Εὐχαριστῶ.	Yes; I am very well. Thank you.
Πήγαινε μέσα.	Go inside.
Ποιὸς εἶνε μέσα;	Who is inside?
Ὁ καλὸς ἄνθρωπος εἶνε μέσα.	The good man is inside.
Αὐτὸς ὁ ἄνθρωπος δὲν εἶνε καλός. Εἶνε κακός.	This man is not good. He is bad.
Ποιὸς εἶνε ἐπάνω;	Who is upstairs?
Ἕνας ἄνθρωπος εἶνε ἐπάνω.	A man is upstairs.
Ποιὸς εἶνε αὐτὸς ὁ ἄνθρωπος;	Who is this man?
Εἶνε ὁ ἀδελφὸς Γιάννης.	It is brother John.
Εἶνε ὁ Γιάννης ἔξω;	Is John outside?
Ὄχι. Ὁ Γιάννης δὲν εἶνε ἔξω. Εἶνε μέσα ἐδῶ.	No. John is not outside. He is in here.
Εἶσθε καλά;	Are you well?
Ἡμεῖς εἴμεθα πολὺ καλά.	We are very well.
Σεῖς πῶς εἶσθε;	How are you?

Ἐγὼ εἶμαι ὀλίγον ἄρρωστος.	I am a little sick.
Ὁ πατέρας καὶ ἡ μητέρα εἶνε πολὺ καλά.	The father and the mother are very well.

Elementary Grammar

The Personal Pronouns are:

ἐγὼ	I
σὺ	thou, you (singular)
αὐτός	he
αὐτὴ	she
αὐτὸ	it
ἡμεῖς (col. ἐμεῖς)	we
σεῖς	you (plural)
αὐτοὶ	they (masculine)
αὐταί (c. αὐτές)	they (feminine)
αὐτὰ	they (neuter)

The third personal pronouns αὐτός, αὐτή, αὐτό (he, she, it) serve also as adjectives and are declined likewise. For example:

Αὐτὸς ὁ ἄνθρωπος	This man
Αὐτοὶ οἱ ἄνθρωποι	These men, these people
Αὐτὴ ἡ κόρη	This girl
Αὐταὶ αἱ κόραι col. αὐτὲς ἡ κόρες	These girls
Αὐτὸ τὸ παιδὶ	This child
Αὐτὰ τὰ παιδιά	These children

* In Greek the definite article is usually placed before a proper name:

Ὁ Γιάννης	(The) John
Ἡ Μαρία	(The) Mary
Τὸν Γεώργιον	(The) George

LESSON 5

ὁ ἄνθρωπος	ô ȧn′thrôpôs	**the man** (*nominative*)
τοῦ ἀνθρώπου	too ȧnthrô′poo	**of the man** (*genitive*)
τὸν ἄνθρωπον	tôn ȧn′thrôpôn	**the man** (*accusative*)
ὦ ἄνθρωπε!	ô ȧn′thropĕ	**O man!**
οἱ ἄνθρωποι	ĭ ȧn′thrôpĭ	**the men** (*nominative*)
τῶν ἀνθρώπων	tôn ȧnthrô′pôn	**of the men** (*genitive*)
τοὺς ἀνθρώπους	toos ȧnthrô′poos	**the men** (*accusative*)
ὦ ἄνθρωποι!	ô ȧn′thrôpĭ	**O men!**
ἡ ζάχαρη	ĭ zȧ′hȧrĭ	**the sugar**
τὸ τσάϊ	tô tsȧ′ĭ	**the tea**
ὁ καφὲς	ô kȧfĕs′	**the coffee**
ἔχω τὴν ζάχαρη	ĕ′ho tĭn zȧ′hȧrĭ	**I have the sugar**
ἡ μουστάρδα	ĭ moostȧr′thȧ	**the mustard**
τὰ χρήματα	tȧ hrĭ′mȧtȧ	**the money**
θέλω	thĕ′lô	**I want, I wish**
θέλεις	thĕ′lĭs	**you want (sing.)**
θέλει	thĕ′lĭ	**he (she, it) wants**
θέλομεν, *col.* θέλομε	thĕ′lômĕn, thĕ′lômĕ	**we want**
θέλετε	thĕ′lĕtĕ	**you want (plural)**
θέλουν	thĕ′loon	**they want**
εἰς, *col.* σὲ *or* σ’	ĭs, sĕ, s	**in, at, to**
μόνον	mô′nôn	**only**
βλέπω	vlĕ′pô	**I see**
ὁ σκύλος	ô skĭ′lôs	**the dog**
δότε, *col.* δόστε	thô′tĕ or thôs′tĕ	**give (plural)**

EXERCISES

Ἔχετε τὸ γάλα;	Have you the milk?
Ναί, ἔχω τὸ γάλα καὶ τὸν καφέ.	Yes, I have the milk and the coffee.
Θέλετε τὴν ζάχαρην;	Do you want the sugar?
Ναί, θέλω τὴν ζάχαρη.	Yes; I want the sugar.
Δότε μου τὴν ζάχαρη καὶ τὸν καφέ, παρακαλῶ.	Give me the sugar and the coffee, please.
Δός μου τὸν καφὲ καὶ τὸ τσάϊ.	Give me the coffee and the tea.
Αὐτὸ τὸ παιδὶ θέλει τὸν καφέ.	This boy wants the coffee.
Δὸς τὸν καφὲ εἰς τὸ παιδί.	Give the coffee to the boy.
Ἔχετε τὸ ἁλάτι;	Have you the salt?
Ναί, ἔχω τὸ ἁλάτι καὶ τὸ πιπέρι.	Yes, I have the salt and the pepper.
Θέλετε τὴν μουστάρδαν;	Do you want the mustard?
Ὄχι. Θέλω μόνον τὸ πιπέρι.	No; I want only the pepper.
Ἡ κόρη θέλει τὸ ἁλάτι.	The girl wants the salt.
Θέλει τὸ ἁλάτι, τὸ πιπέρι καὶ τὴν μουστάρδα.	She wants the salt, the pepper and the mustard.
Ποῖος θέλει τὰ χρήματα;	Who wants the money?
Ἡμεῖς θέλομεν τὰ χρήματα.	We want the money.
Τὸ παιδὶ καὶ ἡ κόρη θέλουν τὰ χρήματα.	The boy and the girl want the money.

Βλέπω ἕνα σκύλον.	I see a dog.
Δόστε τὸ κρέας σ' αὐτὸν τὸν σκύλον.	Give the meat to this dog.

Elementary Grammar

Ἐδῶ εἶναι	ὁ ἄνθρωπος	Here is the man
Ὁ καφὲς	τοῦ ἀνθρώπου	The coffee of the man (the man's coffee)
Βλέπω	τὸν ἄνθρωπον	I see the man
Θέλεις,	ὦ ἄνθρωπε;	Do you want, O man?
Ἐδῶ εἶναι	οἱ ἄνθρωποι	Here are the men
Ὁ καφὲς	τῶν ἀνθρώπων	The coffee of the men (the men's coffee)
Βλέπω	τοὺς ἀνθρώπους	I see the men
Θέλετε,	ὦ ἄνθρωποι;	Do you want, O men?

Masculine nouns ending in **ος** are declined as the noun ἄνθρωπος. Also adjectives ending in **ος** are declined in the same way. Examples:

Ὁ καλὸς σκύλος	The good dog
Τοῦ καλοῦ σκύλου	Of the good dog
Εἰς τὸν καλὸν σκύλον	To the good dog
Οἱ καλοὶ σκύλοι	The good dogs
Τῶν καλῶν σκύλων	Of the good dogs
Εἰς τοὺς καλοὺς σκύλους	To the good dogs

In the genitive singular or plural and in the accusative plural of nouns ending in **ος** and accented on the third syllable from the end, the accent is transferred to the second syllable from the end. This happens also to adjectives ending in **ος**.—For example:

Ὁ ἴδιος ἄνθρωπος	The same man (nom.)
Τοῦ ἰδίου ἀνθρώπου	Of the same man
Οἱ ἴδιοι ἄνθρωποι	The same men (nom.)
Τῶν ἰδίων ἀνθρώπων	Of the same men
Τοὺς ἰδίους ἀνθρώπους	The same men (accus.)
Τὸ χρήσιμον δωμάτιον	The useful room
Τοῦ χρησίμου δωματίου	Of the useful room

LESSON 6

δίδω	**thĭ'thô**	**I give**
δίδεις	**thĭ'thĭs**	**you give** (sing.)
δίδει	**thĭ'thĭ**	**he (she, it) gives**
δίδομεν	**thĭ'thômĕn**	**we give**
δίδετε	**thĭ'thĕtĕ**	**you give** (plural)
δίδουν	**thĭ'thoon**	**they give**
σοῦ δίδω	soo **thĭ'thô**	**I give you**
μοῦ δίδεις	moo **thĭ'thĭs**	**you give me**
παίρνω	pĕr'nô	**I take**
παίρνεις	pĕr'nĭs	**you take**
κύριε	kĭ'rĭĕ	**sir**
κυρία	kĭrĭ'ȧ	**madam**
δεσποινὶς	**thĕspĭnĭs'**	**miss**
ἐὰν	**ĕ ȧn'**	**if**
ἢ	**ĭ**	**or**
τί	**tĭ**	**what**
κάτι	**kȧ'tĭ**	**something**
τίποτε	tĭ'pôtĕ	**nothing, anything**
ὅλος, ὅλη	**ô'lôs, ô'lĭ**	**all** (mas.); **all** (fem.)
ὅλον, *col.* ὅλο	**ô'lôn, ô'lô**	**all** (neuter)
τὸ σπίτι	**tô spĭ'tĭ**	**the home, the house**
ὁ πάγος	**ô pȧ'γôs**	**the ice**
καί, ἐπίσης	**kĕ, ĕpĭ'sĭs**	**and, also**
μὲ	**mĕ**	**with, together with**

EXERCISES

Ποῖος σοῦ δίδει νερό;	Who gives you water?
Αὐτὸς ὁ ἄνθρωπος μοῦ δίδει νερό.	This man gives me water.
Μοῦ δίδει νερὸ καὶ γάλα.	He gives me water and milk.
Ποιὸς σοῦ δίδει τσάϊ;	Who gives you tea?
Σὺ μοῦ δίδεις τσάϊ. Μοῦ δίδεις τσάϊ καὶ ζάχαρη.	You give me tea. You give me tea and sugar.
Θέλω κάτι, κυρία.	I want something, madam.
Θέλετε τυρί;	Do you want cheese?
Ναί. Θέλομε τυρὶ καὶ ψωμί.	Yes. We want cheese and bread.
Πάρετε τυρὶ καὶ βούτυρο.	Take cheese and butter.
Εὐχαριστῶ, κύριε. Δὲν θέλω τυρί. Θέλω μόνον ψωμί.	Thank you, sir. I don't want cheese. I want bread only.
Θέλετε καὶ νερό;	Do you want water too?
Δὲν θέλω τίποτε. Εὐχαριστῶ.	I don't want anything. Thank you.
Δός μου καφὲ καὶ γάλα, παρακαλῶ.	Give me coffee and milk, please.
Παίρνετε καφὲ ἢ τσάϊ;	Do you take coffee or tea?
Δὲν παίρνω τίποτε.	I don't take anything.
Θέλω μόνον ἕνα ποτῆρι νερὸ μὲ πάγον.	I want only a glass of water with ice (iced water).

Δὲν ἔχομε πάγο ἐδῶ. Ὁ πάγος εἶνε εἰς τὸ σπίτι.	We have no ice here. The ice is in the house.
Ἐγὼ θέλω γάλα καὶ ζάχαρη.	I want milk and sugar.
Θέλετε ὅλο τὸ γάλα;	Do you want all the milk?
Ναί. Δότε μου ὅλον τὸ γάλα, παρακαλῶ.	Yes. Give me all the milk, please.

Grammatical Remarks

Βλέπω	I see
Βλέπεις	You see (singular)
Βλέπει	He (she, it) sees
Βλέπομεν	We see
Βλέπετε	You see (plural)
Βλέπουν	They see
Δίδω	I give
Δίδεις	You give (singular)
Δίδει	He (she, it) gives
Δίδομεν	We give
Δίδετε	You give (plural)
Δίδουν	They give

Greek verbs ending in **ω** are accented on one of the last two syllables. Those accented on the syllable before last are inflected as the above examples.

LESSON 7

τὸ βιβλίον	tô vĭvlĭ′ôn	**the book**
τοῦ βιβλίου	too vĭvlĭ′oo	**of the book**
εἰς τὸ βιβλίον	ĭs tô vĭvlĭ′ôn	**in the book**
τὰ βιβλία	tȧ vĭvlĭ′ȧ	**the books**
τῶν βιβλίων	tôn vĭvlĭ′ôn	**of the books**
βλέπω τὰ βιβλία	vlĕ′pô tȧ vĭvlĭ′ȧ	**I see the books**
ἡ πέννα	ĭ pĕ′nȧ	**the pen**
τῆς πέννας	tĭs pĕ′nȧs	**of the pen**
εἰς τὴν πένναν *or* εἰς τὴν πέννα	ĭs tĭn pĕ′nȧn or ĭs tĭn pĕ′nȧ	**to the pen**
ἡ πέννες	ĭ pĕ′nĕs	**the pens**
τῶν πεννῶν	tôn pĕnôn′	**of the pens**
εἰς τὴς πέννες	ĭs tĭs pĕ′nĕs	**to the pens**
τὸ μαχαῖρι	tô mȧhĕ′rĭ	**the knife**
τὸ μαχαῖρι μου	tô mȧhĕ′rĭ moo	**my knife**
ὁ φίλος	ô fĭ′lôs	**the friend** (masc.)
ἡ φίλη	ĭ fĭ′lĭ	**the friend** (fem.)
ἡ γάτα	ĭ γȧ′tȧ	**the cat**
τὸ βιβλίον μου	tô vĭvlĭ′ôn moo	**my book**
τὸ βιβλίον σου	tô vĭvlĭ′ôn soo	**your (thy) book**
τὸ χαρτὶ	tô hȧrrtĭ′	**the paper**
μεγάλος	mĕγȧ′lôs	**large, big** (masc.)
μεγάλη	mĕγȧ′lĭ	" " (fem.)
μεγάλο	mĕγȧ′lô	" " (neuter)
μικρὸς	mĭkrôs′	**small, little** (masc.)
μικρὰ *or* μικρὴ	mĭkrȧ′, mĭkrĭ′	" " (fem.)
μικρὸν *or* μικρὸ	mĭkrôn′, mĭkrô′	" " (neuter)

EXERCISES

Ἔχεις ἕνα βιβλίον;	Have you a book?
Ἔχω ἕνα μεγάλο βιβλίον.	I have a big book.
Ἐγὼ ἔχω ἕνα μικρὸ βιβλίο.	I have a small book.
Τὸ βιβλίο μου εἶνε πολὺ καλό.	My book is very good.
Τὸ χαρτὶ τοῦ βιβλίου σου δὲν εἶνε καλόν.	The paper of your book is not good.
Ὁ φίλος μου ἔχει καλὰ βιβλία.	My friend has good books.
Ἔχει καὶ καλὲς πέννες.	He also has good pens.
Θέλεις ἕνα μαχαῖρι;	Do you want a knife?
Ναί. Θέλω ἕνα μικρὸ μαχαῖρι.	Yes. I want a small knife.
Τὸ μαχαῖρι μου εἶνε πολὺ μεγάλο.	My knife is too big.
Αὐτὴ ἡ πέννα εἶνε πολὺ μικρή.	This pen is very small.
Δός μου μιὰ μεγάλη πέννα.	Give me a big pen.
Βλέπεις αὐτὸ τὸ μικρὸ παιδί;	Do you see this little child?
Εἶνε ὁ μικρὸς ἀδελφός μου.	He is my little brother.
Ἔχει ἕνα μεγάλο σκύλο.	He has a big dog.
Ὄχι. Ὁ σκύλος του δὲν εἶναι μεγάλος. Εἶναι μικρός.	No. His dog is not big. He is small.
Ἡ φίλη μου ἔχει μία κακὴ μικρὴ γάτα.	My (girl) friend has a bad little cat.
Ποῦ εἶνε τὸ μαχαῖρι σου;	Where is your knife?

Τὸ μαχαῖρι μου εἶνε ἐκεῖ ἐπάνω.	My knife is up there.
Θέλετε τὴν πέννα μου;	Do you want my pen?
Δὲν θέλομεν τὴν πέννα σου.	We do not want your pen.
Ἡ πέννα σου δὲν εἶνε πολὺ καλή.	Your pen is not very good.

Grammatical Remarks

Greek nouns ending in **ον** are declined as the noun **βιβλίον**. Also all adjectives ending in **ον** (neuter gender) are inflected likewise. For example:

Τὸ μικρὸν παιδίον	The small boy
Τοῦ μικροῦ παιδίου	Of the small boy (the small boy's)
Εἰς τὸ μικρὸν παιδίον	To the small boy
Τὰ μικρὰ παιδία	The small boys
Τῶν μικρῶν παιδίων	Of the small boys (the small boys')
Εἰς τὰ μικρὰ παιδία	To the small boys

Greek nouns ending in **α** (feminine gender) are declined as the word **πέννα**. In a similar way are inflected adjectives of the feminine gender ending in **α** or **η**. For example:

Ἡ κακὴ γάτα	The bad cat
Τῆς κακῆς γάτας	Of the bad cat
Εἰς τὴν κακὴν γάταν	To the bad cat
Αἱ κακαὶ γάται	The bad cats
(Col.) Αἱ κακαὶς γάταις	" " "
Τῶν κακῶν γατῶν	Of the bad cats
Εἰς τὰς κακὰς γάτας	To the bad cats
(Col.) Σ ταὶς κακαὶς γάταις	" " " "
or Στὲς κακὲς γάτες	" " " "

LESSON 8

ὁ πατέρας μου	ô pȧtĕ'rȧs moo	**my father**
ὁ πατέρας σου	ô pȧtĕ'rȧs soo	**your (thy) father,** *sing.*
ὁ πατέρας του	ô pȧtĕ'rȧs too	**his father**
ὁ πατέρας της	ô pȧtĕ'rȧs tĭs	**her father**
ὁ πατέρας μας	ô pȧtĕ'rȧs mȧs	**our father**
ὁ πατέρας σας	ô pȧtĕ'rȧs sȧs	**your father** (*plural*)
ὁ πατέρας τους	ô pȧtĕ'rȧs toos	**their father**
ἡ ἀδελφή μου	ĭ ȧthelfĭ' moo	**my sister**
ἡ ἀδελφή σου	ĭ ȧthĕlfĭ' soo	**your (thy) sister**
αἱ ἀδελφαί μου	ĕ ȧthĕlfĕ' moo	**my sisters**
αἱ ἀδελφαί μας	ĕ ȧthĕlfĕ' mȧs	**our sisters**
ὀλίγος	ôlĭ'γôs	**little** (masc.)
ὀλίγη	ôlĭ'γĭ	" (fem.)
ὀλίγον	ôlĭ'γôn	" (neuter)
γλυκός, γλυκή, -όν	γlĭkôs', γlĭkĭ', γlĭkôn'	**sweet** (m., f., n.)
ἡ μελάνη	ĭ mĕlȧ'nĭ	**the ink**
ἀλλὰ	ȧlȧ'	**but**
ἄρρωστος, η, ον	ȧ'rôstôs, ȧ'rôstĭ, -ôn	**ill, sick** (m., f., n.)
ἐπίσης	ĕpĭ'sĭs	**also**
κανεὶς	kȧnĭs'	**no one, any one** (m.)*
καμμία	kȧmĭ'ȧ	**no one, any one** (fem.)
κανὲν	kȧnĕn'	**none, anything** (neu.)
κἄτι	kȧ'tĭ	**something**

EXERCISES

Πῶς εἶναι ὁ πατέρας σου; Εἶναι καλά;	How is your father? Is he well?
Ὄχι. Ὁ πατέρας μου δὲν εἶνε καλά. Εἶνε ὀλίγο ἄρρωστος.	No. My father is not well. He is a little ill.
Ἡ μητέρα μου εἶνε πολὺ καλά.	My mother is very well.
Ἡ ἀδελφή μου εἶνε ἐπίσης πολὺ καλά.	My sister also is very well.
Εἶσθε καλοὶ ἢ κακοὶ ἄνθρωποι;	Are you good or bad men?
Εἴμεθα καλοὶ ἄνθρωποι.	We are good men.
Δὲν εἴμεθα κακοί.	We are not bad.
Αἱ ἀδελφαί μου εἶναι πολὺ καλαὶ γυναῖκες.	My sisters are very good women.
Ποῖος εἶναι ἄρρωστος;	Who is sick?
Κανεὶς δὲν* εἶναι ἄρρωστος.	Nobody is sick.
Ὅλοι εἶναι καλὰ ἐδῶ μέσα.	All are well (in) here.
Εἶναι ὁ καφές σου γλυκός;	Is your coffee sweet?
Ὄχι. Ὁ καφές μου δὲν εἶναι πολὺ γλυκός.	No. My coffee is not very sweet.
Θέλετε ζάχαρη;	Do you want sugar?
Ναί. Δότε μου ὀλίγη ζάχαρη.	Yes. Give me some sugar.
Εἶναι οἱ ἀδελφοί σου μικροὶ ἢ μεγάλοι;	Are your brothers small or big?
Οἱ ἀδελφοί μου εἶναι μικροί.	My brothers are small.
Αἱ ἀδελφαί σου εἶνε μεγάλαι.	Your sisters are big.
Ἡ μελάνη σας δὲν εἶνε καλή.	Your ink is not good.
Δό(σ)τε μου καλὴν μελάνην, σᾶς παρακαλῶ.	Give me good ink, please.

Grammatical Remarks

Possessive Pronouns

μου	my
σου	thy, your (singular)
του	his, its
της	her
μας	our
σας	your (plural)
τους or των	their

In Greek the possessive pronouns follow the noun, while in English they precede it. They may retain or drop the definite articles ὁ, ἡ, τό, etc. In general, the possessive pronouns are not accented. Examples:

Τὰ βιβλία μου	My books
Τὰ βιβλία σου	Your books
Τὰ βιβλία του	His books, its books
Τὰ βιβλία της	Her books
Τὰ βιβλία μας	Our books
Τὰ βιβλία σας	Your books (plural)
Τὰ βιβλία τους	Their books

The possessive pronouns are not declined:

Τὸ βιβλίον μου	My book
Τοῦ βιβλίου μου, etc.	Of my book, etc.

---

* In Greek conversation two negatives are sometimes used instead of one. «Κανεὶς δὲν εἶνε ἄρρωστος» literally means "nobody is not sick."

Κανείς, καμμία, κανέν, meaning "no one", is used sometimes in place of the English pronoun "any". F. e. «Εἶνε κανεὶς ἐδῶ;»—"Is any one here?"

LESSON 9

αὐτός	ȧftôs′	**this** (masc.)
αὐτή	ȧftï′	" (fem.)
αὐτό	ȧftŏ′	" (neu.)
αὐτὸς ὁ σκύλος	ȧftôs′ ô skï′lôs	**this dog**
αὐτὴ ἡ γυναῖκα	ȧftï′ ï yĭnĕ′kȧ	**this woman**
αὐτὸ τὸ πρᾶγμα	ȧftŏ′ tô prȧγ′mȧ	**this thing**
τοῦτο τὸ πρᾶγμα	too′tô tô prȧγ′mȧ	**this thing**
ἐκεῖνος	ekï′nôs	**that** (masc.)
ἐκείνη	ĕkï′nĭ	" (fem.)
ἐκεῖνο	ĕkï′nô	" (neu.)
τὸ μολύβι	tô môlï′vĭ	**the pencil**
τὸ τραπέζι	tô trȧpĕ′zĭ	**the table**
τὸ δωμάτιον	tô thômȧ′tĭôn	**the room**
εἰς τὸ δωμάτιον	ĭs tô thômȧ′tĭôn	**in the room**
col. στὸ δωμάτιο	stô thômȧ′tĭô	" " "
ἐπάνω στὸ τραπέζι	ĕpȧ′nô stô trȧpĕ′zĭ	**on the table**
τώρα	tô′rȧ	**now**
πάλιν	pȧ′lĭn	**again**
ὁ δρόμος	ô thrŏ′môs	**the street, the road**
μέ, μαζὺ μὲ	mĕ, mȧzï′ mĕ	**together with**
τόσον	tŏ′sôn	**so, so much**

EXERCISES

Εἶνε αὐτὸ τὸ μαχαῖρι σου;	Is this your knife?
Ναί. Τοῦτο εἶνε τὸ μαχαῖρι μου.	Yes. This is my knife.
Εἶνε ἐκεῖνος ὁ σκύλος σου;	Is that your dog?
Ὄχι, κύριε. Ἐκεῖνος δὲν εἶνε ὁ σκύλος μου.	No, sir. That is not my dog.
Εἶνε ὁ σκύλος τοῦ πατέρα μας.	It is our father's dog (it is the dog of our father).
Ἔχεις πέννα;	Have you a pen?
Ἔχω μιὰ πέννα, ἀλλὰ δὲν ἔχω χαρτί.	I have a pen, but I have no paper.
Ποῦ εἶνε τὸ μολύβι σου;	Where is your pencil?
Τὸ μολύβι μου εἶνε ἐκεῖ.	My pencil is there.
Εἶνε ἐπάνω στὸ τραπέζι.	It is on the table.
Ποῦ εἶνε τὸ τραπέζι;	Where is the table?
Τὸ τραπέζι δὲν εἶνε ἐδῶ. Εἶνε εἰς τὸ μικρὸν δωμάτιον.	The table is not here. It is in the small room.
Εἶνε ὁ ἀδελφός σας στὸ σπίτι;	Is your brother at home?
Ὁ ἀδελφός μου δὲν εἶνε εἰς τὸ σπίτι. Εἶνε εἰς τὸν δρόμον.	My brother is not at home. He is in the street.
Ἡ ἀδελφή μας εἶνε σπίτι.	Our sister is home.
Εἶνε μαζὺ μὲ τὴν μητέρα μας.	She is with our mother.

Ἡ μητέρα μας εἶνε ὀλίγον ἄρρωστη τώρα.	Our mother is a little ill now.
Εἶνε ἄρρωστη πάλιν;	Is she sick again?
Ναί. Δὲν εἶνε τόσον καλά.	Yes. She is not so well.

Grammatical Remarks

The personal pronouns **αὐτός, αὐτή, αὐτὸ (he, she, it)** in Greek serve also as demonstrative pronouns. They are declined the same as adjectives ending in **ος, η, ον.** They may precede or follow the noun to which they refer. Examples:

Αὐτὸς ὁ ἄνθρωπος	or	Ὁ ἄνθρωπος αὐτὸς	This man
Αὐτὴ ἡ γυναῖκα	"	Ἡ γυναῖκα αὐτὴ	This woman
Αὐτὸ τὸ μολύβι	"	Τὸ μολύβι αὐτὸ	This pencil
Αὐτὰ τὰ παιδία	"	Τὰ παιδία αὐτὰ	These children
Αὐτοὶ οἱ ἄνθρωποι	"	Οἱ ἄνθρωποι αὐτοὶ	These men
Αὐτῶν τῶν γυναικῶν	"	Τῶν γυναικῶν αὐτῶν	Of these women
Etc.		Etc.	Etc.

* * *

The preposition **εἰς (to, on, in, at)** in everyday talk is often substituted by the abbreviated forms 'ς, σ' or σε. If the definite article follows the abbreviations σ' or ς', these are merged with the article into a single word. For example:

εἰς τὸ δωμάτιο	or	στὸ δωμάτιο	in the room
εἰς τὸν πατέρα	"	στὸν πατέρα	to the father
εἰς τὴν ἀδελφή μου	"	στὴν ἀδελφή μου	to my sister, etc.
εἰς τοῦτο τὸ τραπέζι	"	σὲ τοῦτο τὸ τραπέζι	on this table
εἰς μίαν ἡμέραν	"	σὲ μίαν ἡμέραν	in one day
εἰς ἕνα μέρος	"	σ' ἕνα μέρος	in a place

LESSON 10

ἐγὼ εἶμαι ἐδῶ	ĕγô′ ï′mĕ ĕthô′	**I am here**
δός μου, δόσε μου	**thôs** moo, **thô′**sĕ moo	**give me**
αὐτὸ εἶνε καλὸν	ȧftô′ ï′nĕ kȧlôn′	**it is good**
μὲ βλέπεις	mĕ vlĕ′pĭs	**you see me**
ὁ φίλος μας	ô fï′lôs mȧs	**our (man) friend**
σεῖς κάμνετε	sïs kȧm′nĕtĕ	**you make, you do**
ἡμεῖς σᾶς βλέπομεν	ïmïs′ sȧs vlĕ′pômĕn	**we see you**
c. μεῖς σᾶς βλέπομε	mïs sȧs vlĕ′pômĕ	" "
δός τους	**thôs′** toos	**give them**
σεῖς τοὺς δίδετε	sïs toos **thï′thĕtĕ**	**you give them**
ἕνα ποτῆρι νερὸ	ĕ′nȧ potï′rï nĕrô′	**a glass of water**
ἀκριβός, ἀκριβή, -όν	ȧkrĭvôs′, ȧkrĭvï′, -vôn′	**dear** *m*; **dear** *f*; **dear** *n*.
γεμᾶτος, γεμάτη, -ον	yĕmȧ′tôs, -tï, -tôn	**full** *m*; **full** *f*; **full** *n*.
ἀδειανός, ή, όν	ȧthïȧnôs′, -ï′, -ôn′	**empty** *m*; *f*; *n*.
πλούσιος, πλούσιον	ploo′sïôs, ploo′sïôn	**rich,** *mas.*; **rich,** *neuter*
πλουσία, *col.* πλούσια	ploosï′ȧ, ploo′sïȧ	**rich,** *feminine*
πτωχός, πτωχή, -όν	ptôhôs′, ptôhï′, ptôhôn′	**poor** *m*; *f*; *n*.
διατὶ	**thïȧtï′**	**why**
διότι	**thïô′tï**	**because**
τεμπέλης	tĕmpĕ′lïs or tĕmbĕ′lïs	**lazy**

EXERCISES

Ἐγὼ εἶμαι ἐδῶ.	I am here.
Ὁ πατέρας μου δὲν εἶναι ἐδῶ.	My father is not here.
Εἶναι στὸ σπίτι.	He is at home.
Εἶσαι ἄρρωστος πάλι;	Are you sick again?
Ὄχι. Δὲν εἶμαι ἄρρωστος. Εἶμαι πολὺ καλὰ τώρα.	No. I am not sick. I am very well now.
Ὁ φίλος μου εἶναι ἄρρωστος.	My friend is sick.
Ὁ φίλος σου ἔχει χρήματα.	Your friend has money.
Ὁ φίλος μου δὲν ἔχει χρήματα. Δὲν εἶναι πλούσιος.	My friend has no money. He is not rich.
Εἶναι πτωχὸς ἄνθρωπος.	He is a poor man.
Διατί εἶναι πτωχός;	Why is he poor?
Εἶναι πτωχὸς διότι εἶναι τεμπέλης.	He is poor because he is lazy.
Ποῦ εἶναι τὰ ϐιϐλία σου;	Where are your books?
Τὰ ϐιϐλία μου εἶναι ἐπάνω στὸ μικρὸ τραπέζι.	My books are on the small table.
Εἶναι καλὰ ϐιϐλία;	Are they good books?
Εἶναι πολὺ καλὰ ϐιϐλία.	They are very good books.
Ποῦ εἶναι ὁ φίλος σου;	Where is your friend?
Εἶναι σ' ἐκεῖνο τὸ δωμάτιον.	He is in that room.
Εἶνε μαζὺ μὲ τὸν ἀδελφό σου.	He is with your brother.
Τί θέλετε τώρα, κύριε;	What do you want now, sir?
Δός μας ἕνα ποτῆρι νερό.	Give us a glass of water.
Δός μου ἕνα ποτῆρι γάλα.	Give me a glass of milk.
Δός μου ἕνα γεμᾶτο ποτῆρι.	Give me a full glass.
Αὐτὸ τὸ ποτῆρι εἶναι ἀδειανό.	This glass is empty.

Grammatical Remarks

DECLENSION OF PERSONAL PRONOUNS

Singular

Case	1st Person	2nd Person	3d Person Masculine	3d Person Feminine	3d Person Neuter
Nomin.	ἐγὼ I	σὺ you (thou)	αὐτὸς he	αὐτὴ she	αὐτὸ it
Genitive	μου my	σου your (thy)	αὐτοῦ *or* του his	αὐτῆς *or* της her	αὐτοῦ *or* του its
Accus.	ἐμέ, μέ, μένα me	σέ, σένα you (thee)	τὸν him	τὴν her	τὸ it

Plural

Case	1st Person	2nd Person	3d Person Masculine	3d Person Feminine	3d Person Neuter
Nomin.	ἡμεῖς *or* 'μεῖς we	σεῖς you	αὐτοὶ they (m.)	αὐταὶ they (f.)	αὐτὰ they (n.)
Genitive	μας our	σας your	αὐτῶν *or* των *or* τους their	αὐτῶν *or* των *or* τους their	αὐτῶν *or* των *or* τους their
Accus.	μᾶς *or* μας us	σᾶς *or* σας you	τοὺς *or* τους them	τοὺς *or* τους them	τοὺς *or* τους them

In the accusative case, personal pronouns are usually accented and precede the verbs:

Τὸν βλέπω	I see him
Μὲ ἔδωσε	He gave me
Μᾶς ἔφερε	He brought us

However, if the verbs are in the imperative mood, the personal pronouns are usually unaccented and follow the verbs:

'Ιδέ τον	See him
Δός με	Give me
Φέρε μας	Bring us

LESSON 11

δύο	thï′ô	**two** (all genders)
τρεῖς	trïs	**three** (masculine and f.)
τρία	trï′á	**three** (neuter)
τέσσαρες	tĕ′sárĕs	**four** (masc. and fem.)
τέσσαρα	tĕ′sárá	**four** (neuter)
πέντε	pĕn′tĕ or pĕn′dĕ	**five** (masc., fem., neu.)
κυττάζω	kĭtá′zô	**I look**
κύτταζε	kï′tázĕ	**look, keep looking**
κύτταξε	kï′táxĕ	**look**
τὸ ἄλογον	tô á′lôγôn	**the horse**
τὸ κάρρον	tô ká′rôn	**the car, the wagon**
τὸ κρεϐϐάτι	tô krĕvá′tĭ	**the bed**
ἡ καθέκλα	ĭ káthĕ′klá	**the chair**
ὁ καθρέπτης	ô káthrĕp′tĭs	**the mirror**
τὸ λεπτὸν	tô lĕp tôn′	**the cent**
τὰ λεπτὰ	tá lĕptá′	**the cents, the money**
πολύς	pôlïs′	**much** (mas. adjective)
πολλὴ	pôlï′	**much** (fem., adjective)
πολὺ	pôlï′	**much** (neu., adjective)
πολλοί, πολλαί, -λά	pôlï′, pôlĕ′, pôlá′	**many** *mas., fem., neu.*
πόσος, πόση, πόσον	pô′sôs, pô′sĭ, pô′sôn	**how much** (adj. m.,f.,n.)
πόσοι, πόσαι, πόσα	pô′sĭ, pô′sĕ, pô′sá	**how many** " "
ὀλίγος,ὀλίγη,ὀλίγον	ôlï′γôs, ôlï′γĭ, ôlï′γôn	**little** " "
ὀλίγοι,ὀλίγαι,ὀλίγα	ôlï′γĭ, ôlï′γĕ, ôlï′γá	**a few** " "
περισσότερος, -η, -ον	pĕrĭsô′tĕrôs, -ĭ, -ôn	**more** " "

EXERCISES

Τί ϐλέπεις εἰς τὸν δρόμον;	What do you see in the street?
Βλέπω ἕνα ἄνθρωπον καὶ ἕνα σκύλον.	I see a man and a dog.

Ἐπίσης ϐλέπω ἕνα ἄλογο καὶ ἕνα κάρρο.	Also I see a horse and a wagon.
Τί ϐλέπεις μέσα στὸ σπίτι;	What do you see in the house?
Βλέπω ἕνα κρεϐϐάτι, δυὸ τραπέζια, ἕνα καθρέπτην καὶ τρεῖς καθέκλες.	I see one bed, two tables, one mirror and three chairs.
Πόσους ἀνθρώπους ϐλέπεις στὸν δρόμο;	How many men do you see in the street?
Βλέπω τρεῖς ἀνθρώπους.	I see three men.
Βλέπω δυὸ ἐργάτες καὶ μιὰ γυναῖκα.	I see two workmen and one woman.
Ἐγὼ ϐλέπω τέσσαρα παιδιά.	I see four children.
Ποῦ εἶναι τὰ χρήματα τῶν ἐργατῶν;	Where is the money of the workmen?
Τὰ χρήματα τῶν ἐργατῶν εἶναι ἐπάνω στὸ τραπέζι.	The workmen's money is on the table.
Ἐκεῖ εἶναι καὶ τὰ ϐιϐλία τῶν παιδιῶν.	There are also the books of the children.
Πόσα χρήματα ἔχεις τώρα μαζύ σου;	How much money have you with you now?
Δὲν ἔχω πολλὰ χρήματα.	I have not much money.
Ἔχω μόνον πέντε λεπτά.	I have only five cents.
Ποιὸς ἔχει περισσότερα χρήματα, σὺ ἢ ὁ φίλος σου;	Who has more money, you or your friend?
Ἐγὼ ἔχω περισσότερα χρήματα.	I have more money.
Ὁ φίλος μου ἔχει ὀλιγώτερα.	My friend has less.

ELEMENTARY GRAMMAR

The First and Second Declensions

Greek masculine nouns ending in **ας**, when not accented on the last syllable, are usually declined as the following example (First Declension):

Nom.	ὁ ταμίας	the treasurer	οἱ ταμίαι(ς)	the treasurers
Gen.	τοῦ ταμίου, c. ταμία	of the treasurer	τῶν ταμιῶν	of the treasurers
Acc.	τὸν ταμία(ν)	the treasurer	τοὺς ταμίας c. ταμίαις	the treasurers
Voc.	ὦ ταμία	O treasurer	ὦ ταμίαι(ς)	O treasurers

Masculine nouns ending in **ης** are usually declined as the following examples (First Declension):

			COLLOQUIAL	
Singular:	**Nom.**	ὁ ἐργάτης	ὁ ἐργάτης	the worker
	Gen.	τοῦ ἐργάτου	τοῦ ἐργάτη	of the worker
	Acc.	τὸν ἐργάτην	τὸν ἐργάτη(ν)	the worker
	Voc.	ὦ ἐργάτα	ὦ ἐργάτη	O worker
Plural:	**Nom.**	οἱ ἐργάται	οἱ ἐργάτες or ἐργάταις	the workers
	Gen.	τῶν ἐργατῶν	τῶν ἐργατῶν	of the workers
	Acc.	τοὺς ἐργάτας	τοὺς ἐργάτες, ἐργάταις	the workers
	Voc.	ὦ ἐργάται	ὦ ἐργάτες	O workers

Nom.	ὁ ποιητὴς	the poet	οἱ ποιηταί	the poets
Gen.	τοῦ ποιητοῦ c. ποιητῆ	of the poet	τῶν ποιητῶν	of the poets
Acc.	τὸν ποιητή(ν)	the poet	τοὺς ποιητάς	the poets
Voc.	ὦ ποιητά	O poet	ὦ ποιηταί	O poets

Feminine nouns ending in **α** and **η** are declined according to the following examples (First Declension):*

Nom.	ἡ ὥρα	the hour	**αἱ** ὧραι,	c. ἡ ὧραις or ὧρες	the hours
Gen.	τῆς ὥρας	of the hour	τῶν ὡρῶν	τῶν ὡρῶν	of the hours
Acc.	τὴν ὥρα(ν)	the hour	**τὰς** ὥρας	τὴς ὥραις, ὧρες	the hours
Nom.	ἡ τιμή	the honor	αἱ τιμαί,	c. αἱ τιμαίς, ἡ τιμές	the honors
Gen.	τῆς τιμῆς	of the honor	τῶν τιμῶν	τῶν τιμῶν	of the honors
Acc.	τὴν τιμή(ν)	the honor	τὰς τιμάς	τὴς τιμαίς, τιμές	the honors

Masculine and feminine nouns ending in **ος** and neuter nouns ending in **ον** are declined as the following examples (Second Declension):*

Nom.	ὁ φίλος	the friend	οἱ φίλοι	the friends
Gen.	τοῦ φίλου	of the friend	τῶν φίλων	of the friends
Acc.	τὸν φίλον	the friend	τοὺς φίλους	the friends
Voc.	ὦ φίλε	O friend	ὦ φίλοι	O friends
Nom.	ἡ νῆσος	the island	αἱ νῆσοι	the islands
Gen.	τῆς νήσου	of the island	τῶν νήσων	of the islands
Acc.	τὴν νῆσον	the island	τὰς νήσους	the islands
Nom., Acc.	τὸ δωμάτιον	the room	τὰ δωμάτια	the rooms
Gen.	τοῦ δωματίου	of the room	τῶν δωματίων	of the rooms

In the colloquial idiom neuter nouns ending in **ι** are usually declined as the following examples:*

Nom.	τὸ παιδί	the child	τὰ παιδιά	the children
Gen.	τοῦ παιδιοῦ	of the child	τῶν παιδιῶν	of the children
Acc.	τὸ παιδί	the child	τὰ παιδιά	the children
Nom.	τὸ τραπέζι	the table	τὰ τραπέζια	the tables
Gen.	τοῦ τραπεζιοῦ	of the table	τῶν τραπεζιῶν	of the tables
Acc.	τὸ τραπέζι	the table	τὰ τραπέζια	the tables

* The vocative case of feminine and neuter nouns has the same form as the nominative.

LESSON 12

προσέχω	prŏsĕ'hŏ	I take care, I look out
πρόσεχε	prŏ'sĕhĕ	take care, look out
πρόσεξε	prŏ'sĕxĕ	take care, look out
ϐλέπω	vlĕ'pŏ	I see
ϐλέπε	vlĕ'pĕ	see
μαῦρος, μαύρη, -ον	måv'rŏs, måv'rĭ, -rŏn	black (masc., fem., neu.)
ἄσπρος, ἄσπρη, -ον	ås'prŏs, ås'prĭ, ås'prŏn	white " " "
ἴδιος	ï'thĭŏs *or* ï'thyŏs	the same, *masculine*
ἰδία, *colloq.* ἴδια	ĭthï'å, ï'thyå	the same, *feminine*
ἴδιον, *col.* ἴδιο	ï'thĭŏn *or* ï'thyŏ	the same, *neuter*
τὸ πρᾶγμα	tŏ pråγ'må	the thing
τὰ πράγματα	tå pråγ'måtå	the things
αὐτὴν τὴν φορὰν	åftïn' tïn fŏrån'	this time
παρακαλῶ *	påråkålŏ'	don't mention it
ἀρέσω	årĕ'sŏ	I like
ἀγαπῶ	åγåpŏ'	I love, I like
ἀγαπᾶς	åγåpås'	you love (thou lovest)
ἀγαπᾷ	åγåpå'	he (she, it) loves
ἀγαπῶμεν	åγåpŏ'mĕn	we love
ἀγαπᾶτε	åγåpå'tĕ	you love (plural)
ἀγαποῦν	åγåpoon'	they love
ἀγάπα	åγå'på	love (imperative)

EXERCISES

Κύτταξε ἐκεῖ, Γιάννη.	Look there, John.
Πρόσεχε. Ἕνας σκύλος εἶναι στὴν κουζίνα.	Look out. A dog is in the kitchen.
Ἀρέσεις αὐτὸν τὸν μαῦρον σκύλον;	Do you like this black dog?
Ὄχι, κύριε· ἀγαπῶ ἐκεῖνον τὸν ἄσπρον σκύλον.	No, sir; I like that white dog.
Τί ἀγαπᾷ ὁ ἀδελφός σου;	What does your brother like?
Ὁ ἀδελφός μου ἀγαπᾷ τὸν ἄσπρον σκύλον ἐπίσης.	My brother likes the white dog too.
Θέλετε τσάϊ ἢ καφέ;	Do you want tea or coffee?
Θέλω καφὲ μὲ γάλα.	I want coffee with milk.
Θέλετε πολὺ γάλα;	Do you want much milk?
Ὄχι. Θέλω πολὺ ὀλίγο γάλα στὸν καφέ μου.	No. I want very little milk in my coffee.
Θέλω μαῦρον καφὲν αὐτὴν τὴν φοράν.	I want black coffee this time.
Δὲν θέλω γάλα εἰς τὸν καφέ μου.	I do not want milk in my coffee.
Τὸ παιδί μου θέλει τὸ ἴδιον πρᾶγμα.	My boy wants the same thing.
Τί εἶναι τοῦτο;	What is this?
Τί εἶναι τοῦτο τὸ πρᾶγμα;	What is this thing?
Εἶναι μολύβι.	It is a pencil.
Ἔχεις πολλὰ μολύβια;	Have you many pencils?
Δὲν ἔχω πολλὰ μολύβια.	I haven't many pencils.
Ἔχω μόνον ὀλίγα.	I have only a few.

Δὸς ἐκεῖνο τὸ μολύβι εἰς τὴν μικρὰν ἀδελφήν σου.	Give that pencil to your little sister.
Τὸ θέλει.	She wants it.
Δός μου ἕνα μολύβι, ἐπίσης.	Give me a pencil, too.
Εὐχαριστῶ πολύ.	I thank you very much.
* Παρακαλῶ, κύριε.	Please don't mention it, sir.

Grammatical Remarks

The imperative mood of verbs not accented on the last syllable, ends in the second person singular in ε, and in the second plural in ετε. For example:

Ἔχω	I have	Ἔχε	Have (Sin.)	Ἔχετε	Have (pl.)
Βλέπω	I see	Βλέπε	See (sin.)	Βλέπετε	See (pl.)
Χύνω	I spill	Χύνε	Spill (sin.)	Χύνετε	Spill (pl.)

If the verb has more than two syllables, the accent in the first person singular of the imperative is transferred to the third syllable from the end.

Προσέχω	I look out	Πρόσεχε	Look out (sin.)
Φυλάσσω	I guard	Φύλασσε	Guard (sin.)
Διαβάζω	I read	Διάβαζε	Read (sin.)

---

*Παρακαλῶ (I pray) is used in answer to εὐχαριστῶ (thank you) taking the place of the English phrase "don't mention it". It is also used when asking for a favor, in place of the English "please". For example:

Δός μου ἕνα μολύβι, παρακαλῶ.	Give me a pencil, please.
Σᾶς εὐχαριστῶ *or* Εὐχαριστῶ.	I thank you.
Παρακαλῶ (*or* Τίποτε).	Don't mention it (it is nothing).

LESSON 13

τὰ ροῦχα	tȧ roo′hȧ	**the clothes**
τὸ καπέλλο(ν)*	tô kȧpĕ′lô	**the hat**
τὸ σακκάκι	to sȧkȧ′kĭ	**the coat**
τὸ ἐπανωφόρι	tô ĕpȧnôfô′rĭ	**the overcoat**
τὸ γελέκο	tô yĕlĕ′ko	**the vest**
τὸ παπούτσι	tô pȧpoo′tsĭ	**the shoe**
τὸ κουμπὶ	tô koombĭ′	**the button**
ἡ τσέπη	ĭ tsĕ′pĭ (chĕ′pĭ)	**the pocket**
τὸ πανταλόνι	tô pȧntȧlô′nĭ	**the trousers**
τὸ κεφάλι	tô kĕfȧ′lĭ	**the head**
καινούρι ος, α, ον	kĕnoo′rĭôs, -ȧ, -ôn	**new** (masc., fem., neu.)
παλαιός, παλαι ά,-όν	pȧlĕôs′, pȧlĕȧ′, pȧleôn′	**old** " " "
καλλίτερ ος, -η, -ον	kȧlĭ′tĕrôs, -tĕrĭ, -tĕrôn	**better** " " "
καλλίτερα	kȧlĭ′tĕrȧ	**better** (adverb)
φέρω, *col.* φέρνω	fĕ′rô, fĕr′nô	**I bring**
πηγαίνω, ὑπάγω	pĭ yĕ′nô, ĭpȧ′γô	**I go**
θέλω νὰ ὑπάγω	thĕ′lô nȧ ĭpȧ′γô	**I want to go**
βάλλω	vȧ′lô	**I put**
col. βάνω *or* βάζω	vȧ′nô *or* vȧ′zô	**I put**
βγάλλω, βγάνω, βγάζω (*col. for* ἐκβάλλω)	vγȧ′lô, vγȧ′nô, vγȧ′zô (*for* ĕkvȧ′lô)	**I put out, I take off**
νά το	nȧ′tô	**there it is**

EXERCISES

Ποῦ εἶναι τὰ ροῦχα μου;	Where are my clothes?
Θέλω νὰ ὑπάγω ἔξω.	I want to go out.
Θέλετε τὸ καλό σας σακκάκι;	Do you want your good coat?
Ναί. Σὲ παρακαλῶ φέρε καὶ τὸ γελέκο μου.	Yes. Please bring my vest also.
Θέλετε τὸ μαῦρο σας πανταλόνι;	Do you want your black trousers?
Ὄχι. Δὲν θέλω τὸ μαῦρο μου πανταλόνι.	No. I do not want my black trousers.
Θέλω τὸ ἄσπρο μου πανταλόνι καὶ τὰ μαῦρα μου παπούτσια.	I want my white trousers and my black shoes.
Βάλε τὸ ἄλλο σου σακκάκι.	Put on your other coat.
Βγάλε αὐτὸ τὸ ἐπανωφόρι.	Take off this overcoat.
Εἶναι πολὺ παλαιόν.	It is too old.
Δὲν ἔχει κουμπιά.	It has no buttons.
Πόσαις τσέπαις ἔχεις εἰς τὸ σακκάκι σου;	How many pockets have you in your coat?
Ἔχω τρεῖς τσέπαις στὸ σακκάκι μου.	I have three pockets in my coat.
Βάλε τὸ καπέλλο σου στὸ κεφάλι σου.	Put your hat on your head.
Δὲν ἀρέσεις τὸ καινούριο μου καπέλλο;	Don't you like my new hat?

Ἐγὼ ἀρέσω καλλίτερα τὸ παλαιό σου καπέλλο.	I like your old hat better.
Θέλω ἕνα καινούριο καπέλλο.	I want a new hat.
Ποῦ εἶναι τὸ παλαιό μου ἐπανωφόρι;	Where is my old overcoat?
Νά το, ἐπάνω στὸ κρεββάτι.	There it is, on the bed.

Grammatical Remarks

* As mentioned elsewhere, in colloquial Greek the final **ν** in nouns or adjectives ending in **ον** is usually omitted. For example:

Μικρὸ καπέλλο	(*for* Μικρὸν καπέλλον)	Small hat
Καλὸ βιβλίο	(*for* Καλὸν βιβλίον)	Good book

Likewise, nouns ending in **ιον** in colloquial Greek often drop the entire syllable **ον**. Examples:

Παιδὶ	(*for* Παιδίον)	Child
Ποτήρι	(" Ποτήριον)	Glass

LESSON 14

τὸ φόρεμα	tô fô′rĕmȧ	the dress
τὸ φουστάνι	tô foostȧ′nĭ	the dress, the skirt
τὸ ὑποκάμισσο	tô ĭpôkȧ′mĭsô	the shirt
τὸ κολάρο (ν)	tô kôlȧ′rô	the collar
τὸ πρόσωπο (ν)	tô prô′sôpô (n)	the face
τά μαλλιὰ	tȧ mȧlĭȧ′ (mȧ lyȧ′)	the hair (the hairs)
νέος	nĕ′ôs	young, new (masc.)
ὁ νέος	ô nĕ′ôs	the young man
νέα	nĕ′ȧ	young, new (fem.)
ἡ νέα	ĭ nĕ′ȧ	the young woman
νέον	nĕ′ôn	young, new (neu.)
γέρων, *col.* γέρος	yĕ′rôn, yĕ′rôs	old (mas.) *or* old man
γραῖα, *col.* γρηὰ	γrĕ′ȧ, γrĭ ȧ′	old (fem.) *or* old woman
καθαρ ός, ή, ὸν	kȧthȧrôs′, kȧthȧrĭ′, -ôn	clean (mas., fem., neu.)
ἀκάθαρτ ος, -η, -ον	ȧkȧ′thȧr tôs, -tĭ, -tôn	dirty " " "
λερός, λερή, λερόν	lĕrôs′, lĕrĭ′, lĕrôn′	dirty " " "
ἔξυπνος, ἔξυπν η, -ον	ĕks′ĭp nôs, -nĭ, -nôn	smart, witty " "
ϐλὰξ (c. ϐλάκας)	vlȧx, vlȧ′kȧs	stupid " "
ἄλλος, ἄλλη, ἄλλο	ȧ′lôs, ȧ′lĭ, ȧ′lô	other " "
ἕνας ἄλλος	ĕ′nȧs ȧ′lôs.	another, mas.
μία ἄλλη *or* μιὰ ἄλλη	mĭ′ȧ ȧ′lĭ	another, fem.
ἓν ἄλλο c. ἕνα ἄλλο	ĕn ȧ′lô *or* ĕ′nȧ ȧ′lô	another, neu.
ὡραῖ ος, ὡραί α, -ον	ôrĕ′ôs, orĕ′ȧ, ôrĕ′ôn	beautiful (mas., f., n.)
δίκαιος, δικαία *	thĭ′kĕôs, thĭkĕ′ȧ	right masc.; right fem.
δίκαιον	thĭ′kĕôn	right neu.
ἄδικος, η, ον	ȧ′thĭkôs, ȧ′thĭkĭ, -kôn	wrong (mas., fem., neu.)
ἔχω δίκαιον **	ĕ′hô thĭ′kĕôn	I am right
ἔχω ἄδικον	ĕ′hô ȧ′thĭkôn	I am wrong

EXERCISES

Αὐτὸ τὸ ὑποκάμισο δὲν εἶναι καθαρό. Εἶναι λερό.	This shirt is not clean. It is dirty.
Παρακαλῶ, φέρε μου ἕνα ἄλλο ὑποκάμισσο καὶ ἕνα καθαρὸ κολλάρο.	Please, bring me another shirt and a clean collar.
Αὐτὸ εἶναι καλλίτερο.	This is better.
Ἡ ἀδελφή μου ἔχει ἕνα καινούριο ἄσπρο φόρεμα.	My sister has a new white dress.
Ἡ μητέρα μας ἔχει ἕνα παλαιὸ μαῦρο φόρεμα.	Our mother has an old black dress.
Ἡ μητέρα μας εἶναι γραῖα.	Our mother is old.
Ἡ ἀδελφή μας εἶναι νέα καὶ ὡραία.	Our sister is young and beautiful.
Τὸ φόρεμά της εἶναι πολὺ ὡραῖον.	Her dress is very pretty.
Δὲν ἀρέσω (or δὲν μοῦ ἀρέσουν) τὰ ροῦχα της.	I do not like her clothes.
Εἶναι πολὺ παλαιά.	They are too old.
Ὁ πατέρας μας ἔχει χρήματα, ἀλλὰ ὁ ἀδελφός μας δὲν ἔχει χρήματα.	Our father has money, but our brother has not any money.
Εἶναι πτωχὸς καὶ γέρων.	He is poor and old.
Αὐτὴ ἡ κόρη εἶναι ὡραία.	This girl is beautiful.
Ὄχι. Δὲν εἶναι ὡραία.	No. She is not beautiful.
Τὸ κεφάλι της εἶνε πολὺ μικρό.	Her head is very small.
Τὸ πρόσωπό της δὲν εἶναι ἄσπρο.	Her face is not white.
Τὰ μαλλιά της εἶνε πολὺ μαῦρα.	Her hair is too black.

Μοῦ ἀρέσει πολὺ καλλίτερα ἡ ἀδελφή της.	I like her sister much better.
Εἶναι ὡραία νέα.	She is a beautiful young woman.
Εἶναι μικρή, ἀλλὰ εἶναι πολὺ ἔξυπνη. Δὲν εἶναι βλάξ.	She is small, but she is very smart. She is not stupid.
Ἡ μητέρα των εἶναι γραῖα· δὲν εἶναι;	Their mother is old; isn't she?
Δὲν ἔχετε δίκαιον· ἔχετε ἄδικον.	You are not right; you are wrong.
Ἡ μητέρα των δὲν εἶναι πολὺ γραῖα· εἶναι ἀκόμη νέα.	Their mother is not very old; she is still young.

Elementary Grammar

* Adjectives with a vowel sound before the masculine ending **ος**, end in the feminine gender in **α**. If the masculine is accented on the third syllable from the end, the accent in the feminine descends to the next syllable. Examples:

Masculine	Feminine	Neuter	
Νέος	Νέα	Νέον	Young
Ὡραῖος	Ὡραία	Ὡραῖον	Beautiful
Ἅγιος	Ἁγία	Ἅγιον	Holy
Δίκαιος	Δικαία	Δίκαιον	Just

—:—

** In Greek we do not say "I am right", "I am wrong", but "I have right", "I have wrong".

LESSON 15

δίδω	thï'thȯ	I give
ἔδιδα	ĕ'thĭthȧ	I was giving, I used to give, I gave
ἔδιδες	ĕ'thĭthĕs	you were giving (sing.)
ἔδιδε	ĕ'thĭthĕ	he (she, it) was giving
ἐδίδαμεν *	ĕthï'thȧmĕn	we were giving
ἐδίδατε	ĕthï'thȧtĕ	you were giving (plur.)
ἔδιδαν	ĕ'thĭthȧn	they were giving
ἔδωσα, ἔδωσες	ĕ'thȯsȧ, ĕ'thȯsĕs	I gave, you gave, sing.
ἔδωσε	ĕ'thȯsĕ	he (she, it) gave
ἐδώσαμεν, ἐδώσατε	ĕthȯ'sȧmĕn, ĕthȯ'sȧtĕ	we gave, you gave, pl.
ἔδωσαν	ĕ'thȯsȧn	they gave
ἔχω δώσει	ĕ'hȯ thȯ'sĭ	I have given
ἔχεις δώσει	ĕ'hĭs thȯ'sĭ	you have given, sing.
ἔχει δώσει	ĕ'hĭ thȯ'sĭ	he (she, it) has given
ἔχομεν δώσει	ĕ'hȯmĕn thȯ'sĭ	we have given
ἔχετε δώσει	ĕ'hĕtĕ thȯ'sĭ	you have given, plural
ἔχουν δώσει	ĕ'hoon thȯ'sĭ	they have given
ἔχω	ĕ'hȯ	I have
εἶχα, εἶχες, εἶχε	ï'hȧ, ï'hĕs, ï'hĕ	I had; you had; he had
εἴχαμεν, εἴχατε	ï'hȧmĕn, ï'hȧtĕ	we had, you had, pl.
εἶχαν	ï'hȧn	they had
θέλω	thĕ'lȯ	I wish, I want
ἤθελα	ï'thĕlȧ	I wished, I was wishing
ἤθελες, *etc.*	ï'thĕlĕs	you wished, etc.
ἠθέλησα, ἠθέλησες	ïthĕ'lĭsȧ, ïthĕ'lĭsĕs	I wished, you wished
ἔχω θελήσει	ĕ'hȯ thĕlï'sĭ	I have wished
φέρω	fĕ'rȯ	I bring
ἔφερα, *col.* ἔφερνα	ĕ'fĕrȧ, ĕ'fĕrnȧ	I was bringing

ἔφερα	ĕ'fĕrȧ	I brought
ἔχω φέρει	ĕ'hô fĕ'rĭ	I have brought
κάμνω	kȧm'nô	I do, I make
ἔκαμνα	ĕ'kȧm nȧ	I was doing
ἔκαμα	ĕ'kȧmȧ	I did
ἔχω κάμει	ĕ'hô kȧ'mĭ	I have done
βάλλω	vȧ'lô	I put
ἔβαλλα	ĕ'vȧlȧ	I was putting
ἔβαλα	ĕ'vȧlȧ	I put (indef. past)
ἔχω βάλει	ĕ'ho vȧ'lĭ	I have put
πηγαίνω	pĭγĕ'nô	I go
ἐπήγαινα	ĕpĭ'γĕnȧ	I was going
ἐπῆγα	ĕpĭ'γȧ	I went
ἔχω ὑπάγει	ĕ'hô ĭpȧ'γĭ	I have gone
σήμερον, σήμερα	sĭ'mĕrôn, sĭ'mĕrȧ	today
χθὲς	h'thĕs	yesterday
προχθὲς	prôh thĕs'	day before yesterday
ὅταν	ô'tȧn	when

EXERCISES

Τί σοῦ ἔδωσε ὁ ἀδελφός μου χθές;	What did my brother give you yesterday?
Χθὲς ὁ ἀδελφός σου μοῦ ἔδωσε ἕνα βιβλίο.	Yesterday your brother gave me a book.
Ποῦ ἔβαλες τὸ βιβλίο αὐτό;	Where did you put this book?
Τὸ ἔβαλα στὸ μεγάλο τραπέζι.	I put it on the large table.
Τί ἐκάματε χθές;	What did you do yesterday?
Χθὲς δὲν ἐκάμαμε τίποτε.	Yesterday we did not do anything.

Προχθὲς ἐπήγαμε στὸ σπίτι τῆς μητέρας μας.	The day before yesterday we went to our mother's house.
Ἔκαμα ἕνα καλὸ πρᾶγμα χθὲς.	I did a good thing yesterday.
Ἔδωσα χρήματα σ' ἕνα πτωχὸν ἄνθρωπον.	I gave money to a poor man.
Καὶ ἐγὼ ἔδιδα χρήματα εἰς τοὺς πτωχοὺς ὅταν εἶχα.	I, too, used to give money to the poor, when I had it.
Ποῦ ἔχεις βάλει τὸ ἐπανωφόρι μου;	Where have you put my overcoat?
Τὸ ἔχω βάλει στὸ δωμάτιόν μου, ἐπάνω σὲ μιὰ καθέκλα.	I have put it in my room, upon a chair.
Πήγαινε νὰ τὸ φέρῃς, παρακαλῶ.	Go and bring it, please.
Τὸ ἔφερα. Αὐτὸ εἶναι;	I have brought it. Is this it?
Θέλεις χρήματα τώρα;	Do you want money now?
Δὲν θέλω χρήματα τώρα. Ἤθελα χρήματα χθές.	I do not want money now. I wanted money yesterday.
Διατί ἤθελες χρήματα χθές;	Why did you want money yesterday?
Δὲν τὰ ἤθελα ἐγώ. Τὰ ἤθελε ὁ πατέρας μου.	I did not want it. My father wanted it.
Ἔχεις φέρει τὸν ἀδελφό σου μαζύ σου;	Have you brought your brother with you?
Ὄχι δὲν τὸν ἔχω φέρει ἐδῶ.	No. I have not brought him here.
Ἐπῆγε μὲ τὴν μητέρα μας.	He went with our mother.

Elementary Grammar

In Greek verbs there are three past tenses in use: the **Imperfect or Continued Past** tense, the **Aorist or Indefinite Past** tense, and the **Perfect or Compound Past** tense.

Though there are some rules for the formation of the past tenses of the regular verbs, yet there are so many exceptions and irregularities, especially among verbs of the most common use, that we have found it preferable to give with each verb its present and past tenses. From these, all the other tenses and moods can be easily formed, as we shall learn later.

In the continued past and indefinite past tenses the vowel ε is placed before verbs beginning with a consonant. Also the accent is raised from the second to the third syllable from the end. Examples:

Present	**Continued Past**	**Indefinite Past**
δίδω I give	ἔδιδα I was giving, I used to give	ἔδοσα (*or* ἔδωσα) I gave
κάμνω I do	ἔκαμνα I was doing, I used to do	ἔκαμα I did
φέρω I bring	ἔφερα I was bringing, I used to bring	ἔφερα I brought

—:—

* Greek words are not accented further than the third syllable from the end; therefore, when a new syllable is added to the end of a word, as in the case of the 1st and 2nd persons plural of the verbs, then the accent automatically descends to the following syllable, so as to fall on the third syllable from the end. For example:

Continued Past		**Indefinite Past**	
Ἔκαμνα	I was doing	Ἔκαμα	I did
Ἔκαμνες	You were doing	Ἔκαμες	You did
Ἔκαμνε	He was doing	Ἔκαμε	He did
Ἐκάμναμεν	We were doing	Ἐκάμαμεν	We did
Ἐκάμνατε	You were doing	Ἐκάματε	You did
Ἔκαμναν	They were doing	Ἔκαμαν	They did

LESSON 16

εἶμαι	ï′mĕ	**I am**
ἤμην, *col.* ἤμουν	ï′mĭn, ï′moon	**I was**
ἦσο, *col.* ἤσουν	ï′sô, ï′soon	**thou wast, you were***
ἦτο, *col.* ἦταν	ï′tô, ï′tȧn	**he (she, it) was**
ἤμεθα, *col.* ἤμαστε	ï′mĕthȧ, ï′mȧstĕ	**we were**
ἦσθε, *col.* ἤσαστε	ïs′thĕ, ï′sȧstĕ	**you were** (plural)
ἦσαν, *col.* ἦταν	ï′sȧn, ï′tȧn	**they were**
ἔρχομαι	ĕr′hômĕ	**I come**
ἠρχόμην	ĭrhô′mĭn	**I was coming**
ἤρχεσο	ïr′hĕsô	**you were coming,** sing.
ἤρχετο	ïr′hĕtô	**he (she,it) was coming**
ἠρχόμεθα	ĭrhô′mĕthȧ	**we were coming**
ἤρχεσθε	ïr′hĕs thĕ	**you were coming,** pl.
ἤρχοντο	ïr′hôntô	**they were coming**
ἦλθα, ἦλθες, *etc.*	ïl′thȧ, ïl′thĕs	**I came, you came, etc.**
ἔχω ἔλθει	ĕ′hô ĕl′thĭ	**I have come**
παίρνω	pĕr′nô	**I take**
ἔπαιρνα	ĕ′pĕrnȧ	**I was taking**
ἐπῆρα	ĕpï′rȧ	**I took**
ἔχω πάρει	ĕ′hô pȧ′rĭ	**I have taken**
ϐλέπω	vlĕ′pô	**I see**
ἔϐλεπα	ĕv′lĕpȧ	**I was seeing**
εἶδα	ï′thȧ	**I saw**
ἔχω ἴδει	ĕ′hô ï′thĭ, ĕhô ĭthï′	**I have seen**
γνωρίζω	γnôrï′zô	**I know**
ἐγνώριζα	ĕγnô′rĭzȧ	**I knew, I used to know**
ἐγνώρισα	ĕγnô′rĭsȧ	**I knew**
ἔχω γνωρίσει	ĕ′hô γnôrï′sĭ	**I have known**
νομίζω	nômï′zô	**I think**

ἐνόμιζα	ĕnô′mĭzȧ	**I was thinking**
ἐνόμισα	ĕnô′mĭsȧ	**I thought**
ἔχω νομίσει	ĕ′hô nômĭ′sĭ	**I have thought**
τὸ σχολεῖον	tô s′hôlĭ′ôn	**the school**
ἀπὸ	ȧpô′	**from, of**
ὅμως	ô′môs	**however**
πάντοτε	pȧn′tôtĕ	**always**

EXERCISES

Ὁ φίλος μας ὁ Γιάννης ἦταν ἐδῶ χθές. Ἦλθε μαζὺ μὲ τὴν μητέρα του.	Our friend John was here yesterday. He came with his mother.
Ἦταν ἡ μητέρα του καλά;	Was his mother well?
Ἐγὼ δὲν τὴν εἶδα. Ἡ ἀδελφή μου τὴν εἶδε. Τὴν γνωρίζει πολὺ καλά.	I did not see her. My sister saw her. She knows her very well.
Ἐγὼ ἐγνώριζα τὸν πατέρα τοῦ Γιάννη ὅταν ἦτο μικρὸ παιδί.	I knew John's father when he was a little child.
Ἐπηγαίναμε μαζὺ στὸ σχολεῖο (*or* ἐπηγαίναμε στὸ σχολεῖο μαζύ).	We were going to (the) school together.
Ἔχεις ἴδει τὰ καινούρια μου ροῦχα;	Have you seen my new clothes?
Ὄχι. Δὲν τὰ ἔχω ἴδει.	No. I have not seen them.
Εἶδα μόνον τὸ καινούριο φόρεμα τῆς ἀδελφῆς σου.	I saw only your sister's new dress.
Εἶδα καὶ τὸ καινούριο της καπέλλο.	I saw her new hat, too.
Ποιὸν εἶδες ὅταν ἤρχεσο ἀπὸ τὸ σπίτι σου;	Whom did you see when you were coming from your house?
Δὲν εἶδα κανένα.	I saw no one.
Εἶδα μόνον ἕνα σκύλον καὶ μιὰ γάτα στὸν δρόμο.	I saw only a dog and a cat in the street.
Δὲν ἔβλεπες καλά, νομίζω. Πολλοὶ ἄνθρωποι ἦσαν εἰς τὸν δρόμον.	You did not see (were not seeing) well, I think. Many people were in the street.
Ἐπήρατε καφὲ χθές;	Did you take coffee yesterday?
Ναί. Χθὲς ἐπῆρα καφέ. Σήμερα ὅμως δὲν ἔχω πάρει τίποτε.	Yes. Yesterday I took coffee. But today I have not taken anything.

Ἐγὼ παίρνω τώρα καφὲ μὲ γάλα.	I take coffee with milk now.
Ὅταν ἤμουν νέος ἔπαιρνα μόνον γάλα.	When I was young I used to take only milk.
Ὁ πατέρας μας ἔπαιρνε μαῦρον καφὲ πάντοτε.	Our father used to take black coffee always.
Ποῦ εἶναι ὁ φίλος σου; Τὸν ἔφερες μαζύ σου;	Where is your friend? Did you bring him with you?
Ὄχι. Δὲν τὸν ἔχω φέρει μαζύ μου.	No. I have not brought him with me.
Δὲν ἤθελε νὰ ἔλθῃ.	He did not want to come.
Ποῦ ἦσουν χθές;	Where were you yesterday?
Χθὲς ἤμουν στὸ σπίτι τῆς ἀδελφῆς μου.	Yesterday I was in my sister's house.

Elementary Grammar

The Perfect Past Tense, as in English, is formed with the auxiliary ἔχω (I have) and the perfect past form of the verb ending in ει (or η). Examples:

Κάμνω	I do
Ἔχω κάμει	I have done
Ἔχεις κάμει	You have done (sin.)
Ἔχει κάμει	He (she, it) has done
Ἔχομεν κάμει	We have done
Ἔχετε κάμει	You have done
Ἔχουν κάμει	They have done

In the same manner, the Pluperfect Tense is formed with the auxiliary εἶχα (I had) and the verb ending in ει or η. For example:

Εἶχα κάμει	I had done
Εἶχες κάμει	You had done (sin.)
Εἶχε κάμει	He (she, it) had done
Εἴχαμεν κάμει	We had done
Εἴχατε κάμει	You had done
Εἶχαν κάμει	They had done

LESSON 17

θὰ ἔχω	thȧ ĕ'hô	I shall have
θὰ ἔχεις	thȧ ĕ'hĭs	you will have, sing.
θὰ ἔχει	thȧ ĕ'hĭ	he (she, it) will have
θὰ ἔχομεν	thȧ ĕ'hômĕn	we shall have
θὰ ἔχετε	thȧ ĕ'hĕtĕ	you will have, plural
θὰ ἔχουν	thȧ ĕ'hoon	they will have
θὰ δίδω „ „	thȧ thĭ'thô	I shall be giving, I shall give
θὰ δίδεις „ „	thȧ thĭ'thĭs	you will give, sing. you will be giving
θὰ δίδει	thȧ thĭ'thĭ	he will be giving
θὰ δίδομεν	thȧ thĭ'thômĕn	we shall be giving
θὰ δίδετε	thȧ thĭ'thĕtĕ	you will be giving, pl.
θὰ δίδουν	thȧ thĭ'thoon	they will be giving
θὰ δώσω	thȧ thô'sô	I shall give
θὰ δώσῃς	thȧ thô'sĭs	you will give, sing.
θὰ δώσῃ	thȧ thô'sĭ	he (she, it) will give
θὰ δώσωμεν	thȧ thô'sômĕn	we shall give
θὰ δώσετε	thȧ thô'sĕtĕ	you will give, pl.
θὰ δώσουν	thȧ thô'soon	they will give
θὰ κάμνω	thȧ kȧm'nô	I shall be doing
θὰ κάμω	thȧ kȧ'mô	I shall do
θὰ κάμῃς *etc.*	thȧ kȧ'mĭs	you will do, etc.
θὰ βλέπω	thȧ vlĕ'pô	I shall be seeing
θὰ ἴδω	thȧ ĭ'thô	I shall see
θὰ παίρνω	thȧ pĕr'nô	I shall be taking
θὰ πάρω	thȧ pȧ'rô	I shall take
θὰ πηγαίνω	thȧ pĭγĕ'nô	I shall be going
θὰ ὑπάγω	thȧ ĭpȧ'γô	I shall go
θὰ βάλω	thȧ vȧ'lô	I shall put

θὰ εἶμαι	thȧ ï′mĕ	**I shall be**
θὰ εἶσαι, *etc.*	thȧ ï′sĕ	**you will be, etc.**
βέβαια	vĕ′vĕȧ	**certainly**
αὔριον	ȧv′rĭôn	**tomorrow**
μεθαύριον	mĕthȧv′rĭôn	**day after tomorrow**
ἡ ἐξοχὴ	ĭ ĕksô hï′	**the open country**
ἡ πόλις	ĭ pô′lĭs	**the city**
πότε	pô′tĕ	**when**
ἐφέτος	ĕfĕ′tôs	**this year**
τοῦ χρόνου	too hrô′noo	**next year**
πέρυσι	pĕ′rĭsĭ	**last year**
πῶς	pôs	**how, that**
τὸ τραῖνο	tô trĕ′nô	**the train**
τὸ αὐτοκίνητον	tô ȧftôkï′nĭtôn	**the automobile, the car**

EXERCISES

Ποῦ θὰ ὑπάγετε σήμερα; (or Ποῦ θὰ πᾶτε σήμερα;)	Where will you go today?
Σήμερα θὰ ὑπάγω εἰς τὴν ἐξοχήν.	Today I shall go to the country.
Θὰ πάρετε τὰ παιδιὰ μαζύ σας;	Will you take the children with you?
Βέβαια. Θὰ τὰ πάρωμεν μαζύ μας.	Certainly. We shall take them with us.
Τί θὰ κάμετε αὔριον;	What will you do tomorrow?
Αὔριον θὰ ὑπάγω νὰ ἴδω τὴν μητέρα μου.	Tomorrow I will go to see my mother.
Ποῦ εἶναι ἡ μητέρα σας;	Where is your mother?
Εἶναι εἰς τὴν πόλιν μὲ τὸν πατέρα μου.	She is in the city with my father.
Πότε θὰ ἴδεις(or ἰδεῖς)τὸν ἀδελφό μου;	When will you see my brother?
Θὰ τὸν ἴδω (or ἰδῶ) μεθαύριον.	I shall see him the day after tomorrow.
Θὰ ἔλθη στὸ σπίτι μας.	He will come to our house.

Ποιὸς ἄλλος θὰ ὑπάγῃ (or θὰ πάῃ) μαζύ του;	Who else will go with him?
Δὲν γνωρίζω. Νομίζω ὁ πατέρας μου θὰ ὑπάγῃ μαζύ του.	I do not know. I think my father will go with him.
Μὲ ποιὸν πηγαίνεις εἰς τὸ σχολεῖον;	With whom do you go to school?
Ἐφέτος πηγαίνω στὸ σχολεῖον μὲ τὴν ἀδελφήν μου.	This year I go to school with my sister.
Τοῦ χρόνου θὰ πηγαίνω μὲ τὸν ἀδελφό μου.	Next year I shall go with my brother.
Θὰ πάρετε καφὲ ἢ τσάϊ;	Will you take coffee or tea?
Ἐγὼ θὰ πάρω καφέ. Ὁ φίλος μου θὰ πάρῃ τσάϊ.	I will take coffee. My friend will take tea.
Ὁ ἀδελφός μου θὰ πάρῃ κρασί.	My brother will take wine.
Ποῦ θὰ βάλετε τό ποτῆρι σας;	Where will you put your glass?
Θὰ τὸ βάλω ἐπάνω σ' ἐκεῖνο τὸ τραπέζι.	I shall put it on that table.
Πῶς θὰ πηγαίνετε εἰς τὴν ἐξοχήν; Μὲ τραῖνο ἢ μὲ αὐτοκίνητο;	How will you go (be going) to the country? By train or by car?
Ἐφέτος θὰ πηγαίνω μὲ αὐτοκίνητον. Πέρυσι ἐπήγαινα μὲ τραῖνο.	This year I shall go (I shall be going) by car. Last year I went (used to go) by train.

Elementary Grammar

THE FUTURE TENSES

Two future tenses are used in Modern Greek: a) The **Continuous Future Tense** and b) the **Momentary Future Tense.**

The Continuous Future Tense is the verb in its present tense preceded by the auxiliary word **θὰ**. For example:

Θὰ δίδω	I shall be giving (or I shall give)
Θὰ δίδεις	You will be giving
Θὰ δίδει	He (she, it) will be giving
Θὰ δίδομεν, κλπ.	We shall be giving, etc.

The Momentary Future is formed with the auxiliary **θὰ** and the verb in its momentary form. (The momentary form of the verb has the stem used in the Modified Perfect or Compound Past Tense.) Examples:

Κάμνω	I do	Βλέπω	I see
Ἔχω κάμει	I have done	Ἔχω ἴδει *or* ἰδεῖ	I have seen
Θὰ κάμω	I shall do	Θὰ ἴδω or θὰ ἰδῶ	I shall see
Θὰ κάμεις	You will do	Θὰ ἴδεις, θὰ ἰδῇς	You will see
Θὰ κάμει	He (she, it) will do	Θὰ ἴδει, θὰ ἰδῇ	He, (she,it) will see
Θὰ κάμομεν	We shall do	Θὰ ἴδομεν, θὰ ἴδωμεν	We shall see
Θὰ κάμετε	You will do	Θὰ ἴδετε	You will see
Θὰ κάμουν	They will do	Θὰ ἴδουν, θὰ ἰδοῦν	They will see

Similar to the auxiliary word θὰ (will) is the auxiliary word **νὰ** (to) with which the Subjunctive mood of the verbs is formed. The verb may be either in continuous or momentary form. Examples:

Θέλω νὰ κάμω	I want to do
Θέλεις νὰ κάμῃς, κλπ.	You want to do, etc.

Or:

Θέλω νὰ κάμνω	I want to do (continuously)
Θέλεις νὰ κάμνῃς, etc.	You want to do " etc.

—:—

In modern Greek verbs two basic forms are used: one signifying continuity, and the other expressing momentary action. Thus there are a continuous past and a momentary past tense, a continuous future and a momentary future tense, a continuous imperative and a momentary imperative mood, a continuous subjunctive and a momentary subjunctive. However, in the present indicative tense the same form is used for expressing both continuous and momentary action or condition. Examples:

	Momentary	**Continuous**
PRESENT	Δίδω — I give	Δίδω — I am giving
PAST	Ἔδωσα — I gave	Ἔδιδον or ἔδιδα — I was giving
FUTURE	Θὰ δώσω — I shall give	Θὰ δίδω — I shall be giving
IMPERATIVE	Δῶσε or Δόσε — Give	Δίδε — Give (be giving)
SUBJUNCTIVE	Νὰ δώσω — To give	Νὰ δίδω—To give (to be giving)

LESSON 18

τὸ χέρι	tô hĕ′ri	the hand, the arm
τὸ πόδι	tô pô′thĭ	the foot, the leg
τὸ στόμα	tô stô′mȧ	the mouth
ἡ κεφαλή, *col.* τὸ κεφάλι	ĭ kĕfȧlĭ′ tô kĕfȧ′lĭ	the head
τὸ μάτι	tô mȧ′tĭ	the eye
τὸ αὐτὶ	tô ȧftĭ′	the ear
τὸ δόντι	tô thôn′tĭ (or thôn′dĭ)	the tooth
δύναμαι	thĭ′nȧmĕ	I can
εἰμπορῶ, *col.* μπορῶ	ĭmpôrô′, ĭmbôrô′, bôrô′	I can or I may
εἰμπόρουν *col.* εἰμπορουῦσα, μπορουῦσα	ĭmbô′roon ĭmbôroo′sȧ bôroo′sȧ	I could or I might
εἰμπόρεσα	ĭmbô′rĕsȧ	I was able
ἔχω εἰμπορέσει	ĕ′hô ĭmbôrĕ′sĭ	I have been able
ἐργάζομαι	ĕrγȧ′zômĕ	I work
περιπατῶ	pĕrĭpȧtô′	I walk
ἐπεριπάτουν	ĕpĕrĭpȧ′toon	I was walking
ἐπεριπάτησα	ĕpĕrĭpȧ′tĭsȧ	I walked
ἔχω περιπατήσει	ĕ′hô pĕrĭpȧtĭ′sĭ	I have walked
τρώγω	trô′γô	I eat
ἔτρωγα	ĕ′trôγȧ	I was eating
ἔφαγα	ĕ′fȧγȧ	I ate
ἔχω φάγει	ĕ′ho fȧ′γĭ	I have eaten
μυρίζομαι	mĭrĭ′zômĕ	I smell
ἀκούω	ȧkoo′ô	I hear
ἄκουα	ȧ′koo ȧ	I was hearing
ἄκουσα	ȧ′koosȧ	I heard
ἔχω ἀκούσει	ĕ′ho ȧkoo′sĭ	I have heard
μασσῶ	mȧsô′	I chew

ἐμάσσων	ĕmȧ'sȏn	**I was chewing**
ἐμάσσησα	ĕmȧ'sĭsȧ	**I chewed**
ἔχω μασσήσει	ĕ'hȏ mȧsĭ'sĭ	**I have chewed**
πίνω	pĭ'nȏ	**I drink**
ἔπινα	ĕ'pĭnȧ	**I was drinking**
ἔπια	ĕ'pĭȧ	**I drank**
ἔχω πίει, *col.* πιῆ	ĕ'hȏ pĭ'ĭ, ĕ'hȏ p'hĭ	**I have drunk**

EXERCISES

Τί εἰμπορεῖς νὰ κάμνῃς μὲ τὰ χέρια σου;	What can you do with your hands?
Εἰμπορῶ νὰ ἐργάζωμαι μὲ τὰ χέρια μου.	I can work with my hands.
Τί εἰμπορεῖς νὰ κάμνῃς μὲ τὰ πόδια σου;	What can you do with your feet?
Εἰμπορῶ νὰ περιπατῶ μὲ τὰ πόδια μου.	I can walk with my feet.
Τί εἰμπορεῖς νὰ κάμνῃς μὲ τὸ στόμα σου;	What can you do with your mouth?
Εἰμπορῶ νὰ τρώγω καὶ νὰ πίνω μὲ τὸ στόμα μου.	I can eat and drink with my mouth.
Τί κάμνεις μὲ τὴν μύτην σου;	What do you do with your nose?
Μυρίζομαι μὲ τὴν μύτην μου.	I smell with my nose.
Εἰμπορεῖς νὰ ἴδῃς μὲ τὴν μύτην σου;	Can you see with your nose?
Ὄχι. Δὲν εἰμπορῶ νὰ ἴδω μὲ τὴν μύτην μου.	No. I can not see with my nose.
Βλέπω μὲ τὰ μάτια μου.	I see with my eyes.
Ἀκούω μὲ τὰ αὐτιά μου.	I hear with my ears.
Μασσῶ μὲ τὰ δόντια μου.	I chew with my teeth.
Πηγαίνω ἐδῶ καὶ ἐκεῖ μὲ τὰ πόδια μου.	I go here and there with my feet.
Πόσα πόδια ἔχομεν;	How many feet have we?
Ἔχομεν δύο πόδια.	We have two feet.
Ἐπίσης ἔχομεν δύο χέρια.	We also have two hands.
Ἔχομεν μόνον μίαν κεφαλήν.	We have only one head.

Τί θέλετε νὰ πιῆτε; **Τσάϊ, καφέ, ἢ γάλα;**	What do you want to drink? Tea, coffee, or milk?
Ἐγὼ θὰ πιῶ τσάϊ. Ἡ μητέρα μου θὰ πιῇ καφέ.	I shall drink tea. My mother will drink coffee.

Elementary Grammar

Τὸ στόμα	The mouth	Τὸ πρᾶγμα	The thing
Τοῦ στόματος	Of the mouth	Τοῦ πράγματος	Of the thing
Τὰ στόματα	The mouths	Τὰ πράγματα	The things
Τῶν στομάτων	Of the mouths	Τῶν πραγμάτων	Of the things

Neuter nouns ending in **α** are declined as above, that is by adding the ending **τος** for the genitive singular, **τα** for the nominative and accusative plural, and **των** for the genitive plural. In the genitive plural the accent descends on the syllable before last.

—:—

The verbs δύναμαι and εἰμπορῶ (or in abbreviation μπορῶ) both mean "I can" or "I may". The verb εἰμπορῶ or ἠμπορῶ (col. μπορῶ) is more commonly used in everyday conversation. It is conjugated as follows:

Εἰμπορῶ	I can
Εἰμπορεῖς	You can (singular)
Εἰμπορεῖ	He (she, it) can
Εἰμποροῦμεν	We can
Εἰμπορεῖτε	You can (plural)
Εἰμποροῦν	They can
Εἰμπόρουν or εἰμποροῦσα	I could
Εἰμπόρεις or εἰμποροῦσες	You could (sin.)
Εἰμπόρει or εἰμποροῦσε	He (she, it) could
Εἰμποροῦμεν or εἰμπορούσαμε	We could
Εἰμπορεῖτε or εἰμπορούσατε	You could (pl.)
Εἰμπόρουν or εἰμποροῦσαν	They could
Εἰμπόρεσα or μπόρεσα, etc.	I was able
Θὰ εἰμπορέσω, θὰ μπορέσω, etc.	I shall be able
Ἔχω εἰμπορέσει or μπορέσει, etc.	I have been able

LESSON 19

ὁ λαιμὸς	ô lĕmôs′	**the neck, the throat**
τὸ δάκτυλον	tô thȧk′tĭlôn	**the finger**
ἡ γλῶσσα	ĭ γlô′sȧ	**the tongue**
γειά σου!	yȧ′soo	**hello!**
ὁ Γεώργιος, Γεώργης	ô yĕ ôr′γĭôs, o yôr′γĭs	**George**
ζεστὸς	zĕstôs′	**hot**
κρύος	krĭ′ôs	**cold**
κρυώνω	krĭô′nô	**I am cold**
ἐκρύωνα	ĕkrĭ′ônȧ	**I was cold**
ἐκρύωσα	ĕkrĭ′ôsȧ	**I caught (felt) cold**
ἔχω κρυώσει	ĕ′hô krĭ ô′sĭ	**I have caught cold**
ἡ φωτιὰ	ĭ fôtĭȧ′	**the fire**
τὸ κάρβουνο, τὰ κάρβουνα	tô kȧr′voonô tȧ kȧr′voonȧ	**the coal** **the coal,** pl.
τὸ ξύλον, τὰ ξύλα	tô ksĭ′lôn, tȧ ksĭ′lȧ	**the wood**
τὸ σπίρτον	tô spĭr′tôn	**the match**
τὸ κουτὶ	tô kootĭ′	**the box**
ὁμιλῶ	ômĭlô′	**I talk, I speak**
ὁμιλεῖς	ômĭlĭs′	**you talk,** sing.
ὁμιλεῖ	ômĭlĭ′	**he (she, it) talks**
ὁμιλοῦμεν	ômĭloo′mĕn	**we talk**
ὁμιλεῖτε	ômĭlĭ′tĕ	**you talk,** pl.
ὁμιλοῦν	ômĭloon′	**they talk**
ὡμίλουν c. ὡμιλοῦσα	ômĭ′loon, ômĭloo′sȧ	**I was talking**
ὡμίλεις c. ὡμιλοῦσες	ômĭ′lĭs, ômĭloo′sĕs	**you were talking,** sing.
ὡμίλει c. ὡμιλοῦσε	ômĭ′lĭ, ômĭloo′sĕ	**he(she, it)was talking**
ὡμιλοῦμεν *or* ὡμιλούσαμε	ômĭloo′mĕn or ômĭloo′sȧmĕ	**we were talking** " " "
ὡμιλεῖτε *or* ὡμιλούσατε	ômĭlĭ′tĕ or ômĭloo′sȧtĕ	**you were talking,** plur. " " "

ὡμίλουν *or* ὡμιλοῦσαν	ômĭ'loon *or* ômĭloo'sȧn	**they were talking** " " "
ὡμίλησα, *c.* μίλησα	ômĭ'lĭsȧ, mĭ'lĭsȧ	**I talked**
ὡμίλησες, *etc.*	ômĭ'lĭsĕs	**you talked,** etc.
ἔχω ὁμιλήσει	ĕ'hô ômĭlĭ'sĭ	**I have talked**
θὰ ὁμιλῶ	thȧ ômĭlô'	**I shall be talking**
θὰ ὁμιλήσω	thȧ ômĭlĭ'sô	**I shall talk**
πῶς, ποῦ	pôs, poo	**that** (conjunction)

EXERCISES

Ποῦ εἶναι ἡ γλῶσσά σου;	Where is your tongue?
Ἡ γλῶσσά μου εἶναι μέσα εἰς τὸ στόμα μου.	My tongue is in my mouth.
Τί κάμνεις μὲ τὴν γλῶσσάν σου;	What do you do with your tongue?
Ὁμιλῶ μὲ τὴν γλῶσσάν μου.	I speak with my tongue.
Ποῖος ὁμιλεῖ τώρα;	Who is speaking now?
Ὁ πατέρας μας ὁμιλεῖ μαζὺ μὲ τὸν φίλον του.	Our father is speaking with his friend.
Χθὲς ὡμίλει μὲ τὸν ἀδελφόν σου.	Yesterday he spoke (was speaking) with your brother.
Θέλω νὰ ἰδῶ τὸν λαιμόν σου.	I want to see your neck.
Εἶναι ὁ λαιμός σου καὶ τὰ χέρια σου καθαρά;	Are your neck and your hands clean?
Ναί. Ὁ λαιμός μου καὶ τὰ χέρια μου εἶναι πολὺ καθαρά.	Yes. My neck and my hands are very clean.
Κύτταξε τὰ δάκτυλά μου.	Look at my fingers.
Εἶναι ἐπίσης πολὺ καθαρά.	They are also very clean.
Γειά σου, Γεώργιε. Τί κάνεις;	Hello, George. How do you do?
Εἶμαι πολὺ καλά. Εὐχαριστῶ.	I am very well. Thank you.
Κρυώνεις;	Are you cold?
Ὄχι δὲν κρυώνω. Εἶμαι πολὺ ζεστός. Μόνον τὰ πόδια μου εἶναι κρύα.	No, I am not cold. I am very warm. Only my feet are cold.
Κάμε φωτιά.	Make a fire.

Νά, ἐδῶ εἶναι κάρβουνα καὶ ξύλα.	Look, here are coal and wood.
Πάρε ἕνα σπίρτο ἀπὸ τὸ κουτί.	Take a match from the box.
Τί βλέπετε στὸ δρόμο;	What do you see in the street?
Βλέπω ἄνδρες, γυναῖκες καὶ παιδιά.	I see men, women and children.
Ἐγὼ βλέπω μόνον δύο ἄνδρες ποὺ περιπατοῦν καὶ ὁμιλοῦν στὸ δρόμο.	I see only two men who are walking and talking in the street.
Θέλεις νὰ φάγῃς κάτι;	Do you want to eat something?
Ὄχι, εὐχαριστῶ. Σήμερα ἔφαγα καλά. Ἔφαγα κρέας, ψωμὶ καὶ τυρί, καὶ ἔπια ἕνα ποτῆρι γάλα.	No, thank you. Today I ate well. I ate meat, bread and cheese, and I drank a glass of milk.
Ἔχει φάγει ὁ ἀδελφός σου;	Has your brother eaten?
Νομίζω πῶς δὲν ἔχει φάγει.	I think that he has not eaten.
Δόστε του κάτι νὰ φάγῃ, σᾶς παρακαλῶ.	Give him something to eat, please.

Conjugation of Verbs Accented on the Last Syllable

ὁμιλῶ	I talk	ἀγαπῶ	I love
ὁμιλεῖς	you talk (sin.)	ἀγαπᾷς	you love (sin.)
ὁμιλεῖ	he (she, it) talks	ἀγαπᾷ	he (she, it) loves
ὁμιλοῦμεν	we talk	ἀγαπῶμεν	we love
ὁμιλεῖτε	you talk (pl.)	ἀγαπᾶτε	you love (pl.)
ὁμιλοῦν	they talk	ἀγαποῦν	they love
ὡμίλουν	I was talking, I talked	ἠγάπων	I was loving, I loved
ὡμίλεις	you were talking (sin.)	ἠγάπας	you were loving (sin.)
ὡμίλει	he was talking	ἠγάπα	he was loving
ὡμιλοῦμεν	we were talking	ἠγαπῶμεν	we were loving
ὡμιλεῖτε	you were talking (pl.)	ἠγαπᾶτε	you were loving (pl.)
ὡμίλουν	they were talking	ἠγάπων	they were loving
ὡμίλησα, etc.	I talked	ἠγάπησα, etc.	I loved
ἔχω ὁμιλήσει	I have talked	ἔχω ἀγαπήσει	I have loved
θὰ ὁμιλῶ	I shall be talking, or	θὰ ἀγαπῶ	I shall be loving, or
θὰ ὁμιλήσω	I shall talk	θὰ ἀγαπήσω	I shall love
νὰ ὁμιλῶ	to be talking, or	νὰ ἀγαπῶ	to be loving, or
νὰ ὁμιλήσω	to talk	νὰ ἀγαπήσω	to love

ὁμίλει	be talking, talk	ἀγάπα	be loving, love
ὁμίλησε	talk	ἀγάπησε	love

Verbs accented on the last syllable in writing and cultured conversation are inflected as the above examples. However, in common conversation the above verbs ὁμιλῶ and ἀγαπῶ might be formed as follows: (Colloquially the verb ὁμιλῶ is abbreviated as μιλῶ.)

μιλῶ	I talk	ἀγαπῶ	I love
μιλᾷς	you talk (sin.)	ἀγαπᾷς	you love (sin.)
μιλᾷ	he (she, it) talks	ἀγαπᾷ	he (she, it) loves
μιλοῦμε	we talk	ἀγαποῦμε	we love
μιλᾶτε	you talk (pl.)	ἀγαπᾶτε	you love (pl.)
μιλοῦν	they talk	ἀγαποῦν	they love
μιλοῦσα	I was talking	ἀγαποῦσα	I was loving, I loved
μιλοῦσες	you were talking (sin.)	ἀγαποῦσες	you were loving (sin.)
μιλοῦσε	he was talking	ἀγαποῦσε	he (she, it) was loving
μιλούσαμε	we were talking	ἀγαπούσαμε	we were loving
μιλούσατε	you were talking (pl.)	ἀγαπούσατε	you were loving (pl.)
μιλοῦσαν	they were talking	ἀγαποῦσαν	they were loving
μίλησα, etc.	I talked	ἀγάπησα, etc.	I loved
ἔχω μιλήσει	I have talked	ἔχω ἀγαπήσει	I have loved
θὰ μιλῶ	I shall be talking, or	θὰ ἀγαπῶ	I shall be loving, or
θὰ μιλήσω	I shall talk	θὰ ἀγαπήσω	I shall love
νὰ μιλῶ	to be talking, or	νὰ ἀγαπῶ	to be loving, or
νὰ μιλήσω	to talk	νὰ ἀγαπήσω	to love
μίλησε	talk (sin.)	ἀγάπησε	love (sin.)
μιλῆστε	talk (pl.)	ἀγαπῆστε	love (pl.)
μίλα	be talking, talk (sin.)	ἀγάπα	be loving, love (sin.)
μιλᾶτε	be talking, talk (pl.)	ἀγαπᾶτε	be loving, love (pl.)

LESSON 20

τὸ πρωΐ	tô prô ï′	the morning
ἡ ἡμέρα	ĭ ĭmĕ′rȧ	the day
ἡ ἑσπέρα	í ĕspĕ′rȧ	the evening
τὸ βράδυ	tô vrȧ′thĭ	the evening
ἡ νύκτα	ĭ nĭk′tȧ	the night
καλημέρα	kȧlĭmĕ′rȧ	good morning
καλησπέρα	kȧlĭspĕ′rȧ	good evening
καληνύκτα	kȧlĭ nĭk′tȧ	good night
χαίρετε	hĕ′rĕtĕ	good bye
τί ἔχεις; τί ἔπαθες;	tĭ ĕ′hĭs, tĭ ĕ′pȧthĕs	what is the matter with you?
ἠξεύρω (γνωρίζω)	ĭksĕv′rô (γnôrĭ′zô)	I know
ἤξευρα	ĭ′ksĕvrȧ	I knew
ὁ πονοκέφαλος	ô pônôkĕ′fȧlôs	(the) headache
τὸ κρυολόγημα	tô krĭ ôlô′γĭmȧ	(the) cold
τὸ μαγαζί	tô mȧγȧzĭ′	the store
ἡ ἐργασία	ĭ ĕrrγȧsĭ′ȧ	the work
ἐργάζομαι	ĕrrγȧ′zômĕ	I work
ἐργάζεσαι	ĕrγȧ′zĕsĕ	you work, sing.
ἐργάζεται	ĕrγȧ′zĕtĕ	he (she, it) works
ἐργαζόμεθα	ĕrγȧzô′mĕthȧ	we work
ἐργάζεσθε	ĕrγȧ′zĕsthĕ	you work, plural
ἐργάζονται	ĕrrγȧ′zôntĕ	they work
τὸ ἐργοστάσιον	tô ĕrγôstȧ′sĭôn	the factory

EXERCISES

Καλημέρα, Γεῶργο. Τί κάνεις;	Good morning, George. How do you do?
Πολὺ καλά, Γιάννη. Πῶς εἶσθε σεῖς;	Very well, John. How are you?
Δὲν εἶμαι τόσον καλὰ σήμερα. Εἶμαι ἄρρωστος.	I am not so well today. I am sick.
Εἶσαι ἄρρωστος; Τί ἔχεις;	Are you sick? What is the matter with you?
Δὲν εἰξεύρω.	I do not know.
Εἶμαι πολὺ ζεστός.	I am very warm.
Ἔχω πονοκέφαλο.	I have a headache.
Τὰ πόδια μου εἶναι κρύα.	My feet are cold.
Δὲν εἶναι τίποτε. Εἶναι μόνον ἕνα μικρὸν κρυολόγημα.	It is nothing. It is only a little cold.
Εἶναι ἐδῶ ὁ πατέρας σου;	Is your father here?
Ὁ πατέρας μου δὲν εἶναι ἐδῶ. Εἶναι ἔξω. Εἶναι στὸ μαγαζί.	My father is not here. He is out. He is in the store.
Θὰ ὑπάγῃς καὶ σὺ ἐκεῖ;	Will you go there too?
Ὄχι. Δὲν θὰ ὑπάγω τώρα. Θὰ ὑπάγω τὸ πρωΐ.	No. I shall not go now. I shall go in the morning.
Ὁ φίλος μου θὰ ὑπάγῃ τὸ βράδυ.	My friend will go in the evening.
Ἐγὼ πηγαίνω εἰς τὴν ἐργασίαν μου τώρα.	I am going to my work now.
Ποῦ ἐργάζεσαι;	Where do you work?
Ἐργάζομαι εἰς ἕνα ἐργοστάσιον κουμπιῶν.	I work in a button factory.
Τί κάμνετε ἐκεῖ;	What do you make there?
Κάμνομεν κουμπιὰ διὰ ὑποκάμισσα.	We make buttons for shirts.
Ὁ ἀδελφός σου ἐργάζεται καὶ αὐτός;	Is your brother working too?
Ναί. Ἐργάζεται τὴν νύκτα.	Yes. He works at night.

Intransitive and Passive Verbs

In general, transitive verbs end in ω (δίδω — I give, παίρνω — I take, ἀγαπῶ—I love). Intransitive verbs may end in ω (πηγαίνω—I go, χαίρω—I rejoice, νομίζω—I think), or μαι (ἔρχομαι—I come, γίνομαι—I become, ἐργάζομαι—I work, κοιμῶμαι—I sleep). Passive verbs end in μαι (δίδομαι—I am given, παίρνομαι—I am taken, ἀγαπῶμαι—I am loved).

In the indicative present, verbs ending in μαι are inflected as the following examples:

δίδομαι	I am given	ἔρχομαι	I come
δίδεσαι	you are given (sin.)	ἔρχεσαι	you come (sin.)
δίδεται	he (she, it) is given	ἔρχεται	he (she, it) comes
διδόμεθα	we are given	ἐρχόμεθα	we come
δίδεσθε	you are given (pl.)	ἔρχεσθε	you come
δίδονται	they are given	ἔρχονται	they come
βλέπομαι	I am seen	ἀγαπῶμαι	I am loved
βλέπεσαι	you are seen (sin.)	ἀγαπᾶσαι	you are loved (sin.)
βλέπεται	he (she, it) is seen	ἀγαπᾶται	he (she, it) is loved
βλεπόμεθα	we are seen	ἀγαπώμεθα	we are loved
βλέπεσθε	you are seen (pl.)	ἀγαπᾶσθε	you are loved (pl.)
βλέπονται	they are seen	ἀγαπῶνται	they are loved

—:—

We must remind the student that in Greek the 2nd person singular of pronouns and verbs is used when speaking to intimate friends or younger persons. A person addressing a familiar friend may say: "Πῶς εἶσαι; 'Εργάζεσαι; — How art thou? Dost thou work?" instead of "Πῶς εἶσθε; 'Εργάζεσθε; — How are you? Do you work?"

However, when addressing persons with whom we are not familiar, in polite conversation the second person plural is generally used. For example: "Καλημέρα, Κυρία Πολίτου. Τί κάμνετε; (instead of 'τί κάμνεις;') — Good morning, Mrs. Polites. How do you do?"

LESSON 21

τὰ γλυκὰ	tȧ γlĭkȧ′	**the sweets, the candies**
ἡ σοκολάτα	ĭ sȯkȯlȧ′tȧ	**the chocolate**
πάρα πολὺ	pȧ′rȧ polĭ′	**too much**
ἡ σοῦπα	ĭ soo′pȧ	**the soup**
μερικός, μερική, -όν	mĕrĭkȯs′, mĕrĭkĭ′, -ȯn′	**some** (masc., fem., neu.)
ἡ πατάτα	ĭ pȧtȧ′tȧ	**the potato**
τὰ μακαρόνια	tȧ mȧkȧrȯ′nĭȧ	**the macaroni**
ὅποιος δήποτε	ȯ′pĭȯs thĭ′pȯtĕ	**anybody,** masc.
ὅποια δήποτε	ȯ′pĭȧ thĭ′pȯtĕ	**anybody,** fem.
ὅ,τι δήποτε	ȯ′tĭ thĭ′pȯtĕ	**anything**
πεινῶ	pĭnȯ′	**I am hungry**
ἐπείνων, *c.* ἐπεινοῦσα	ĕpĭ′nȯn, ĕpĭnoo′sȧ	**I was hungry**
ἐπείνασα	ĕpĭ′nȧsȧ	**I felt hungry**
ἔχω πεινάσει	ĕ′ho pĭnȧ′sĭ	**I have been hungry**
κάθημαι	kȧ′thĭmĕ	**I sit, I sit down**
ἐκαθήμην, ἐκαθήμουν	ĕkȧthĭ′mĭn, -moon	**I was sitting**
ἐκάθησα	ĕkȧ′thĭsȧ	**I sat**
θὰ καθήσω	thȧ kȧthĭ′sȯ	**I shall sit**
καθήσατε	kȧthĭ′sȧtĕ	**sit down,** pl.
ψητὸ ϐωδινὸ	psĭtȯ′ vȯthĭnȯ′	**roast beef**
ἡ σαλάτα	ĭ sȧlȧ′tȧ	**the salad**
τὸ χοιρομέρι	tȯ hĭrȯmĕ′rĭ	**the ham**
τὸ αὐγὸ(ν)	tȯ ȧv γȯ′	**the egg**
τὸ κουτάλι	tȯ kootȧ′lĭ	**the spoon**
τὸ πηροῦνι	tȯ pĭroo′nĭ	**the fork**
ἡ μπύρα	ĭ bĭ′rȧ	**the beer**
διψῶ	thĭpsȯ′	**I am thirsty**
ἐδίψων, *col.* διψοῦσα	ĕthĭ′psȯn, thĭpsoo′sȧ	**I was thirsty**
ἐδίψασα	ĕthĭ′psȧsȧ	**I felt thirsty**
ἔχω διψάσει	ĕ′hȯ thĭpsȧ′sĭ	**I have been thirsty**
τὸ φλυτζάνι	tȯ flĭ tzȧ′nĭ	**the cup**

EXERCISES

Ἔχω κάτι διὰ σέ.	I have something for you.
Τί εἶναι;	What is it?
Εἶναι ἕνα κουτὶ γλυκά.	It is a box of candies.
Σᾶς εὐχαριστῶ πολύ, κύριε. Εἶσθε πολὺ καλός.	I thank you very much, sir. You are very kind.
Εἶναι καλὰ γλυκά. Ἀγαπῶ τὴς σοκολάτες πάρα πολύ.	They are good candies. I like chocolates very much.
Εἰμπορεῖς νὰ μοῦ δώσῃς κάτι νὰ φάγω;	Can you give me something to eat?
Μάλιστα, κύριε. Θέλετε ἕνα πιάτο σούπα;	Yes, sir. Do you want a plate of soup?
Ὄχι. Δὲν θέλω σούπα.	No. I don't want soup.
Δός μου μερικὸ κρέας.	Give me some meat.
Θέλετε πατάτες ἢ μακαρόνια;	Do you want potatoes or macaroni?
Δός μου ὅ,τι δήποτε. Πεινῶ πολύ.	Give me anything. I am very hungry.
Καθήσατε, κύριε. Θὰ σᾶς φέρω ἀπὸ ὅλα.	Sit down, sir. I will bring you everything.
Θέλω ψητὸ βωδινὸ καὶ σαλάτα.	I want roast beef and salad.
Φέρε μου χοιρομέρι καὶ αὐγά.	Bring me ham and eggs.
Τώρα φέρε μου ἕνα μαχαῖρι, ἕνα κουτάλι καὶ ἕνα πηροῦνι.	Now, bring me a knife, a spoon and a fork.
Τί θὰ πιῆτε (or πίετε), κύριε;	What will you drink, sir?
Θέλετε τσάϊ ἢ καφέ;	Do you want tea or coffee?
Φέρε μου ἕνα ποτῆρι μπύρα, ἂν ἔχετε. Διψῶ πολύ.	Bring me a glass of beer, if you have any. I am very thirsty.
Ἂν δὲν ἔχετε μπύρα, φέρε μου ἕνα φλυτζάνι καφὲ καὶ ἕνα ποτῆρι νερό.	If you haven't any beer, bring me a cup of coffee and a glass of water.
Ποῦ πηγαίνετε τώρα;	Where are you going now?
Πηγαίνω σπῆτι.	I am going home.
Χαίρετε.	Good bye.

—:—

In Greek we do not say "a plate of soup, a glass of water", but "a plate soup (ἕνα πιάτο σοῦπα), a glass water (ἕνα ποτῆρι νερό)", etc.

LESSON 22

ὁ ἰατρός, *col.* γιατρός	ô ĭătrôs′ or yătrôs′	**the doctor**
τὸ παράθυρον	tô pără′thĭrôn	**the window**
ὁ κρεοπώλης	ô krĕôpô′lĭs	**the butcher**
col. ὁ χασάπης	ô hăsă′pĭs	" "
ὁ παντοπώλης	ô păntôpô′lĭs	**the grocer**
col. ὁ μπακάλης	ô băkă′lĭs	" "
τὸ χρῶμα	tô hrô′mă	**the color**
κόκκινος, κόκκινη, ον	kô′kĭnôs, kô′kĭnĭ, -ôn	**red** (masc., fem., neu.)
κίτρινος, κίτρινη, -ον	kĭ′trĭnôs, kĭtrĭnĭ, -ôn	**yellow** " " "
πράσινος, -η, -ον	pră′sĭnôs, prăsĭnĭ, -ôn	**green** " " "
γαλανός, -ή, -όν	γălănôs′, γălănĭ′, -ôn′	**blue** " " "
καστανός, -ή, -όν	kăstănôs′, -ĭ′, -ôn′	**brown** " " "
φορῶ	fôrô′	**I wear**
ἐφόρουν *or* ἐφοροῦσα	ĕfô′roon, ĕforoo′să	**I was wearing**
ἐφόρεσα	ĕfô′rĕsă	**I wore**
ἔχω φορέσει	ĕ′hô fôrĕ′sĭ	**I have worn**
τὸ φροῦτο(ν)	tô froo′tô	**the fruit**
τὸ μῆλον	tô mĭ′lôn	**the apple**
τὸ πορτοκάλλι	tô pôrtôkă′lĭ	**the orange**
ἡ ϐανάνα	ĭ vănă′nă	**the banana**
τὸ ἀπίδι	tô ăpĭ′thĭ	**the pear**
κανεὶς	kănĭs′	**nobody**
κάποιος	kă′pĭôs	**somebody**
ὅμοιος, ὁμοία, ὅμοιον	ô′mĭôs, ômĭ′ă, ô′mĭon	**alike** (masc., fem., neu.)
ὡσὰν	ôsăn′	**like, as**
ὁ διάδρομος	ô thĭă′thrômôs	**the corridor**
ἡ αἴθουσα, ἡ σάλα	ĭ ĕ′thoosă, ĭ să′lă	**the hall, the parlor**
ἡ Μαρία	ĭ mărĭ′ă	**Mary**
ἡ Ἑλένη	ĭ ĕlĕ′nĭ	**Helen**
πρίν, πρότερον	prĭn, prô′tĕrôn	**before**

EXERCISES

Τὸ σπίτι τοῦ ἰατροῦ εἶναι μεγάλο.	The doctor's house is large.
Τὰ παράθυρά του εἶναι μικρά.	Its windows are small.
Τοῦ κρεοπώλου τὸ παιδὶ εἶναι μικρό.	The butcher's boy is small.
Ἡ κόρη τοῦ παντοπώλου εἶναι μεγάλη.	The daughter of the grocer (the grocer's daughter) is big.
Ποῖον εἶναι τὸ χρῶμα τοῦ φορέματός σου;	What is the color of your dress?
Τὸ φόρεμά μου εἶνε μαῦρο.	My dress is black.
Τὸ ἐπανωφόρι τοῦ ἀδελφοῦ μου εἶνε ἄσπρο.	My brother's coat is white.
Ἡ Μαρία φορεῖ ἕνα κόκκινο ἐπανωφόρι μὲ μεγάλες τσέπες.	Mary is wearing (wears) a red coat with large pockets.
Μαρία, ἔλα κάτω, παρακαλῶ, καὶ δός μας κάτι νὰ φάγωμεν. Πεινῶμεν πολύ.	Mary, come down, please, and give us something to eat. We are very hungry.
Ἔχεις κάτι νὰ μᾶς δώσῃς;	Have you something to give us?
Δὲν ἔχω τίποτε.	I haven't anything.
Ἔχω μόνον ὀλίγα φροῦτα.	I have only some fruit.
Δός μας ἕνα μῆλο καὶ δύο πορτοκάλλια.	Give us an apple and two oranges.
Τί εἶναι τὸ χρῶμα αὐτοῦ τοῦ μήλου;	What is the color of this apple?
Αὐτὸ τὸ μῆλο ἔχει κόκκινο χρῶμα.	This apple has a red color.
Ἐκεῖνο τὸ ἀπίδι ἔχει πράσινο χρῶμα.	That pear has a green color.
Τὸ χρῶμα αὐτῆς τῆς βανάνας εἶναι κίτρινο.	The color of this banana is yellow.
Τὰ μάτια τῆς Μαρίας εἶναι καστανά.	Mary's eyes are brown.
Τὰ μάτια τῆς Ἑλένης εἶναι γαλανά. Εἶναι ὡσὰν τὰ μάτια τοῦ πατέρα της.	Helen's eyes are blue. They are like her father's eyes (like the eyes of her father).
Ποιὸς εἶναι στὴ σάλα;	Who is in the parlor?
Κανεὶς δὲν εἶνε στὴ σάλα τώρα.	Nobody is in the parlor now.
Κάποιος ἦταν στὸ διάδρομο πρίν.	Somebody was in the corridor before.
Νομίζω κάποιος εἶνε κάτω.	I think some one is downstairs.
Ναί, ὁ μπακάλης εἶναι κάτω μαζὺ μὲ τὸν παπποῦ μας.	Yes, the grocer is downstairs with our grandfather.

Τί κάμνουν;	What are they doing?
Πίνουν καφὲ καὶ ὁμιλοῦν.	They are drinking coffee and talking.

Elementary Grammar

In the vernacular, masculine nouns ending in ς and accented on the last syllable (with the exception of nouns ending in ος, for which see Lesson 5), are usually declined as the following examples:

	Singular		Plural	
Nom.	ὁ καφὲς	the coffee	οἱ καφέδες	the coffees
Gen.	τοῦ καφὲ	of the coffee	τῶν καφέδων	of the coffees
Accus.	τὸν καφὲ	the coffee	τοὺς καφέδες	the coffees
Voc.	ὦ καφὲ	O coffee	ὦ καφέδες	O coffees
Nom.	ὁ παπᾶς	the priest	οἱ παπάδες	the priests
Gen.	τοῦ παπᾶ	of the priest	τῶν παπάδων	of the priests
Accus.	τὸν παπᾶ	the priest	τοὺς παπάδες	the priests
Voc.	ὦ παπᾶ	O priest	ὦ παπάδες	O priests

In the same idiom feminine nouns ending in οῦ are declined as follows:

	Singular		Plural	
Nom.	ἡ ἀλεποῦ	the fox	ἡ ἀλεποῦδες	the foxes
Gen.	τῆς ἀλεποῦς	of the fox	τῶν ἀλεπούδων	of the foxes
Accus.	τὴν ἀλεποῦ	the fox	τὴς ἀλεποῦδες	the foxes
Voc.	ὦ ἀλεποῦ	O fox	ὦ ἀλεποῦδες	O foxes
Nom.	ἡ μαϊμοῦ	the monkey	ἡ μαϊμοῦδες	the monkeys
Gen.	τῆς μαϊμοῦς	of the monkey	τῶν μαϊμούδων	of the monkeys
Accus.	τὴν μαϊμοῦ	the monkey	τὴς μαϊμοῦδες	the monkeys
Voc.	ὦ μαϊμοῦ	O monkey	ὦ μαϊμοῦδες	O monkeys

—:—

In Greek the definite article usually accompanies proper names. For example: " 'Ο Γεώργιος εἶνε ἐδῶ—(the) George is here. 'Η Μαρία ἦλθε—(the) Mary came. Τοῦ Γιάννη τὸ καπέλλο—(the) John's hat", etc.

LESSON 23

ἀγοράζω	ἀγôrá'zô	I buy
ἀγόραζα	ἀγô'rázá	I was buying, I bought
ἀγόρασα	ἀγô'rásá	I bought
ἔχω ἀγοράσει	ĕ'ho ἀγôrá'sĭ	I have bought
τὸ λάδι	tô lá'thĭ	the oil
τὸ ξύδι	tô xĭ'thĭ (ksĭ'thĭ)	the vinegar
ἡ μποτίλια	ĭ bôtĭ'lĭá	the bottle
ἡ σακοῦλα	ĭ sákoo'lá	the bag
τὸ ἀλεῦρι	tô álĕv'rĭ	the flour
ἡ λίτρα	ĭ lĭ'trá	the pound
τὸ λεμόνι	tô lĕmô'nĭ	the lemon
χρειάζομαι	hrĭá'zômĕ	I need
ἐχρειαζόμην	ĕhrĭázô'mĭn	I was in need, I needed
ἐχρειάσθην	ĕhrĭá'sthĭn	I needed
ἔχω χρειασθῆ	ĕ'hô hrĭásthĭ'	I have needed
ὅ,τι δήποτε ἄλλο	ô'tĭth ĭ'pôtĕ á'lô	anything else
ἀνοίγω	ánĭ'γô	I open
ἄνοιγα	á'nĭγá	I was opening
ἄνοιξα	á'nĭxá	I opened
ἔχω ἀνοίξει	ĕ'ho ánĭ'ksĭ	I have opened
κλείω, *col.* κλείνω	klĭ'ô, klĭ'nô	I close
ἔκλεια *col.* ἔκλεινα	ĕ'klĭá or ĕ'klĭná	I was closing, I closed
ἔκλεισα	ĕ'klĭsá	I closed
ἔχω κλείσει	ĕ'ho klĭ'sĭ	I have closed
ἡ θύρα	ĭ thĭ'rá	the door
μπαίνω	bĕ'nô	I go in, I come in
ἔμπαινα	ĕm'bĕná	I was going in
ἐμπῆκα	ĕmbĭ'ká	I went in
ἔχω μπῆ	ĕ'hô bĭ	I have gone in
λέγω	lĕ'γô	I say, I tell
ἔλεγα	ĕ'lĕγá	I was saying

εἶπα	i'pȧ	**I said**
ἔχω εἰπῆ	ĕ'hô ĭpĭ'	**I have said**
ὁ κύριος Πολίτης	ô kĭ'rĭôs pôlĭ'tĭs	**Mr. Politis,** nominative
Κύριε Πολίτη	kĭ'rĭĕ pôlĭ'tĭ	**Mr. Politis,** vocative

EXERCISES

Γιάννη, πήγαινε κάτω καὶ ἀγόρασε μιὰ μποτίλια λάδι καὶ μιὰ μποτίλια ξύδι.	John, go downstairs and buy a bottle of oil and a bottle of vinegar.
Θέλετε καὶ * μιὰ μποτίλια κρασί;	Do you also want a bottle of wine?
Ὄχι· πάρε μιὰ σακκοῦλα ἀλεῦρι, μιὰ λίτρα τυρὶ καὶ δύο λεμόνια.	No; get a bag of flour, a pound of cheese and two lemons.
Ἀγόρασε ἐπίσης καὶ ὅ,τι δήποτε ἄλλο χρειαζόμεθα.	Also buy anything else we need.
Ὁ Γιάννης πηγαίνει εἰς τοῦ μπακάλη.	John goes to the grocer's.
Ἀνοίγει τὴν θύραν.	He opens the door.
Μπαίνει μέσα καὶ κλείνει τὴν θύραν.	He goes in and closes the door.
Λέγει εἰς τὸν μπακάλην:	He says to the grocer:
«Κύριε Πολίτη, δός μου μιὰ σακκοῦλα ἀλεῦρι, μιὰ μποτίλια ξύδι καὶ μιὰ λίτρα ἄσπρο τυρί.	"Mr. Polites, give me a bag of flour, a bottle of vinegar and a pound of white cheese.
«Δός μου ἐπίσης δύο λεμόνια καὶ μιὰ μποτίλια κόκκινο κρασί.»	"Also give me two lemons and one bottle of red wine."
Ὁ μπακάλης εἶπε εἰς τὸν Γιάννη:	The grocer said to John:
«Θέλετε τίποτε ἄλλο;»	"Do you want anything else?"
Ὁ Γιάννης εἶπε: «Θέλω μιὰ μποτίλια λάδι καὶ μιὰ λίτρα φασόλια.	John said: "I want a bottle of oil and a pound of beans.
«Θὰ ἀγοράσω καὶ μιὰ λίτρα βούτυρο.»	"I shall also buy a pound of butter."

—:—

* In Greek the conjunction καὶ (and) is also used in the meaning of "also, too". For example:

Δός μου κ α ὶ μιὰ λίτρα τυρί. —Give me a l s o a pound of cheese.

Θέλεις κ α ὶ βούτυρο; — Do you want butter t o o ?

LESSON 24

ἐρωτῶ	ĕrôtô′	**I ask**
ἠρώτων	ĭrô′tôn	**I was asking**
ἠρώτησα	ĭrô′tĭsȧ	**I asked**
ἔχω ἐρωτήσει	ĕ′hô ĕrôtĭ′sĭ	**I have asked**
τὸ καρβέλι	tô kȧrvĕ′lĭ	**the loaf**
ὁ τενεκὲς	ô tĕnĕkĕs′	**the can**
ἡ τομάτα	ĭ tômȧ′tȧ	**the tomato**
τὸ κρομμύδι	tô krômĭ′thĭ	**the onion**
μισός, μισή, μισόν	mĭsôs′, mĭsĭ′, mĭsôn′	**half** (masc., fem., neu.)
τὸ ρύζι	tô rĭ′zĭ	**the rice**
κατόπιν	kȧtô′pĭn	**after, afterwards**
ἓξ	ĕx	**six**
ἑπτὰ	ĕptȧ′	**seven**
ὀκτὼ	ôktô′	**eight**
ἐννέα	ĕnĕ′ȧ	**nine**
δέκα	thĕ′kȧ	**ten**
ἀξίζει	ȧksĭ′zĭ	**it costs**
πόσον ἀξίζουν	pô′sôn ȧksĭ′zoon	**how much they cost**
τὸ δολλάριον	tô thôlȧ′rĭôn	**the dollar**
τὸ λεπτόν· τὰ λεπτὰ	tô lĕptôn′; tȧ lĕptȧ′	**the cent; the money**
τὰ ρέστα	tȧ rĕs′tȧ	**the change**
μετρῶ· ἐμέτρησα	mĕtrô′, ĕmĕ′trĭsȧ	**I count; I counted**
ἔχω μετρήσει	ĕ′hô mĕtrĭ′sĭ	**I have counted**
ὅλα τὰ πράγματα	ô′lȧ tȧ prȧγ′mȧtȧ	**everything, all things**
εἰπέ μου	ĭpĕ′ moo	**tell me**

EXERCISES

Ὁ μπακάλης ἐρωτᾷ τὸν Γιάννη: «Τί ἄλλο θέλετε;»	The grocer asks John: "What else do you want?"
Ὁ Γιάννης εἶπε: «Θέλω ἕνα καρβέλι ψωμί, ἕνα τενεκὲ τομάτες καὶ μιὰ λίτρα κρομμύδια.	John said: "I want a loaf of bread, a can of tomatoes and a pound of onions.
Δόστε με καὶ μισὴ λίτρα ρύζι καὶ ἓξ καλὰ αὐγά.»	Give me also half a pound of rice and six good eggs."
Ὁ μπακάλης ἔδωσε στὸν Γιάννη ὅλα τὰ πράγματα ποῦ ἤθελε. Κατόπιν τὸν ἠρώτησε:	The grocer gave John everything he wanted. Then he asked him:
«Θὰ πάρετε τίποτε ἄλλο;»	"Will you have anything else?"
Ὁ Γιάννης εἶπε: «Ναί· θὰ πάρω ἑπτὰ λίτρες πατάτες, ὀκτὼ κόκκινα μῆλα, ἐννέα κίτρινες βανάνες, καὶ δέκα πράσινα ἀπίδια.»	John said: "Yes; I'll take seven pounds of potatoes, eight red apples, nine yellow bananas, and ten green pears."
Ὁ Κύριος Πολίτης ἠρώτησε πάλιν τὸν Γιάννην: «Χρειάζεσθε τίποτε ἄλλο;»	Mr. Polites asked John again: "Do you need anything else?"
Ὁ Γιάννης εἶπε: «Δὲν χρειάζομαι ἄλλο τίποτε. Εἰπέ με μόνον πόσον ἀξίζουν αὐτὲς ἡ μικρὲς πατάτες.»	John said: "I don't need anything else. Only tell me how much are these small potatoes."
Ὁ μπακάλης λέγει: «Αὐτὲς ἡ μικρὲς πατάτες εἶναι νέες. Ἀξίζουν ἑπτὰ λεπτὰ (σὲντς) ἡ λίτρα.	The grocer says: "These small potatoes are new. They cost seven cents a pound.
Ἐκεῖνες ἐκεῖ ἡ μεγάλες εἶναι παλαιὲς πατάτες. Εἶνε μόνον ἓξ σὲντς ἡ λίτρα.»	Those large ones are old potatoes. They are only six cents a pound."
Ὁ Γιάννης ἀγόρασε τρεῖς λίτρες μεγάλες πατάτες.	John bought three pounds of large potatoes.

Ὁ μπακάλης ἔφερε ὅλα ἐπάνω στὸ τραπέζι.	The grocer brought everything on the table.
Ἐπῆρε μία μεγάλη σακκοῦλα καὶ ἔβαλε ὅλα τὰ πράγματα μέσα σ' αὐτή.	He took a big bag and put everything in it.
Ὁ Γιάννης ἐρώτησε τὸν Κύριον Πολίτην πόσον ἀξίζουν ὅλα μαζύ.	John asked Mr. Polites how much they cost all together.
Ὁ κύριος Πολίτης τὸν εἶπε: «Τέσσαρα δολλάρια καὶ δέκα σέντς.»	Mr. Polites told him: "Four dollars and ten cents."
Ὁ Γιάννης ἔδωσε στὸν κύριον Πολίτην πέντε δολλάρια.	John gave Mr. Polites five dollars.
Ὁ κύριος Πολίτης ἔδωσε στὸν Γιάννη τὰ ρέστα του.	Mr. Polites gave John his change.
Ὁ Γιάννης εἶπε «χαίρετε» εἰς τὸν κύριον Πολίτην.	John said "goodbye" to Mr. Polites.
Ἐπῆρε τὴν σακκοῦλα μὲ τὰ πράγματα καὶ ἐπῆγε σπίτι.	He took the bag with the things and went home.

The word σπίτι (house, home) is used exactly as the English parallel "home". It serves as a noun, meaning "house", or as an adverb, meaning "at home" or "to the house". Examples:

Μεγάλο σπίτι	A big house.
Ὁ πατέρας μου εἶνε στὸ σπίτι.	My father is at home.
Πηγαίνω σπίτι.	I am going home.

LESSON 25

ὁ υἱός, *col.* γυιὸς	ô ĭôs′, or yôs	**the son**
ἡ θυγάτηρ, *col.* θυγατέρα	ĭ thĭγà′tĭr or thĭγà-tĕ′rà	**the daughter** " "
τὸ μετάξι	tô mĕtà′xĭ	**the silk**
μετάξινος, -η, -ον	mĕtà′xĭnôs, -ĭ, -ôn	**made of silk, silken**
τὰ ὑποδήματα	tà ĭpôthĭ′màtà	**the shoes**
τὸ ζευγάρι	tô zĕvγà′rĭ	**the pair**
ἰδικός μου, δικός μου, ὁ ἰδικός μου	ĭthĭkôs′ moo or ô ĭthĭkôs′ moo	**mine** "
ἰδικός σου	ĭthĭkôs′ soo	**thine, yours** (sing.)
ἰδικός του	ĭthĭkôs′ too	**his**
ἰδικός της	ĭthĭkôs′ tĭs	**hers**
ἰδικός μας	ĭthĭkôs′ màs	**ours**
ἰδικός σας	ĭthĭkôs′ sàs	**yours,** plural
ἰδικός των	ĭthĭkôs′ tôn	**theirs**
ὁ χρυσὸς	ô hrĭsôs′	**the gold**
χρυσός, χρυσῆ, -ό	hrĭsôs′, hrĭsĭ′, hrĭsô′	**made of gold**
ὁ ἄργυρος *col.* τὸ ἀσῆμι	ô àr′γĭrôs, tô àsĭ′mĭ	**the silver** " "
ἀσημένιος	àsĭmĕ′nĭôs	**made of silver**
τὸ σημάδι	tô sĭmà′thĭ	**the mark**
ἡ πλευρὰ	ĭ plĕvrà′	**the side**
τὸ ὡρολόγιον *col.* ρολόγι	to ôrôlô′γĭôn rôlô′γĭ, rôlô′yĭ	**the watch, the clock** " " "
τὸ βαμβάκι	tô vàmvà′kĭ	**the cotton**
βαμβακερὸς	vàmvàkĕrôs′	**made of cotton**
ἡ κάλτσα	ĭ kàl′tsà	**the stocking, the sock**
ὅτι	ô′tĭ	**that**

EXERCISES

Ποιὸς εἶνε αὐτὸς ὁ νέος;	Who is this young man?
Αὐτὸς ὁ νέος εἶναι υἱός μου.	This young man is my son.
Ἐκείνη ἡ νέα εἶνε θυγάτηρ μου.	That young woman is my daughter.
Ἡ θυγατέρα μου ἔχει ἕνα ὡραῖο μετάξινο φόρεμα καὶ ἕνα ὡραῖο ζευγάρι ὑποδήματα.	My daughter has a pretty silk dress and a fine pair of shoes.
Εἶναι αὐτὴ ἡ πένα ἰδική σας;	Is this pen yours?
Αὐτὴ ἡ χρυσῆ πένα δὲν εἶναι ἰδική μου. Εἶναι τοῦ πατέρα μου.	This gold pen is not mine. It is my father's.
Τὸ χρυσὸ ὡρολόγι εἶνε δικό σου.	The gold watch is yours.
Ἐκεῖνο τὸ ἀσημένιο μαχαῖρι εἶνε δικό σου, ἐπίσης.	That silver knife is yours, too.
Πῶς γνωρίζεις ὅτι εἶνε ἰδικόν μου;	How do you know that it is mine?
Τὸ γνωρίζω διότι ἔχει ἕνα σημάδι εἰς τὴν πλευράν.	I know it because it has a mark on the side.
Αὐτὸς εἶνε τοῦ ἀδελφοῦ σου ὁ σκύλος;	Is this your brother's dog?
Ὄχι· δὲν εἶνε ἰδικός του· εἶνε ἰδικός μας.	No; he is not his; he is ours.
Δὲν εἶνε ἰδικός σας· δὲν εἶνε ἰδικός των. Εἶνε ὁ δικός μου σκύλος.	He is not yours; he is not theirs. He is my dog.
Ἔχεις ἕνα ζευγάρι μετάξινες κάλτσες;	Have you a pair of silk stockings?
Ὄχι, κύριε· ἔχω ἕνα ζευγάρι βαμβακερὲς κάλτσες.	No, sir; I have a pair of cotton socks (stockings).
Ἡ ἀδελφή μου ἔχει ἕνα ὡραῖο ζευγάρι μετάξινες κάλτσες.	My sister has a fine pair of silk stockings.
Ὁ ἀδελφός μου ἔχει ἄσπρες μετάξινες κάλτσες.	My brother has white silk socks.

LESSON 26

τὸ παποῦτσι (*col.*)	tô pápoo′tsĭ	**the shoe**
ὁ παπουτσῆς	ô pápootsïs′	**the shoemaker**
τὸ δέρμα	tô **thĕr′má**	**the leather**
δερμάτινος, -η, -ον	**thĕrmá′tĭnôs**, -ĭ, -ôn	**made of leather**
τὸ εἶδος	tô **ï′thôs**	**the kind**
τί εἴδους	tï **ï′thoos**	**of what kind**
εὐθηνός, εὐθηνή, -όν	ĕf thĭ nôs′, -nï′, -nôn′	**cheap** (mas., fem., neu.)
ἀκριβός, ή, ὸν	ákrĭ-vôs,′ -vï′, -vôn′	**expensive** " " "
τὸ κιβώτιον, τὸ κουτὶ	tô kĭvô′tĭôn, tô kootï′	**the box**
τὸ μωρὸ	tô môrô′	**the baby**
εὔμορφος, -η, -ον	ĕv′môrfôs, -ĭ, -ôn	**pretty** (mas., fem., neu.)
προσέχω	prôsĕ′hô	**I take care**
ἐπρόσεχα	ĕprô′sĕhá	**I was taking care**
ἐπρόσεξα	ĕprô′sĕxá	**I took care**
ἔχω προσέξει	ĕ′ho prôsĕ′xĭ	**I have taken care**
μία κυρία	mï′á kĭrï′á	**a lady**
τὸ ὕφασμα	tô ï′fásmá (ï′fázma)	**the cloth**
ὁ ράπτης	ô ráp′tĭs	**the tailor**
μετὰ	mĕtá′	**after; with**
τὸ φαγητὸν	tô fáγĭtôn′	**the meal, the dinner**
μετὰ τὸ φαγητὸν	mĕtá′ tô fáγĭtôn′	**after dinner**
τὸ δεῖπνον	tô thïp′nôn	**the supper**
ἔτσι	ĕ′tsĭ	**so, in this manner**
δὲν εἶν’ ἔτσι;	thĕn ïn ĕ′tsĭ	**isn’t it so?**

EXERCISES

Ἐκεῖνος ὁ παπουτσῆς κάμνει καλὰ δερμάτινα παπούτσια. Ἂν θέλετε ἕνα ζευγάρι, μπορεῖτε νὰ πᾶτε εἰς αὐτόν.	That shoemaker makes good leather shoes. If you want a pair, you can go to him.
Εἶναι καλὰ μῆλα αὐτά;	Are these good apples?
Τί εἶδος μῆλα θέλετε, κύριε;	What kind of apples do you want, sir?
Αὐτὰ εἶνε εὐθηνὰ μῆλα.	These are cheap apples.
Ἐκεῖνα τὰ μῆλα εἰς τὸ κιβώτιον δὲν εἶνε εὐθηνά.	Those apples in the box are not cheap.
Εἶνε πολὺ ἀκριβά.	They are very expensive.
Ποιὰ εἶνε ἐκείνη ἡ κυρία;	Who is that lady?
Δὲν τὴν γνωρίζω.	I do not know her.
Ἔχει ἕνα εὔμορφο μωρό.	She has a beautiful baby.
Τὸ μωρὸ δὲν εἶνε δικό της. Αὐτὴ μόνον προσέχει τὸ παιδὶ ἐκεῖνο.	The baby is not hers. She only takes care of that child.
Ἔχω ἕνα κομμάτι καλὸ ὕφασμα.	I have a piece of good cloth.
Θέλω νὰ κάμω ἕνα ἐπανωφόρι διὰ τὸ παιδί μου.	I want to make an overcoat for my boy.
Θὰ ὑπάγω εἰς τὸν ράπτην μετὰ τὸ φαγητόν.	I shall go to the tailor after dinner.
Αὐτὸς θὰ κάμῃ τὸ ἐπανωφόρι διὰ τὸν υἱόν μου.	He will make the overcoat for my son.
Πήγαινε στὴν ἐργασία σου μετὰ τὸ φαγητόν. Μπορεῖς νὰ πᾶς εἰς τοῦ ράπτου μετὰ τὸ δεῖπνον.	Go to your work after dinner. You can go to the tailor's after supper.
Δὲν εἶνε ἔτσι, κυρία;	Isn't it so, madam?
Ἔχετε δίκαιον, φίλε μου.	You are right, my friend.
Πρέπει νὰ προσέχωμεν πολὺ τὴν ἐργασίαν μας.	We must be very careful about our work.
Ποῦ εἶναι τώρα ὁ υἱός σας;	Where is your son now?
Εἶνε στὴν πόλιν μαζὺ μὲ τὴν ἀδελφή μου.	He is in the city with my sister.
Ἐπῆγαν ν' ἀγοράσουν ροῦχα καὶ παπούτσια.	They have gone to buy clothes and shoes.

LESSON 27

ἡ βροχὴ	ί vrôhï′	the rain
βρέχω	vrĕ′hô	I wet
βρέχει	vrĕ′hĭ	it rains
ἔβρεχε	ĕ′vrĕhĕ	it was raining
ἔβρεξε	ĕ′vrĕxĕ	it rained
ἔχει βρέξει	ĕ′hĭ vrĕ′xĭ	it has rained
ὁ καιρὸς	ô kĕrôs′	the weather, the time
μένω	mĕ′nô	I stay, I live
ἔμενα	ĕ′mĕnȧ	I was staying
ἔμεινα	ĕ′mĭnȧ	I stayed
ἔχω μείνει	ĕ′hô mï′nĭ	I have stayed
ζῶ	zô	I live
ἔζων	ĕ′zôn	I was living
ἔζησα	ĕ′zĭsȧ	I lived
ἔχω ζήσει	e′hô zï′sĭ	I have lived
τραγουδῶ	trȧγoothô′	I sing
ἐτραγούδουν	ĕtrȧγoo′thoon	I was singing
ἐτραγούδησα	ĕtrȧγoo′thĭsȧ	I sang
ἔχω τραγουδήσει	e′hô traγoothï′sĭ	I have sung
τὸ δένδρον	tô thĕn′thrôn	the tree
ἡ χλόη	ĭ hlô′ĭ	the grass
τὸ πουλὶ	tô poolï′	the bird
ὁ ἀέρας	ô ȧĕ′rȧs	the air, the wind
ὑγιεινός, -ή, -όν	ĭ γĭ ĭ nôs′, -ï′, -ôn′	healthy, healthful
μόνος, μόνη, μόνον	mô′nôs, mô′nĭ, mô′non	alone (mas., fem., neu.)
εὐχαριστημένος,η,ον	ĕfhȧrĭstĭmĕ′nos, -ĭ,-ôn	pleased " " "
ἡ διασκέδασις	ĭ thĭȧskĕ′thȧsĭs	good time, amusement

EXERCISES

Ἤμην εἰς τὴν ἐξοχὴν χθές.	I was in the country yesterday.
Ἔβρεχε;	Was it raining?
Ὄχι. Δὲν ἔβρεχε.	No. It was not raining.
Εἴχαμε ὡραῖον καιρόν.	We had fine weather.
Ἀγαπῶ νὰ μένω εἰς τὴν ἐξοχήν.	I like to live in the country.
Καὶ ἐγὼ ἀγαπῶ νὰ ζῶ εἰς τὴν ἐξοχήν.	I also like to live in the country.
Δὲν μοῦ ἀρέσει νὰ ζῶ εἰς τὴν πόλιν.	I do not like to live in the city.
Ἀγαπῶ τὰ δένδρα καὶ τὴν χλόην.	I like the trees and the grass.
Ἀγαπῶ νὰ ἀκούω τὰ πουλιὰ νὰ τραγουδοῦν.	I like to hear the birds sing.
Ὁ ἀέρας τῆς ἐξοχῆς εἶναι τόσον ὑγιεινός.	The air of the country is so healthful.
Πότε εἶχες ὑπάγει εἰς τὴν ἐξοχήν;	When did you go (had you gone) to the country?
Ἤμουν στὴν ἐξοχὴν χθές.	I was in the country yesterday.
Ἦσο μόνος;	Were you alone?
Ὄχι. Δὲν ἤμουν μόνος.	No. I was not alone.
Οἱ φίλοι μου ἦσαν ἐκεῖ μαζύ μου.	My friends were there with me.
Ἔμειναν πολὺ εὐχαριστημένοι.	They were much pleased.
Εἴχομεν πολλὴν διασκέδασιν ὅλην τὴν ἡμέραν.	We had much fun (diversion) all day.
Θὰ πᾶμε (or θὰ ὑπάγωμεν) πάλιν στὴν ἐξοχὴν αὔριον.	We shall go to the country again tomorrow.
Θὰ πάρωμεν μαζύ μας καὶ τὴν μητέρα μας.	We shall take our mother with us, too.

—:—

In Greek it is not required to place the subject before the verb, or the object immediately after. They may precede or follow the verb, or be separated from it by other words. For example, the sentence "John saw a dog yesterday" may be expressed correctly in several ways with the same words:

Ὁ Γιάννης εἶδε ἕνα σκύλο χθές.
Ὁ Γιάννης εἶδε χθὲς ἕνα σκύλο.
Ἕνα σκύλο εἶδε χθὲς ὁ Γιάννης.
Ἕνα σκύλο εἶδε ὁ Γιάννης χθές.
Χθὲς ὁ Γιάννης εἶδε ἕνα σκύλο. Etc.

LESSON 28

τὸ β̌ράδυ	tô vrá'thĭ	the evening
λυποῦμαι	lĭpoo'mĕ	I am sorry
ἐλυπούμην	ĕlĭpoo'mĭn	I was sorry
ἐλυπήθην	ĕlĭpĭ'thĭn	I felt sorry
ἔχω λυπηθῆ	ĕ'hô lĭpĭthĭ'	I have been sorry
χαίρω	hĕ'rô	I am glad
ἔχαιρον *col.* ἔχαιρα	ĕ'hĕrôn, ĕ'hĕrȧ	I was glad (contin.past)
ἐχάρην	ĕhȧ'rĭn	I was glad (indef. past)
ἔχω χαρῆ	e'hô hȧrĭ'	I have been glad
εὐτυχὴς	ĕf tĭ hĭs'	happy
ἡ ὀμπρέλλα	ĭ ômbrĕ'lȧ	the umbrella
τὴν περασμένη ἑβδομάδα	tĭn pĕrȧzmĕ'nĭ ĕvthômȧ'thȧ	last week
τὸ γράμμα	tô γrȧ'mȧ	the letter
ἀρκετός, ή, ὸν	ȧrketôs', arkĕtĭ', ôn'	enough (mas., fem., neu.)
γίνομαι	yĭ'nômĕ	I become
ἐγινόμην	ĕyĭnô'mĭn	I was becoming
ἔγινα	ĕ'yĭnȧ	I became
ἔχω γίνει	ĕ'hô yĭ'nĭ	I have become
προχθὲς	prôh thĕs'	day before yesterday
ἐντελῶς	ĕntĕlôs' *or* ĕndĕlôs'	fully, entirely
ἄνθρωποι	ȧn'thrôpĭ	men, people
ἕως	ĕ'ôs	till, until

EXERCISES

Χθὲς ὁ καιρὸς ἦτο πολὺ κακὸς εἰς τὴν πόλιν.	Yesterday the weather was very bad in the city.
Ἔβρεχε ὅλην τὴν ἡμέραν.	It rained (was raining) all day.
Ἐγὼ ἤμουν σπῆτι ἀπὸ τὸ πρωῒ ἕως τὸ βράδυ.	I was at home from morning till night.
Λυποῦμαι πολὺ ποῦ τὸ ἀκούω.	I am very sorry to hear it.
Εἶχες τὴν ὀμπρέλλα σου μαζύ σου;	Did you have your umbrella with you?
Ναί. Εἶχα μιὰ ὀμπρέλλα, ἀλλὰ δὲν ἦτο καλή.	Yes. I had an umbrella, but it was not good.
Ποῦ ἦτο ὁ φίλος σου τὴν περασμένη ἑβδομάδα;	Where was your friend last week?
Ἦτο μαζύ σου εἰς τὴν ἐξοχήν;	Was he with you in the country?
Ὄχι. Δὲν ἦτο εἰς τὴν ἐξοχήν.	No. He was not in the country.
Ἦτο εἰς τὴν πόλιν ὅλον τὸν καιρόν.	He was in the city all the time.
Ἦτο εὐτυχὴς διότι εἶχε γράμμα ἀπὸ τὸν πατέρα του.	He was happy because he had a letter from his father.
Χαίρω νὰ τὸ ἀκούω.	I am glad to hear it.
Εἶχε χρήματα;	Had he any money?
Εἶχε ἀρκετὰ χρήματα.	He had enough money.
Ἦτο πολὺ πτωχὸς ὅταν ἦτο νέος, ἀλλὰ τώρα ἔγινε πλούσιος μὲ τὴν ἐργασία του.	He was very poor when he was young, but now he has become rich by his work.
Ἦσο ἄρρωστος προχθές;	Were you ill day before yesterday?
Ναί. Ἤμουν ἄρρωστος.	Yes. I was ill.
Τί εἶχες;	What was the matter with you? (What had you?)
Εἶχα ἕνα μικρὸν πονοκέφαλον.	I had a slight (little) headache.
Τώρα εἶμαι ἐντελῶς καλά.	Now I am perfectly well.
Πόσοι ἄνθρωποι ἦσαν στὸ σπίτι σου χθὲς τὸ βράδυ;	How may people were at your house last night?
Ἦσαν ὀκτὼ ἢ ἐννέα ἄνθρωποι.	There were eight or nine people.

LESSON 29

ἔλα, ἐλᾶτε	ĕ′là, ĕlà′tĕ	**come** sing.; **come** plural
πρέπει	prĕ′pĭ	**must, it is necessary**
ἔπρεπε	ĕ′prĕpĕ	**should, it was necessary**
πρέπει νὰ ὑπάγω	prĕ′pĭ nà ĭpà′γô	**I must go**
πρέπει νὰ ὑπάγῃς	prĕ′pĭ nà ĭpà′γĭs	**you must go** (sing.)
πρέπει νὰ ὑπάγῃ	prĕ′pĭ nà ĭpà′γĭ	**he (she, it) must go**
πρέπει νὰ ὑπάγωμεν	prĕ′pĭ nà ĭpà′γômĕn	**we must go**
πρέπει νὰ ὑπάγετε	prĕ′pĭ nà ĭpà′γĕtĕ	**you must go** (plural)
πρέπει νὰ ὑπάγουν	prĕ′pĭ nà ĭpà′γoon	**they must go**
ἔπρεπε νὰ ὑπάγω, *etc.*	ĕ′prĕpĕ nà ĭpà′γô	**I should go, etc.**
φεύγω	fĕv′γô	**I go away**
ἔφευγα	ĕ′fĕv γà	**I was going away**
ἔφυγα	ĕ′fĭγà	**I went away**
ἔχω φύγει	e′hô fĭ′γĭ	**I have gone away**
φύγε· φύγετε	fĭ′γĕ; fĭ′γetĕ	**go away** s.; **go away** pl.
γρήγορος, η, ον	γrĭ′γôrôs, -ĭ, -ôn	**quick, fast** (m., f., n.)
γρήγορα	γrĭ′γôrà	**quickly, soon**
ἀργός, ή, όν	àrγôs′, àrγĭ′, àrγôn′	**slow, late** (m. f. n.)
ἀργὰ	àrγà′	**slowly, late**
εὑρίσκω	evrĭ′skô	**I find**
ηὗρα	ĭv′rà	**I found**
ἔχω εὕρῃ *or* εὑρῇ	ĕ′hô ev′rĭ *or* ĕvrĭ′	**I have found**
κοιμῶμαι	kĭmô′mĕ	**I sleep**
κοιμᾶσαι	kĭmà′sĕ	**you sleep**
κοιμᾶται	kĭmà′tĕ	**he (she, it) sleeps**
κοιμώμεθα	kĭmô′mĕthà	**we sleep**
κοιμᾶσθε	kĭmà′sthĕ	**you sleep** (plural)
κοιμῶνται	kĭmôn′tĕ	**they sleep**
τί ἔπαθες;	tĭ ĕ′pathĕs	**what is the matter with you?**

ἀκόμη	ȧkô′mĭ	**yet**
σήκω	sĭ′kô	**get up**
κάμε γρήγορα	kȧ′mĕ γrĭ′γôrȧ	**hurry, make haste**
ἕτοιμος, η, ον	ĕ′tĭmôs,ĕ′tĭmĭ,ĕ′tĭmôn	**ready** (mas. fem. neu.)

EXERCISES

Ἐλᾶτε γρήγορα, παιδιά μου. Πρέπει νὰ φύγωμεν.	Come quickly, my boys. We must go away.
Δὲν εἰμποροῦμεν νὰ μείνωμεν ἐδῶ περισσότερον.	We cannot stay here any longer.
Δὲν ἔχομεν καιρόν.	We have no time.
Εἶσαι πολὺ ἀργός, Γιάννη.	You are very slow, John.
Τί ἔπαθες;	What is the matter with you?
Δὲν εἰμπορῶ νὰ εὕρω τὰ παπούτσια μου.	I can't find my shoes.
Δὲν εἰξεύρω ποῦ εἶνε.	I don't know where they are.
Δὲν γνωρίζω ποῦ τὰ ἔβαλα χθὲς τὸ βράδυ.	I don't know where I put them last night (last evening).
Νά! Τὰ ηὗρα. Τώρα θὰ βάλω τὸ ἐπανωφόρι μου καὶ θὰ ἔλθω μαζύ σας.	There! I have found them. Now I shall put on my coat and come with you.
Ποῦ εἶναι ὁ Γεώργιος;	Where is George?
Ὁ Γεώργιος κοιμᾶται ἀκόμη.	George is still sleeping.
Σήκω, Γεώργιε. Μὴ κοιμᾶσαι τόσον πολύ.	Get up, George. Don't sleep so much (so long).
Ημεῖς εἴμεθα ἐντελῶς ἕτοιμοι νὰ φύγωμεν.	We are quite ready to leave.

Ἂν θέλῃς νὰ ἔλθῃς μαζύ μας, κάμε γρήγορα.	If you want to come with us, hurry (make haste).
Θὰ ὑπάγωμεν εἰς τὴν πόλιν.	We shall go to the city.
Θὰ πᾶμε νὰ ἴδωμεν τὴν Καν Ἑλένην.	We shall go to see Mrs. Helen.
Πρέπει νὰ ἔλθῃς καὶ σὺ μαζύ μας.	You must come with us too.
Ἡ κυρία Ἑλένη θὰ χαρῇ νὰ μᾶς ἰδῇ ὅλους.	Mrs. Helen will be very glad to see us all.

Grammatical Remarks

The verb "π ρ έ π ε ι" is always used with the conjunction **νὰ**:

Πρέπει νὰ ἴδω	I must see.
Πρέπει νὰ ἴδῃς	You must see.
Πρέπει νὰ ἴδωμεν	We must see.
Πρέπει νὰ ἴδουν.	They must see, etc.

Ἔπρεπε νὰ ὑπάγω	I should go, I ought to go.
Ἔπρεπε νὰ ὑπάγῃς	You should go, you ought to go.
Ἔπρεπε νὰ ὑπάγῃ	He (she, it) should go.
Ἔπρεπε νὰ ὑπάγωμεν	We should go.
Ἔπρεπε νὰ ὑπάγετε	You should go. (pl.)
Ἔπρεπε νὰ ὑπάγουν	They should go.

LESSON 30

περιμένω	pĕrĭmĕ′nô	I wait, I am waiting
ἐπερίμενα	ĕpĕrĭ′mena	I was waiting
ἐπερίμεινα	ĕpĕrĭ′mĭnȧ	I waited
ἔχω περιμείνη	ĕ′hô pĕrĭmĭ′nĭ	I have waited
τὸ τρὰμ	tô trȧm	the trolley car
τρέχω	trĕ′hô	I run
ἔτρεχα	ĕ′trĕhȧ	I was running
ἔτρεξα	ĕ′trĕxȧ	I ran
ἔχω τρέξει	ĕ′hô trĕ′xĭ	I have run
στέκομαι	stĕ′komĕ	I stay, I stop
ἐστεκόμην	ĕstĕkô′mĭn	I was staying, stopping
ἐστάθην	ĕstȧ′thĭn	I stayed, I stopped
ἔχω σταθῆ	ĕ′hô stȧthĭ′	I have stayed, stopped
στάσου	stȧ′soo	stay, stop (imperative)
ἡ σκάλα	ĭ skȧ′lȧ	the stairs
τὸ πάτωμα	tô pȧ′tômȧ	the floor
τὸ χαλὶ	tô hȧlĭ′	the carpet, the rug
ὁ Παῦλος	o pȧv′lôs	Paul
ἡ εἰκών, *col.* εἰκόνα	ĭ ĭkôn′, ĭ ĭkô′nȧ	the picture
ὁ τοῖχος	ô tĭ′hôs	the wall
ὁ σύζυγος	ô sĭ′zĭγôs	the husband
ἡ σύζυγος	ĭ sĭ′zĭγôs	the wife
πᾶμε, ἄς ὑπάγωμεν	pȧ′mĕ, ȧs ĭpȧ′γômĕn	let us go
ἡ στέγη	ĭ stĕ′γĭ	the roof
χάνω	hȧ′nô	I lose

ἔχανα	ĕ'hȧnȧ	**I was losing**
ἔχασα	ĕ'hȧsȧ	**I lost**
θὰ χάσω	thȧ hȧ'sô	**I shall lose**
τὸ ἀπόγευμα	tô ȧpô'γĕvmȧ	**the afternoon**
ἀργά· ἐνωρὶς	ȧrγȧ'; ĕnôrĭs'	**late; early**
πλησίον· μακρὰν	plĭsĭ'ôn; mȧkrȧn'	**near; far**

EXERCISES

Τώρα εἴμεθα ὅλοι ἕτοιμοι.	Now we are all ready.
Ἐδῶ πρέπει νὰ περιμένωμε τὸ τράμ.	Here we must wait for the trolley.
Ἐγὼ νομίζω πῶς εἶναι καλλίτερα νὰ περιπατήσωμεν.	I think it is better to walk.
Δὲν εἶνε μακρὰν ἀπ' ἐδῶ.	It is not far from here.
Εἶναι πολὺ πλησίον.	It is very near.
Πάντοτε μοῦ ἀρέσει (ἀρέσω) νὰ περιπατῶ, ὅταν ὁ καιρὸς εἶνε ὡραῖος.	Always I like to walk, when the weather is fine.
Λέγουν ὅτι εἶνε πολὺ ὑγιεινὸν νὰ περιπατῇ κανείς.	They say that it is very healthful to walk.
Μὴ τρέχεις, Γιάννη. Στάσου καὶ περίμενέ μας.	Don't run, John. Stop and wait for us.
Αὐτὸ εἶνε τὸ σπῆτι τῆς Κας Ἑλένης.	This is Mrs. Helen's house.
Εἶνε ὡραῖον σπῆτι.	It is a beautiful house.
Ἡ σκάλες του εἶναι τόσον καθαρές.	Its stairs are so clean.
Ὅλα εἶνε πολὺ καθαρὰ ἐδῶ.	Everything is clean here.
Ἕνα ὡραῖο χαλὶ εἶνε εἰς τὸ πάτωμα.	A fine rug is on the floor.
Ὡραῖες εἰκόνες εἶνε εἰς τοὺς τοίχους.	Beautiful pictures are on the walls.
Ὁ κύριος Παῦλος λέγει ὅτι ἡ σύζυγός του δὲν εἶνε στὸ σπίτι.	Mr. Paul says that his wife is not at home.

Λυπούμεθα ὅτι δὲν εἰμποροῦμεν νὰ τὴν περιμένωμεν.	We are very sorry we cannot wait for her.
Εἶνε πολὺ ζέστη ἐδῶ.	It is very warm here.
Ἄς πᾶμε εἰς τὴν στέγην νὰ πάρωμεν ὀλίγον ἀέρα.	Let us go on the roof to get a little air.
Δὲν ἔχομεν καιρὸν νὰ χάσωμεν.	We have no time to lose.
Πρέπει νὰ πᾶμε στῆς ἀδελφῆς μου τὸ σπίτι.	We must go to my sister's house.
Ὁ σύζυγός της εἶνε πολὺ ἄρρωστος.	Her husband is very sick.
Δὲν εἰμπορεῖτε νὰ μείνετε ὀλίγον περισσότερον;	Can't you stay a little longer (more)?
Μπορεῖτε νὰ πᾶτε ἐκεῖ τὸ ἀπόγευμα.	You can go there in the afternoon.
Δὲν εἶνε τόσον ἀργὰ ἀκόμη.	It is not so late yet.
Εἶνε ἀρκετὰ ἀργά.	It is late enough.
Πρέπει νὰ πηγαίνωμεν.	We must be going.
Χαίρετε, Κύριε Παῦλε.	Good bye, Mr. Paul.

Elementary Grammar

As mentioned in a previous lesson, the Greek verbs have two basic forms or stems. One signifying action or condition in continuity, and the other momentary or finished action or condition. For instance, in the verb τρέχω (I run) the stem τρεχ signifies continuity and the modified form τρεξ means momentary action.

In the indicative present tense only the continuity stem is used:

τρέχ ω	I run, I am running
τρέχ εις	you run, you are running (sin.)
τρέχ ει	he (she, it) runs, is running
τρέχ ομεν	we run, we are running
τρέχ ετε	you run, you are running (pl.)
τρέχ ουν	they run, they are running

For the past tenses, the continuity stem (with the usual vowel increase at the beginning of the verb) is used for the continuous or imperfect past; the momentary modified form (also with a vowel increase) is used for the momentary or finished past; also the momentary form with the ending ει is used for the compound or perfected past. Examples:

ἔ τρεχ α	I was running, I ran	ἔ τρεξ α	I ran
ἔτρεχ ες	you were running	ἔ τρεξ ες	you ran
ἔ τρεχ ε	he was running	ἔ τρεξ ε	he ran
ἐ τρέχ αμεν	we were running	ἐ τρέξ αμεν	we ran
ἐ τρέχ ατε	you were running	ἐ τρέξ ατε	you ran
ἔ τρεχ αν	they were running	ἔ τρεξ αν	they ran

ἔχω τρέξ ει	I have run	εἶχα τρέξ ει	I had run
ἔχεις τρέξ ει	you have run	εἶχ ες τρέξ ει	you had run
ἔχει τρέξ ει,	he has run	εἶχε τρέξ ει	he had run

In the future tenses and in the imperative and subjunctive moods, the continuity stem is used to denote duration, while the momentary modified form is used in all other cases.

θὰ τρέχ ω	I shall be running	θὰ τρέξ ω	I shall run
θὰ τρέχ εις	you will be running	θὰ τρέξ εις	you will run
θὰ τρέχ ει	he will be running	θὰ τρέξ ει	he will run
θὰ τρέχ ομεν	we shall be running	θὰ τρέξ ομεν	we shall run
θὰ τρέχ ετε	you will be running	θὰ τρέξ ετε	you will run
θὰ τρέχ ουν	they will be running	θὰ τρέξ ουν	they will run

ἂς τρέχ ω	let me be running	ἂς τρέξ ω	let me run
τρέχ ε	be running (sin.)	τρέξ ε	run (sin.)
ἂς τρέχ η	let him be running	ἂς τρέξ η	let him run
ἂς τρέχ ωμεν	let us be running	ἂς τρέξ ωμεν	let us run
τρέχ ετε	be running (pl.)	τρέξ ατε	run (pl.)
ἂς τρέχ ουν	let them be running	ἂς τρέξ ουν	let them run

Πρέπει νὰ τρέχ ω	I must be running, or, I must run
Πρέπει νὰ τρέχ ης	you must be running, or, you must run
Θέλω νὰ τρέχ ω	I want to be running, or, I want to run
Πρέπει νὰ τρέξω, etc.	I must run, etc.

LESSON 31

λαμβάνω *col.* παίρνω	lȧmvȧ'nô or pĕr'nô	**I take**
ἐλάμβανα, *c.* ἔπαιρνα	ĕlȧm'vȧnȧ, ĕ'pĕrnȧ	**I was taking**
ἔλαβα, *col.* ἐπῆρα	ĕ'lȧvȧ, ĕpï'rȧ	**I took**
ἔχω λάβει,	ĕ'hô lȧ'vĭ	**I have taken**
col. ἔχω πάρει	ĕ'hô pȧ'rĭ	" "
ὁ ἐξάδελφος	ô ĕxȧ'thĕlfôs	**the cousin** (male)
ἡ ἐξαδέλφη	ĭ ĕxȧthĕl'fĭ	**the cousin** (female)
τὸ πορτοφόλι	to pôrtôfô'lĭ	**the pocketbook**
βοηθῶ	vôïthô'	**I help**
ἐβοήθουν *c.* βοηθοῦσα	ĕvôï'thoon, voïthoo'sȧ	**I was helping**
ἐβοήθησα	ĕvôï'thĭsȧ	**I helped**
ἔχω βοηθήσει	ĕ'hô voïthĭ'sĭ	**I have helped**
ὁ ὁποῖος	ô ôpï'ôs	**who, which** (masc.)
ἡ ὁποία	ĭ ôpï'ȧ	" " (fem.)
τὸ ὁποῖον	tô ôpï'ôn	" " (neu.)
πληρώνω	plĭrô'nô	**I pay**
ἐπλήρωνα	ĕplï'rônȧ	**I was paying**
ἐπλήρωσα	ĕplï'rôsȧ	**I paid**
ἔχω πληρώσει	ĕ'hô plĭrô'sĭ	**I have paid**
δύναμαι· δύνασαι	thï'nȧmĕ; thï'nȧsĕ	**I can; you can** (sin.)
δύναται	thï'nȧtĕ	**he (she, it) can**
δυνάμεθα	thĭnȧ'mĕthȧ	**we can**
δύνασθε	thï'nȧs thĕ	**you can** (plural)
δύνανται	thï'nȧntĕ	**they can**
ἠδυνάμην	ïthĭnȧ'mĭn	**I could**
ἠδυνήθην	ïthĭnï'thĭn	**I was able**

EXERCISES

Εἶδα τὸν ἐξάδελφόν σου χθές.	I saw your cousin yesterday.
Ποῦ τὸν εἶδες;	Where did you see him?
Τὸν εἶδα εἰς τὸν δρόμον μὲ τὴν σύζυγόν του.	I saw him in the street with his wife.
Ἔχετε ἴδει τὴν μικράν μου ἀδελφήν;	Have you seen my little sister?
Ὄχι. Δὲν τὴν ἔχω ἴδει.	No. I have not seen her.
Ἔχασες τὰ χρήματά σου;	Have you lost your money?
Ναί. Ἔχασα ὅλα μου τὰ χρήματα χθές.	Yes. I lost all my money yesterday.
Ποῦ τὰ εἶχες;	Where did you have it?
Τὰ εἶχα μέσα εἰς τὸ πορτοφόλι μου.	I had it in my purse.
Δὲν ηὗρες τὸ πορτοφόλι σου ἀκόμη;	Didn't you find your purse yet?
Ναί. Τὸ ηὗρα.	Yes. I found it.
Ἦτο εἰς τὴν κρεββατοκάμαρά μου, κάτω ἀπὸ τὸ τραπέζι.	It was in my bedroom under the table.
Ποῖος τὸ ἔβαλεν ἐκεῖ;	Who put it there?
Δὲν γνωρίζω ποιὸς τὸ ἔβαλε ἐκεῖ.	I don't know who put it there.
Νομίζω πῶς τὸ μωρὸ τὸ ἔβαλε ἐκεῖ.	I think (that) the baby put it there.
Ἔκαμα ἕνα καλὸ πρᾶγμα σήμερα.	I did a good thing today.
Τί καλὸ πρᾶγμα ἔκαμες;	What good thing did you do?
Εἶδα ἕνα πτωχὸν ἄνθρωπον στὸν δρόμο σήμερα τὸ πρωΐ.	I saw a poor man in the street this morning.
Μοῦ εἶπε πῶς δὲν εἰμποροῦσε νὰ ἐργασθῇ διότι ἦτο ἄρρωστος.	He told me that he could not work because he was sick.
Μοῦ ἐζήτησε χρήματα διὰ νὰ ἀγοράσῃ κάτι νὰ φάγῃ.	He asked me for money to buy something to eat.
Εἶπε πῶς ἐπεινοῦσε πολύ.	He said he was very hungry.
Δὲν εἶχε φάγει τίποτε διὰ δύο ἡμέρας.	He had not eaten anything for two days.
Ἐλυπήθην πολὺ δι' αὐτόν.	I was very sorry for him.
Τοῦ ἔδωσα δύο δολλάρια.	I gave him two dollars.
Ἔκαμες ἕνα πολὺ καλὸ πρᾶγμα.	You did a very good thing.
Ἐβοήθησες ἕνα πτωχὸν γέροντα, ὁ ὁποῖος δὲν ἠδύνατο νὰ ἐργασθῇ.	You helped a poor old man, who could not work.
Ὁ Θεὸς θὰ σοῦ τὸ πληρώσῃ μιὰ μέρα. *	God will pay you for it some day.

Elementary Grammar

The verbs **δύναμαι** and **εἰμπορῶ** are synonymous, meaning "I can, I may". «Δύναμαι» is used more by the purists and in writing, while «εἰμπορῶ» (or «ἠμπορῶ») is used in everyday talk.

δύναμαι	εἰμπορῶ	I can, I may
δύνασαι	εἰμπορεῖς	you can
δύναται	εἰμπορεῖ	he (she, it) can
δυνάμεθα	εἰμπορoῦμεν	we can
δύνασθε	εἰμπορεῖτε	you can (pl.)
δύνανται	εἰμπορoῦν	they can
ἠδυνάμην	εἰμπορoῦσα	I could, I might
ἠδύνασο	εἰμπορoῦσες	you could (sin.)
ἠδύνατο	εἰμπορoῦσε	he (she, it) could
ἠδυνάμεθα	εἰμπορούσαμεν	we could
ἠδύνασθε	εἰμπορούσατε	you could (pl.)
ἠδύναντο	εἰμπορoῦσαν	they could

Θὰ δύναμαι or θὰ δυνηθῶ
Θὰ εἰμπορῶ or θὰ εἰμπορέσω } I shall be able

Ἔχω δυνηθῆ or ἔχω εἰμπορέσει — I have been able, etc.

—:—

* In ordinary conversation many words beginning with unaccented vowels or diphthongs may be abbreviated by dropping the initial vowel or diphthong. For example:

μπορῶ	*for*	εἰμπορῶ	I can, I may
μέρα	»	ἡμέρα	day
ξάδελφος	»	ἐξάδελφος	cousin
πλήρωσα	»	ἐπλήρωσα	I paid
δώσαμε	»	ἐδώσαμεν	we gave
πάγει (or πάει)	»	ὑπάγει	goes, etc.

LESSON 32

ἀφήνω	ȧfĭ'nô	**I let, I leave, I allow**
ἄφηνα	ȧ'fĭnȧ	**I was letting**
ἄφησα	ȧ'fĭsȧ	**I let, I left, I allowed**
ἔχω ἀφήσει	ĕ'hô ȧfĭ'sĭ	**I have let, left, allowed**
γυρίζω, ἐπιστρέφω	γĭrĭ'zô, ĕpĭstrĕ'fô	**I turn or return**
ἐγύριζα, ἐπέστρεφα	ĕγĭ'rĭzȧ, ĕpĕ'strĕfȧ	**I was (re)turning**
ἐγύρισα, ἐπέστρεψα	ĕγĭ'rĭsȧ, ĕpĕs'trĕpsȧ	**I turned or returned**
ἔχω γυρίσει, ἔχω ἐ-πιστρέψει	ĕ'hô γĭrĭ'sĭ, ĕ'hô ĕpĭ-strĕ'psĭ	**I have turned,returned**
ἐρχόμενος, η, ον	ĕrhô'mĕnôs, -ĭ, -on	**coming** (m., f., n.)
περασμένος, η, ον	pĕrȧsmĕ'nôs, -ĭ, -ôn	**passed or past** (f.m.n.)
ὁ μήν, *col.* ὁ μῆνας	ô mĭn, ô mĭ'nȧs	**the month**
τὸν περασμένο μῆνα	tôn pĕrȧzmĕ'nô mĭ'na	**last month**
τὸ ἔτος, ὁ χρόνος	tô ĕ'tôs, ô hrô'nôs	**the year**
τὸ παρελθὸν ἔτος	tô pȧrĕlthôn' ĕ'tôs	**last year**
ἐργάζομαι	ĕrγȧ'zômĕ	**I work**
εἰργαζόμην	ĭrγȧzô'mĭn	**I was working**
εἰργάσθην	ĭrγȧs'thĭn	**I worked**
θὰ ἐργασθῶ	thȧ ĕrγȧsthô'	**I shall work**
ἐργάζου *or* ἐργάσου	ĕrγȧ'zoo or ĕrγȧ'soo	**work** (imperative)
ἡ Κυριακὴ	ĭ kĭrĭȧkĭ'	**Sunday**
ἡ Δευτέρα	ĭ thĕftĕ'rȧ	**Monday**
ἡ Τρίτη	ĭ trĭ'tĭ	**Tuesday**
ἡ Τετάρτη	ĭ tĕtȧr'tĭ	**Wednesday**
ἡ Πέμπτη	ĭ pĕm'ptĭ	**Thursday**
ἡ Παρασκευὴ	ĭ pȧrȧskĕvĭ'	**Friday**
τὸ Σάββατον	tô sȧ'vȧtôn	**Saturday**
ἐλεύθερος	ĕlĕf'thĕrôs	**free**
χθὲς τὸ βράδυ	hthĕs tô vrȧ'thĭ	**last night**
ἐκοιμήθην	ĕkĭmĭ'thĭn	**I slept**
col. ἐκοιμήθηκα	ĕkĭmĭ'thĭkȧ	

θὰ κοιμηθῶ	thȧ kĭmĭthȯ′	**I shall sleep**
θὰ κοιμῶμαι	thȧ kĭmȯ′mĕ	**I shall be sleeping**
κουρασμένος, η, ον	koorȧzmĕ′nȯs, -ĭ, -ȯn	**tired**
στὰ πόδια μου	stȧ pȯ′thĭȧ moo	**on my feet**
ἀπόψε	ȧpȯ′psĕ	**tonight, this evening**

EXERCISES

Θὰ ὑπάγω εἰς τὴν πόλιν αὔριον.	I shall go to the city tomorrow.
Θὰ ἔλθετε μαζύ μου;	Will you come with me?
Ναί, θὰ ἔλθω, ἂν ὁ πατέρας μου μὲ ἀφήσῃ.	Yes, I will come, if my father will let me.
Θὰ ὑπάγω καὶ θὰ τὸ εἴπω εἰς τὸν πατέρα σου.	I shall go and tell it to your father.
Ὁ πατέρας σου δὲν θὰ σὲ ἀφήσῃ νὰ ὑπάγῃς μαζύ μου.	Your father will not let you go with me.
Λέγει ὅτι ὁ καιρὸς δὲν εἶνε πολὺ καλός.	He says that the weather is not very good.
Νομίζω πῶς θὰ βρέξῃ αὔριον.	I think(that)it will rain tomorrow.
Δὲν μὲ μέλει ἂν θὰ βρέξῃ ἢ ὄχι.	I do not care whether it will rain or not.
Πόσον καιρὸν θὰ μείνετε εἰς τὴν πόλιν;	How long will you stay in the city?
Θὰ μείνω ἐκεῖ τρεῖς ἡμέρας.	I will stay there three days.
Θὰ γυρίσω τὴν ἐρχομένην ἡμέραν, τὴν Δευτέραν.	I shall come back the next day, Monday.
Τί θὰ κάμετε τὸν ἐρχόμενον μῆνα;	What will you do next month?
Τὸν ἐρχόμενον μῆνα θὰ ὑπάγω εἰς ἐργασίαν.	Next month I shall go to work.
Ἂν ἐργασθῇς ὅλον τὸν καιρὸν θὰ ἔχῃς χρήματα τὸ ἐρχόμενον ἔτος.	If you work all the time, you will have money next year.
Ἔτσι νομίζω καὶ ἐγώ.	I think so, too.
Ἤμην πτωχὸς τὸ παρελθὸν ἔτος.	I was poor last year.
Δὲν εἶμαι τόσον πτωχὸς τώρα.	I am not so poor now.
Τὸ ἐρχόμενον ἔτος θὰ εἶμαι πλούσιος.	Next year I shall be rich.
Ποῦ θὰ πᾶτε τὴν ἐρχομένην Τρίτην;	Where will you go next Tuesday?
Τὴν ἐρχομένην Τρίτην θὰ πᾶμε εἰς * τοῦ ἐξαδέλφου μου.	Next Tuesday we shall go to my cousin's.

Θὰ μείνωμεν ἐκεῖ τὴν Τετάρτην, Πέμπτην καὶ Παρασκευήν.	We shall stay there Wednesday, Thursday and Friday.
Θὰ γυρίσωμεν σπῆτι τὸ Σάββατον.	We shall return home Saturday.
Θὰ σᾶς ἴδωμεν πάλιν τὴν Κυριακήν, ἂν εἶσθε ἐλεύθερος.	We shall see you again Sunday, if you are free.
Ἦλθα σπῆτι ἀργὰ χθὲς τὸ βράδυ.	I came home late last night.
Δὲν ἐκοιμήθην ἀρκετά.	I did not sleep enough.
Εἶμαι τόσον κουρασμένος σήμερα.	I am so tired today.
Δὲν εἰμπορῶ νὰ σταθῶ στὰ πόδια μου.	I cannot stand on my feet.
Δὲν θὰ κάμω τὸ ἴδιον πρᾶγμα πάλιν.	I shall not do the same thing again.
Θὰ κοιμηθῶ ἐνωρὶς ἀπόψε.	I will sleep early tonight.
Θὰ κοιμῶμαι ἐνωρὶς ἄλλην φοράν.	I will sleep early next time.

Intransitive and Passive Verbs Ending in ομαι

Indicative Present

χάν ομαι	I am lost	ἐργάζ ομαι	I work, I am working
χάν εσαι	you are lost	ἐργάζ εσαι	you work, you are working
χάν εται	he is lost	ἐργάζ εται	he works
χαν όμεθα	we are lost	ἐργαζ όμεθα	we work
χάν εσθε	you are lost	ἐργάζ εσθε	you work
χάν ονται	they are lost	ἐργάζ ονται	they work

Imperfect or Continuous Past

ἐ χαν όμην	I was being lost	εἰργαζ όμην	I was working, I worked
ἐ χάν εσο	you were being lost	εἰργάζ εσο	you were working
ἐ χάν ετο	he was being lost	εἰργάζ ετο	he was working
ἐ χαν όμεθα	we were being lost	εἰργαζ όμεθα	we were working
ἐ χάν εσθε	you were being lost	εἰργάζ εσθε	you were working
ε χάν οντο	they were being lost	εἰργάζ οντο	they were working

Finished Past or Aorist

ἐ χά θην, c. χά θηκα	I was lost	εἰργάσθην, c. ἐργάσθηκα	I worked
ἐ χά θης, χά θηκες	you were lost	εἰργάσθης, ἐργάσθηκες	you worked
ἐ χά θη, χά θηκε	he was lost	εἰργάσθη, ἐργάσθηκε	he worked
ἐ χάθημεν, χαθήκαμε	we were lost	εἰργάσθημεν, ἐργασθήκαμε	we worked
ἐ χάθητε, χαθήκατε	you were lost	εἰργάσθητε, ἐργασθήκατε	you worked
ἐ χά θησαν, χα θῆκαν	they were lost	εἰργάσθησαν, ἐργάσθηκαν	they worked

Perfected or Compound Past

ἔχω χα θῇ	I have been lost	ἔχω ἐργα σθῇ	I have worked
ἔχεις χα θῇ	you have been lost	ἔχεις ἐργα σθῇ	you have worked
ἔχει χα θῇ	he has been lost	ἔχει ἐργα σθῇ	he has worked
ἔχομεν χα θῇ	we have been lost	ἔχομεν ἐργα σθῇ	we have worked
ἔχετε χα θῇ	you have been lost	ἔχετε ἐργα σθῇ	you have worked
ἔχουν χα θῇ	they have been lost	ἔχουν ἐργα σθῇ	they have worked

Duration Future

θὰ χάν ομαι	I shall be lost	θὰ ἐργάζ ομαι	I shall be working
θὰ χάν εσαι,	you will be lost	θὰ ἐργάζ εσαι,	you will be working

Momentary Future

θὰ χα θῶ	I shall be lost	θὰ ἐργασθῶ	I shall work
θὰ χα θῇς	you will be lost	θὰ ἐργασθῇς	you will work
θὰ χα θῇ	he will be lost	θὰ ἐργασθῇ	he will work
θὰ χα θῶμεν, col. θὰ χα θοῦμε	we shall be lost	θὰ ἐργασθῶμεν, *or* col. θὰ ἐργασθοῦμε	we shall work
θὰ χα θῆτε	you will be lost	θὰ ἐργασθῆτε	you will work
θὰ χα θοῦν	they will be lost	θὰ ἐργασθοῦν	they will work

Duration Imperative

νὰ (or ἄς) χάνεσαι	be lost	νὰ ἐργάζεσαι *or* ἐργάζου	work
νὰ χάνεται	let him be lost	νὰ ἐργάζεται	let him work
νὰ χανώμεθα	let us be lost	νὰ ἐργαζώμεθα	let us work
νὰ χάνεσθε	be lost	νὰ ἐργάζεσθε or ἐργάζεσθε	work (pl.)
νὰ χάνωνται	let them be lost	νὰ ἐργάζωνται	let them work

Momentary Imperative

νὰ χα θῇς or χάσου	be lost	νὰ ἐργασθῇς or ἐργάσου	work
νὰ χα θῇ	let him be lost	νὰ ἐργασθῇ	let him work
νὰ χαθῶμεν, or col. νὰ χαθοῦμε	let us be lost	νὰ ἐργασθῶμεν, or col. νὰ ἐργασθοῦμε	let us work
νὰ χαθῆτε, χαθῆτε	be lost	νὰ ἐργασθῆτε, ἐργασθῆτε	work
νὰ χα θοῦν	let them be lost	νὰ ἐργασθοῦν	let them work

—:—

* «Εἰς τοῦ ἐξαδέλφου μου» corresponds to the English expression "to my cousin's." The full phrase would be «εἰς τοῦ ἐξαδέλφου μου τὸ σπίτι»—"to my cousin's house." The word "σπίτι—house" may be omitted in the Greek, as in the English language.

LESSON 33

ζητῶ —	zĭtô′	I ask, I look for
ἐζήτουν	ĕzĭ′toon	I was asking
ἐζήτησα	ĕzĭ′tĭsȧ	I asked, I looked for
ἔχω ζητήσει	ĕhô zĭtĭ′sĭ	I have asked
ἕνδεκα	ĕn′thĕkȧ	eleven
δώδεκα	thô′thĕkȧ	twelve
δέκα τρία	thĕ′kȧ trĭ′ȧ	thirteen
δέκα τέσσαρα	thĕ′kȧ tĕ′sȧrȧ	fourteen
δέκα πέντε	thĕ′kȧ pĕn′tĕ	fifteen
δέκα ἕξ	thĕ′kȧ ĕx	sixteen
εἴκοσι	ĭ′kôsĭ	twenty
εἴκοσι ἕν, εἴκοσι ἕνα	ĭ′kôsĭ ĕn, ĭ′kôsĭ ĕ′nȧ	twenty-one
εἴκοσι δύο	ĭ′kôsĭ thĭ′ô	twenty-two
τὸ ὄνομα	tô ô′nômȧ	the name
ὀνομάζω	ônômȧ′zô	I name
ὀνομάζομαι	ônômȧ′zômĕ	I am named
πόσον ἐτῶν	pô′sôn ĕtôn′	how old
ἡ δουλειὰ	ĭ thoolĭȧ′	the work, the business
ὁ μάγειρος	ô mȧ′γĭrôs	the cook
μαγειρεύω	mȧγĭrĕv′ô	I cook
ἐμαγείρευσα	ĕmȧγĭ′rĕfsȧ	I cooked
κάθε	kȧ′thĕ	every
ἡ κουζίνα	ĭ koozĭ′nȧ	the kitchen
ἡ χώρα	ĭ hô′rȧ	the country
ὁ Ἰταλὸς	ô ĭtȧlôs′	the Italian
ἡ Ἰταλίς c. Ἰταλίδα	ĭ ĭtȧlĭs′, ĭtȧlĭ′thȧ	the Italian lady
ὁ Γάλλος	ô γȧ′lôs	the Frenchman
ἡ Γαλλίς c. Γαλλίδα	ĭ γȧlĭs′, γȧlĭ′thȧ	the French lady
ὁ Ἕλλην	ô ĕ′lĭn	the Greek
Ἑλληνίς c. Ἑλληνίδα	ĕlĭnĭs′, ĕlĭnĭ′thȧ	Greek lady

Ἀμερικανὸς	ȧmĕrĭkȧnȯs′	**American (man)**
Ἀμερικανίς, *c.*-νίδα	ȧmĕrĭkȧ nïs′, -nï′**th**ȧ	**American lady**
κατάγομαι	kȧtȧ′γȯmĕ	**I come from**
ἡ Ἀμερικὴ	ĭ ȧmĕrĭkï′	**America**
Ἡ Ἑλλὰς	ĭ ĕlȧs′	**Greece**
τῆς Ἑλλάδος	tĭs ĕlȧ′**th**ȯs	**of Greece**
τὴν Ἑλλάδα	tĭn ĕlȧ′**th**ȧ	**Greece** (accusative)
ἐννοῶ	ĕnȯ ȯ′	**I understand**
ἐνόησα	ĕnȯ′ĭsȧ	**I understood**
Ἀγγλικά· Ἑλληνικά	ȧnglĭkȧ′; ĕlĭnĭkȧ′	**English; Greek**
ἐγεννήθην	ĕ yĕnï′thĭn	**I was born**

EXERCISES

Θέλεις ἐργασίαν; Ζητεῖς ἐργασίαν;	Do you want work? Are you looking for work?
Ναί, κύριε. Θέλω ἐργασίαν.	Yes, sir. I want work.
Ποῦ μένεις;	Where do you live?
Μένω εἰς τὸ Εἴκοσι Ὁδὸς Ἐλευθερίας.	I live at Twenty Liberty Street.
Ποῖον εἶνε τὸ ὄνομά σου;	What is your name?
Ὀνομάζομαι Γεώργιος Μῆτρος.	My name is George Metros.
Πόσων ἐτῶν εἶσαι;	How old are you?
Εἶμαι εἴκοσι ἓξ ἐτῶν.	I am twenty-six years old.
Τί ἐργασίαν εἰμπορεῖς νὰ κάμῃς;	What work can you do?
Ποιὰ εἶνε ἡ δουλειά σου;	What is your business?
Εἶμαι μάγειρος.	I am a cook.
Εἰμπορῶ νὰ μαγειρεύω καὶ νὰ κάμνω κάθε δουλειὰ τῆς κουζίνας.	I can cook and do any kitchen work.
Ἀπὸ ποίαν χώραν ἔρχεσαι (or κατάγεσαι);	From what country do you come? (Where do you come from?)
Εἶσαι Ἰταλὸς ἢ Γάλλος;	Are you an Italian or a Frenchman?

Ὄχι, κύριε. Εἶμαι Ἀμερικανός.	No, sir. I am an American.
Ἐγεννήθην ἐδῶ. Ὁ πατέρας μου εἶνε Ἕλλην.	I was born here. My father is a Greek.
Ἐγεννήθη εἰς τὴν Ἑλλάδα.	He was born in Greece.
Ὁμιλεῖς Ἑλληνικά;	Do you speak Greek?
Ὄχι καλά. Ἐννοῶ Ἑλληνικά, ἀλλὰ δὲν εἰμπορῶ νὰ ὁμιλῶ πολὺ καλά.	Not well. I understand Greek, but I cannot speak very well.
Ὁμιλῶ ἀρκετὰ καλὰ Ἀγγλικά.	I speak English well enough.
Ἐγεννήθην στὴν Ἀμερική.	I was born in America.
Ὁ ἀδελφός μου ἐγεννήθη στὴν Ἑλλάδα.	My brother was born in Greece.
Ὁμιλεῖ Ἑλληνικὰ πολὺ ὡραῖα.	He speaks Greek very well (nicely).
Δὲν ὁμιλεῖ τόσον καλὰ Ἀγγλικά.	He does not speak English so well.
Ἐπίσης ὁμιλεῖ Γαλλικὰ καὶ Ἰταλικά.	He also speaks French and Italian.

Elementary Grammar

Adverbs are formed from adjectives with the ending α (and in the puristic language ως):

καθαρός—καθαρά (or καθαρῶς)	clean — cleanly
κακός — κακά (or κακῶς)	bad — badly
καλὸς — καλὰ (or καλῶς)	good — well
ὡραῖος — ὡραῖα	beautiful — beautifully
γρήγορος — γρήγορα	quick — quickly

LESSON 34

τριάντα (Pur. τριάκοντα)	trĭàn'tȧ, trĭȧ'kȏnta	**thirty**
σαράντα	sȧrȧn'tȧ (*or* sȧrȧn'dȧ)	**forty**
πενῆντα	pĕnïn'tȧ (pĕnïn'dȧ)	**fifty**
ἑξῆντα	ĕxïn'tȧ (or ĕksïn'dȧ)	**sixty**
ἑβδομῆντα	ĕvthȏmïn'tȧ	**seventy**
ὀγδοῆντα	ȏγthȏïn'tȧ	**eighty**
ἐνενῆντα	ĕnĕnïn'tȧ	**ninety**
ἑκατὸ(ν)	ĕkȧtȏ(n)'	**one hundred**
διακόσιοι, -αι, -α	thĭȧkȏ'sĭ ĭ, -ĕ, -ȧ	**two hundred** (m. f. n.)
τριακόσιοι, -αι, -α	trĭȧkȏ'sĭ ĭ, -ĕ, -ȧ	**three hundred** (m. f. n.)
τετρακόσιοι, -αι, -α	tĕtrȧkȏ'sĭ ĭ, -ĕ, -ȧ	**four hundred** "
πεντακόσιοι, -αι, -α	pĕntȧkȏ'sĭ ĭ, -ĕ, -ȧ	**five hundred** "
ἑξακόσιοι, -αι, -α	ĕxȧkȏ'sĭ ĭ, -ĕ, -ȧ	**six hundred** "
ἑπτακόσιοι, -αι, -α	ĕptȧkȏ'sĭ ĭ, -ĕ, -ȧ	**seven hundred** "
ὀκτακόσιοι, -αι, -α	ȏktȧkȏ'sĭ ĭ, -ĕ, -ȧ	**eight hundred** "
ἐννεακόσιοι, -αι, -α	ĕnĕȧkȏ'sĭ ĭ, -ĕ, -ȧ	**nine hundred** "
χίλιοι, χίλιαι, χίλια	hï'lĭ ĭ, hï'lĭĕ, hï'lĭȧ	**one thousand** "
δύο χιλιάδες	thï'ȏ hĭlĭȧ'thĕs	**two thousand**
κερδίζω	kĕrrthï'zȏ	**I earn, I win**
ἐκέρδιζα	ĕkĕr'thĭzȧ	**I was earning**
ἐκέρδισα	ĕkĕr'thĭsȧ	**I earned, I won**
ἔχω κερδίσει	ĕ'hȏ kĕrrthï'sĭ	**I have earned**
τὸ ἐνοίκιον	tȏ ĕnï'kĭȏn	**the rent**
τὸ μέρος	tȏ mĕ'rȏs	**the place, the part**
ἡ πόλις	ĭ pȏ'lĭs	**the city**
τῆς πόλεως	tĭs pȏ'lĕȏs	**of the city**
ἡ θέσις *	ĭ thĕ'sĭs	**the place, the position**
τῆς θέσεως	tĭs thĕ'sĕȏs	**of the place**
ἡ οἰκογένεια	ĭ ĭkȏγĕ'nĭȧ	**the family**
πόσον ἔχει; **	pȏ'sȏn ĕ'hĭ	**how much does it cost?**

EXERCISES

Πόσα χρήματα θέλεις νὰ κερδίζῃς τὴν ἑβδομάδα;	How much money do you want to make (to earn) a week?
Θέλω τριάντα δολλάρια τὴν ἑβδομάδα.	I want thirty dollars a week.
Τὸ περασμένο ἔτος ἐκέρδιζα σαράντα δύο δολλάρια.	Last year I was making forty-two dollars.
Πόσον ἐνοίκιον πληρώνετε;	How much rent do you pay?
Πληρώνομεν πενῆντα πέντε δολλάρια τὸν μῆνα.	We pay fifty-five dollars a month.
Εἰς ποῖον μέρος τῆς πόλεως μένετε;	In what part of the town do you live?
Μένομεν εἰς τὸν ἀριθμὸν διακόσια ὀγδοῆντα, Ὁδὸς Πάρκ.	We live at number two hundred and eighty Park Street.
Πέρυσι ἐμέναμεν εἰς τὸ τετρακόσια εἴκοσι πέντε, Ὁδὸς Κολόμβου.	Last year we were living at four twenty five Columbus Street.
Ἡμεῖς δὲν μποροῦμεν νὰ πληρώνωμεν τριάντα δολλάρια τὴν ἑβδομάδα.	We cannot pay thirty dollars a week.
Θὰ σὲ πληρώνωμεν εἰκοσιπέντε δολλάρια δι' αὐτὴν τὴν ἐργασίαν.	We shall pay you twenty-five dollars for this work.
Εἰκοσιπέντε δολλάρια δὲν εἶνε ἀρκετά, κύριε.	Twenty-five dollars is not enough, sir.
Ἄφησα τὴν ἄλλην μου θέσιν διότι ἤθελα νὰ κερδίζω περισσότερα χρήματα.	I left my other place because I wanted to earn more money.
Δὲν εἰμπορῶ νὰ ζήσω μὲ εἰκοσιπέντε δολλάρια τὴν ἑβδομάδα.	I cannot live on twenty-five dollars a week.
Ἔχω οἰκογένειαν—γυναῖκα καὶ τρία παιδιά.	I have a family—a wife and three children.

Ὅλα τὰ πράγματα εἶνε πολὺ ἀκριβὰ τώρα.	All things are very expensive now.
Τὸ ψωμὶ ἔχει δώδεκα σὲντς ἡ λίτρα.	Bread is twelve cents a pound.
Τὸ τυρὶ δεκαοκτὼ σέντς.	Cheese, eighteen cents.
Ἡ πατάτες εἰκοσιδύο σὲντς ἡ πέντε λίτρες.	Potatoes, twenty-two cents the five pounds.
Τὸ γάλα ἕνδεκα σὲντς ἡ μποτίλια.	Milk, eleven cents a bottle.

Elementary Grammar

* Feminine nouns ending in ις, ordinarily used in well spoken Greek, are declined as follows:

Nom.	ἡ πόλις	the city	ἡ θέσις	the place
Gen.	τῆς πόλεως	of the city	τῆς θέσεως	of the place
Accus.	τὴν πόλιν	the city	τὴν θέσιν	the place
Nom.	αἱ πόλεις	the cities	αἱ θέσεις	the places
Gen.	τῶν πόλεων	of the cities	τῶν θέσεων	of the places
Accus.	τὰς πόλεις	the cities	τὰς θέσεις	the places

In the vernacular the ending η is used for pure Greek feminine nouns ending in ις unaccented. Accordingly, in poetry and unrefined conversation "πόλη, θέση, etc." may be used in place of "πόλις, θέσις, etc."

—:—

** In Greek the verb ἔ χ ω is used to signify the cost of articles: «Ἡ πατάτες ἔχουν τρία σὲντς ἡ λίτρα»—"Potatoes are three cents a pound."

LESSON 35

ἡ ὥρα	ĭ ô′rȧ	the hour, the time
τί ὥρα	tĭ′ ô′rȧ	what time
ἡ ὥρα εἶναι μία	ĭ ô′rȧ ĭ′nĕ mĭ′ȧ	it is one o'clock
μία καὶ τέταρτον	mĭ′ȧ kĕ tĕ′tȧrtôn	a quarter past one
μία παρὰ τέταρτον	mĭ′ȧ pȧrȧ′ tĕ′tartôn	a quarter to one
ἓξ παρὰ πέντε λεπτὰ	ĕx pȧrȧ′ pĕn′tĕ lĕptȧ′	five minutes to six
ἓξ καὶ πέντε	ĕx kĕ pĕn′tĕ	five past six
ἓξ καὶ μισὴ	ĕx kĕ mĭsĭ′	half past six
περίπου	pĕrĭ′poo	about, almost
ἀκριϐῶς	ȧkrĭvôs′	exactly
κρατῶ	krȧtô′	I hold, I keep
ἐκράτουν *c.* κρατοῦσα	ĕkrȧ′toon, krȧtoo′sȧ	I was holding *or* keeping
ἐκράτησα	ĕkrȧ′tĭsȧ	I held, I kept
ἔχω κρατήσει	ĕ′hô krȧtĭ′sĭ	I have held, have kept
τὸ λάθος	tô lȧ′thôs	the mistake, the error
τὰ λάθη	tȧ lȧ′thĭ	the mistakes
ἔχω λάθος	ĕ′hô lȧ′thôs	I am mistaken
πηγαίνει ἐμπρὸς	pĭγĕ′nĭ ĕmprôs′	is fast (goes forward)
πηγαίνει πίσω	pĭγĕ′nĭ pĭ′sô	is slow (goes backward)
σωστός, σωστή, -όν	sôstôs′, sôstĭ′, -ôn′	right (m. f. n.)
φθάνω	fthȧ′nô	I arrive, I reach
ἔφθασα	ĕ′fthȧsȧ	I arrived
θὰ φθάσω	thȧ fthȧ′sô	I shall arrive
αὐτὸ σημαίνει	ȧftô′ sĭmĕ′nĭ	this means
ἀργῶ	ȧrγô′	I am late, I am slow
ἤργησα, *col.* ἄργησα	ĭrr′γĭsȧ or ȧrr′γĭsȧ	I was late

θὰ ἀργήσω	thȧ ȧrrγĭ′sô	I shall be late	
ἐντὸς ὀλίγου	ĕntôs′ ôlĭ′γoo	in a little while	
ὑποχρεώνω	ĭpôhrĕô′nô	I oblige	
ὑπεχρέωσα	ĭpĕhrĕ′ôsȧ, ĭpôhrĕ′ôsȧ	I obliged	
θὰ ὑποχρεώσω	thȧ ĭpôhrĕô′sô	I shall oblige	
ὑποχρεωμένος, η, ον	ĭpôhrĕomĕn′ôs, -ĭ, -ôn	obliged	(m. f. n.)

EXERCISES

Τί ὥρα εἶναι;	What time is it?
Εἰμπορεῖτε νὰ μοῦ πῆτε τὴν ὥραν, παρακαλῶ;	Can you tell me the time, please?
Μάλιστα, κύριε. Εἶνε περίπου δέκα.	Yes, sir. It is about ten (o'clock.)
Ὄχι, ἔχω λάθος. * Εἶνε μόνον ἐννέα καὶ μισή.	No, I am mistaken. It is only half past nine.
Δὲν εἶνε ἐννέα καὶ μισή. Εἶνε δέκα παρὰ εἴκοσι.	It is not half past nine. It is twenty (minutes) to ten.
Αὐτὸ τὸ ὡρολόγι πηγαίνει ἐμπρός.	This watch is fast.
Τὸ ἄλλο πηγαίνει πίσω.	The other one is slow.
Τὸ ἰδικό μου ὡρολόγι κρατεῖ πάντοτε καλὴν ὥραν.	My watch keeps good time always.
Εἶνε ἀκριβῶς ἐννέα καὶ εἰκοσιπέντε λεπτά, μὲ τὸ ἰδικόν μου ὡρολόγι.	It is exactly twenty-five minutes past nine by my watch.
Αὐτή εἶνε ἡ σωστὴ ὥρα;	Is that the right time?
Ὄχι, κύριε. Τὸ ὡρολόγι σου πηγαίνει δύο λεπτὰ ὀπίσω.	No, sir. Your watch is two minutes slow.
Ἡ σωστὴ ὥρα εἶνε ἐννέα καὶ εἰκοσιεπτὰ λεπτά.	The right time is twenty-seven minutes past nine.
Τί ὥραν θὰ ἔλθῃ τὸ τραῖνον;	What time will the train come?

Τὸ τραῖνον θὰ φθάσῃ ἐδῶ εἰς τὰς ἕνδεκα καὶ σαρανταπέντε.	The train will arrive here at eleven forty-five.
Δὲν γνωρίζω τί σημαίνει αὐτό.	I don't know what that means.
Σημαίνει δώδεκα παρὰ τέταρτον.	It means a quarter to twelve.
Τὸ τραῖνο ἀργεῖ. Εἶνε δώδεκα παρὰ πέντε καὶ δὲν ἔφθασε ἀκόμη.	The train is late. It is five to twelve and it hasn't arrived yet.
Περιμείνατε ὀλίγον ἀκόμη. Θὰ φθάσῃ ἐντὸς ὀλίγου.	Wait a little longer. It will arrive soon.
Δὲν εἰμπορῶ νὰ περιμένω περισσότερον. Θὰ φύγω καὶ θὰ γυρίσω ἐντὸς ὀλίγου.	I can't wait any longer. I'll go away and return in a little while.
Σᾶς παρακαλῶ νὰ μὲ περιμένετε ἐδῶ.	I beg you to wait for me here.
Θὰ μὲ ὑποχρεώσετε πολύ.	You will oblige me very much.

Neuter Nouns Ending in ος

Nom. and Accus.	τὸ λάθος	the mistake	τὸ πλάτος	the width
Gen.	τοῦ λάθους	of the mistake	τοῦ πλάτους	of the width
Nom. and Accus.	τὰ λάθη	the mistakes	τὰ πλάτη	the widths
Gen.	τῶν λαθῶν	of the mistakes	τῶν πλατῶν	of the widths
Nom. and Accus.	τὸ ὕψος	the height	τὸ μέγεθος	the size
Gen.	τοῦ ὕψους	of the height	τοῦ μεγέθους	of the size
Nom. and Accus.	τὰ ὕψη	the heights	τὰ μεγέθη	the sizes
Gen.	τῶν ὑψῶν	of the heights	τῶν μεγεθῶν	of the sizes

---

* In Greek we may say "I have a mistake — ἔχω λάθος" instead of "I make a mistake." However, we can also say, as in English "κάμνω λάθος— I make a mistake".

LESSON 36

πρῶτος, πρώτη, πρῶτον	prô'tôs, prô'tĭ, prô'tôn	first (m., f., n.)
δεύτερος, δευτέρα, -τερον	thĕf'tĕrôs, -tĕ'rȧ, -tĕrôn	second "
τρίτος, τρίτη, τρίτον	trï'tôs, trï'tĭ, trï'tôn	third "
τέταρτος, -τάρτη, -ταρτον	tĕ'tȧrtôs, -tȧr'tĭ, -tȧrtôn	fourth "
πέμπτος	pĕm'ptôs	fifth (m.)
ἕκτος	ĕk'tôs	sixth
ἕβδομος	ĕv'thômôs	seventh
ὄγδοος	ôγ'thô ôs	eighth
ἔνατος	ĕ'nȧtôs	ninth
δέκατος	thĕ'kȧtôs	tenth
ἑνδέκατος	ĕnthĕ'kȧtôs	eleventh
δωδέκατος	thôthĕ'kȧtôs	twelfth
δέκατος τρίτος	thĕ'kȧtôs trï'tôs	thirteenth
εἰκοστὸς	íkôstôs'	twentieth
εἰκοστὸς πρῶτος	íkôstôs' prô'tôs	twenty-first
τριακοστὸς	trĭȧkôstôs'	thirtieth
τεσσαρακοστὸς	tĕsȧrȧkôstôs'	fortieth
πεντηκοστὸς	pĕntĭkôstôs'	fiftieth
ἑκατοστὸς	ĕkȧtôstôs'	one hundredth
χιλιοστὸς	hĭlĭôstôs'	one thousandth
ὁ νότος, νότιος	ô nô'tôs, nô'tĭos	the south, southern
ὁ βορρᾶς, βόρειος	ô vôrȧs', vô'rĭôs	the north, northern
ἡ ἀνατολή, ἀνατολικὸς	ĭ ȧnȧtôlĭ', ȧnȧtôlĭkôs'	the east, eastern
ἡ δύσις, δυτικὸς	ï thï'sĭs, thĭtĭkôs'	the west, western
ἡ ὁδός, ὁ δρόμος	ĭ ôthôs', ô thrô'môs	the street, the road
ἡ λεωφόρος	ĭ lĕôfô'rôs	the avenue
ὁ ἀριθμὸς	ô ȧrĭthmôs'	the number
ἡ σειρὰ	ĭ sĭrȧ'	the line, the turn
τρίτη φορὰ	trï'tĭ fôrȧ'	third time
τὸ τέλος	tô tĕ'lôs	the end
τὸ κατάστημα	tô kȧtȧ'stĭmȧ	the store
τὸ τηλέφωνον	tô tĭlĕ'fônôn	the telephone

τηλεφωνῶ	tīlĕfônô′	**I telephone**
ἂν καί, μολονότι	àn kĕ, môlônô′tĭ	**although**

EXERCISES

Νά, ἦλθε τὸ τραῖνο.	Look, the train has come.
Σὲ ὀλίγην ὥραν θὰ ἴδωμεν τοὺς φίλους μας.	In a little while we shall see our friends.
Νὰ ὁ κύριος 'Αποστόλου. Εἶνε ὁ τέταρτος ἀπὸ τὰ δεξιά.	There is Mr. Apostolou. He is the fourth from the right.
Νὰ καὶ ἡ κόρη του ἡ 'Ελένη. Τὴν γνωρίζετε;	Here is also his daughter Helen. Do you know her?
Εἶνε ἡ ἑβδόμη στὴν σειράν.	She is the seventh in the line.
Δὲν τὴν γνωρίζω καλά, μολονότι εἶναι ἡ τρίτη φορὰ ποὺ τὴν βλέπω (or: ποὺ τὴν ἔχω ἰδῇ).	I don't know her well, though it is the third time that I have seen her (that I see her).
Ποῖος εἶνε ὁ κύριος ποῦ ἔρχεται πέμπτος ἀπὸ τὸ τέλος;	Who is the gentleman who comes fifth from the end?
Αὐτὸς εἶνε ὁ θεῖός της. Ἔχει κατάστημα εἰς τὸ Σικᾶγον.	He is her uncle. He has a store in Chicago.
Γνωρίζετε ποῦ μένει;	Do you know where he lives?
Ναί. Μένει εἰς τὴν Δυτικὴν Τεσσαρακοστὴν 'Οδόν, ἀριθμὸς ἑκατὸν ἑξῆντα τρία.	He lives in West Fortieth Street, number one hundred and sixty-three.
Θὰ ὑπάγετε νὰ τὸν ἴδητε;	Will you go to see him?
Ὄχι. 'Αλλὰ θὰ τοῦ τηλεφωνήσω.	No. But I'll telephone him.
Ποῦ μένει ἡ κόρη του;	Where does his daughter live?
Ἡ κόρη του μένει εἰς τὴν Δεκάτην πέμπτην λεωφόρον.	His daughter lives on Fifteenth Avenue.
Πόσον καιρὸν μένει ἐκεῖ;	How long has she lived (is she living) there?
Μένει ἐκεῖ ὀκτὼ ἔτη. Πρὶν ἔμενε εἰς τὴν Νότιον 'Ογδόην 'Οδόν.	She has lived (is living) there eight years. Before she lived (was living) on South Eighth Street.

The numerical adjectives usually end in **τος** for the masculine, **τη** for the feminine, and **τον** for the neuter gender. Examples:

	MASCULINE	FEMININE	NEUTER	
10—Δέκα	Δέκατος	Δεκάτη	Δέκατον	Tenth
20—Εἴκοσι	Εἰκοστός	Εἰκοστή	Εἰκοστόν	Twentieth
23—Εἰκοσιτρία	Εἰκοστὸς τρίτος	Εἰκοστὴ τρίτη	Εἰκοστὸν τρίτον	Twenty-third

LESSON 37

κανεὶς	kȧnïs′	**nobody** (m.)
καμμία or καμμιὰ	kȧmï′ȧ, kȧmĭȧ′	**nobody** (f.)
κανὲν or κανένα	kȧnĕn′, kȧnĕ′nȧ	**no one, nothing** (n.)
τὸ ξενοδοχεῖον	tô ksĕnôthôhï′ôn	**the restaurant, hotel**
τὸ ἑστιατόριον	tô ĕstĭȧtô′rĭôn	**the restaurant**
τὸ πρόγευμα	tô prô′γĕvmȧ	**the breakfast**
τριγύρω, γύρω	trĭγï′rô, γï′rô	**around**
ἀπέναντι	ȧpĕ′nȧntĭ	**opposite**
ἀπέναντι στὸν δρόμον	ȧpĕ′nȧntĭ stôn thrô′mô	**across the street**
πιάνω, ἔπιασα	pĭȧ′nô, ĕ′pĭȧsȧ	**I catch, I caught**
θὰ πιάσω	thȧ pĭȧ′sô	**I shall catch**
γεῦμα μικρὸν	γĕv′mȧ mĭkrôn′	**lunch**
ὁ σερβιτόρος	ô sĕr-vĭtô′rôs	**the waiter**
ὁ κατάλογος φαγητῶν	ô kȧtȧ′lôγôs fȧγĭtôn′	**the bill of fare**
συγχωρῶ· ἐσυγχώρησα	sĭng hôrô′; ĕsĭng hô′rĭsȧ	**I pardon; I pardoned**
μὲ συγχωρεῖτε	mĕ sĭnhôrï′tĕ	**pardon me**
κάτω ἀπὸ τὴν πετσέτα	kȧ′tô ȧpô′ tĭn pĕtsĕ′tȧ	**under the napkin**
φοβοῦμαι, ἐφοβήθην	fôvoo′mĕ, ĕfôvï′thĭn	**I am afraid, I was afraid**
ἔχω φοβηθῆ	ĕ′hô fôvĭthï′	**I have been afraid**
ὁ φόβος	ô fô′vôs	**the fear**
μήπως	mï′pôs	**lest, that**
ζεστός, or θερμὸς	zĕstôs′, thĕrrmôs′	**warm** *or* **hot**
ἡ συγγνώμη	ĭ sĭnγnô′mĭ	**the pardon**
διαβάζω· ἐδιάβασα	thĭȧvȧ′zô; ĕthĭȧ′vȧsa	**I read; I read**
λησμονῶ· ἐλησμόνησα	lĭzmônô′; ĕlĭzmô′nĭsȧ	**I forget; I forgot**
τὸ γυαλί· τὰ γυαλιὰ	tô yalï′; tȧ yȧlĭȧ′	**the glass; the glasses**

EXERCISES

Εἶνε κανὲν ξενοδοχεῖον ἐδῶ τριγύρω;	Is there a restaurant around here?
Πεινῶ πολύ.	I am very hungry.
Δὲν ἔφαγα τίποτε ἀπὸ τὸ πρωΐ.	I have not eaten anything since this morning.
Εἶναι ἕνα ξενοδοχεῖον ἀπέναντι στὸν δρόμον.	There is a restaurant across the street.
Εἶναι πολὺ καλὸν μέρος.	It is a very good place.
Ἐγὼ πάντοτε τρώγω ἐκεῖ τὸ πρόγευμά μου.	I always eat my breakfast there.
Νά, ἐδῶ εἴμεθα.	Here we are.
Ἂς καθήσωμεν πλησίον εἰς τὸ παράθυρον.	Let us sit near the window.
Παρακαλῶ κλείσατε αὐτὸ τὸ παράθυρον.	Please close this window.
Φοβοῦμαι μήπως πάρω κρύον.	I am afraid that I may catch cold.
Σερβιτόρε, φέρε μας τὸν κατάλογον τῶν φαγητῶν, παρακαλῶ.	Waiter, bring us the bill of fare, please.
Συγγνώμην, κύριε· εἶνε κάτω ἀπὸ τὴν πετσέταν σας.	Pardon me, sir; it is under your napkin.
Δὲν εἰμπορῶ νὰ φάγω αὐτὴν τὴν σοῦπαν. Εἶναι κρύα.	I can't eat this soup. It is cold.
Σᾶς ζητῶ συγγνώμην, κύριε. Ἦτο ζεστὴ ὅταν τὴν ἔφερα.	I beg your pardon, sir. It was hot when I brought it.
Τώρα ἂς ἴδωμεν τί εἶνε εἰς τὸν κατάλογον.	Now, let us see what is in the bill of fare.
Δὲν βλέπω καλά. Ἐλησμόνησα τὰ γυαλιά μου. Τὰ ἄφησα στὸ σπίτι. Διάβασέ τον δι' ἐμέ, παρακαλῶ.	I can't see well. I forgot my glasses. I left them at home. Read it for me, please.

The pronouns "κανείς, καμμία, κανέν" mean "no one, nobody". However, they may also be used in the meaning of "any". For example:

«Ποῖος εἶνε ἐδῶ;» — «Κανείς.»	"Who is here?" — "Nobody."
«Εἶνε κανεὶς ἐδῶ;»	"Is there anybody here?"
«Δὲν βλέπω κανένα.»	"I don't see anybody."

LESSON 38

τὸ φαγητὸν	tô fȧγĭtôn′	**something to eat, meal**
ψητός, ψητή, ψητὸν	psĭtôs′, psĭtĭ′, psĭtôn′	**roast** *or* **baked (m.,f.,n.)**
ἡ μπριζόλα	ĭ brĭzô′lȧ	**the steak, the chop**
τὸ βωδινὸν	tô vôthĭnôn′	**the beef**
τὸ μοσχάρι	tô môs **h**ȧ′rĭ	**the veal**
τὸ χοιρινὸν	tô **h**ĭrĭnôn′	**the pork**
τὸ ἀρνάκι	tô ȧrrnȧ′kĭ	**the lamb**
μαγειρευμένο	mȧγĭrĕvmĕ′nô	**cooked**
ἡ κοτολέττα	ĭ kôtôlĕ′tȧ	**the cutlet**
τηγανίζω· ἐτηγάνισα	tĭγȧnĭ′zô; ĕtĭγȧ′nĭsȧ	**I fry; I fried**
τὸ ψάρι· τὰ ψάρια	tô psȧ′rĭ; tȧ psȧ′rĭȧ	**the fish; the fishes**
τὸ κοτόπουλον	tô kôtô′poolôn	**the chicken**
τὸ φασόλι· τὰ φασόλια	tô fȧsô′lĭ; tȧ fȧsô′lĭȧ	**the bean; the beans**
ψήνω· ἔψησα	psĭ′nô; ĕ′psĭsȧ	**I bake, I roast; I baked**
καλοψημένος	kȧlôpsĭmĕ′nôs	**well baked, well done**
βράζω· ἔβρασα	vrȧ′zô; ĕ′vrȧsȧ	**I boil; I boiled**
τῆς σχάρας	tĭs skȧ′rȧs (s**h**ȧ′rȧs)	**broiled (of the grate)**
χύνω· ἔχυσα	**h**ĭ′nô; ĕ′**h**ĭsȧ	**I spill; I spilled**
λερώνω· ἐλέρωσα	lĕrô′nô; ĕlĕ′rôsȧ	**I soil; I soiled**
δὲν πειράζει	**th**ĕn pĭrȧ′zĭ	**it doesn't matter**
ἡ σάλτσα	ĭ sȧl′tsȧ	**the sauce**
παντὸς εἴδους	pȧntôs′ ĭ′**th**oos	**of all kinds**
ἡ ζαχαριέρα	ĭ zȧ**h**ȧrĭĕ′rȧ	**the sugar bowl**
τὸ ἐπιδόρπιον	tô ĕpĭ**th**ôr′pĭôn	**the dessert**
τὸ τραπεζομάνδηλον	tô trȧpĕzômȧn′**th**ĭlôn	**the tablecloth**
ἕνας κύριος	ĕ′nȧs kĭ′rĭôs	**a gentleman**
τὸ ριζόγαλον	tô rĭzô′γȧlôn	**the rice pudding**
ἡ πήττα	ĭ pĭ′tȧ	**the pie, the cake**
ἡ φέτα	ĭ fĕ′tȧ	**the slice**
τὸ πεπόνι	tô pĕpô′nĭ	**the melon**

EXERCISES

Τί ἔχετε νὰ φάγωμεν; (Τί φαγητὰ ἔχετε;)	What have you to eat? (What meals have you?)
Ἔχομεν βωδινὴ μπριζόλα, μοσχάρι ψητό, ἀρνάκι μαγειρευμένο.	We have beefsteak, roast veal, lamb stew.
Ἐπίσης ἔχομεν τηγανητὸ ψάρι, φασόλια ψητά, κοτόπουλο τῆς σχάρας, καὶ σαλάτας παντὸς εἴδους.	We also have fried fish, baked beans, broiled chicken and all kinds of salads.
Θὰ πάρω μιὰ μπριζόλα βωδινὴ καλοψημένη.	I'll have a beefsteak well done.
Φέρε μου μιὰ κοτολέττα μοσχάρι.	Bring me a veal cutlet.
Ἔχετε διόλου βραστὲς πατάτες;	Have you any boiled potatoes?
Βέβαια ἔχομεν.	Certainly we have.
Παρακαλῶ, δός μου μερικὴ σάλτσα.	Please give me some sauce.
Θέλετε καφὲ ἢ τσάϊ;	Do you want coffee or tea?
Ἐγὼ θὰ πάρω ἕνα φλυτζάνι καφέ.	I'll take a cup of coffee.
Φέρε ἕνα ποτῆρι κόκκινο κρασὶ γιὰ μέ.	Bring a glass of red wine for me.
Νὰ ὁ καφές σας, κύριε.	Here is your coffee, sir.
Νὰ καὶ ἡ ζαχαριέρα, ἂν θέλετε περισσότερη ζάχαρη.	Here is also the sugar bowl, if you want more sugar.
Τί ἔκαμα!	What have I done!
Ἔχυσα τὸν καφέ μου.	I have spilled my coffee.
Ἐλέρωσα τὸ τραπεζομάνδυλον.	I soiled the tablecloth.
Λυποῦμαι πολὺ διὰ τοῦτο.	I am very sorry for this.
Δὲν πειράζει, κύριοι. Αὐτὸ δὲν εἶνε τίποτε. *	Never mind, gentlemen. That is nothing.
Τί ἐπιδόρπιον θὰ πάρετε;	What dessert will you have?
Ἐγὼ θὰ πάρω ριζόγαλον.	I'll take rice pudding.
Ἐγὼ θέλω μιὰ φέτα πεπόνι.	I want a slice of melon.

* In Greek conversation the use of two negatives instead of one is allowed in the same sentence. For instance, we may say: «Αὐτὸ δὲν εἶνε τίποτε», instead of «Αὐτὸ εἶνε τίποτε» — "This is nothing."

LESSON 39

εὔκολος	ĕf'kôlôs	easy
εὐκολώτερος	ĕfkôlô'tĕrôs	easier
εὐκολώτατος	ĕfkôlô'tàtôs	easiest
δύσκολος	thĭs'kôlôs	hard, difficult
δυσκολώτερος	thĭskôlô'tĕrôs	harder
δυσκολώτατος	thĭskôlô'tàtôs	hardest
ὡραῖος	ôrĕ'ôs	pretty, beautiful
ὡραιότερος	ôrĕô'tĕrôs	prettier
ὡραιότατος	ôrĕô'tàtôs	prettiest
σκληρὸς	sklĭrôs',	tough, hard
σκληρότερος	sklĭrô'tĕrôs	tougher
σκληρότατος	sklĭrô'tàtôs	toughest
θερμός, ζεστὸς	thĕrmôs', zĕstôs'	hot
θερμότερος	thĕrmô'tĕrôs	hotter
θερμότατος	thĕrmô'tàtôs	hottest
γλυκύς, γλυκὸς	γlĭkĭs', γlĭkôs'	sweet
γλυκύτερος, γλυκότερος	γlĭkĭ'tĕrôs, γlĭkô'tĕrôs	sweeter
γλυκύτατος, γλυκότατος	γlĭkĭ'tàtôs, γlĭkô'tàtôs	sweetest
προσεκτικὸς	prôsĕktĭkôs'	careful
προσεκτικώτερος	prôsĕktĭkô'tĕrôs	more careful
προσεκτικώτατος	prôsĕktĭkô'tàtôs	most careful
ἤ, παρά, ἀπὸ	ĭ, pàrà', àpô'	than
τὰ σταφύλια	tà stàfĭ'lĭà	the grapes
τὸ μέλι	tô mĕ'lĭ	the honey
ὁ θεῖος· ἡ θεία	ô thĭ'ôs; ĭ thĭ'à	the uncle; the aunt
καλός· καλλίτερος	kàlôs; kàlĭ'tĕrôs	good; better
κάλλιστος, ὁ καλλίτερος	kà'lĭstôs, ô kàlĭ'tĕrôs	best, the best
κακός· χειρότερος	kàkôs'; hĭrô'tĕrôs	bad; worse
χείριστος, ὁ χειρότερος	hĭ'rĭstôs, ô hĭrô'tĕrôs	worst; the worst
πολύς, πολλοὶ	pôlĭs', polĭ'	much, many
περισσότερος, -τεροι	pĕrĭsô'tĕrôs, pĕrĭsô'tĕrĭ	more (sin.), more (pl.)

πλεῖστος, πλεῖστοι	plï'stôs, plï'stï	**most (sin.), most (pl.)**
ὀλίγος· ὀλιγώτερος	ôlï'γôs; ôlïγô'tĕros	**little; less**
ἐλάχιστος	ĕlȧ'hïstôs	**least**
τόσον . . . ὅσον	tô'sôn......ô'sôn	**so much ...... as**
ἀληθής· ἡ ἀλήθεια	ȧlïthïs'; ï ȧlï'thïȧ	**true; the truth**
τὸ ψεῦμα· ὁ ψεύστης	tô psĕv'mȧ; ô psĕf'stïs	**the lie; the liar**
ὁ γείτων· ἡ γειτόνισσα	ô yï'tôn; ï yïtô'nïsȧ	**neighbor,m. neighbor,f.**
δυνατός· ἀδύνατος	thïnȧtôs'; ȧthï'nȧtôs	**strong; weak**
τίμιος· ἄτιμος	tïmïôs; ȧ'tïmôs	**honest; dishonest**
βαρύς· ἐλαφρὸς	vȧrïs'; ĕlȧfrôs'	**heavy; light**
δοκιμάζω· ἐδοκίμασα	thôkïmȧ'zô; ĕthôkï'mȧsȧ	**I try; I tried**
σηκώνω· ἐσήκωσα	sïkô'nô; ĕsï'kôsȧ	**I lift; I lifted**
κινῶ· ἐκίνησα	kïnô'; ĕkï'nïsȧ	**I move; I moved**
κινοῦμαι · ἐκινήθην	kïnoo'mĕ; ĕkïnï'thïn	**I am moved;I was moved**
σπάζω· ἔσπασα	spȧ'zô; ĕ'spȧsȧ	**I break; I broke**
προσπαθῶ· προσπάθησα	prôspȧthô'; prôspȧ'thïsȧ	**I try; I tried**
ὁ κόσμος	ô kôz'môs	**the world; the people**

EXERCISES

Τὰ σταφύλια εἶνε γλυκά.	Grapes are sweet.
Ἡ ζάχαρις εἶνε γλυκυτέρα ἀπὸ τὰ σταφύλια, ἀλλὰ τὸ μέλι εἶνε τὸ γλυκύτερον πρᾶγμα ἀπὸ ὅλα.	Sugar is sweeter than grapes, but honey is the sweetest thing of all.
Σήμερον εἶνε ζεστά, ἀλλὰ ἦτο ζεστότερα χθές.	Today it is warm, but it was warmer yesterday.
Ἡ ἐργασία μου εἶνε ἀρκετὰ δύσκολος, ἀλλὰ ἡ ἰδική σου εἶνε δυσκολωτέρα ἀπὸ τὴν ἰδικήν μου.	My work is hard enough, but yours is harder than mine.
Τοῦ Ἰωάννου ἡ ἐργασία εἶνε ἡ δυσκολωτάτη (or ἡ πειὸ δύσκολη).	John's work is the hardest.
Ἡ ἐργασία σου εἶνε εὔκολος.	Your work is easy.
Εἶνε εὐκολωτέρα ἀπὸ τὴν ἰδική μου.	It is easier than mine.
Ὁ πατήρ σου εἶνε καλὸς ἄνθρωπος, ἀλλὰ ὁ ἰατρὸς εἶνε καλλίτερος ἀπὸ τὸν πατέρα σου.	Your father is a good man, but the doctor is better than your father.

Ὁ θεῖός μου εἶνε ὁ καλλίτερος ἄνθρωπος εἰς τὴν πόλιν.	My uncle is the best man in (the) town.
Ἔκαμες ἓν κακὸν πρᾶγμα χθές, ἀλλὰ αὐτὸ ποῦ ἔκαμες σήμερον τὸ πρωῒ ἦτο χειρότερον. Τώρα προσπαθεῖς νὰ κάμῃς τὸ χειρότερον πρᾶγμα ἀπὸ ὅλα.	You did a bad thing yesterday, but what you did this morning was worse. Now you are trying to do the worst thing of all.
Ἔχω περισσότερα χρήματα ἀπὸ σέ, ἀλλὰ ὁ ἀδελφός μου ἔχει τὰ περισσότερα.	I have more money than you, but my brother has the most.
Ποτὲ δὲν εἰμπορῶ νὰ εἴπω ψεῦμα· πάντοτε λέγω τὴν ἀλήθειαν· ἀλλ' ὁ περισσότερος κόσμος δὲν ἀγαπᾷ νὰ ἀκούῃ τὴν ἀλήθειαν.	I can never tell a lie; I always tell the truth; but most people do not like to hear the truth.
Ὁ φίλος σου ἔσπασε αὐτὸ τὸ ποτῆρι. Πρέπει νὰ εἶναι προσεκτικώτερος ἄλλην φοράν.	Your friend broke this glass. He must be more careful next time.
Ὁ φίλος μου λέγει πὼς δὲν τὸ ἔσπασε αὐτὸς. Ὁ Γιάννης δὲν εἶναι ψεύστης. Τὸν γνωρίζω πολὺ καλά.	My friend says that he did not break it. John is not a liar. I know him very well.
Δὲν εἶσαι τόσον ἀδύνατος. Εἶσαι τόσον δυνατὸς ὅσον ὁ πατέρας μου, ἀλλὰ ὁ γείτονάς μας εἶνε δυνατώτερος ἀπὸ σέ.	You are not so weak. You are as strong as my father, but our neighbor is stronger than you.
Σὺ ἔχεις ὀλίγα χρήματα, ἀλλ' ἐγὼ ἔχω ὀλιγώτερα ἀπὸ σέ.	You have little money, but I have less than you.
Ὁ φίλος μου ἔχει τὰ ὀλιγώτερα· δὲν ἔχει σχεδὸν τίποτε.	My friend has the least; he has almost nothing.
Εἶνε ἡ φίλη σου ὡραιοτέρα ἀπὸ αὐτὴν τὴν κόρην;	Is your friend prettier than this girl?
Ἡ φίλη μου εἶνε ἡ ὡραιοτέρα κόρη ἐδῶ τριγύρω.	My friend is the prettiest girl around here.
Τοῦτο τὸ κιβώτιον δὲν εἶνε ἐλαφρόν· εἶνε τόσον βαρὺ ὅσον μπορεῖ νὰ εἶνε.	This box is not light; it is as heavy as it can be.
Εἶνε βαρύτερον ἀπὸ τὸ ἄλλο.	It is heavier than the other.
Δὲν μπορῶ νὰ τὸ σηκώσω.	I cannot lift it.
Δὲν μπορῶ νὰ τὸ κινήσω.	I cannot move it.

Degrees of Comparison

The comparison of adjectives is expressed with the endings **τερος, τερα, τερον** for the comparative degree, and **τατος, τατη, τατον** for the superlative.

	MASCULINE	FEMININE	NEUTER	
Positive	Πτωχός	πτωχή	πτωχόν	Poor
Comparative	Πτωχότερος	πτωχοτέρα	πτωχότερον	Poorer
Superlative	Πτωχότατος	πτωχοτάτη	πτωχότατον	Poorest
Positive	Βαθὺς	βαθεῖα	βαθύ	Deep
Comparative	Βαθύτερος	βαθυτέρα	βαθύτερον	Deeper
Superlative	Βαθύτατος	βαθυτάτη	βαθύτατον	Deepest

The second subject of comparison in the spoken language is in the accusative case preceded by the preposition **ἀπὸ** (than, of).

'Ο Γιάννης εἶνε δυνατώτερος ἀπὸ τὸν Παῦλον.
John is stronger than Paul.

'Η ἀδελφή σου εἶνε ὡραιοτέρα ἀπὸ αὐτὴν τὴν κόρην.
Your sister is prettier than this girl.

Σὺ εἶσαι μικρότερος ἀπὸ ἐμέ.
You are smaller than I.

In the written or purified language the second part of comparison may also be expressed by the genitive case. For example:

John is stronger than Paul.
'Ο Γιάννης εἶνε δυνατώτερος τοῦ Παύλου.

'Η ἀδελφή σου εἶνε ὡραιοτέρα αὐτῆς τῆς κόρης.
Your sister is prettier than this girl.

Σὺ εἶσαι μικρότερος ἐμοῦ.
You are smaller than I.

The superlative degree of adjectives usually ends in **τατος, τατη, τατον.**

Ἡ ζάχαρη εἶνε γλυκυτάτη.	Sugar is sweetest.
Ἡ ἀδελφή μου εἶνε ὡραιοτάτη.	My sister is most beautiful.

However, if the adjective in superlative is preceded by the definite articles **ὁ, ἡ, τὸ,** the superlative degree may also be expressed with the endings **τερος, τέρα, τερον:**

Ἡ ἀδελφή μου εἶνε ἡ ὡραιοτέρα κόρη εἰς τὴν πόλιν αὐτήν.

My sister is the prettiest girl in this town.

Ὁ Γιάννης εἶνε ὁ δυνατώτερος ἄνθρωπος ἐδῶ.

John is the strongest man here.

The comparative degrees of the adjectives καλός, κακός, πολύς, and a few others, are formed irregularly:

Καλός — καλλίτερος — κάλλιστος	Good — better — best
Κακός — χειρότερος — χείριστος	Bad — worse — worst
Πολύς — περισσότερος — πλεῖστος	Much, many — more — most

Adjectives ending in **ης** in the masculine and feminine genders, end in the neuter gender in **ες.** Such adjectives in the comparative degrees end in **έστερος, έστατος:**

	MASCULINE	FEMININE	NEUTER	
Positive	Εὐτυχής	εὐτυχής	εὐτυχές	Happy
Comparative	Εὐτυχέστερος	εὐτυχεστέρα	εὐτυχέστερον	Happier
Superlative	Εὐτυχέστατος	εὐτυχεστάτη	εὐτυχέστατον	Happiest

Adverbs usually end in **α** in all degrees of comparison.

Positive	Γρήγορα	Quickly	Βέβαια	Surely
Comparative	Γρηγορώτερα	More quickly	Βεβαιότερα	More surely
Superlative	Γρηγορώτατα	Most quickly	Βεβαιότατα	Most surely

LESSON 40

ἀλλάσσω, c. ἀλλάζω	àlà'sô, àlà'zô	**I change**
ἄλλαξα	à'làksà	**I changed**
ἡ εὐχαρίστησις	ĭ ĕfhàrĭ'stĭsĭs	**the pleasure**
μονός, μονή, μονὸν	mônôs', mônĭ', mônôn'	**single (m., f., n.)**
διπλός, διπλῆ, διπλὸν	thĭplôs', thĭplĭ', thĭplôn'	**double (m., f., n.)**
τὸ τέταρτον	tô te'tàrtôn	**the fourth, the quarter**
ἡ δεκάρα	ĭ thĕkà'rà	**the dime**
ἡ πεντάρα	ĭ pentà'rà	**the five-cent coin**
τὸ λεπτὸν	tô lĕptôn'	**the cent**
ἡ καρφίτσα	ĭ kàrfĭ'tsà	**the pin**
καρφώνω· ἐκάρφωσα	kàrfô'nô; ĕkàr'fôsà	**I stick, I nail; I stuck**
ὁ λαιμοδέτης	ô lĕmôthĕ'tĭs	**the necktie**
ἐξοδεύω· ἐξώδευσα	ĕksôthĕ'vô; ĕksô'thĕfsà	**I spend; I spent**
οἰκονομῶ· οἰκονόμησα	ĭkônômô'; ĭkônô'mĭsà	**I save; I saved**
ἄεργος, ἀργὸς	à'ĕrrγôs, àrrγôs'	**idle, unemployed**
τρέχω	trĕ'hô	**I run**
τρέχων, c. τρέχωντας	trĕ'hôn, trĕ'hôntàs	**running**
προσέχω	prôsĕ'hô	**I watch, I take care**
προσέχων, c. προσέχωντας	prôsĕ'hôn, prôsĕ'hôntàs	**watching**
τὸ δακτυλίδιον	tô thàktĭlĭ'thĭôn	**the ring**
τὸ δῶρον	tô thô'rôn	**the present**
φιλῶ· ἐφίλησα	fĭlô'; ĕfĭ'lĭsà	**I kiss; I kissed**
τὸ φιλὶ	tô fĭlĭ'	**the kiss**
τρελλός, τρελλή, τρελλὸν	trĕlôs', trĕlĭ', trĕlôn'	**crazy (m., f., n.)**
κάπως	kà'pôs	**somewhat**
στρογγυλὸς	strôngkĭlôs'	**round**
ἴσιος, ἴσια, ἴσιον	ĭ'sĭôs, ĭ'sĭà, ĭ'sĭôn	**straight (m., f., n.)**
παίζω· ἔπαιξα	pĕ'zô; ĕ'pĕxà	**I play; I played**
δένω· ἔδεσα	thĕ'nô; ĕ'thĕsà	**I tie; I tied**
τὸ τόπι· τὸ κουβάρι	tô tô'pĭ; tô koovà'rĭ	**the ball**
τὸ δέμα	tô thĕ'mà	**the package**

ὁ σπάγγος	ô spȧn′gôs	**the string, the cord**
ρίπτω· ἔρριψα	rĭp′tô; ĕ′rĭpsȧ	**I throw, I drop; I threw**
κόπτω· ἔκοψα	kôp′tô; ĕ′kôpsȧ	**I cut; I cut**
τὸ ψαλίδι	tô psȧlĭ′thĭ	**the scissors**
κτυπῶ· ἐκτύπησα	ktĭpô′; ĕktĭ′pĭsȧ	**I hit, I knock; I knocked**
κτυπῶ τὸ κουδοῦνι	ktĭpô′ tô koothoo′nĭ	**I ring the bell**

EXERCISES

Βλέπω ἔχεις πολλὰ χρήματα.	I see you have much money.
Εἰμπορεῖς νὰ μοῦ ἀλλάξῃς πέντε δολλάρια;	Can you change five dollars for me?
Μετ' εὐχαριστήσεως. 'Εδῶ εἶνε τέσσαρα μονὰ δολλάρια, ἓν μισὸ δολλάριον, ἓν τέταρτον, μία δεκάρα, δύο πεντάρες καὶ πέντε λεπτά.	With pleasure. Here are four single dollars, a half dollar, a quarter, a dime, two nickels and five pennies.
Κύτταξε! Εἶνε μία καρφίτσα ἐπάνω στὸ πάτωμα.	Look! There is a pin on the floor.
Σήκωσέ την. Θέλω νὰ τὴν καρφώσω εἰς τὸν λαιμοδέτην μου.	Pick it up. I want to stick it in my necktie.
Πόσον ἐπλήρωσες διὰ τὸ νέον σου ἐπανωφόρι;	How much did you pay for your new overcoat?
'Επλήρωσα μόνον δεκαπέντε δολλάρια δι' αὐτό.	I paid only fifteen dollars for it.
Νομίζω εἶνε ἀρκετὰ εὐθηνά.	I think it is cheap enough.
Δὲν εἰμπορῶ νὰ ἐξοδεύω πολλά, ὅπως γνωρίζεις.	I can't spend much, (as) you know.
Πρέπει νὰ οἰκονομῶ μερικὰ χρήματα διὰ τὸν πατέρα μου.	I must save some money for my father.
Δὲν ἐργάζεται ὁ πατήρ σου;	Isn't your father working?
Δὲν ἐργάζεται· εἶνε ἄεργος τώρα.	He is not working; he is idle now.
'Ο Γιάννης ἦτο πολὺ εὐτυχὴς χθὲς τὸ βράδυ.	John was very happy last night.
῎Εδωσε εἰς τὴν ἀδελφήν του ἕνα ὡραῖο δακτυλίδι.	He gave his sister a beautiful ring.
'Αλήθεια; Τί δῶρον ἔδωσε ἡ ἀδελφή του εἰς αὐτόν;	Is that so? What present did his sister give him?
῎Εβαλε τὰ χέρια της γύρω εἰς τὸν λαιμόν του καὶ τὸν ἐφίλησεν εἰς τὰ χείλη.	She put her arms around his neck and kissed him on the lips.

Ὁ Γιάννης ἀγαπᾷ τὴν ἀδελφήν του τόσον πολύ.	John loves his sister so much.
Εἶνε τρελλὸς δι' αὐτήν.	He is crazy about her.
Ἡ ἀδελφή του εἶνε ὡραία κόρη· δέν εἶνε;	His sister is a beautiful girl; isn't she?
Δὲν νομίζω ὅτι εἶνε τόσον ὡραία.	I don't think she is so beautiful.
Τὸ κεφάλι της εἶνε κἄπως στρογγυλόν, καὶ ἡ μύτη της δὲν εἶνε ἴσια.	Her head is rather round, and her nose is not straight.
Ἔλα ἐδῶ τρέχωντας· σὲ θέλω νὰ μοῦ δέσῃς ἕνα δέμα.	Come here quickly (running); I want you to tie a package for me.
Νὰ ἕνα κουβάρι σπάγγος.	Here is a ball of cord.
Κόψε τὸν σπάγγο μὲ τὸ ψαλίδι.	Cut the cord with the scissors.
Τὸ δέμα εἶνε ἕτοιμον τώρα.	The package is ready now.
Πάρε το ἀπέναντι, προσέχωντας νὰ μὴ τὸ ρίψῃς κάτω.	Take it across the street, taking care not to drop it.
Κτύπησε τὸ κουδοῦνι καὶ δός το εἰς τὴν κυρίαν Παύλου.	Ring the bell and give it to Mrs. Paul.

—:—

In the written language the participle present of verbs ending in ω is formed with the endings ων (m.), ουσα (f.), ον (n.). In the colloquial idiom the participle present ends in ωντας (or οντας), which is common to all genders and is not declined. Examples:

	MASCULINE	FEMININE	NEUTER	COLLOQUIAL	
Sin.: Nom.	τρώγων	τρώγουσα	τρῶγον	τρώγωντας *or* τρώγοντας	
Gen.	τρώγοντος	τρωγούσης	τρώγοντος		eating
Acc.	τρώγοντα	τρώγουσαν	τρῶγον		
Pl.: Nom.	τρώγοντες	τρώγουσαι	τρώγοντα	τρώγωντας *or* τρώγοντας	
Gen.	τρωγόντων	τρωγουσῶν	τρωγόντων		eating
Acc.	τρώγοντας	τρωγούσας	τρώγοντα		
Likewise:	πίνων	πίνουσα	πίνον	πίνωντας *or* πίνοντας	drinking
And:	ἀγαπῶν	ἀγαπῶσα	ἀγαπῶν	ἀγαπῶντας	loving

Verbs ending in μαι form the participle present with the ending μενος (f. μενη, n. μενον) and the participle past aorist with θείς (f. θεῖσα, n. θέν, or -είς -εῖσα -έν), and participle perfect with -μένος, -μένη, -μένον:

	PARTICIPLE PRESENT	PARTICIPLE PAST
λύνομαι, I am untied	λυνόμενος, being untied	λυθείς, λυμένος, untied
ψήνομαι, I am roasted	ψηνόμενος, being roasted	ψηθείς, ψημένος, roasted
κόπτομαι, I am cut	κοπτόμενος, being cut	κοπείς, (κε)κομμένος, cut
ἀγαπῶμαι, I am loved	ἀγαπώμενος, being loved	ἀγαπηθείς, -ημένος, loved
ἔρχομαι, I come	ἐρχόμενος, coming	
κοιμῶμαι, I sleep	κοιμώμενος, sleeping	

LESSON 41[1]

σοφός	sôfôs′	**wise; wise man**
ἀρχαῖος, παλαιός	ȧr hĕ′ôs, pȧlĕôs′	**ancient, old**
’Αθηναῖος	ȧthĭnĕ′ôs	**Athenian**
βασιλικός	vȧsĭlĭkôs′	**royal**
ταπεινός	tȧpĭnôs′	**humble**
φιλόπατρις	fĭlô′pȧtrĭs	**patriotic** (m., f.)
ὑπηρετῶ· ὑπηρέτησα	ĭpĭrĕtô′; ïpĭrĕ′tĭsȧ	**I serve; I served**
ἡ πατρίς (τῆς πατρίδος)	ĭ pȧtrĭs′ (tĭs pȧtrĭ′thôs)	**the country, the native**
c. ἡ πατρίδα (τῆς -ίδας)	ĭ pȧtrĭ′thȧ (tĭs -ĭ′thȧs)	**land, the fatherland**
ὁ πόλεμος	ô pô′lĕmôs	**the war**
πιστεύω· ἐπίστευσα	pĭstĕ′vô; ĕpĭ′stĕfsȧ	**I believe; I believed**
ἡ μετριότης (τῆς -ότητος)	ĭ mĕtrĭô′tĭs (tĭs -ô′tĭtôs)	**(the) moderation**
ὁ κανών (τοῦ κανόνος)	ô kȧnôn′ (too kȧnô′nôs)	**the rule**
ἡ ζωή, ὁ βίος	ĭ zôĭ′, ô vĭ′ôs	**the life**
πᾶς, πᾶσα, πᾶν (παντός)	pȧs, pȧ′sȧ, pȧn	**every, all** (m., f., n.)
τὸ μέτρον	tô mĕ′trôn	**the measure, moderation**
ἄριστος, κάλλιστος	ȧ′rĭstôs, kȧ′lĭstôs	**best**
ταξειδεύω· ἐταξείδευσα	tȧxĭthĕ′vô; ĕtȧxĭ′thĕfsȧ	**I travel; I traveled**
σπουδάζω· ἐσπούδασα	spoothȧ′zô; ĕspoo′thȧsȧ	**I study; I studied**
τὸ ἔθιμον	tô ĕ′thĭmôn	**the custom, the habit**
ὁ νόμος	ô nô′môs	**the law**
ὁ λαός	ô lȧ ôs′	**the people**
βαρύνομαι, c. βαρυέμαι	vȧrĭ′nômĕ (vȧrĭĕ′mĕ)	**I am wearied, I am tired**
ἐβαρύνθην, c. ἐβαρέθηκα	ĕvȧrĭn′thĭn, ĕvȧrĕ′thĭkȧ	**I was wearied**
ἔχω βαρυνθῆ, c. βαρεθῆ	ĕ′hô vȧrĭnthĭ′, vȧrĕthĭ′	**I have been wearied**
ἡ φιλονεικία	ĭ fĭlônĭkĭ′ȧ	**the quarrel**
τηρῶ· ἐτήρησα	tĭrô′, ĕtĭ′rĭsȧ	**I keep, I observe; I kept**
τηροῦμαι· ἐτηρήθην	tĭroo′mĕ; ĕtĭrĭ′thĭn	**I am kept; I was kept**
γράφω· ἔγραψα	γrȧ′fô; ĕ′γrȧpsȧ	**I write; I wrote**
στρέφω· ἔστρεψα	strĕ′fô; ĕ′strĕpsȧ	**I turn; I turned**
ἔχω στρέψει· ἐστράφην	ĕ′hô strĕ′psĭ; ĕstrȧ′fĭn	**I have turned; was turned**
ἡ προσοχή	ĭ prôsôhĭ′	**the attention**
ἡ ἀνακούφισις	ĭ ȧnȧkoo′fĭsĭs	**the relief**
ἄθλιος· ἡ ἀθλιότης	ȧth′lĭôs; ĭ ȧthlĭô′tĭs	**miserable; the misery**

1 The following lessons are in the simplified literary idiom, much used by Greek writers of our times.

Ο ΣΟΛΩΝ	SOLON
Ὁ Σόλων ἦτο ἕνας ἀπὸ τοὺς ἑπτὰ σοφοὺς τῆς Ἑλλάδος.	Solon was one of the seven wise men of Greece.
Ἦτο Ἀθηναῖος ἀπὸ ἀρχαίαν βασιλικὴν οἰκογένειαν.	He was an Athenian of an old royal family.
Ἦτο ταπεινός, δίκαιος καὶ φιλόπατρις καὶ εἶχε ὑπηρετήσει τὴν πατρίδα του εἰς τὸν πόλεμον.	He was humble, upright and patriotic, and had served his country in war.
Ἐπίστευεν ὅτι ἡ μετριότης εἰς ὅλα πρέπει νὰ εἶναι ὁ κανὼν τῆς ζωῆς μας.	He believed that moderation in everything should be the rule in (our) life.
Ἔλεγε: «Πᾶν μέτρον ἄριστον.»	He used to say: "Moderation in all is the best thing."
Ὁ Σόλων εἶχε ταξειδεύσει εἰς πολλὰς χώρας διὰ νὰ σπουδάσῃ τὰ ἔθιμα καὶ τοὺς νόμους ἄλλων λαῶν.	Solon had traveled in many lands to study the habits and laws of other peoples.
Οἱ Ἀθηναῖοι εἶχον βαρυνθῇ ἀπὸ τὰς φιλονεικίας μεταξὺ πλουσίων καὶ πτωχῶν, καί, βλέποντες ὅτι οἱ νόμοι τῆς πόλεως δὲν ἐτηροῦντο, ἐζήτησαν ἀπὸ τὸν Σόλωνα νὰ γράψῃ νέους νόμους δι' αὐτούς.	The Athenians had been wearied with the quarrels between the rich and the poor, and, finding (seeing) that the laws of the city were not observed, asked Solon to write new laws for them.
Ὁ Σόλων ἔστρεψε πρῶτον τὴν προσοχήν του εἰς τὴν ἀνακούφισιν τῆς ἀθλιότητος τῶν πτωχῶν.	Solon turned his attention first to relieving the misery of the poor.

Feminine nouns ending in ίς (accented) are usually declined as follows:

Nom.	ἡ πατρίς	the country	αἱ πατρίδες	the countries
Gen.	τῆς πατρίδος	of the country	τῶν πατρίδων	of the countries
Acc.	τὴν πατρίδα	the country	τὰς πατρίδας	the countries

Feminine nouns ending in ης (unaccented) are usually declined as follows:

Nom.	ἡ ἀθλιότης	the misery	αἱ ἀθλιότητες	the miseries
Gen.	τῆς ἀθλιότητος	of the misery	τῶν ἀθλιοτήτων	of the miseries
Acc.	τὴν ἀθλιότητα	the misery	τὰς ἀθλιότητας	the miseries

LESSON 42

καταργῶ· κατήργησα	kȧtȧrrγô'; kȧtĭrr'γĭsȧ	**I cancel; I canceled**
τὸ χρέος· τὰ χρέη	tô hrĕ'ôs; tȧ hrĕ'ĭ	**the debt; the debts**
δημόσιος· ἰδιωτικός	thĭmô'sĭôs; ĭthĭôtĭkôs'	**public; private**
ἀπαγορεύω· ἀπηγόρευσα	ȧpȧγôrĕ'vô; ȧpĭγô'rĕfsȧ	**I prohibit; I prohibited**
ἔχω ἀπαγορεύσει	ĕ'hô ȧpȧγôrĕf'sĭ	**I have prohibited**
πωλῶ· ἐπώλησα	pôlô'; ĕpô'lĭsȧ	**I sell; I sold**
πωλοῦμαι· ἐπωλήθην	pôloo'mĕ; ĕpôlĭ'thĭn	**I am sold; I was sold**
ὁ δοῦλος· ἡ δούλη	ô thoo'lôs; ĭ thoo'lĭ	**the slave**
ἡ δουλεία	ĭ thoolĭ'ȧ	**slavery**
ὁ ὀφειλέτης· ἡ ὀφειλέτις	ô ôfĭlĕ'tĭs; ĭ ôfĭlĕ'tĭs	**the debtor**
ἡ ἐκκλησία	ĭ ĕklĭsĭ'ȧ	**the church; the assembly**
ὁ δῆμος	ô thĭ'môs	**the citizens, the people**
ὁ πολίτης	ô pôlĭ'tĭs	**the citizen**
ἄνω, ἐπάνω	ȧ'nô, ĕpȧ'nô	**above, over**
τὸ δικαίωμα· ἡ ψῆφος	tô thĭkĕ'ômȧ; ĭ psĭ'fôs	**the right; the vote**
ψηφίζω· ἐψήφισα	psĭfĭ'zô; ĕpsĭ'fĭsȧ	**I vote; I voted**
ἀποφασίζω· ἀπεφάσισα	ȧpôfȧsĭ'zô; ȧpĕfȧ'sĭsȧ	**I decide; I decided**
ἡ εἰρήνη	ĭ ĭrĭ'nĭ	**the peace**
σπουδαῖος	spoothĕ'ôs	**important**
τὸ ζήτημα	tô zĭ'tĭmȧ	**the matter, the question**
ἡ ἐξουσία	ĭ ĕxoosĭ'ȧ	**the authority**
εἰς τὰς χεῖρας, στὰ χέρια	ĭs tȧs hĭ'rȧs, stȧ hĕ'rĭȧ	**in the hands**
ὁ Ἄρειος Πάγος	ô ȧ'rĭôs pȧ'γôs	**the Areopagus**
ἀνώτατον δικαστήριον	ȧnô'tȧtôn thĭkȧstĭ'rĭôn	**supreme court**
ὁ φύλαξ (τοῦ φύλακος) c. φύλακας	ô fĭ'lȧx (too fĭ'lȧkôs) fĭ' lȧkȧs	**the guardian**
τιμωρῶ· θὰ τιμωρήσω	tĭmôrô'; thȧ tĭmôrĭ'sô	**I punish; I shall punish**
ἐτιμώρουν, ἐτιμώρησα	ĕtĭmô'roon; ĕtĭmô'rĭsȧ	**I punished**
κακοῦργος	kȧkoorr'γôs	**criminal**
ὁ συνωμότης, ἡ -ότις	ô sĭnômô'tĭs	**the conspirator**
ἐναντίον	ĕnȧntĭ'ôn	**against**
τὸ κράτος, ἡ πολιτεία	tô krȧ'tôs, ĭ pôlĭtĭ'ȧ	**the state**
ἐπιβλέπω· ἐπέβλεπον	ĕpĭvlĕ'pô; ĕpĕ'vlĕpôn	**I supervise; I supervised**
ἡ ἐφαρμογή	ĭ ĕfȧrrmôγĭ'	**fitting; enforcement**
ἡ μόρφωσις	ĭ môrr'fôsĭs	**the education**
φροντίζω· ἐφρόντισα	frôntĭ'zô; ĕfrôn'tĭsȧ	**I provide; I provided**

Κατήργησε ὅλα τὰ χρέη παντὸς εἴδους, δημόσια καὶ ἰδιωτικά.

He canceled all debts of every kind, public and private.

Ἀπηγόρευσε νὰ πωλοῦνται ὡς δοῦλοι οἱ ὀφειλέται ποὺ δὲν εἰμποροῦσαν νὰ πληρώσουν τὰ χρέη των.

He prohibited the sale into slavery of debtors who could not pay their debts.

Ἤνοιξε τὴν Ἐκκλησίαν τοῦ Δήμου εἰς ὅλους τοὺς πολίτας, πλουσίους ἢ πτωχούς. Ὅλοι οἱ Ἀθηναῖοι ἄνω τῶν εἴκοσι ἐτῶν ἔλαβον τὸ δικαίωμα νὰ ψηφίζουν.

He opened the Popular Assembly to all the citizens, rich or poor. All Athenians over twenty years old had the right to vote.

Ἀπεφάσιζαν δι' εἰρήνην ἢ πόλεμον καὶ ἄλλα σπουδαῖα ζητήματα.

They decided on peace or war and other important matters.

Ὅλη ἡ ἐξουσία ἦτο εἰς χεῖρας τοῦ λαοῦ.

All authority was in the hands of the people.

Ὁ Ἄρειος Πάγος (τὸ Ἀνώτατον Δικαστήριον) ἔγινε ὁ φύλαξ τῶν νόμων.

The Areopagus (the Supreme Court) became the guardian of the laws.

Ἐτιμώρει τοὺς κακούργους καὶ τοὺς συνωμότας ἐναντίον τοῦ Κράτους.

It punished the criminals and the conspirators against the State.

Ἐπέβλεπε τὴν ἐφαρμογὴν τῶν νόμων καὶ ἐφρόντιζε διὰ τὴν μόρφωσιν τῶν παιδίων.

It supervised the enforcement of the laws and provided for the education of children.

Many nouns ending in ξ are declined according to the following example:

Nom.	ὁ φύλαξ	the keeper	οἱ φύλακες	the keepers
Gen.	τοῦ φύλακος	of the keeper	τῶν φυλάκων	of the keepers
Acc.	τὸν φύλακα	the keeper	τοὺς φύλακας	the keepers

Likewise many nouns ending in ψ are declined as follows:

Nom.	ἡ λαῖλαψ	the storm	αἱ λαίλαπες	the storms
Gen.	τῆς λαίλαπος	of the storm	τῶν λαιλάπων	of the storms
Acc.	τὴν λαίλαπα	the storm	τὰς λαίλαπας	the storms

Feminine nouns ending in accented άς are usually declined as follows:

Nom.	ἡ κοιλάς	the valley	αἱ κοιλάδες	the valleys
Gen.	τῆς κοιλάδος	of the valley	τῶν κοιλάδων	of the valleys
Acc.	τὴν κοιλάδα	the valley	τὰς κοιλάδας	the valleys

LESSON 43

ἡ ἡλικία	ï ïlĭkï'á	**the age**
διδάσκω· ἐδίδαξα	thĭthá'skô; ĕthï'tháxá	**I teach; I taught**
διδάσκομαι· ἐδιδασκόμην	thĭthá'skômĕ; -kô'mĭn	**I am taught; I was t.**
ἡ ἀνάγνωσις· ἡ γραφή	ï áná'γnôsĭs; ï γráfï'	**reading; writing**
ἡ μουσική	ï moosĭkï'	**music**
τὸ κολύμβημα	tô kôlïm'vĭmá	**swimming**
ἡ γυμναστική	ï yĭmnástĭkï'	**gymnastics, exercise**
ὁρκίζομαι	ôrrkï'zômĕ	**I swear, I take an oath**
ὡρκιζόμην· ὡρκίσθην	ôrrkĭzô'mĭn; ôrrkïs'thĭn	**I swore**
ὑπακούω· ὑπήκουσα	ĭpákoo'ô; ĭpï'koosá	**I obey; I obeyed**
ἡ τάξις· ἡ ὑπόσχεσις	ï tá'xĭs; ï ĭpôs'hĕsĭs	**the order; the promise**
ὑπόσχομαι· ὑπεσχέθην	ĭpôs'hômĕ; ĭpĕs hĕ'thĭn	**I promise; I promised**
θὰ ὑποσχεθῶ	thá ĭpôs hĕthô'	**I shall promise**
ὁ ὅρκος	ô ôrr'kôs	**the oath**
ἑπόμενος	ĕpô'mĕnôs	**next, following**
ἀναγκάζω	ánángá'zô	**I compel**
ἡ ἀλλαγή	ï áláγï'	**the change**
ἐπισκέπτομαι· ἐπεσκέφθη	ĕpĭskĕp'tômĕ; ĕpĕskĕf'thĭ	**I visit; he visited**
ἡ Μικρὰ 'Ασία	ĭ mĭkrá' ásï'á	**Asia Minor**
ὅπου, ποῦ	ôpoo, poo	**where**
ὁ ποταμός, c· τὸ ποτάμι	ô pôtámôs'; tô pôtá'mĭ	**the river**
ἡ ἄμμος	ï á'môs	**the sand**
ὁ βασιλεύς (τοῦ βασιλέως)	ô vásĭlĕfs' (vásĭlĕ'ôs)	**the king** (of the king)
ὑπερβολικά, πάρα πολύ	ïpĕrrvôlĭká', pá'rá polï'	**exceedingly**
φιλοξενῶ· ἐφιλοξένησα	fĭloxĕnô'; ĕfĭlôxĕ'nĭsá	**I entertain; I entertained**
τὸ ἀνάκτορον, τὰ -ρα	tô ánák'tôrôn, tá -rá	**the palace, the palaces**
δεικνύω, c· δείχνω	thĭknï'ô, thïh'nô	**I show**
ἔδειξα· θὰ δείξω	ĕthĭxá; thá thï'xô	**I showed; I shall show**
ὁ θησαυρός	ô thĭsávrôs'	**the treasure**
ἡ δόξα	ï thô'xá	**the glory**
ἐνάρετος	ĕná'rĕtôs	**virtuous, upright**
οὔτε...οὔτε	oo'tĕ... oo'tĕ	**neither... nor**
τὸ τέκνον	tô tĕk'nôn	**the child**
πίπτω, c· πέφτω· θὰ πέσω	pïp'tô, pĕf'tô; thá pĕ'sô	**I fall; I shall fall**
ἔπεσα· πεσμένος	ĕ'pĕsá; pĕzmĕ'nôs	**I fell; fallen**
γενναῖος· γενναίως	yĕnĕ'ôs; yĕnĕ'ôs	**brave; bravely**
ὑπερασπίζομαι· -ζόμενος	ĭpĕráspï'zômĕ; -zô'mĕnôs	**I defend; defending**

Μετὰ τὸ ἕβδομον ἔτος τῆς ἡλικίας των τὰ παιδιὰ ἔπρεπε νὰ πηγαίνουν εἰς σχολεῖα ὅπου ἐδιδάσκοντο ἀνάγνωσιν καὶ γραφήν, μουσικήν, κολύμβημα καὶ γυμναστικήν.	After their seventh year children were required to attend schools where they were taught reading and writing, music, swimming and gymnastics.
Οἱ νέοι ὡρκίζοντο ὅτι θὰ ἀγαποῦν τὴν πατρίδα των καὶ θὰ ὑπακούουν εἰς τοὺς νόμους της.	Young men took the oath to love their country and obey its laws.
Ὁ Σόλων, ἀφοῦ ἔκαμε τοὺς νόμους του καὶ ἔβαλε τάξιν εἰς τὰ πράγματα, ἔκαμε τοὺς Ἀθηναίους νὰ ὑποσχεθοῦν μὲ ὅρκον ὅτι δὲν θὰ ἀλλάξουν τίποτε διὰ τὰ ἑπόμενα δέκα ἔτη.	Solon, after enacting his laws and putting things in order, made the Athenians promise upon oath that they would not change anything for the next ten years.
Τότε ἔφυγεν ἀπὸ τὰς Ἀθήνας διὰ νὰ μὴ ἀναγκασθῇ νὰ κάμῃ καμμίαν ἀλλαγὴν εἰς τοὺς νόμους του.	Then he left Athens so that he would not be compelled to make any change in his laws.
Πρῶτον ἐπεσκέφθη τὸν φίλον του Θαλῆν εἰς τὴν Μικρὰν Ἀσίαν.	First he visited his friend Thales in Asia Minor.
Κατόπιν ὁ Σόλων ἐπῆγεν εἰς τὴν Λυδίαν.	Afterwards Solon went to Lydia.
Ἡ Λυδία ἦτο πλουσία χώρα ὅπου εὑρίσκετο ὁ ποταμὸς Πακτωλός, τοῦ ὁποίου ἡ ἄμμος εἶχε χρυσόν.	Lydia was a rich country where flowed (was found) the river Pactolus whose sand(s) contained gold.
Βασιλεύς της ἦτο ὁ Κροῖσος, ὁ ὁποῖος ἦτο ὑπερβολικὰ πλούσιος.	Its king was Croesus, who was exceedingly rich.
Ἐφιλοξένησε τὸν Σόλωνα εἰς τὰ ἀνάκτορά του, τοῦ ἔδειξε τοὺς θησαυρούς του καὶ ὅλην τὴν δόξαν του καὶ εἶπε:	He entertained Solon in his palace (palaces), showed him his treasures and all his glory and said:
«Σόλων, ποῖον νομίζεις τὸν εὐτυχέστερον ἄνθρωπον εἰς τὸν κόσμον;»	"Solon, whom do you think the happiest man in the world?"
«Ἕνα(ν) τίμιον ἄνθρωπον ὀνομαζόμενον Τέλλον,» εἶπεν ὁ Σόλων, «ὁ ὁποῖος ἔζησε βίον ἐνάρετον, δὲν ἦτο οὔτε πλούσιος οὔτε πτωχός, εἶχε καλὰ τέκνα καὶ ἔπεσε γενναίως ὑπερασπιζόμενος τὴν πατρίδα του.»	"An honest man named Tellos," said Solon, "who lived an upright life, was neither rich nor poor, had good children and died (fell) bravely defending his country."

LESSON 44

δυσαρεστῶ· -στοῦμαι	thĭsărĕstŏ'; -stoo'mĕ	**I displease; am displeased**
δυσηρεστήθην	thĭsĭrĕstĭ'thĭn	**I was displeased**
ὁ νικητής	ŏ nĭkĭtĭs'	**the the victor, the winner**
ὁ ἀγών (τοῦ ἀγῶνος)	ŏ ȧγŏn' (too ȧγŏ'nŏs)	**the struggle; the contest**
οἱ 'Ολυμπιακοὶ ἀγῶνες	ĭ ŏlĭmpĭȧkĭ' ȧγŏ'nĕs	**the Olympic games**
τὸ βῶδι· τὰ βώδια	tŏ vŏ'thĭ; tȧ vŏ'thyȧ	**the ox; the oxen**
τραβῶ· ἐτράβηξα	trȧvŏ'; ĕtrȧ'vĭxȧ	**I pull; I pulled**
ἡ ἅμαξα, τὸ ἁμάξι	ĭ ȧ'mȧxȧ, tŏ ȧmȧ'xĭ	**the carriage**
ὁ ναός	ŏ nȧŏs'	**the temple**
ἀποθνήσκω, c. πεθαίνω	ȧpŏthnĭ'skŏ, pĕthĕ'nŏ	**I die**
ἀπέθανον· πεθαμένος	ȧpĕ'thȧnŏn; pĕthȧmĕ'nos	**I died; dead**
ὁ θάνατος	ŏ thȧ'nȧtŏs	**death**
εἰρηνικός· εἰρηνικά	ĭrĭnĭkŏs'; ĭrĭnĭkȧ'	**peaceful; peacefully**
χωρίς, ἄνευ	hŏrĭs'; ȧ'nĕf	**without**
ὁ πόνος· ἡ λύπη	ŏ pŏ'nŏs; ĭ lĭ'pĭ	**the pain; the sorrow**
ἀπαντῶ· ἀπήντησα	ȧpȧntŏ'; ȧpĭn'tĭsȧ	**I reply, I meet; I replied**
οὐδείς (g. οὐδενός, ac. οὐδένα)	oothĭs' (oothĕnŏs', -ĕ'nȧ)	**no one**
πρὸ τοῦ τέλους	prŏ too tĕ'loos	**before the end**
μακαρίζω	mȧkȧrĭ'zŏ	**I consider happy**
θυμώνω	thĭmŏ'nŏ	**I get angry; I anger**
ἐθύμωσα· θυμωμένος	ĕthĭ'mŏsȧ; thĭmŏmĕ'nŏs	**I got angry; angered**
ἡ ἀπάντησις	ĭ ȧpȧn'tĭsĭs	**the answer**
διώκω, c. διώχνω	thĭŏ'kŏ, thĭŏh'nŏ	**I drive away**
ἔδιωξα	ĕ'thĭŏxȧ	**I drove away**

Ὁ Κροῖσος δυσηρεστήθη καὶ ἠρώτησε ποῖος ἦτο ὁ κατόπιν εὐτυχέστερος.

Croesus was displeased and asked who was (the) next happiest.

«Δύο ἀδελφοὶ ὀνομαζόμενοι Κλέοβις καὶ Βίτων,» εἶπεν ὁ Σόλων. «Ἦσαν νικηταὶ εἰς τοὺς 'Ολυμπιακοὺς ἀγῶνας καὶ εἶχον μεγάλην ἀγάπην πρὸς τὴν μητέρα των.

"Two brothers called Cleobis and Biton," said Solon. "They were winners at the Olympic games and had great love for their mother.

«Μίαν ἡμέραν ποὺ τὰ βώδια εἶχον ἀργήσει νὰ ἔλθουν, οἱ ἀδελφοὶ ἐπῆ-

"One day, when the oxen were late in coming, the brothers took

ραν τὴν θέσιν των καὶ ἐτράβηξαν τὴν ἅμαξαν εἰς τὸν ναὸν ὅπου ἡ μητέρα των ἤθελε νὰ ὑπάγῃ.	their place and pulled the carriage to the temple where their mother wanted to go.
«Ἀπέθανον εἰρηνικά, χωρὶς πόνον καὶ χωρὶς λύπην.»	"They died peacefully, without pain and without grief."
«Καὶ τί νομίζεις δι' ἐμέ;» ἠρώτησεν ὁ Κροῖσος. «Δὲν πιστεύεις πῶς εἶμαι εὐτυχής;»	"And what do you think of me?" asked Croesus. "Don't you believe I am happy?"
Ὁ Σόλων ἀπήντησε: «Οὐδένα πρὸ τοῦ τέλους μακάριζε:—Μὴ θεωρῇς κανένα εὐτυχῆ πρὸ τοῦ θανάτου του.»	Solon replied: "Deem no man happy before the end: — Consider no one happy before his death."
Ὁ Κροῖσος ἐθύμωσε ἀπὸ τὴν ἀπάντησιν αὐτὴν καὶ ἔδιωξε τὸν Σόλωνα.	Croesus was angered at this answer and sent Solon away.

Nouns ending in ων are declined according to the following examples:

Nom.	ὁ κανών	the rule	οἱ κανόνες	the rules
Gen.	τοῦ κανόνος	of the rule	τῶν κανόνων	of the rules
Acc.	τὸν κανόνα	the rule	τοὺς κανόνας	the rules
Nom.	ὁ ἀγών	the struggle	οἱ ἀγῶνες	the struggles
Gen.	τοῦ ἀγῶνος	of the struggle	τῶν ἀγώνων	of the struggles
Acc.	τὸν ἀγῶνα	the struggle	τοὺς ἀγῶνας	the struggles
Nom.	ὁ γείτων	the neighbor	οἱ γείτονες	the neighbors
Gen.	τοῦ γείτονος	of the neighbor	τῶν γειτόνων	of the neighbors
Acc.	τὸν γείτονα	the neighbor	τοὺς γείτονας	the neighbors
Nom.	ὁ γέρων	the old man	οἱ γέροντες	the old men
Gen.	τοῦ γέροντος	of the old man	τῶν γερόντων	of the old men
Acc.	τὸν γέροντα	the old man	τοὺς γέροντας	the old men
Nom.	ὁ κώδων	the bell	οἱ κώδωνες	the bells
Gen.	τοῦ κώδωνος	of the bell	τῶν κωδώνων	of the bells
Acc.	τὸν κώδωνα	the bell	τοὺς κώδωνας	the bells
Nom.	ὁ Σόλων	Solon		
Gen.	τοῦ Σόλωνος	Solon's, of Solon		
Acc.	τὸν Σόλωνα	Solon		

LESSON 45

ἐν τούτοις	ĕn too'tĭs	**however**
ὁ νοῦς (τοῦ νοῦ, τὸν νοῦν)	ŏ noos, too noo, tŏn noon	**the mind**
ὁ στρατός	ŏ strătŏs'	**the army**
νικῶ· ἐνίκησα	nĭkŏ'; ĕnĭ'kĭsă	**I defeat; I defeated**
νικῶμαι· ἐνικήθην	nĭkŏ'mĕ; ĕnĭkĭ'thĭn	**I am defeated; I was defeated**
ὁ, ἡ, αἰχμάλωτος	ĕhmă'lŏtŏs	**the prisoner**
θέτω· ἔθεσα	thĕ'tŏ; ĕ'thĕsă	**I place; I placed**
τὸ πῦρ, ἡ πυρά, c. φωτιά	tŏ pĭr, ĭ pĭră', ĭ fŏtyă'	**the fire**
καίω· ἔκαυσα, c. ἔκαψα	kĕ'ŏ; ĕ'kăfsă, ĕ'kăpsă	**I burn; I burned**
θὰ καύσω, c. θὰ κάψω	thă kăf'sŏ, thă kă'psŏ	**I shall burn**
καίομαι· θὰ καῶ	kĕ'ŏmĕ; thă kăŏ'	**I am burned; I shall be burned**
ἐκάην, c. ἐκάηκα	ĕkă'ĭn, ĕkă'ĭkă	**I was burned**
ζωντανός	zŏntănŏs'	**alive**
τότε	tŏ'tĕ	**then**
ἐνθυμοῦμαι· ἐνθυμήθην	ĕnthĭmoo'mĕ	**I remember; I remembered**
ὁ λόγος	ŏ lŏ'γŏs	**the word; the reason**
οἱ λόγοι, τὰ λόγια	ĭ lŏ'γĭ, tă lŏ'γyă	**the words**
φωνάζω· ἐφώναξα	fŏnă'zŏ; ĕfŏ'năxă	**I cry; I cried**
σημαίνω· ἐσήμαινον	sĭmĕ'nŏ; ĕsĭ'mĕnŏn	**I mean; I meant**
διηγοῦμαι· διηγήθην	thĭĭγoo'mĕ; thĭĭγĭ'thĭn	**I narrate; I narrated**
ἡ ἱστορία	ĭ ĭstŏrĭ'ă	**the story; the history**
ἡ συνάντησις	ĭ sĭnăn'tĭsĭs	**the meeting**
ἡ ἐντύπωσις	ĭ ĕntĭ'pŏsĭs	**the impression**
χαρίζω· ἐχάρισα	hărĭ'zŏ; ĕhă'rĭsă	**I donate, I spare; I donated**
ὁ, ἡ, σύμβουλος	sĭm'voolŏs	**the adviser**
ὑπόλοιπος· ὑπόλοιπον	ĭpŏ'lĭpŏs; ĭpŏ'lĭpŏn	**remaining; remainder**

Ἐν τούτοις, οἱ λόγοι τοῦ Σόλωνος γρήγορα ἦλθον εἰς τὸν νοῦν του.

However, Solon's words soon came to his mind.

Εἰς πόλεμον ἐναντίον τοῦ Κύρου, βασιλέως τῶν Περσῶν, ὁ στρατὸς τοῦ Κροίσου ἐνικήθη καὶ ὁ ἴδιος ὁ Κροῖσος συνελήφθη αἰχμάλωτος.

In a war against Cyrus, king of the Persians, Croesus' army was defeated and Croesus himself was taken prisoner.

Τὸν ἔθεσαν ἐπάνω εἰς μίαν πυρὰν διὰ νὰ καῇ ζωντανός. Τότε ὁ Κροῖσος ἐνθυμήθη τὰ λόγια τοῦ Σόλωνος καὶ ἐφώναξε: «Σόλων, Σόλων, Σόλων!»

They placed him over a fire to be burned alive. Then Croesus remembered Solon's words and cried: "Solon, Solon, Solon!"

Ὁ Κῦρος τὸν ἤκουσε καὶ ἠρώτησε τί ἐσήμαινον ἐκεῖνα τὰ λόγια.	Cyrus heard him and asked what those words meant.
Ὁ Κροῖσος διηγήθη τὴν ἱστορίαν τῆς συναντήσεώς του μὲ τὸν Ἀθηναῖον σοφόν.	Croesus told the story of his meeting with the Athenian sage.
Ἡ ἱστορία ἔκαμε τόσην ἐντύπωσιν εἰς τὸν Κῦρον, ὥστε ἐχάρισε τὴν ζωὴν εἰς τὸν Κροῖσον καὶ τὸν ἔκαμε σύμβουλόν του διὰ τὸ ὑπόλοιπον τοῦ βίου του (τῆς ζωῆς του).	The story made such an impression on Cyrus that he spared Croesus' life and made him his adviser for the rest of his life.

Nouns ending in εύς are usually declined as follows:

Nom.	ὁ βασιλεύς	the king	οἱ βασιλεῖς	the kings
Gen.	τοῦ βασιλέως	of the king	τῶν βασιλέων	of the kings
Acc.	τὸν βασιλέα	the king	τοὺς βασιλεῖς	the kings
Voc.	ὦ βασιλεῦ	O king	ὦ βασιλεῖς	O kings

Nouns ending in ωρ are generally declined as follows:

Nom.	ὁ ῥήτωρ	the orator	οἱ ῥήτορες	the orators
Gen.	τοῦ ῥήτορος	of the orator	τῶν ῥητόρων	of the orators
Acc.	**τὸν ῥήτορα**	the orator	τοὺς ῥήτορας	the orators
Voc.	ὦ ῥῆτορ	O orator	ὦ ῥήτορες	O orators

Adjectives ending in the masculine and feminine gender in ης and in the neuter in ες are declined according to the following examples:

SINGULAR	*Masc. and Fem.*	*Neuter*	*Masc. and Fem.*	*Neuter*
Nom.	ἀληθής, true	ἀληθὲς	συνήθης, usual	σύνηθες
Gen.	ἀληθοῦς	ἀληθοῦς	συνήθους	συνήθους
Acc.	ἀληθῆ	ἀληθὲς	συνήθη	σύνηθες
PLURAL				
Nom.	ἀληθεῖς	ἀληθῆ	συνήθεις	συνήθη
Gen.	ἀληθῶν	ἀληθῶν	συνήθων	συνήθων
Acc.	ἀληθεῖς	ἀληθῆ	συνήθεις	συνήθη

Adjectives ending in the masculine in ύς usually have the feminine in εῖα and the neuter in ύ. They are declined as follows:

	SINGULAR			*PLURAL*		
	Masculine	*Feminine*	*Neuter*	*Masculine*	*Feminine*	*Neuter*
Nom.	ταχύς, fast	ταχεῖα	ταχύ	ταχεῖς	ταχεῖαι	ταχέα
Gen.	ταχέος	ταχείας	ταχέος	ταχέων	ταχειῶν	ταχέων
Acc.	ταχύν	ταχεῖαν	ταχύ	ταχεῖς	ταχείας	ταχέα

CONJUGATION OF GREEK VERBS

THE REGULAR VERB ΖΗΛΕΥΩ

INDICATIVE

Present

ζηλεύω	I envy
ζηλεύεις	you envy
ζηλεύει	he envies
ζηλεύομε(ν)	we envy
ζηλεύετε	you envy
ζηλεύουν	they envy

Imperfect or Long Past

ἐζήλευον	c. ἐζήλευα	I was envying
ἐζήλευες	ἐζήλευες	you were envying
ἐζήλευε	ἐζήλευε	he was envying
ἐζηλεύομεν	ἐζηλεύαμε	we were envying
ἐζηλεύετε	ἐζηλεύατε	you were envying
ἐζήλευον	ἐζήλευαν	they were envying

Aorist

ἐζήλευσα	I envied
ἐζήλευσες	you envied
ἐζήλευσε	he envied
ἐζηλεύσαμεν	we envied
ἐζηλεύσατε	you envied
ἐζήλευσαν	they envied

Perfect

ἔχω ζηλεύσει	I have envied
ἔχεις ζηλεύσει	you have envied
ἔχει ζηλεύσει	he has envied
ἔχομεν ζηλεύσει	we have envied
ἔχετε ζηλεύσει	you have envied
ἔχουν ζηλεύσει	they have envied

Momentary Future

θὰ ζηλεύσω	I shall envy
θὰ ζηλεύσῃς	you will envy
θὰ ζηλεύσῃ	he will envy
θὰ ζηλεύσωμεν	we shall envy
θὰ ζηλεύσετε	you will envy
θὰ ζηλεύσουν	they will envy

Duration Future

θὰ ζηλεύω	I shall be envying
θὰ ζηλεύεις	you will be envying
θὰ ζηλεύει	he will be envying
θὰ ζηλεύομεν	we shall be envying
θὰ ζηλεύετε	you will be envying
θὰ ζηλεύουν	they will be envying

Future Perfect

θὰ ἔχω ζηλεύσει	I shall have envied
θὰ ἔχεις ζηλεύσει	you will have "
θὰ ἔχει ζηλεύσει	he will have "
θὰ ἔχωμεν ζηλεύσει	we will have "
θὰ ἔχετε ζηλεύσει	you will have "
θὰ ἔχουν ζηλεύσει	they will have "

Pluperfect

εἶχον ζηλεύσει	I had envied
εἶχες ζηλεύσει	you had envied
εἶχε ζηλεύσει	he had envied
εἴχομεν ζηλεύσει	we had envied
εἴχετε ζηλεύσει	you had envied
εἶχον ζηλεύσει	they had envied

DURATION IMPERATIVE

ζήλευε	envy
νὰ (or ἂς) ζηλεύῃ	let him envy
ζηλεύετε	envy
νὰ (or ἂς) ζηλεύουν	let them envy

MOMENTARY IMPERATIVE (Aorist)

ζήλευσον, c. ζήλευσε	envy
νὰ (or ἂς) ζηλεύσῃ	let him envy
ζηλεύσατε	envy
νὰ (or ἂς) ζηλεύσουν	let them envy

CONDITIONAL (I would envy, you would envy, etc.)

θὰ ἐζήλευον, θὰ ἐζήλευες, θὰ ἐζήλευε, θὰ ἐζηλεύομεν, θὰ ἐζηλεύετε, θὰ ἐζήλευον.
c. θὰ ἐζήλευα, θὰ ἐζήλευες, θὰ ἐζήλευε, θὰ ἐζηλεύαμε, θὰ ἐζηλεύατε, θὰ ἐζήλευαν.

CONDITIONAL PAST (I woull have envied, etc.)

θὰ εἶχον (εἶχα) ζηλεύσει, θὰ εἶχες ζηλεύσει, θὰ εἶχε ζηλεύσει, etc.

PARTICIPLE PRESENT

ζηλεύων (f. ζηλεύουσα, n. ζηλεῦον), col. ζηλεύοντας or ζηλεύωντας, envying.

PARTICIPLE PAST (Aorist): ζηλεύσας (f. ζηλεύσασα, n. ζηλεῦσαν), having envied.

PASSIVE VOICE — ΖΗΛΕΥΟΜΑΙ

INDICATIVE

Present		Imperfect or Long Past	
ζηλεύομαι	I am envied	ἐζηλευόμην	I was envied
ζηλεύεσαι	you are envied	ἐζηλεύεσο	you were envied
ζηλεύεται	he is envied	ἐζηλεύετο	he was envied
ζηλευόμεθα	we are envied	ἐζηλευόμεθα	we were envied
ζηλεύεσθε	you are envied	ἐζηλεύεσθε	you were envied
ζηλεύονται	they are envied	ἐζηλεύοντο	they were envied

Aorist			Perfect	
ἐζηλεύθην	c. ἐζηλεύθηκα	I was envied	ἔχω ζηλευθῆ	I have been envied
ἐζηλεύθης	ἐζηλεύθηκες	you were "	ἔχεις ζηλευθῆ	you have been "
ἐζηλεύθη	ἐζηλεύθηκε	he was "	ἔχει ζηλευθῆ	he has been "
ἐζηλεύθημεν	ἐζηλευθήκαμε	we were "	ἔχομεν ζηλευθῆ	we have been "
ἐζηλεύθητε	ἐζηλευθήκατε	you were "	ἔχετε ζηλευθῆ	you have been "
ἐζηλεύθησαν	ἐζηλεύθηκαν	they were "	ἔχουν ζηλευθῆ	they have been "

Duration Future		Momentary Future	
θὰ ζηλεύομαι	I shall be envied	θὰ ζηλευθῶ	I shall be envied
θὰ ζηλεύεσαι	you will be envied	θὰ ζηλευθῆς	you will be envied
θὰ ζηλεύεται	he will be envied	θὰ ζηλευθῆ	he will be envied
θὰ ζηλευόμεθα	we shall be envied	θὰ ζηλευθῶμεν c. θὰ ζηλευθοῦμε	we shall be envied
θὰ ζηλεύεσθε	you will be envied	θὰ ζηλευθῆτε	you will be envied
θὰ ζηλεύονται	they will be envied	θὰ ζηλευθοῦν	they will be envied

Future Perfect	Pluperfect
θὰ ἔχω ζηλευθῆ, I shall have been envied	εἶχον ζηλευθῆ, I had been envied

(Duration)	IMPERATIVE (Momentary)	
νὰ (or ἂς) ζηλεύεσαι	νὰ (or ἂς) ζηλευθῆς	be envied
νὰ (or ἂς) ζηλεύεται	νὰ (or ἂς) ζηλευθῆ	let him be envied
νὰ (or ἂς) ζηλεύεσθε	ζηλευθῆτε, νὰ (or ἂς) ζηλευθῆτε	be envied
νὰ (or ἂς) ζηλεύωνται	νὰ (or ἂς) ζηλευθοῦν	let them be envied

CONDITIONAL (I would be envied)

θὰ ἐζηλευόμην, θὰ ἐζηλεύεσο, θὰ ἐζηλεύετο, θὰ ἐζηλευόμεθα, etc.

CONDITIONAL PAST (I would have been envied)

θὰ εἶχον ζηλευθῆ, θὰ εἶχες ζηλευθῆ, θὰ εἶχε ζηλευθῆ, θὰ εἴχομεν ζηλευθῆ, etc.

PARTICIPLE PRESENT

ζηλευόμενος (f. ζηλευομένη, n. ζηλευόμενον), being envied.

(Aorist) PARTICIPLE PAST (Perfect)

ζηλευθείς (f. ζηλευθεῖσα, n. ζηλευθέν), or, ζηλευμένος (f.-μένη, n.-μένον), envied.

GENERAL REMARKS

Augment. In the imperfect and aorist of the indicative, verbs beginning with a consonant are prefixed with the *augment* ἐ:

γράφω — ἔγραφον — ἔγραψα	I write — I was writing — I wrote

Those beginning with a vowel (in puristic Greek) change the initial vowel from ἀ or ἐ to ἡ and from ὀ to ὠ:

ἀκούω — ἤκουον — ἤκουσα	I hear — I was hearing — I heard
ἐλπίζω — ἤλπιζον — ἤλπισα	I hope — I was hoping — I hoped
ὁμιλῶ — ὡμίλουν — ὡμίλησα	I speak — I was speaking — I spoke

Verbs beginning with a diphthong change αι to ῃ, αυ and ευ to ηυ, οι to ῳ:

αἰσθάνομαι — ᾐσθανόμην — ᾐσθάνθην	I feel — I was feeling — I felt
αὐξάνω — ηὔξανον — ηὔξησα	I grow — I was growing — I grew

Compound verbs whose first part is a preposition (ἀνὰ or ἀν, ἀντὶ or αντ, ἀπὸ or ἀπ or ἀφ, διὰ or δι, εἰς, ἐκ or ἐξ, ἐν or ἐγ or ἐμ, ἐπὶ or ἐπ or ἐφ, κατὰ or κατ or καθ, μετὰ or μετ or μεθ, παρὰ or παρ, περί, πρό, πρός, σύν or συγ or συλ or συμ, ὑπέρ, ὑπὸ or ὑπ or ὑφ) in the puristic language take the augment between the preposition and the verb stem:

προσθέτω — προσέθετον - προσέθεσα	I add — I was adding — I added
ἐνδύω — ἐνέδυον — ἐνέδυσα	I dress — I was dressing — I dressed

The prepositions (except περὶ and πρὸ) drop their final vowel before the augment ἐ:

καταπίπτω — κατέπεσα	I fall — I fell
ἐπιτρέπω — ἐπέτρεψα	I permit — I permitted

If the verb begins with the preposition ἐκ, it changes ἐκ to ἐξ before the augment ἐ:

ἐκλέγω — ἐξέλεξα	I choose — I chose

If the prepositions ἐν and σὺν in the present tense have taken the euphonic forms of ἐγ or ἐμ, and συγ - συλ - συμ or συρ, they resume their original forms before the augment ἐ:

ἐγκλείω (ἐν-κλείω) — ἐνέκλεισα	I enclose — I enclosed
ἐμπίπτω (ἐν-πίπτω) — ἐνέπεσα	I fall in — I fell in
συλλέγω (σὺν-λέγω) — συνέλεξα	I collect — I collected
συμβάλλω (σὺν-βάλλω) — συνέβαλον	I contribute — I contributed

In the spoken language the augment is necessarily used in the imperfect and aorist singular of disyllabic verbs accented on their first syllable. In all other cases it may be used or omitted at will:

τρέχω — ἔτρεχα — ἔτρεξα	I run — I was running — I ran
ρίπτω — ἔρριπτα — ἔρριψα	I throw — I was throwing — I threw
νομίζω — ἐνόμιζα or νόμιζα	I think — I was thinking

In compound verbs it is placed at the beginning of the verb, or may be omitted entirely:

ἀγαπῶ — ἀγάπησα or ἠγάπησα	I love, I was loving — I loved
προχωρῶ — ἐπροχώρησα or προχώρησα	I advance — I advanced
παραδίδω — ἐπαράδοσα or παράδοσα	I deliver — I delivered

COMMON GREEK VERBS

Regularly, Greek verbs form the aorist (momentary past) with the vowel increase or augment at the beginning of the verb stem and the endings σα, σες, σε, σαμεν, σατε, σαν; the perfect with the auxiliary ἔχω and the verb ending in σει; and the momentary future with the auxiliary θὰ and the endings σω, σεις, σει, etc.

The passive voice regularly forms the aorist in θην (c.θηκα) with the augment prefixed; the aorist participle in θείς without the augment; the momentary future with the auxiliary θὰ and the terminations θῶ, θῆς, etc; the perfect with the auxiliary ἔχω and the verb ending in θῆ (or θεῖ); and the perfect participle with the ending μένος.

In most cases, however, the verb undergoes various changes in forming the aorist, perfect and momentary future tenses; therefore, we have found it advisable to give here a list of common Greek verbs with their most important changes.

In the following list the indicative present, aorist, perfect and passive past participle (of the aorist) of verbs most common in the Greek language are given. Verbs ending in ω and ομαι are conjugated as the verbs ζηλεύω, ζηλεύομαι (pp.139, 140). Verbs ending in ῶ (άω) are conjugated as the verb ἀγαπῶ and those ending in ῶ (έω) are conjugated as the verb ὁμιλῶ (pages 69 and 70).

Compound verbs not listed below are conjugated as the simple verbs of their second part, with the augment placed between the preposition and the verb for the formation of the imperfect and aorist indicative.

PRESENT	AORIST	PERFECT	PAST PARTICIPLE PASSIVE
	A		
ἀγαπῶ (άω), I love	ἠγάπησα,ἀγάπησα	ἔχω ἀγαπήσει	ἀγαπηθείς,-μένος
ἀγγέλλω, I announce	ἤγγειλα	ἔχω ἀγγείλει	ἀγγελθείς
ἁγιάζω, I sanctify	ἡγίασα, ἅγιασα	ἔχω ἁγιάσει	ἁγιασθείς,-μένος
ἀγκαλιάζω, I embrace	ἀγκάλιασα	ἔχω ἀγκαλιάσει	ἀγκαλιασθείς
ἀγνοῶ (έω), I ignore	ἠγνόησα, ἀγνόησα	ἔχω ἀγνοήσει	ἀγνοηθείς
ἀγοράζω, I buy	ἠγόρασα,ἀγόρασα	ἔχω ἀγοράσει	ἀγορασθείς
ἀγορεύω, I speak	ἠγόρευσα	ἔχω ἀγορεύσει	ἀγορευθείς
ἀγριεύω, I get angry	ἠγρίευσα,ἀγρίευσα	ἔχω ἀγριεύσει	ἀγριευμένος
ἀγρυπνῶ (έω), I am awake	ἠγρύπνησα, ἀγρύ-	ἔχω ἀγρυπνήσει	ἀγρυπνηθείς
ἄγω, I lead, I bring	ἤγαγον, ἔφερα	ἔχω ἀγάγει	ἀχθείς, ἠγμένος
ἀγωνίζομαι, I struggle	ἠγωνίσθην	ἔχω ἀγωνισθῆ	ἀγωνισθείς
ἀδειάζω, I empty	ἄδειασα	ἔχω ἀδειάσει	ἀδειασθείς
ἀδιαφορῶ, I am indifferent	ἀδιαφόρησα	ἔχω ἀδιαφορήσει	
ἀδικῶ (έω), I wrong	ἠδίκησα, ἀδίκησα	ἔχω ἀδικήσει	ἀδικηθείς
ἀδρανῶ (έω),I am inactive	ἠδράνησα,ἀδρά-	ἔχω ἀδρανήσει	ἀδρανηθείς
ἀερίζω, I air	ἀέρισα	ἔχω ἀερίσει	ἀερισθείς
ἀθετῶ (έω), I violate	ἠθέτησα, ἀθέτησα	ἔχω ἀθετήσει	ἀθετηθείς
ἀθροίζω, I add	ἤθροισα,ἄθροισα	ἔχω ἀθροίσει	ἀθροισθείς
ἀθυμῶ (έω), I feel blue	ἠθύμησα,ἀθύμησα	ἔχω ἀθυμήσει	
ἀθωῶ, ἀθωώνω, I acquit	ἠθώωσα,ἀθώωσα	ἔχω ἀθωώσει	ἀθωωθείς
αἰσθάνομαι, I feel	ἠσθάνθην,αἰσθάνθηκα	» αἰσθανθῆ	αἰσθανθείς
αἰσχύνω, I shame	ἤσχυνα	ἔχω αἰσχύνει	αἰσχυνθείς

PRESENT	AORIST	PERFECT	PAST PARTICIPLE PASSIVE
αἰτῶ (έω), I ask	ἤτησα	ἔχω αἰτήσει	αἰτηθείς
ἀκμάζω, I flourish	ἤκμασα	ἔχω ἀκμάσει	
ἀκολουθῶ (έω), I follow	ἠκολούθησα, ἀκο-	ἔχω ἀκολουθήσει	ἀκολουθηθείς
ἀκονίζω, I sharpen	ἠκόνισα,ἀκόνισα	ἔχω ἀκονίσει	ἀκονισθείς
ἀκουμϐῶ (άω), I lean	ἀκούμϐησα	ἔχω ἀκουμϐήσει	ἀκουμϐισμένος
ἀκούω, I hear	ἤκουσα, ἄκουσα	ἔχω ἀκούσει	ἀκουσθείς,-σμένος
ἀκυρῶ, ἀκυρώνω, I annul	ἠκύρωσα,ἀκύρωσα	ἔχω ἀκυρώσει	ἀκυρωθείς
ἀλέθω, I grind	ἤλεσα, ἄλεσα	ἔχω ἀλέσει	ἀλεσθείς,-σμένος
ἀλείφω, I smear, I coat	ἤλειψα, ἄλειψα	ἔχω ἀλείψει	ἀλειφθείς,-ειμμένος
ἀληθεύω, I am true	ἠλήθευσα,ἀλή-	ἔχω ἀληθεύσει	
ἁλιεύω, I fish	ἡλίευσα	ἔχω ἁλιεύσει	ἁλιευθείς
ἀλλάσσω,ἀλλάζω,I change	ἤλλαξα,ἄλλαξα	ἔχω ἀλλάξει	ἀλλαχθείς,ἀλλαγείς
ἀλλοιῶ, ἀλλοιώνω, I alter	ἠλλοίωσα	ἔχω ἀλλοιώσει	ἀλλοιωθείς
ἁμαρτάνω, I sin	ἡμάρτησα,-ἁμάρ-	ἔχω ἁμαρτήσει	
ἀμϐλύνω, I blunt	ἤμϐλυνα,ἄμϐλυνα	ἔχω ἀμϐλύνει	ἀμϐλυνθείς
ἀμείϐω, I reward	ἤμειψα	ἔχω ἀμείψει	ἀμειφθείς
ἀμελῶ (έω), I neglect	ἠμέλησα,ἀμέλησα	ἔχω ἀμελήσει	ἀμεληθείς
ἀμύνομαι, I defend	ἠμύνθην	ἔχω ἀμυνθῇ	ἀμυνθείς
ἀμφιϐάλλω, I doubt	ἀμφέϐαλον, -ϐαλα	ἔχω ἀμφιϐάλει	
ἀναϐαίνω, I go up	ἀνέϐην, ἀνέϐηκα	ἔχω ἀναϐῇ	(ἀναϐάς)
ἀναγγέλλω, I announce	ἀνήγγειλα	ἔχω ἀναγγείλει	ἀναγγελθείς
ἀναγινώσκω, I read	ἀνέγνωσα	ἔχω ἀναγνώσει	ἀναγνωσθείς
ἀναγκάζω, I compel	ἠνάγκασα	ἔχω ἀναγκάσει	ἀναγκασθείς
ἀναγνωρίζω, I recognize	ἀνεγνώρισα	ἔχω ἀναγνωρίσει	ἀναγνωρισθείς
ἀναθέτω, I commission	ἀνέθεσα	ἔχω ἀναθέσει	ἀνατεθείς,-θειμένος
ἀνακαλύπτω, I discover	ἀνεκάλυψα	ἔχω ἀνακαλύψει	ἀνακαλυφθείς
ἀνακοινῶ, I communicate	ἀνεκοίνωσα	ἔχω ἀνακοινώσει	ἀνακοινωθείς
ἀνακουφίζω, I relieve	ἀνεκούφισα	ἔχω ἀνακουφίσει	ἀνακουφισθείς
ἀναλαμϐάνω, I assume	ἀνέλαϐον, -λαϐα	ἔχω ἀναλάϐει	ἀναληφθείς
ἀναμένω, I wait	ἀνέμεινα	ἔχω ἀναμείνει	
ἀναμιγνύω, I mix	ἀνέμιξα	» ἀναμίξει	ἀναμιχθείς,-ιγμένος
ἀνανεῶ,ἀνανεώνω, I renew	ἀνενέωσα	ἔχω ἀνανεώσει	ἀνανεωθείς
ἀναπαύω, I rest	ἀνέπαυσα	ἔχω ἀναπαύσει	ἀναπαυθείς
ἀναπνέω, I breathe	ἀνέπνευσα	ἔχω ἀναπνεύσει	
ἀναπληρῶ, -ώνω, I replace	ἀνεπλήρωσα	ἔχω ἀναπληρώσει	ἀναπληρωθείς
ἀναπτύσσω, I develop	ἀνέπτυξα	» ἀναπτύξει	ἀναπτυχθείς,-γμένος
ἀνάπτω, I light	ἤναψα	ἔχω ἀνάψει	ἀναφθείς,ἀναμμένος
ἀναστενάζω, I sigh	ἀνεστέναξα	ἔχω ἀναστενάξει	
ἀναστήνω, I revive	ἀνέστησα	ἔχω ἀναστήσει	ἀναστηθείς
ἀνατέλλω, I rise	ἀνέτειλα	ἔχω ἀνατείλει	
ἀνατρέπω, I overthrow	ἀνέτρεψα	ἔχω ἀνατρέψει	ἀνατραπείς
ἀνατρέφω, I bring up	ἀνέθρεψα	ἔχω ἀναθρέψει	ἀνατραφείς
ἀναφέρω, I report	ἀνέφερον, -ρα	ἔχω ἀναφέρει	ἀναφερθείς
ἀναφωνῶ (έω), I exclaim	ἀνεφώνησα	ἔχω ἀναφωνήσει	ἀναφωνηθείς
ἀνατριχιάζω, I shudder	ἀνετρίχιασα	» ἀνατριχιάσει	ἀνατριχιασμένος
ἀναχωρῶ (έω), I depart	ἀνεχώρησα	ἔχω ἀναχωρήσει	
ἀνεγείρω, I erect	ἀνήγειρα	ἔχω ἀνεγείρει	ἀνεγερθείς
ἀνέχομαι, I tolerate	ἠνέχθην	ἔχω ἀνεχθῇ	ἀνεχθείς
ἀνήκω, I belong	ἀνῆκον, ἀνῆκα		
ἀνησυχῶ (έω), I worry	ἀνησύχησα	ἔχω ἀνησυχήσει	
ἀνθίζω, ἀνθῶ, I blossom	ἤνθησα,ἄνθισα	ἔχω ἀνθίσει	ἀνθισμένος
ἀνίσταμαι, I rise	ἀνέστην	ἔχω ἀναστῇ	ἀναστηθείς
ἀνοίγω, I open	ἤνοιξα, ἄνοιξα	ἔχω ἀνοίξει	ἀνοιχθείς,-οιγμένος
ἀνορθῶ, -θώνω, I restore	ἀνώρθωσα	ἔχω ἀνορθώσει	ἀνορθωθείς

PRESENT	AORIST	PERFECT	PAST PARTICIPLE PASSIVE
ἀνταμείβω, I reward	ἀντήμειψα	ἔχω ἀνταμείψει	ἀνταμειφθείς
ἀνταμώνω, I meet	ἀντάμωσα	ἔχω ἀνταμώσει	ἀνταμωθείς
ἀντέχω, I resist, I endure	ἀντέσχον	ἔχω ἀνθέξει	
ἀντηχῶ (έω), I resound	ἀντήχησα	ἔχω ἀντηχήσει	
ἀντιδρῶ (άω), I react	ἀντέδρασα	ἔχω ἀντιδράσει	
ἀντικαθιστῶ (άω) I replace	ἀντικατέστησα	» ἀντικαταστήσει	ἀντικατασταθείς
ἀντικρύζω, I face	ἀντίκρυσα	ἔχω ἀντικρύσει	ἀντικρυσθείς
ἀντιστοιχῶ, I correspond	ἀντεστοίχησα	ἔχω ἀντιστοιχήσει	
ἀξίζω, I am worth, I deserve	ἤξισα, ἄξισα	ἔχω ἀξίσει	
ἀξιῶ,-ώνω, I claim; I enable	ἠξίωσα, ἀξίωσα	ἔχω ἀξιώσει	ἀξιωθείς
ἀπαιτῶ (έω), I demand	ἀπήτησα, ἀπαίτησα	ἔχω ἀπαιτήσει	ἀπαιτηθείς
ἀπαλλάσσω, I release	ἀπήλλαξα	» ἀπαλλάξει	ἀπαλλαγείς,-αχθείς
ἀπαντῶ (άω), I meet	ἀπήντησα, ἀπάντησα	ἔχω ἀπαντήσει	ἀπαντηθείς
ἀπατῶ (άω), I cheat	ἠπάτησα, ἀπάτησα	ἔχω ἀπατήσει	ἀπατηθείς
ἀπειλῶ, I menace	ἠπείλησα	ἔχω ἀπειλήσει	ἀπειληθείς
ἀπελπίζω, I disappoint	ἀπήλπισα, ἀπέλπισα	ἔχω ἀπελπίσει	ἀπελπισθείς
ἀπεργῶ (έω), I strike	ἀπήργησα, ἀπέρ-	ἔχω ἀπεργήσει	
ἀπέρχομαι, I go away	ἀπῆλθον, ἀπῆλθα	ἔχω ἀπέλθει	
ἀπευθύνω, I direct	ἀπηύθυνα	ἔχω ἀπευθύνει	ἀπευθυνθείς
ἀπέχω, I am distant	ἀπέσχον	ἔχω ἀπόσχει	
ἁπλώνω, I spread	ἥπλωσα, ἅπλωσα	ἔχω ἁπλώσει	ἁπλωθείς
ἀποβαίνω, I become	ἀπέβην	ἔχω ἀποβῇ	(ἀποβάς, -ᾶσα, -άν)
ἀποβάλλω, I reject	ἀπέβαλον, -λα	ἔχω ἀποβάλει	ἀποβληθείς
ἀποβιβάζω, I land	ἀπεβίβασα	ἔχω ἀποβιβάσει	ἀποβιβασθείς
ἀποβλέπω, I consider	ἀπέβλεψα	ἔχω ἀποβλέψει	
ἀποδεικνύω, I prove	ἀπέδειξα	» ἀποδείξει	ἀποδειχθείς,-γμένος
ἀποκρίνομαι, I answer	ἀπεκρίθην	ἔχω ἀποκριθῇ	ἀποκριθείς
ἀποκτῶ (άω), I acquire	ἀπέκτησα	ἔχω ἀποκτήσει	ἀποκτηθείς
ἀπολαύω, I enjoy	ἀπήλαυσα	ἔχω ἀπολαύσει	ἀπολαυσθείς
ἀπολογοῦμαι, I apologize	ἀπελογήθην	ἔχω ἀπολογηθῇ	ἀπολογηθείς
ἀπομονῶ, -νώνω, I isolate	ἀπεμόνωσα	ἔχω ἀπομονώσει	ἀπομονωθείς
ἀπονέμω, I bestow	ἀπένειμον, -μα	ἔχω ἀπονείμει	ἀπονεμηθείς
ἀπορροφῶ (άω), I absorb	ἀπερρόφησα	ἔχω ἀπορροφήσει	ἀπορροφηθείς
ἀπορῶ (έω), I wonder	ἠπόρησα, ἀπόρησα	ἔχω ἀπορήσει	
ἀποσπῶ (άω), I detach	ἀπέσπασα	ἔχω ἀποσπάσει	ἀποσπασθείς
ἀποσύρω, I withdraw	ἀπέσυρον, -ρα	ἔχω ἀποσύρει	ἀποσυρθείς
ἀποτείνω, I address	ἀπέτεινα	ἔχω ἀποτείνει	ἀποταθείς
ἀποτελῶ (έω), I constitute	ἀπετέλεσα	ἔχω ἀποτελέσει	ἀποτελεσθείς
ἀποτυγχάνω, I fail	ἀπέτυχον, -χα	ἔχω ἀποτύχει	
ἀποφασίζω, I decide	ἀπεφάσισα	ἔχω ἀποφασίσει	ἀποφασισθείς
ἀποφεύγω, I avoid	ἀπέφυγον, -γα	» ἀποφύγει	ἀποφευχθείς,-γμένος
ἀπωθῶ (έω), I repel	ἀπώθησα	ἔχω ἀπωθήσει	ἀπωθηθείς
ἀράσσω, ἀράζω, I moor	ἤραξα, ἄραξα	ἔχω ἀράξει	ἀραχθείς, ἀραγμένος
ἀραιῶ, -ώνω, I thin out	ἠραίωσα, ἀραίωσα	ἔχω ἀραιώσει	ἀραιωθείς
ἀργῶ (έω), I am late	ἤργησα, ἄργησα	ἔχω ἀργήσει	
ἀρέσκω, ἀρέσω, I please	ἤρεσα, ἄρεσα	ἔχω ἀρέσει	ἀρεσθείς
ἀριθμῶ (έω), I number	ἠρίθμησα, ἀρί-	ἔχω ἀριθμήσει	ἀριθμηθείς
ἀρκῶ (έω), I suffice	ἤρκεσα, ἄρκεσα	ἔχω ἀρκέσει	ἀρκεσθείς
ἁρμόζω, I fit	ἥρμοσα, ἅρμοσα	ἔχω ἁρμόσει	ἁρμοσθείς
ἀρνοῦμαι (έομαι), I deny	ἠρνήθην, ἀρνήθηκα	ἔχω ἀρνηθῇ	ἀρνηθείς
ἁρπάζω, I snatch	ἥρπασα, ἅρπαξα	ἔχω ἁρπάσει	ἁρπασθείς
ἀρρωστῶ,-ταίνω, I fall sick	ἀρρώστησα	ἔχω ἀρρωστήσει	
ἀρχίζω, I begin	ἤρχισα, ἄρχισα	ἔχω ἀρχίσει	ἀρχισθείς
ἀσθενῶ (έω), I am ill	ἠσθένησα	ἔχω ἀσθενήσει	

PRESENT	AORIST	PERFECT	PAST PARTICIPLE PASSIVE
ἀσκῶ (έω), I train	ἤσκησα	ἔχω ἀσκήσει	ἀσκηθείς
ἀσπάζομαι, I kiss	ἠσπάσθην	ἔχω ἀσπασθῆ	ἀσπασθείς
ἀστράπτει, it lightens	ἤστραψε, ἄστραψε	ἔχει ἀστράψει	
ἀσχολοῦμαι, I am occupied	ἠσχολήθην,ἀσχολή-	ἔχω ἀσχοληθῆ	ἀσχοληθείς
ἀτακτῶ (έω), I misbehave	ἠτάκτησα, ἀτάκ-	ἔχω ἀτακτήσει	
ἀτυχῶ(έω), I have ill luck	ἠτύχησα, ἀτύχησα	ἔχω ἀτυχήσει	
αὐξάνω, I increase, I grow	ηὔξησα, αὔξησα	ἔχω αὐξήσει	αὐξηθείς,ηὐξημένος
ἀφαιρῶ(έω), I take away	ἀφήρεσα,ἀφαίρεσα	» ἀφαιρέσει	-ρεθείς,ἀφῃρημένος
ἀφηγοῦμαι(έομαι),I relate	ἀφηγήθην	ἔχω ἀφηγηθῆ	ἀφηγηθείς
ἀφιερῶ, -ρώνω, I dedicate	ἀφιέρωσα	ἔχω ἀφιερώσει	ἀφιερωθείς
ἀφίνω, I leave	ἄφισα,ἄφησα,ἀφῆκα	ἔχω ἀφήσει	ἀφεθείς,ἀφημένος
ἀφορῶ (άω), I concern	ἀπέϐλεψα	ἔχω ἀποϐλέψει	
ἀφοσιοῦμαι, I am devoted	ἀφωσιώθην,-θηκα	ἔχω ἀφοσιωθῆ	ἀφοσιωθείς
ἀφρίζω, I froth, I foam	ἤφρισα, ἄφρισα	ἔχω ἀφρίσει	ἀφρισθείς,-σμένος
ἀψηφῶ (έω), I defy	ἠψήφησα,ἀψήφησα	ἔχω ἀψηφήσει	ἀψηφηθείς

Β

βαδίζω, I walk	ἐϐάδισα	ἔχω βαδίσει	
βαίνω, I go on	ἔϐην	ἔχω βῆ	(βάς, βᾶσα, βάν)
βάζω, βάνω, I put	ἔϐαλα	ἔχω ϐάλει	βαλθείς, βαλμένος
βάλλω, I put	ἔϐαλον, ἔϐαλα	ἔχω ϐάλει	ϐληθείς, ϐεϐλημένος
βαπτίζω, I baptize	ἐϐάπτισα	ἔχω ϐαπτίσει	ϐαπτισθείς
βαρύνω, I burden, I weigh	ἐϐάρυνα	ἔχω ϐαρύνει	βαρυνθείς
ϐαρῶ (άω), I beat	ἐϐάρεσα	ἔχω ϐαρέσει	ϐαρεθείς
βασίζω, I base	ἐϐάσισα	ἔχω ϐασίσει	ϐασισθείς
βασιλεύω, I reign	ἐϐασίλευσα	ἔχω ϐασιλεύσει	ϐασιλευθείς
βασκαίνω, I bewitch	ἐϐάσκανα	ἔχω ϐασκάνει	ϐασκανθείς,-αμένος
βαστάζω, I carry	ἐϐάστασα	» ϐαστάσει	ϐασταχθείς,-γμένος
βάφω, I dye	ἔϐαψα	ἔχω ϐάψει	ϐαφείς, ϐαμμένος
βγάζω, I put out	ἔϐγαλα	ἔχω ϐγάλει	ϐγαλθείς,ϐγαλμένος
βγαίνω, I go out	ἐϐγῆκα	ἔχω ϐγῆ, ἔχω ἔϐγη	ϐγαλμένος
βεϐαιῶ, -ώνω, I assure	ἐϐεϐαίωσα	ἔχω ϐεϐαιώσει	ϐεϐαιωθείς
βιάζω, I force	ἐϐίασα	ἔχω ϐιάσει	ϐιασθείς
βλάπτω, I harm	ἔϐλαψα	ἔχω ϐλάψει	ϐλαϐείς,-αμμένος
βλαστάνω, I grow, I sprout	ἐϐλάστησα	ἔχω ϐλαστήσει	
βλασφημῶ (έω), I curse	ἐϐλασφήμησα	ἔχω ϐλασφημήσει	ϐλασφημηθείς
βλέπω, I see, I look	εἶδον, εἶδα	ἔχω ἴδει or ἰδῆ	ὁραθείς,ἰδωμένος
βοηθῶ (έω), I help	ἐϐοήθησα	ἔχω ϐοηθήσει	ϐοηθηθείς
βόσκω, I pasture, I graze	ἐϐόσκησα	ἔχω ϐοσκήσει	ϐοσκηθείς
βουλλώνω, I seal	ἐϐούλλωσα	ἔχω ϐουλλώσει	ϐουλλωθείς
βουτῶ (άω), I dip	ἐϐούτησα	ἔχω ϐουτήσει	ϐουτηθείς
βοῶ (έω), I shout, I roar	ἐϐόησα	ἔχω ϐοήσει	
βραδύνω, I am late	ἐϐράδυνα	ἔχω ϐραδύνει	ϐραδυνθείς
βράζω, I boil	ἔϐρασα	ἔχω ϐράσει	ϐρασθείς
βρέχω, I wet	ἔϐρεξα	ἔχω ϐρέξει	ϐραχείς, ϐρεγμένος
βροντῶ (άω), I thunder	ἐϐρόντησα	ἔχω ϐροντήσει	
βρωμῶ (άω), I stink	ἐϐρώμησα	ἔχω ϐρωμήσει	ϐρωμισμένος

Γ

γελῶ (άω), I laugh	ἐγέλασα	ἔχω γελάσει	γελασθείς
γεμίζω, I fill	ἐγέμισα	ἔχω γεμίσει	γεμισθείς
γεννῶ (άω), I give birth	ἐγέννησα	ἔχω γεννήσει	γεννηθείς
γέρνω, I lean, I incline	ἔγυρα	ἔχω γύρει	γερμένος,γυρμένος
γίνομαι, I become	ἔγινα, ἔγεινα	ἔχω γίνει	γινωμένος
γλύφω, γλείφω, I lick	ἔγλειψα, ἔγλυψα	ἔχω γλύψει	γλυφθείς,-υμμένος

PRESENT	AORIST	PERFECT	PAST PARTICIPLE PASSIVE
γνωρίζω, I know; I advise	ἐγνώρισα	ἔχω γνωρίσει	γνωρισθείς
γράφω, I write	ἔγραψα	ἔχω γράψει	γραφείς,-αμμένος
γυμνάζω, I exercise	ἐγύμνασα	ἔχω γυμνάσει	γυμνασθείς
γυρίζω, I turn	ἐγύρισα	ἔχω γυρίσει	γυρισθείς
	Δ		
δαγκάνω, I bite	ἐδάγκασα	ἔχω δαγκάσει	δαγκασθείς
δακρύω, δακρύζω, I weep	ἐδάκρυσα	ἔχω δακρύσει	δακρυσμένος
δανείζω, I lend	ἐδάνεισα	ἔχω δανείσει	δανεισθείς
δαπανῶ (άω), I spend	ἐδαπάνησα	ἔχω δαπανήσει	δαπανηθείς
δεικνύω, I show	ἔδειξα	ἔχω δείξει	δειχθείς, (δε) δειγμένος
δειπνῶ (έω), I take supper	ἐδείπνησα	ἔχω δειπνήσει	
δένω, I tie, I bind	ἔδεσα	ἔχω δέσει	δεθείς, (δε) δεμένος
δέχομαι, I accept, I receive	ἐδέχθην, ἐδέχθηκα	ἔχω δεχθῆ	δεχθείς, (δε) δεγμένος
δηλῶ, δηλώνω, I declare	ἐδήλωσα	ἔχω δηλώσει	δηλωθείς
δημοσιεύω, I publish	ἐδημοσίευσα	ἔχω δημοσιεύσει	δημοσιευθείς
διαβάζω, I read	ἐδιάβασα	ἔχω διαβάσει	διαβασθείς
διαβαίνω, I pass	διέβην, διάβηκα	ἔχω διαβῆ	(διαβάς)
διάγω, I live	διήγαγον	ἔχω διαγάγει	
διαδίδω, I spread	διέδοσα, διέδωσα	ἔχω διαδόσει	διαδοθείς
διαθέτω, I dispose	διέθεσα	ἔχω διαθέσει	διατεθείς,-θειμένος
διαιρῶ (έω), I divide	διήρεσα, ἐδιαίρεσα	» διαιρέσει	διαιρεθείς,διηρημένος
διακόπτω, I interrupt	διέκοψα, διάκοψα	»διακόψει	διακοπείς,-κεκομμένος
διακρίνω, I distinguish	διέκρινα	»διακρίνει	διακριθείς,-κεκριμένος
διαλέγω, I select	ἐδιάλεξα	» διαλέξει	διαλεχθείς,-λεγμένος
διαλύω, I dissolve	διέλυσα, ἐδιάλυσα	ἔχω διαλύσει	διαλυθείς
διαπλέω, I sail through	διέπλευσα	ἔχω διαπλεύσει	διαπλευσθείς
διαρκῶ (έω), I last	διήρκεσα,διάρκεσα	ἔχω διαρκέσει	
διασκεδάζω, I amuse	διεσκέδασα,ἐδιασκ-	ἔχω διασκεδάσει	διασκεδασθείς
διασπῶ (άω), I break	διέσπασα	ἔνω διασπάσει	διασπασθείς
διασταυρῶ, -ρώνω, I cross	διεσταύρωσα, **ἐδια-**	ἔχω διασταυρώσει	διασταυρωθείς
διατάσσω, I order	διέταξα, ἐδιάταξα	» διατάξει	διαταχθείς,-αγμένος
διατελῶ (έω), I am, I remain	διετέλεσα	ἔχω διατελέσει	
διατηρῶ (έω), I keep	διετήρησα	ἔχω διατηρήσει	διατηρηθείς
διαφέρω, I differ	διέφερον, διέφερα	ἔχω διαφέρει	
διαφωνῶ (έω), I disagree	διεφώνησα	ἔχω διαφωνήσει	
διαψεύδω, I give the lie	διέψευσα	ἔχω διαψεύσει	διαψευσθείς
διδάσκω, I teach	ἐδίδαξα	ἔχω διδάξει	διδαχθείς,-αγμένος
δίδω, δίνω, I give	ἔδοσα, ἔδωσα	» δόσει,δώσει	δοθείς, (δε) δομένος
διεγείρω, I rouse, I incite	διήγειρα	ἔχω διεγείρει	διεγερθείς
διευθετῶ (έω), I arrange	διηυθέτησα, διευθέ-	ἔχω διευθετήσει	διευθετηθείς
διευθύνω, I direct	διηύθυνα, διεύθυνα	ἔχω διευθύνει	διευθυνθείς
διηγοῦμαι (έομαι), I relate	διηγήθην,διηγήθηκα	ἔχω διηγηθῆ	διηγηθείς
δικάζω, I judge, I try	ἐδίκασα	ἔχω δικάσει	δικασθείς
δικαιῶ, -ώνω, I do justice	ἐδικαίωσα	ἔχω δικαιώσει	δικαιωθείς
διοικῶ (έω), I govern	διώκησα, διοίκησα	ἔχω διοικήσει	διοικηθείς
διοργανῶ,-ώνω, I organize	διωργάνωσα	ἔχω διοργανώσει	διοργανωθείς
διορθῶ, -θώνω, I correct	διώρθωσα,ἐδιόρθω-	ἔχω διορθώσει	διορθωθείς
διπλώνω, I fold, I wrap	ἐδίπλωσα	ἔχω διπλώσει	διπλωθείς
διστάζω, I hesitate	ἐδίστασα	ἔχω διστάσει	
διψῶ (άω), I am thirsty	ἐδίψησα, ἐδίψασα	ἔχω διψάσει	διψασμένος
διώκω, διώχνω, I chase	ἐδίωξα, ἔδιωξα	ἔχω διώξει	διωχθείς, διωγμένος
δοκιμάζω, I try	ἐδοκίμασα	ἔχω δοκιμάσει	δοκιμασθείς
δοξάζω, I glorify	ἐδόξασα	ἔχω δοξάσει	δοξασθείς

PRESENT	AORIST	PERFECT	PAST PARTICIPLE PASSIVE
δουλεύω, I work; I serve	ἐδούλευσα	ἔχω δουλεύσει	δουλευθείς
δραπετεύω, I escape	ἐδραπέτευσα	ἔχω δραπετεύσει	
δρέπω, I pick, I gather	ἔδρεψα	ἔχω δρέψει	δρεφθείς
δρῶ (δράω), I act, I do	ἔδρασα	ἔχω δράσει	δρασθείς,δεδραμένος
δύναμαι, I can	ἠδυνήθην,ἠμπόρεσα	ἔχω δυνηθῆ	δυνηθείς
δυστυχῶ(έω),I have ill luck	ἐδυστύχησα	ἔχω δυστυχήσει	
δύω, I set, I sink	ἔδυσα	ἔχω δύσει	δυθείς
δωρῶ (έω), I present	ἐδώρησα	ἔχω δωρήσει	δωρηθείς

E

ἐγγίζω, I touch	ἤγγισα	ἔχω ἐγγίσει	ἐγγισθείς
ἐγγυῶμαι(άο),I guarantee	ἠγγυήθην,ἐγγυήθηκα	ἔχω ἐγγυηθῆ	ἐγγυηθείς
ἐγείρω, I raise	ἤγειρα	ἔχω ἐγείρει	ἐγερθείς
ἐγκρίνω, I approve	ἐνέκρινα	» ἐγκρίνει	ἐγκριθείς,-κεκριμένος
εἰδοποιῶ (έω), I notify	εἰδοποίησα	ἔχω εἰδοποιήσει	εἰδοποιηθείς
εἰσάγω, I introduce	εἰσήγαγον, -γα	» εἰσαγάγει	εἰσαχθείς,-σηγμένος
εἰσέρχομαι, I come in	εἰσῆλθον, εἰσῆλθα	ἔχω εἰσέλθει	(εἰσελθών)
εἰσπράττω, I collect	εἰσέπραξα,εἴσπραξα	» εἰσπράξει	εἰσπραχθείς,-γμένος
ἐκβάλλω, I put or take out	ἐξέβαλον, -λα	ἔχω ἐκβάλει	ἐκβληθείς
ἐκδικῶ (έω), I avenge	ἐξεδίκησα,ἐκδίκησα	ἔχω ἐκδικήσει	ἐκδικηθείς
ἐκδιώκω, I chase out	ἐξεδίωξα	ἔχω ἐκδιώξει	ἐκδιωχθείς,-γμένος
ἐκλέγω, I choose	ἐξέλεξα, ἔκλεξα	ἔχω ἐκλέξει	ἐκλεχθείς,-εγείς
ἐκπαιδεύω, I educate	ἐξεπαίδευσα	ἔχω ἐκπαιδεύσει	ἐκπαιδευθείς
ἐκπληρῶ, -ώνω, I fulfill	ἐξεπλήρωσα,ἐκπλή-	ἔχω ἐκπληρώσει	ἐκπληρωθείς
ἐκπλήττω,-ήσσω,I surprise	ἐξέπληξα	ἔχω ἐκπλήξει	ἐκπλαγείς
ἐκσπῶ (άω), I burst out	ἐξέσπασα	ἔχω ἐκσπάσει	
ἐκτείνω, I extend	ἐξέτεινα, ἔκτεινα	» ἐκτείνει	ἐκταθείς,ἐκτεταμένος
ἐκτελῶ (έω), I perform	ἐξετέλεσα,ἐκτέλεσα	ἔχω ἐκτελέσει	ἐκτελεσθείς
ἐκτιμῶ (άω), I value	ἐξετίμησα,ἐκτίμησα	ἔχω ἐκτιμήσει	ἐκτιμηθείς
ἐκφράζω, I express	ἐξέφρασα, ἔκφρασα	ἔχω ἐκφράσει	ἐκφρασθείς
ἐλαττῶ, -ώνω, I diminish	ἠλάττωσα,ἐλάττωσα	ἔχω ἐλαττώσει	ἐλαττωθείς
ἐλευθερῶ, -ώνω, I free	ἠλευθέρωσα, ἐλευ-	ἔχω ἐλευθερώσει	ἐλευθερωθείς
ἐλεῶ (έω), I have mercy	ἠλέησα, ἐλέησα	ἔχει ἐλεήσει	ἐλεηθείς
ἐλπίζω, I hope	ἤλπισα, ἔλπισα	ἔχω ἐλπίσει	ἐλπισθείς
ἐμβαίνω, I enter, I go in	ἐμβῆκα, μπῆκα	ἔχω ἔμβει, ἔχω μπῆ	(ἐμβάς)
ἐμβάλλω, I put in	ἐνέβαλον, ἐνέβαλα	ἔχω ἐμβάλει	ἐμβληθείς
ἐμπαίζω, I mock	ἐνέπαιξα, ἔμπαιξα	ἔχω ἐμπαίξει	ἐμπαιχθείς,-γμένος
ἐμπήγω, I drive in	ἐνέπηξα, ἔμπηξα	ἔχω ἐμπήξει	ἐμπηχθείς,-γμένος
ἐμπίπτω, I fall in.	ἐνέπεσα	ἔχω ἐμπέσει	(ἐμπεσών)
ἐμπνέω, I inspire	ἐνέπνευσα, ἔμπνευ-	ἔχω ἐμπνεύσει	ἐμπνευσθείς
ἐμποδίζω, I prevent	ἠμπόδισα,ἐμπόδισα	ἔχω ἐμποδίσει	ἐμποδισθείς
ἐμφανίζω, I show, I present	ἐνεφάνισα, ἐμφά-	ἔχω ἐμφανίσει	ἐμφανισθείς
ἐμφυσῶ (άω), I blow in	ἐνεφύσησα, ἐμφύ-	ἔχω ἐμφυσήσει	ἐμφυσηθείς
ἐμῶ (έω), I vomit	ἤμεσα, ἔμεσα	ἔχω ἐμέσει	ἐμεθείς,-εσμένος
ἐνάγω, I sue	ἐνήγαγον, ἐνήγαγα	ἔχω ἐναγάγει	ἐναχθείς,-ηγμένος
ἐνδιαφέρω, I concern	ἐνδιέφερον,-ρα	ἔχω ἐνδιαφέρει	ἐνδιαφερθείς
ἐνδίδω, I give in	ἐνέδοσα, ἔνδωσα	ἔχω ἐνδόσει or ἐνδώσει	
ἐνδύω, I dress	ἐνέδυσα, ἔνδυσα	ἔνω ἐνδύσει	ἐνδυθείς,ἐνδεδυμένος
ἐνεργῶ (έω), I act	ἐνήργησα,ἐνέργησα	ἔχω ἐνεργήσει	ἐνεργηθείς
ἐνθυμοῦμαι, I remember	ἐνεθυμήθην, ἐνθυ-	ἔχω ἐνθυμηθῆ	ἐνθυμηθείς
ἐνισχύω, I strengthen	ἐνίσχυσα	ἔχω ἐνισχύσει	ἐνισχυθείς
ἐννοῶ (έω), I understand	ἐνόησα	ἔχω ἐννοήσει	ἐννοηθείς
ἐνοχλῶ (έω), I annoy	ἠνόχλησα,ἐνόχλησα	ἔχω ἐνοχλήσει	ἐνοχληθείς
ἐντείνω, I strain, I exert	ἐνέτεινα, ἔντεινα	» ἐντείνει	ἐνταθείς,ἐντεταμένος

PRESENT	AORIST	PERFECT	PAST PARTICIPLE PASSIVE
ἐνσκήπτω, I fall upon	ἐνέσκηψα	ἔχω ἐνσκήψει	
ἐντρέπομαι, I am ashamed	ἐντράπην, -πηκα	ἔχω ἐντραπῆ	ἐντραπείς
ἑνῶ, ἑνώνω, ἑνόνω, I unite	ἥνωσα, ἕνωσα	ἔχω ἑνώσει	ἑνωθείς, ἡνωμένος
ἐξάγω, I take out, I export	ἐξήγαγον, ἐξήγαγα	ἔχω ἐξαγάγει	ἐξαχθείς,-ηγμένος
ἐντυπῶ, -ώνω, I impress	ἐνετύπωσα, ἐντύ-	ἔχω ἐντυπώσει	ἐντυπωθείς
ἐξαίρω, I exalt; I stress	ἐξῆρα	ἔχω ἐξάρει	ἐξαρθείς,ἐξηρμένος
ἐξαντλῶ (έω), I exhaust	ἐξήντλησα, ἐξάν-	ἔχω ἐξαντλήσει	ἐξαντληθείς
ἐξελίσσω, I unfold	ἐξείλιξα	ἔχω ἐξελίξει	ἐξελιχθείς,-ιγμένος
ἐξετάζω, I examine	ἐξήτασα, ἐξέτασα	ἔχω ἐξετάσει	ἐξετασθείς
ἐξηγῶ (έω), I explain	ἐξήγησα	ἔχω ἐξηγήσει	ἐξηγηθείς
ἐξογκῶ, -ώνω, I swell	ἐξώγκωσα	ἔχω ἐξογκώσει	ἐξογκωθείς
ἐξοδεύω, I spend	ἐξώδευσα	ἔχω ἐξοδεύσει	ἐξοδευθείς
ἐξολοθρεύω, I exterminate	ἐξωλόθρευσα	ἔχω ἐξολοθρεύσει	ἐξολοθρευθείς
ἐξοφλῶ (έω), I pay off	ἐξώφλησα	ἔχω ἐξοφλήσει	ἐξοφληθείς
ἐξυπνῶ (έω), I wake	ἐξύπνησα	ἔχω ἐξυπνήσει	ἐξυπνηθείς
ἑορτάζω, I celebrate	ἑώρτασα	ἔχω ἑορτάσει	ἑορτασθείς
ἐπαινῶ (έω), I praise	ἐπήνεσα, ἐπαίνεσα	ἔχω ἐπαινέσει	ἐπαινεθείς
ἐπιβαίνω, I get upon, I ride	ἐπέβην	ἔχω ἐπιβῆ	(ἐπιβάς)
ἐπιβάλλω, I impose	ἐπέβαλον, ἐπέβαλα	ἔχω ἐπιβάλει	ἐπιβληθείς
ἐπιδρῶ (άω), I influence	ἐπέδρασα	ἔχω ἐπιδράσει	
ἐπιθέτω, I lay on, I apply	ἐπέθεσα	» ἐπιθέσει	ἐπιτεθείς,-τεθειμένος
ἐπιθεωρῶ (έω), I inspect	ἐπεθεώρησα, ἐπιθ-	ἔχω ἐπιθεωρήσει	ἐπιθεωρηθείς
ἐπιθυμῶ (έω), I wish	ἐπεθύμησα, ἐπιθύμ-	ἔχω ἐπιθυμήσει	ἐπιθυμηθείς
ἐπιμένω, I insist	ἐπέμεινα, ἐπίμεινα	ἔχω ἐπιμείνει	
ἐπισκέπτομαι, I visit	ἐπεσκέφθην	ἔχω ἐπισκεφθῆ	ἐπισκεφθείς
ἐπιστρέφω, I return	ἐπέστρεψα	ἔχω ἐπιστρέψει	ἐπιστραφείς
ἐπιτρέπω, I allow	ἐπέτρεψα	» ἐπιτρέψει	ἐπιτραπείς,-αμμένος
ἐπιτυγχάνω, I succeed	ἐπέτυχον, ἐπέτυχα	ἔχω ἐπιτύχει	ἐπιτυχημένος
ἐργάζομαι, I work	εἰργάσθην	ἔχω ἐργασθῆ	ἐργασθείς
ἐρεθίζω, I irritate	ἠρέθισα, ἐρέθισα	ἔχω ἐρεθίσει	ἐρεθισθείς
ἐρευνῶ (άω), I search	ἠρεύνησα,ἐρεύνησα	ἔχω ἐρευνήσει	ἐρευνηθείς
ἔρχομαι, I come	ἦλθον, ἦλθα	ἔχω ἔλθει	(ἐλθών)
ἐρωτῶ (άω), I ask	ἠρώτησα, ἐρώτησα	ἔχω ἐρωτήσει	ἐρωτηθείς
ἑτοιμάζω, I prepare	ἡτοίμασα,ἑτοίμασα	ἔχω ἑτοιμάσει	ἑτοιμασθείς
εὐκαιρῶ (έω), I have time	ηὐκαίρησα, εὐκαί-	ἔχω εὐκαιρήσει	
εὐκολύνω, I facilitate	ηὐκόλυνα,εὐκόλυνα	ἔχω εὐκολύνει	εὐκολυνθείς
εὐλογῶ (έω), I bless	εὐλόγησα	ἔχω εὐλογήσει	εὐλογηθείς
εὐνοῶ (έω), I favor	ηὐνόησα, εὐνόησα	ἔχω εὐνοήσει	εὐνοηθείς
εὑρίσκω, I find	εὗρον, ηὗρα, εὕρηκα	ἔχω εὕρει or εὑρῆ	εὑρεθείς
εὐσπλαγχνίζομαι, I pity	εὐσπαγχνίσθην	»εὐσπλαγχνισθῆ	εὐσπλαγχνισθείς
εὐτυχῶ (έω), I prosper	ηὐτύχησα,εὐτύχησα	ἔχω εὐτυχήσει	
εὐφραίνω, I delight	ηὔφρανα, εὔφρανα	ἔχω εὐφράνει	εὐφρανθείς
εὐχαριστῶ (έω), I thank	εὐχαρίστησα, ηὐχα-	ἔχω εὐχαριστήσει	εὐχαριστηθείς
εὔχομαι, I wish	ηὐχήθην, εὐχήθηκα	ἔχω εὐχηθῆ	εὐχηθείς
εὐωδιάζω, I smell sweetly	εὐωδίασα	ἔχω εὐωδιάσει	εὐωδιασθείς
ἐφαρμόζω, I apply	ἐφήρμοσα,ἐφάρμοσα	ἔχω ἐφαρμόσει	ἐφαρμοσθείς
ἐφιστῶ (άω), I direct, I fix	ἐπέστησα	ἔχω ἐπιστήσει	ἐπιστηθείς
ἔχω, I have. (imp.εἶχον,-α)	ἔσχον, εἶχα	ἔχω λάβει	(σχεθείς)

Z

ζαλίζω, I make dizzy	ἐζάλισα	ἔχω ζαλίσει	ζαλισθείς
ζαρώνω, I wrinkle	ἐζάρωσα	ἔχω ζαρώσει	ζαρωθείς
ζεσταίνω, I heat, I warm	ἐζέστανα	ἔχω ζεστάνει	ζεσταθείς
ζηλεύω, I envy	ἐζήλευσα	ἔχω ζηλεύσει	ζηλευθείς

PRESENT	AORIST	PERFECT	PAST PARTICIPLE PASSIVE
ζημιῶ, -ώνω, I damage	ἐζημίωσα	ἔχω ζημιώσει	ζημιωθείς
ζητῶ (έω), I seek	ἐζήτησα	ἔχω ζητήσει	ζητηθείς
ζυγίζω, I weigh	ἐζύγισα	ἔχω ζυγίσει	ζυγισθείς
ζυμώνω, I knead	ἐζύμωσα	ἔχω ζυμώσει	ζυμωθείς
ζῶ (ζάω),I live;(imp.**ἔζων**)	ἔζησα	ἔχω ζήσει	(ζήσας)
ζώνω, I girdle	ἔζωσα	ἔχω ζώσει	ζωσθείς
	Η		
ἡγοῦμαι, I lead	ἡγήθην	ἔχω ἡγηθῆ	ἡγηθείς
ἠμπορῶ (έω), I can, I may	ἠμπόρεσα	ἔχω ἠμπορέσει	δυνηθείς
ἠρεμῶ (έω), I am calm	ἠρέμησα	ἔχω ἠρεμήσει	
ἡσυχάζω, I am quiet	ἡσύχασα	ἔχω ἡσυχάσει	ἡσυχασθείς
ἡττῶμαι, I am defeated	ἡττήθην	ἔχω ἡττηθῆ	ἡττηθείς
ἠχῶ (έω), I echo, I sound	ἤχησα	ἔχω ἠχήσει	ἠχηθείς
	Θ		
θάλλω, I bloom, I flourish	ἀνέθηλα	ἔχω θάλει or θαλλήσει	
θάπτω, I bury	ἔθαψα	ἔχω θάψει	ταφείς, (τε)θαμμένος
θαυμάζω, I admire	ἐθαύμασα	ἔχω θαυμάσει	θαυμασθείς
θέλγω, I charm	ἔθελξα	ἔχω θέλξει	θελχθείς
θέλω, I want, I wish	ἠθέλησα	ἔχω θελήσει	
θερμαίνω, I warm, I heat	ἐθέρμανα	ἔχω θερμάνει	θερμανθείς
θέτω, I put	ἔθεσα	ἔχω θέσει	τεθείς, τεθειμένος
θεωρῶ (έω), I consider	ἐθεώρησα	ἔχω θεωρήσει	θεωρηθείς
θίγω, I touch	ἔθιξα	ἔχω θίξει	θιχθείς, θιγμένος
θλίβω, I squeeze, I afflict	ἔθλιψα	ἔχω θλίψει	θλιβείς,(τε)θλιμμένος
θρηνῶ (έω), I mourn	ἐθρήνησα	ἔχω θρηνήσει	θρηνηθείς
θραύω, I break	ἔθραυσα	ἔχω θραύσει	θραυσθείς
θυμώνω, I get angry	ἐθύμωσα	ἔχω θυμώσει	θυμωθείς
	Ι		
ἱδρώνω, I sweat	ἵδρωσα	ἔχω ἱδρώσει	ἱδρωμένος
ἱδρύω, I found	ἵδρυσα	ἔχω ἱδρύσει	ἱδρυθείς
ἱππεύω, I ride	ἵππευσα	ἔχω ἱππεύσει	ἱππευθείς
ἵσταμαι, I stand, I stop	ἐστάθην	ἔχω σταθῆ	σταθείς, στημένος
ἰσχύω, I am in force	ἴσχυσα	ἔχω ἰσχύσει	(ἰσχυθείς)
	Κ		
καθαρίζω, I clean	ἐκαθάρισα	ἔχω καθαρίσει	καθαρισθείς
κάθημαι, I sit	ἐκάθησα	ἔχω καθήσει	καθισμένος
καθίσταμαι, I become	κατέστην	ἔχω καταστῆ	καταστάς,-σταθείς
καθιστῶ, I render	κατέστησα	ἔχω καταστήσει	κατασταθείς
καίω, I burn	ἔκαυσα	ἔχω καύσει	καείς, καμμένος
καλύπτω, I cover	ἐκάλυψα	» καλύψει	καλυφθείς,-υμμένος
καλῶ, I call	ἐκάλεσα	ἔχω καλέσει	κληθείς,καλεσμένος
κάμνω, I make	ἔκαμον, ἔκαμα	ἔχω κάμει	καμωμένος
κάμπτω, I bend	ἔκαμψα	» κάμψει	καμφθείς, (κε)καμμένος
κανονίζω, I regulate	ἐκανόνισα	ἔχω κανονίσει	κανονισθείς
καπνίζω, I smoke	ἐκάπνισα	ἔχω καπνίσει	καπνισθείς
καρφώνω, I nail	ἐκάρφωσα	ἔχω καρφώσει	καρφωθείς
καταβαίνω, I descend	**κατέβην,κατέβηκα**	ἔχω καταβῆ	(καταβάς)
καταβάλλω, I put down	κατέβαλον, -**βαλα**	ἔχω καταβάλει	καταβληθείς
καταγράφω, I list	κατέγραψα	ἔχω καταγράψει	καταγραφείς
κατακτῶ (άω), I conquer	κατέκτησα	ἔχω κατακτήσει	κατακτηθείς
καταντῶ (άω), I become	κατήντησα	ἔχω καταντήσει	
καταπαύω, I cease, I stop	κατέπαυσα	ἔχω καταπαύσει	
καταπιέζω, I oppress	κατεπίεσα	ἔχω καταπιέσει	καταπιεσθείς

PRESENT	AORIST	PERFECT	PAST PARTICIPLE PASSIVE
καταπίνω, I swallow	κατέπιον, κατάπια	ἔχω καταπίει	καταποθείς
καταργῶ (έω), I abolish	κατήργησα	ἔχω καταργήσει	καταργηθείς
καταρτίζω, I form	κατήρτισα	ἔχω καταρτίσει	καταρτισθείς
κατασκευάζω, I make	κατεσκεύασα	» κατασκευάσει	κατασκευασθείς
καταστρέφω, I destroy	κατέστρεψα	» καταστρέψει	καταστραφείς
κατάσχω, I seize	κατέσχον,-σχεσα	ἔχω κατασχέσει	κατασχεθείς
καταφεύγω, I take refuge	κατέφυγον, -φυγα	ἔχω καταφύγει	
καταχρῶμαι (άο), I abuse	κατεχράσθην, -ηκα	ἔχω καταχρασθῇ	καταχρασθείς
κατέχω, I possess	κατέσχον	ἔχω καθέξει	
κατηγορῶ (έω), I accuse	κατηγόρησα	ἔχω κατηγορήσει	κατηγορηθείς
κατηχῶ (έω), I catechize	κατήχουν, -χοῦσα	ἔχω κατηχήσει	κατηχηθείς
κατοικῶ (έω), I reside	κατώκησα, κατοίκ-	ἔχω κατοικήσει	κατοικηθείς
κατορθῶ, -ώνω, I achieve	κατώρθωσα	ἔχω κατορθώσει	κατορθωθείς
καυχῶμαι(άομαι), I boast	ἐκαυχήθην, -θηκα	ἔχω καυχηθῇ	καυχηθείς
κεῖμαι, I lie	(imp. ἐκείμην).		
κελαδῶ(έω), I sing, I chirp	ἐκελάδησα	ἔχω κελαδήσει	
κεντῶ (άω), I prick	ἐκέντησα	ἔχω κεντήσει	κεντηθείς
κερδίζω, I gain	ἐκέρδισα	ἔχω κερδίσει	κερδισθείς
κερνῶ (άω), I treat	ἐκέρασα	ἔχω κεράσει	κερασθείς
κηδεύω, I bury	ἐκήδευσα	ἔχω κηδεύσει	κηδευθείς
κηρύττω, I proclaim	ἐκήρυξα	ἔχω κηρύξει	κηρυχθείς,-υγμένος
κινδυνεύω, I am in danger	ἐκινδύνευσα	ἔχω κινδυνεύσει	
κινῶ (έω), I move	ἐκίνησα	ἔχω κινήσει	κινηθείς
κλαίω, I weep	ἔκλαυσα, ἔκλαψα	ἔχω κλαύσει	κλαυσθείς
κλειδώνω, I lock	ἐκλείδωσα	ἔχω κλειδώσει	κλειδωθείς
κλείω, κλείνω, I close	ἔκλεισα	ἔχω κλείσει	κλεισθείς,κλεισμένος
κλέπτω, I steal	ἔκλεψα	ἔχω κλέψει	κλαπείς, κλεμμένος
κλίνω, I bend, I incline	ἔκλινον, ἔκλινα	ἔχω κλίνει	κλιθείς, κεκλιμένος
κλονίζω, I shake	ἐκλόνισα	ἔχω κλονίσει	κλονισθείς
κοιμῶμαι (άομαι), I sleep	ἐκοιμήθην, -ήθηκα	ἔχω κοιμηθῇ	κοιμηθείς
κοινωνῶ,έω I communicate	ἐκοινώνησα	ἔχω κοινωνήσει	κοινωνηθείς
κολακεύω, I flatter	ἐκολάκευσα	ἔχω κολακεύσει	κολακευθείς
κολλῶ (άω), I stick	ἐκόλλησα	ἔχω κολλήσει	κολληθείς
κολυμϐῶ (άω), I swim	ἐκολύμϐησα	ἔχω κολυμϐήσει	
κομίζω, I carry	ἐκόμισα	ἔχω κομίσει	κομισθείς
κοπιάζω, I labor	ἐκοπίασα	ἔχω κοπιάσει	
κόπτω, I cut	ἔκοψα	ἔχω κόψει	κοπείς, (κε) κομμένος
κοσμῶ (έω), I adorn	ἐκόσμησα	ἔχω κοσμήσει	κοσμηθείς
κοστίζω, I cost	ἐκόστισα	ἔχω κοστίσει	
κουνῶ (άω), I shake	ἐκούνησα	ἔχω κουνήσει	κουνηθείς
κουράζω, I tire	ἐκούρασα	ἔχω κουράσει	κουρασθείς
κουρεύω, I cut the hair	ἐκούρευσα	ἔχω κουρεύσει	κουρευθείς
κράζω, I call, I cry out	ἔκραξα	ἔχω κράξει	
κρατῶ (έω), I keep, I hold	ἐκράτησα	ἔχω κρατήσει	κρατηθείς
κραυγάζω, I shout, cry out	ἐκραύγασα	ἔχω κραυγάσει	
κρέμαμαι, I hang	ἐκρεμάσθην	ἔχω κρεμασθῇ	κρεμασθείς
κρεμῶ (άω), I hang	ἐκρέμασα	ἔχω κρεμάσει	κρεμασθείς
κρημνίζω, I demolish	ἐκρήμνισα	ἔχω κρημνίσει	κρημνισθείς
κρίνω, I judge	ἔκρινον, ἔκρινα	ἔχω κρίνει	κριθείς, κεκριμένος
κρούω, I knock	ἔκρουσα	ἔχω κρούσει	κρουσθείς
κρύπτω, I hide	ἔκρυψα	ἔχω κρύψει	κρυφθείς, κρυμμένος
κτενίζω, I comb	ἐκτένισα	ἔχω κτενίσει	κτενισθείς
κτίζω, I build	ἔκτισα	ἔχω κτίσει	κτισθείς
κτυπῶ (άω), I beat	ἐκτύπησα	ἔχω κτυπήσει	κτυπηθείς

PRESENT	AORIST	PERFECT	PAST PARTICIPLE PASSIVE
κυβερνῶ (άω), I govern	ἐκυβέρνησα	ἔχω κυβερνήσει	κυβερνηθείς
κυλίω, I roll	ἐκύλισα	ἔχω κυλίσει	κυλισθείς
κυματίζω, I wave	ἐκυμάτισα	ἔχω κυματίσει	
κυνηγῶ (έω), I hunt	ἐκυνήγησα	ἔχω κυνηγήσει	κυνηγηθείς
κύπτω, I stoop	ἔκυψα	ἔχω κύψει	
κυρῶ, κυρώνω, I ratify	ἐκύρωσα	ἔχω κυρώσει	κυρωθείς
κυττάζω, I look	ἐκύτταζα	ἔχω κυττάξει	κυτταχθείς,-γμένος
	Λ		
λαλῶ (έω), I speak	ἐλάλησα	ἔχω λαλήσει	λαληθείς
λαμβάνω, I take	ἔλαβον, ἔλαβα	ἔχω λάβει	ληφθείς, εἰλημμένος
λάμπω, I shine	ἔλαμψα	ἔχω λάμψει	
λατρεύω, I worship	ἐλάτρευσα	ἔχω λατρεύσει	λατρευθείς
λέγω, I say	εἶπον, εἶπα	ἔχω εἴπει	λεχθείς, εἰρημένος
λείπω, I am missing, I fail	ἔλειψα	ἔχω λείψει	λειφθείς
λειτουργῶ (έω), I function	ἐλειτούργησα	ἔχω λειτουργήσει	λειτουργηθείς
λερώνω, I soil	ἐλέρωσα	ἔχω λερώσει	λερωθείς
λευκαίνω, I bleach	ἐλεύκανα	ἔχω λευκάνει	λευκανθείς
λήγω, I end	ἔληξα	ἔχω λήξει	
λησμονῶ (έω), I forget	ἐλησμόνησα	ἔχω λησμονήσει	λησμονηθείς
ληστεύω, I rob	ἐλήστευσα	ἔχω ληστεύσει	ληστευθείς
λογαριάζω, I calculate	ἐλογάριασα	ἔχω λογαριάσει	λογαριασθείς
λογίζομαι, I consider	ἐλογίσθην, -ίσθηκα	ἔχω λογισθῆ	λογισθείς
λούω, I bathe	ἔλουσα	ἔχω λούσει	λουσθείς
λυώνω, I melt	ἔλυωσα	ἔχω λυώσει	λυωθείς
λυπῶ (έω), I grieve	ἐλύπησα	ἔχω λυπήσει	λυπηθείς
λυσσῶ (άω), I rage	ἐλύσσαξα	ἔχω λυσσάξει	λυσσασμένος
	Μ		
μαγειρεύω, I cook	ἐμαγείρευσα	ἔχω μαγειρεύσει	μαγειρευθείς
μαγεύω, I bewitch	ἐμάγευσα	ἔχω μαγεύσει	μαγευθείς
μαδῶ (άω), I pluck	ἐμάδησα	ἔχω μαδήσει	μαδηθείς
μαζεύω, I gather	ἐμάζευσα	ἔχω μαζεύσει	μαζευθείς
μακρύνω, I lengthen	ἐμάκρυνα	ἔχω μακρύνει	μακρυνθείς
μαλάσσω, I soften	ἐμάλαξα	ἔχω μαλάξει	μαλαχθείς,-αγμένος
μαλώνω, I scold	ἐμάλωσα	ἔχω μαλώσει	μαλωθείς
μανθάνω, I learn	ἔμαθον, ἔμαθα	ἔχω μάθει	μαθημένος
μαντεύω, I guess	ἐμάντευσα	ἔχω μαντεύσει	μαντευθείς
μαραίνω, I fade	ἐμάρανα	ἔχω μαράνει	μαρανθείς, -αμένος
μαρτυρῶ (έω), I witness	ἐμαρτύρησα	ἔχω μαρτυρήσει	μαρτυρηθείς
μασσῶ (άω), I chew	ἐμάσσησα	ἔχω μασσήσει	μασσηθείς
ματαιῶ, -ώνω, I frustrate	.ἐματαίωσα	ἔχω ματαιώσει	ματαιωθείς
μαυρίζω, I blacken	ἐμαύρισα	ἔχω μαυρίσει	μαυρισθείς
μεγαλώνω, I grow	ἐμεγάλωσα	ἔχω μεγαλώσει	μεγαλωθείς
μεθῶ (άω), I get drunk	ἐμέθυσα	ἔχω μεθύσει	μεθυσθείς
μειδιῶ (άω), I smile	ἐμειδίασα	ἔχω μειδιάσει	
μελετῶ (άω), I study	ἐμελέτησα	ἔχω μελετήσει	μελετηθείς
μέλλω, I am about to	(imp. ἔμελλον)		
μένω, I remain	ἔμεινα	ἔχω μείνει	
μεριμνῶ (άω), I take care	ἐμερίμνησα	ἔχω μεριμνήσει	μεριμνηθείς
μεταβαίνω, I go	μετέβην	ἔχω μεταβῆ	(μεταβάς)
μεταβάλλω, I change	μετέβαλον, -λα	ἔχω μεταβάλει	μεταβληθείς
μετανοῶ (έω), I repent	μετενόησα, μετανό-	ἔχω μετανοήσει	μετανοημένος
μετριάζω, I moderate	ἐμετρίασα	ἔχω μετριάσει	μετριασθείς
μετρῶ (έω), I measure	ἐμέτρησα	ἔχω μετρήσει	μετρηθείς

PRESENT	AORIST	PERFECT	PAST PARTICIPLE PASSIVE
μηνύω, I send word	ἐμήνυσα	ἔχω μηνύσει	μηνυθείς
μιμοῦμαι(έομαι), I imitate	ἐμιμήθην, -μίθηκα	ἔχω μιμηθῇ	μιμηθείς
μισθῶ, -ώνω, I hire	ἐμίσθωσα	ἔχω μισθώσει	μισθωθείς
μισῶ (έω), I hate	ἐμίσησα	ἔχω μισήσει	μισηθείς
μοιράζω, I divide	ἐμοίρασα	ἔχω μοιράσει	μοιρασθείς
μολύνω, I pollute	ἐμόλυνα	ἔχω μολύνει	μολυνθείς,-υσμένος
μορφῶ, -ώνω, I form	ἐμόρφωσα	ἔχω μορφώσει	μορφωθείς
μοχθῶ (έω), I toil	ἐμόχθησα	ἔχω μοχθήσει	
μυκῶμαι (άομαι), I roar	ἐμυκήθην	ἔχω μυκηθῇ	μυκηθείς
μυρίζω, I smell	ἐμύρισα	ἔχω μυρίσει	μυρισθείς
μυῶ (έω), I initiate	ἐμύησα	» μυήσει	μυηθείς, (με) μυημένος
μωραίνω, I make stupid	ἐμώρανα	ἔχω μωράνει	μωρανθείς,-αμένος

Ν

ναρκῶ, -ώνω, I benumb	ἐνάρκωσα	ἔχω ναρκώσει	ναρκωθείς
ναυαγῶ (έω), I am wrecked	ἐναυάγησα	ἔχω ναυαγήσει	
ναυλῶ, -ώνω, I charter	ἐναύλωσα	ἔχω ναυλώσει	ναυλωθείς
νεύω, I make a sign, I nod	ἔνευσα	ἔχω νεύσει	
νηστεύω, I fast	ἐνήστευσα	ἔχω νηστεύσει	νηστευθείς
νικῶ (άω), I vanquish	ἐνίκησα	ἔχω νικήσει	νικηθείς
νίπτω, I wash	ἔνιψα	ἔχω νίψει	νιφθείς, (νε) νιμμένος
νοθεύω, I adulterate	ἐνόθευσα	ἔχω νοθεύσει	νοθευθείς
νομίζω, I think	ἐνόμισα	ἔχω νομίσει	νομισθείς
νυκτώνει, it is getting dark	ἐνύκτωσε	ἔχει νυκτώσει	νυκτωθείς
νυστάζω, I feel sleepy	ἐνύσταξα	ἔχω νυστάξει	νυσταγμένος

Ξ

ξενυκτῶ,άω, I pass the night	ἐξενύκτησα	ἔχω ξενυκτήσει	ξενυκτημένος
ξερνῶ, ξερνάω, I vomit	ἐξέρασα	ἔχω ξεράσει	ξερασθείς
ξεύρω, ξέρω, I know	(imp. ἤξευρον, ἤξευρα)		
ξηραίνω, I dry	ἐξήρανα	ἔχω ξηράνει	ξηρανθείς, -αμένος
ξυνίζω, I turn sour	ἐξύνισα	ἔχω ξυνίσει	ξυνισθείς
ξύνω, I scratch, I scrape	ἔξυσα	ἔχω ξύσει	ξυσθείς
ξυρίζω, I shave	ἐξύρισα	ἔχω ξυρίσει	ξυρισθείς

Ο

οἰκονομῶ (έω), I save	ᾠκονόμησα, οἰκονό-	ἔχω οἰκονομήσῃ	οἰκονομηθείς
ὁμαλύνω, I level, I smooth	ὡμάλυνα	ἔχω ὁμαλύνει	ὁμαλυνθείς
ὁμιλῶ (έω), I talk	ὡμίλησα	ἔχω ὁμιλήσει	ὁμιληθείς
ὀμνύω, I swear	ὤμοσα	ἔχω ὀμόσει	ὀμοσθείς
ὁμοιάζω, I resemble	ὡμοίασα	ἔχω ὁμοιάσει	ὁμοιασθείς
ὁμολογῶ (έω), I confess	ὡμολόγησα	ἔχω ὁμολογήσει	ὁμολογηθείς
ὀνομάζω, I name	ὠνόμασα	ἔχω ὀνομάσει	ὀνομασθείς
ὀξύνω, I sharpen	ὤξυνα	ἔχω ὀξύνει	ὀξυνθείς, ὠξυσμένος
ὁπλίζω, I arm	ὥπλισα	ἔχω ὁπλίσει	ὁπλισθείς
ὀργανῶ, -ώνω, I organize	ὠργάνωσα	ἔχω ὀργανώσει	ὀργανωθείς
ὀργίζω, I make angry	ὤργισα	ἔχω ὀργίσει	ὀργισθείς
ὁρίζω, I define	ὥρισα	ἔχω ὁρίσει	ὁρισθείς
ὁρμῶ (άω), I rush upon	ὥρμησα	ἔχω ὁρμήσει	ὁρμηθείς
ὀφείλω, I owe	(imp. ὤφειλον, ὤφειλα)		
ὀχυρῶ, -ώνω, I fortify	ὠχύρωσα	ἔχω ὀχυρώσει	ὀχυρωθείς

Π

παγώνω, I freeze	ἐπάγωσα	ἔχω παγώσει	παγωμένος
παίζω, I play	ἔπαιξα	ἔχω παίξει	παιχθείς, παιγμένος
παίρνω, I take	ἐπῆρα	ἔχω πάρει	παρθείς, παρμένος
παλαίω, I wrestle	ἐπάλαισα	ἔχω παλαίσει	παλαισθείς

PRESENT	AORIST	PERFECT	PAST PARTICIPLE PASSIVE
πάλλω, I palpitate	ἔπαλα	ἔχω πάλει	
πανηγυρίζω, I celebrate	ἐπανηγύρισα	ἔχω πανηγυρίσει	πανηγυρισθείς
παραβαίνω, I transgress	παρέβην, -έβηκα	ἔχω παραβῆ	(παραβάς)
παραβάλλω, I compare	παρέβαλον, -βαλα	ἔχω παραβάλει	παραβληθείς
παραγγέλλω, I order	παρήγγειλα	ἔχω παραγγείλει	παραγγελθείς
παράγω, I produce	παρήγαγον, -αγα	» παραγάγει	παραχθείς,-γμένος
παραδίδω, I deliver	παρέδοσα, -έδωκα	ἔχω παραδώσει	παραδοθείς
παρακαλῶ (έω), I beg	παρεκάλεσα	ἔχω παρακαλέσει	παρακληθείς
παραλαμβάνω, I receive	παρέλαβον, -λαβα	ἔχω παραλάβει	παραληφθείς
παραπονοῦμαι, I complain	παρεπονέθην,-έθηκα	ἔχω παραπονεθῆ	παραπονεθείς
παρεξηγῶ, I misinterpret	παρεξήγησα	ἔχω παρεξηγήσει	παρεξηγηθείς
παρέρχομαι, I pass	παρῆλθον,παρῆλθα	ἔχω παρέλθει	(παρελθών)
παρέχω, I grant, I give	παρέσχον	ἔχω παράσχει	παρασχεθείς
παρηγορῶ (έω), I console	παρηγόρησα	ἔχω παρηγορήσει	παρηγορηθείς
παριστάνω, I represent	παρέστησα	ἔχω παραστήσει	παρασταθείς
παροτρύνω, I urge	παρώτρυνα	ἔχω παροτρύνει	παροτρυνθείς
παρουσιάζω, I present	παρουσίασα	ἔχω παρουσιάσει	παρουσιασθείς
πάσχω, I suffer	ἔπαθον, ἔπαθα	ἔχω πάθει	παθημένος
πατῶ (έω), I step	ἐπάτησα	ἔχω πατήσει	πατηθείς
παύω, I cease	ἔπαυσα	ἔχω παύσει	παυθείς
παχύνω, I fatten	ἐπάχυνα	ἔχω παχύνει	παχυνθείς
πείθω, I persuade	ἔπεισα	ἔχω πείσει	πεισθείς
πεινῶ (άω), I am hungry	ἐπείνασα	ἔχω πεινάσει	πεινασμένος
πειράζω, I tease	ἐπείραξα	ἔχω πειράξει	πειραχθείς,-αγμένος
πειρῶμαι (άομαι), I try	ἐπειράθην	»πειραθῆ	πειραθείς,πεπειραμένος
πενθῶ (έω), I mourn	ἐπένθησα	ἔχω πενθήσει	
περιμένω, I wait	ἐπερίμεινα	ἔχω περιμείνει	
περιορίζω, I limit	περιώρισα	ἔχω περιορίσει	περιορισθείς
περιπατῶ (έω), I walk	ἐπεριπάτησα	ἔχω περιπατήσει	
περιποιοῦμαι, I entertain	ἐπεριποιήθην, -θηκα	ἔχω περιποιηθῆ	περιποιηθείς
περισσεύω, I am left over	ἐπερίσσευσα	ἔχω περισσεύσει	
περνῶ (άω), I pass	ἐπέρασα	ἔχω περάσει	περασμένος
πετῶ (άω), I fly, I throw	ἐπέταξα	ἔχω πετάξει	πεταχθείς, -γμένος
πηγαίνω, I go	ἐπῆγα	ἔχω ὑπάγει	
πηδῶ (άω), I jump	ἐπήδησα	ἔχω πηδήσει	πηδηθείς
πιάνω, I catch	ἔπιασα	ἔχω πιάσει	πιασθείς
πιέζω, I press	ἐπίεσα	ἔχω πιέσει	πιεσθείς
πικραίνω, I embitter	ἐπίκρανα	ἔχω πικράνει	πικρανθείς,-αμένος
πίνω, I drink	ἔπιον, ἔπια	ἔχω πίει	ποθείς, πιωμένος
πίπτω, I fall	ἔπεσα	ἔχω πέσει	πεσμένος
πιστεύω, I believe	ἐπίστευσα	ἔχω πιστεύσει	πιστευθείς
πλακώνω, I crush	ἐπλάκωσα	ἔχω πλακώσει	πλακωθείς
πλανῶμαι (άο), I wander	ἐπλανήθην, -ήθηκα	ἔχω πλανηθῆ	πλανηθείς
πλάττω, I create, I form	ἔπλασα	ἔχω πλάσει	πλασθείς
πλέκω, I knit	ἔπλεξα	ἔχω πλέξει	πλεχθείς, -εγμένος
πλέω, I sail	ἔπλευσα	ἔχω πλεύσει	πλευσθείς
πληγώνω, I wound	ἐπλήγωσα	ἔχω πληγώσει	πληγωθείς
πλημμυρῶ (έω), I overflow	ἐπλημμύρησα	ἔχω πλημμυρήσει	πλημμυρισθείς
πληροφορῶ (έω), I inform	ἐπληροφόρησα	» πληροφορήσει	πληροφορηθείς
πληρῶ (όω, -ώνω) I fill	ἐπλήρωσα	ἔχω πληρώσει	πληρωθείς
πληρώνω, I pay	ἐπλήρωσα	ἔχω πληρώσει	πληρωθείς
πλησιάζω, I approach	ἐπλησίασα	ἔχω πλησιάσει	πλησιασθείς
πλήττω, πλήσσω, I strike	ἔπληξα	ἔχω πλήξει	πληγείς,-ηγμένος
πλύνω, πλένω, I wash	ἔπλυνα	ἔχω πλύνει	πλυθείς

PRESENT	AORIST	PERFECT	PAST PARTICIPLE PASSIVE
πνέω, I blow	ἔπνευσα	ἔχω πνεύσει	πνευσθείς
πνίγω, I choke, I drown	ἔπνιξα	ἔχω πνίξει	πνιγείς, πνιγμένος
ποθῶ (έω), I desire	ἐπόθησα	ἔχω ποθήσει	ποθηθείς
ποικίλλω, I vary	ἐποίκιλα	ἔχω ποικίλει	ποικιλθείς
ποιῶ (έω), I make, I do	ἐποίησα	ἔχω ποιήσει	ποιηθείς
πολεμῶ (έω), I fight	ἐπολέμησα	ἔχω πολεμήσει	πολεμηθείς
πονῶ (έω), I am in pain	ἐπόνεσα	ἔχω πονέσει	πονεθείς
ποτίζω, I water	ἐπότισα	ἔχω ποτίσει	ποτισθείς
πράττω, I do	ἔπραξα	ἔχω πράξει	πραχθείς,-αγμένος
πρέπω, I befit	ἔπρεψα	ἔχω πρέψει	
προάγω, I promote	προήγαγον, -γα	» προαγάγει	προαχθείς,-ηγμένος
προβαίνω, I proceed	προέβην	ἔχω προβῇ	(προβάς)
προβάλλω, I offer; I pop out	προέβαλον, ἐπρόβαλα	» προβάλει	προβληθείς
προδίδω, I betray	ἐπρόδοσα	ἔχω προδόσει	προδοθείς
προικίζω, I endow	ἐπροίκισα	ἔχω προικίσει	προικισθείς
προλέγω, I foretell	προεῖπον, προεῖπα	» προείπει	προρρηθείς,-ειρημένος
προμηθεύω, I furnish	ἐπρομήθευσα	ἔχω προμηθεύσει	προμηθευθείς
προνοῶ (έω), I provide	ἐπρονόησα	ἔχω προνοήσει	προνοηθείς
προξενῶ (έω), I cause	ἐπροξένησα	ἔχω προξενήσει	προξενηθείς
προοδεύω, I progress	προώδευσα	ἔχω προοδεύσει	προωδευμένος
προορίζω, I destine	προώρισα	ἔχω προορίσει	προορισθείς
προσεύχομαι, I pray	προσηυχήθην,-ευχήθηκα	» προσευχηθῇ	προσευχηθείς
προσέχω, I take care	ἐπρόσεξα	ἔχω προσέξει	
προσθέτω, I add	προσέθεσα, ἐπρόσθεσα	» προσθέσει	προστεθείς
προσκαλῶ (έω), I invite	προσεκάλεσα, ἐπροσκά-	» προσκαλέσει	προσκληθείς
προσκυνῶ (έω), I worship	προσεκύνησα, ἐπροσκύ-	» προσκυνήσει	προσκυνηθείς
προσπαθῶ (έω), I try	προσεπάθησα, ἐπροσπά-	» προσπαθήσει	
προστάζω, I order	ἐπρόσταξα	ἔχω προστάξει	προσταχθείς
προστατεύω, I protect	ἐπροστάτευσα	ἔχω προστατεύσει	προστατευθείς
προσφέρω, I offer	προσέφερον, ἐπρόσφερα	» προσφέρει	προσφερθείς
προτείνω, I propose	ἐπρότεινα	ἔχω προτείνει	προταθείς
προτιμῶ (άω), I prefer	ἐπροτίμησα	ἔχω προτιμήσει	προτιμηθείς
προχωρῶ (έω), I advance	ἐπροχώρησα	ἔχω προχωρήσει	προχωρημένος
πταίω, I am guilty	ἔπταισα	ἔχω πταίσει	
πτοῶ (έω), I frighten	ἐπτόησα	ἔχω πτοήσει	πτοηθείς
πτύω, I spit	ἔπτυσα	ἔχω πτύσει	πτυσθείς
πυροβολῶ (έω), I fire	ἐπυροβόλησα	ἔχω πυροβολήσει	πυροβοληθείς
πωλῶ (έω), I sell	ἐπώλησα	ἔχω πωλήσει	πωληθείς

Ρ

ράπτω, I sew	ἔρραψα	ἔχω ράψει	ραφθείς, (ἐρ) ραμμένος
ρέω, I flow	ἔρρευσα	ἔχω ρεύσει	
ρίπτω, I throw	ἔρριψα	ἔχω ρίψει	ριφθείς, (ἐρ) ριμμένος
ροφῶ (άω, έω), I sip	ἐρρόφησα	ἔχω ροφήσει	ροφηθείς

Σ

σαπίζω, I rot	ἐσάπισα	ἔχω σαπίσει	σαπισμένος
σαρώνω, I sweep	ἐσάρωσα	ἔχω σαρώσει	σαρωθείς
σβύνω, I extinguish	ἔσβεσα, ἔσβυσα	ἔχω σβύσει	σβεσθείς, σβυσμένος
σέβομαι, I respect	ἐσεβάσθην	ἔχω σεβασθῇ	σεβασθείς
σείω, I shake	ἔσεισα	ἔχω σείσει	σεισθείς
σηκώνω, I lift, I raise	ἐσήκωσα	ἔχω σηκώσει	σηκωθείς
σημαίνω, I signify; I ring	ἐσήμανα	ἔχω σημάνει	σημανθείς,-ασμένος
σημειῶ, -ώνω, I mark	ἐσημείωσα	ἔχω σημειώσει	σημειωθείς

PRESENT	AORIST	PERFECT	PAST PARTICIPLE PASSIVE
σιγῶ (άω), I am silent	ἐσίγησα	ἔχω σιγήσει	σιγηθείς
σιωπῶ (άω), I keep silent	ἐσιώπησα	ἔχω σιωπήσει	σιωπηθείς
σκαλίζω, I poke, I dig	ἐσκάλισα	ἔχω σκαλίσει	σκαλισθείς
σκάπτω, I dig	ἔσκαψα	ἔχω σκάψει	σκαφθείς,ἐσκαμμένος
σκεπάζω, I cover	ἐσκέπασα	ἔχω σκεπάσει	σκεπασθείς
σκέπτομαι, I think	ἐσκέφθην	ἔχω σκεφθῆ	σκεφθείς,ἐσκεμμένος
σκληρύνω, I harden	ἐσκλήρυνα	ἔχω σκληρύνει	σκληρυνθείς
σκοπεύω, I intend; I aim	ἐσκόπευσα	ἔχω σκοπεύσει	σκοπευθείς
σκορπίζω, I scatter	ἐσκόρπισα	ἔχω σκορπίσει	σκορπισθείς
σκοτίζω, I darken; I bother	ἐσκότισα	ἔχω σκοτίσει	σκοτισθείς
σκύπτω, I stoop	ἔσκυψα	ἔχω σκύψει	σκυμμένος
σπάζω, I break	ἔσπασα	ἔχω σπάσει	σπασθείς,σπασμένος
σπαταλῶ (άω), I waste	ἐσπατάλησα	ἔχω σπαταλήσει	σπαταληθείς
σπείρω, I sow	ἔσπειρα	ἔχω σπείρει	σπαρθείς,-αρμένος
σπεύδω, I hasten	ἔσπευσα	ἔχω σπεύσει	ἐσπευσμένος
σπογγίζω, I wipe	ἐσπόγγισα	ἔχω σπογγίσει	σπογγισθείς
σπουδάζω, I study	ἐσπούδασα	ἔχω σπουδάσει	σπουδασμένος
σπρώχνω, I push	ἔσπρωξα	ἔχω σπρώξει	σπρωχθείς,-γμένος
στάζω, I drip	ἔσταξα	ἔχω στάξει	
σταματῶ (άω), I stop	ἐσταμάτησα	ἔχω σταματήσει	σταματηθείς
στέκω, στέκομαι, I stand	ἐστάθην, ἐστάθηκα	ἔχω σταθῆ	σταθείς
στέλλω, I send	ἔστειλα	» στείλει	σταλείς, (ἐ) σταλμένος
στενάζω, I sigh	ἐστέναξα	ἔχω στενάξει	
στέργω, I consent	ἔστερξα	ἔχω στέρξει	
στερεῶ, -ώνω, I make firm	ἐστερέωσα	ἔχω στερεώσει	στερεωθείς
στερῶ (έω), I deprive	ἐστέρησα	ἔχω στερήσει	στερηθείς
στέφω, I crown	ἔστεψα	» στέψει	στεφθείς, (ἐ) στεμμένος
στήνω, I set up	ἔστησα	ἔχω στήσει	στηθείς, (ἐ) στημένος
στηρίζω, I support	ἐστήριξα	ἔχω στηρίξει	στηριχθείς,-ιγμένος
στοιχίζω, I cost	ἐστοίχισα	ἔχω στοιχίσει	
στολίζω, I adorn, I dress	ἐστόλισα	ἔχω στολίσει	στολισθείς
στοχάζομαι, I imagine	ἐστοχάσθην,-άσθηκα	ἔχω στοχασθῆ	στοχασθείς
στρέφω, I turn	ἔστρεψα	» στρέψει	στραφείς,ἐστραμμένος
στρώνω, I strew, I spread	ἔστρωσα	ἔχω στρώσει	στρωθείς, -μένος
συγγράφω, I write	συνέγραψα	ἔχω συγγράψει	συγγραφείς
συγκινῶ (έω), I move	συνεκίνησα,ἐσυγκί-	ἔχω συγκινήσει	συγκινηθείς
συγκρίνω, I compare	συνέκρινα,ἐσύγκρι-	ἔχω συγκρίνει	συγκριθείς
συγχωρῶ (έω), I pardon	συνεχώρησα,ἐσυγχώ-	» συγχωρήσει	συγχωρηθείς
συζητῶ (έω), I discuss	συνεζήτησα,ἐσυζήτησα	» συζητήσει	συζητηθείς
συλλαμβάνω, I catch	συνέλαβον,συνέλαβα	ἔχω συλλάβει	συλληφθείς
συλλέγω, I collect	συνέλεξα	ἔχω συλλέξει	συλλεχθείς
συμβαίνει, it happens	συνέβη, συνέβηκε	ἔχει συμβῆ	
συμβάλλω, I contribute	συνέβαλον, -λα	ἔχω συμβάλει	συμβληθείς
συμβουλεύω, I advise	συνεβούλευσα,ἐσυμβ-	» συμβουλεύσει	συμβουλευθείς
συμπαθῶ, έω, I sympathize	συνεπάθησα,ἐσυμπ-	ἔχω συμπαθήσει	συμπαθηθείς
συμπίπτω, I coincide	συνέπεσα	ἔχω συμπέσει	
συμπράττω, I cooperate	συνέπραξα	ἔχω συμπράξει	συμπραχθείς
συμφωνῶ (έω), I agree	συνεφώνησα,ἐσυμφ-	ἔχω συμφωνήσει	συμφωνηθείς
συναινῶ (έω), I consent	συνήνεσα,συναίνεσα	ἔχω συναινέσει	
συναντῶ (άω), I meet	συνήντησα	ἔχω συναντήσει	συναντηθείς
συνάπτω, I join	συνῆψα	» συνάψει	συναφθείς,συνημμένος
συνδέω, I connect	συνέδεσα,ἐσύνδεσα	» συνδέσει	συνδεθείς,-δεδεμένος
συνεννοοῦμαι (έομαι), I come to an understanding	συνενοήθην or συνενοήθηκα	ἔχω συνεννοηθῆ	συνεννοηθείς συνεννοημένος

PRESENT	AORIST	PERFECT	PAST PARTICIPLE PASSIVE
συνηθίζω, I accustom	συνήθισα,ἐσυνήθισα	ἔχω συνηθίσει	συνηθισμένος
συνιστῶ (άω), I recommend	συνέστησα	ἔχω συστήσει	συστηθείς,-ημένος
συνοδεύω, I accompany	συνώδευσα	ἔχω συνοδεύσει	συνοδευθείς
συντείνω, I contribute	συνέτεινα	ἔχω συντείνει	
συντελῶ (έω), I contribute	συνετέλεσα	ἔχω συντελέσει	συντελεσθείς
συντηρῶ (έω), I keep	συνετήρησα,ἐσυντή-	ἔχω συντηρήσει	συντηρηθείς
συντρίβω, I crush	συνέτριψα,ἐσύντρι-	» συντρίψει	συντριβείς, -ιμμένος
συρρέω, I flow together	συνέρρευσα	ἔχω συρρεύσει	
σύρω, I drag, I pull	ἔσυρα	ἔχω σύρει	συρθείς
σφάζω, I slay	ἔσφαξα	ἔχω σφάξει	σφαγείς,ἐσφαγμένος
σφάλλω, I err	ἔσφαλον, ἔσφαλα	ἔχω σφάλει	ἐσφαλμένος
σφίγγω, I hold tight	ἔσφιξα	ἔχω σφίξει	σφιχθείς, (ἐ) σφιγμένος
σφυρίζω, I whistle	ἐσφύριξα	ἔχω σφυρίξει	σφυριχθείς
σχεδιάζω, I plan	ἐσχεδίασα	ἔχω σχεδιάσει	σχεδιασθείς
σχετίζω, I relate	ἐσχέτισα	ἔχω σχετίσει	σχετισθείς
σχίζω, I tear	ἔσχισα	ἔχω σχίσει	σχισθείς, (ἐ) σχισμένος
σώζω, I save	ἔσωσα	ἔχω σώσει	σωθείς, (σε) σωσμένος
σωρεύω, I pile	ἐσώρευσα	ἔχω σωρεύσει	σωρευθείς

T

ταράσσω, I agitate, disturb	ἐτάραξα	ἔχω ταράξει	ταραχθείς, -γμένος
τάσσω, I order, I place	ἔταξα	ἔχω τάξει	ταχθείς, (τε) ταγμένος
ταχύνω, I quicken	ἐτάχυνα	ἔχω ταχύνει	ταχυνθείς
τείνω, I tend	ἔτεινα	ἔχω τείνει	ταθείς, τεταμένος
τελειώνω, I finish	ἐτελείωσα	ἔχω τελειώσει	τελειωθείς
τελῶ (έω), I perform	ἐτέλεσα	» τελέσει	τελεσθείς,τετελεσμένος
τέρπω, I delight	ἔτερψα	ἔχω τέρψει	τερφθείς
τηγανίζω, I fry	ἐτηγάνισα	ἔχω τηγανίσει	τηγανισθείς
τηρῶ (έω), I keep	ἐτήρησα	ἔχω τηρήσει	τηρηθείς
τιμῶ (άω), I honor	ἐτίμησα	ἔχω τιμήσει	τιμηθείς
τιμωρῶ (έω), I punish	ἐτιμώρησα	ἔχω τιμωρήσει	τιμωρηθείς
τινάσσω, τινάζω, I shake	ἐτίναξα	ἔχω τινάξει	τιναχθείς,-αγμένος
τολμῶ (άω), I dare	ἐτόλμησα	ἔχω τολμήσει	τολμηθείς
τονίζω, I accent	ἐτόνισα	ἔχω τονίσει	τονισθείς
τονῶ, τονώνω, I strengthen	ἐτόνωσα	ἔχω τονώσει	τονωθείς
τραβῶ (άω), I pull, I draw	ἐτράβηξα	» τραβήξει	τραβηχθείς,-ηγμένος
τραγουδῶ (άω), I sing	ἐτραγούδησα	ἔχω τραγουδήσει	τραγουδηθείς
τρελλαίνω, I drive mad	ἐτρέλλανα	ἔχω τρελλάνει	τρελλαθείς
τρέμω, I tremble	(imp.ἔτρεμον,ἔτρεμα)		
τρέπω, I turn, I change	ἔτρεψα	» τρέψει	τραπείς, (τε) τραμμένος
τρέφω, I feed	ἔθρεψα	ἔχω θρέψει	τραφείς, θρεμμένος
τρέχω, I run	ἔτρεξα	ἔχω τρέξει	
τρίβω, I rub	ἔτριψα	» τρίψει	τριφθείς,τριβείς,-ιμμένος
τρίζω, I creak	ἔτριξα	ἔχω τρίξει	
τρομάζω, I frighten	ἐτρόμαξα	ἔχω τρομάξει	τρομαγμένος
τροχίζω, I sharpen	ἐτρόχισα	ἔχω τροχίσει	τροχισθείς
τρυγῶ, άω, I gather grapes	ἐτρύγησα	ἔχω τρυγήσει	τρυγηθείς
τρυπῶ (άω), I make a hole	ἐτρύπησα	ἔχω τρυπήσει	τρυπηθείς
τρώγω, I eat	ἔφαγον, ἔφαγα	ἔχω φάγει	φαγωθείς
τσιμπῶ (άω), I pinch	ἐτσίμπησα	ἔχω τσιμπήσει	τσιμπηθείς
τυγχάνω, I happen	ἔτυχον, ἔτυχα	ἔχω τύχει	
τυλίσσω, I wind; I wrap	ἐτύλιξα	ἔχω τυλίξει	τυλιχθείς, -ιγμένος
τυπῶ, τυπώνω, I print	ἐτύπωσα	ἔχω τυπώσει	τυπωθείς
τυραννῶ (έω), I torture	ἐτυράννησα	ἔχω τυραννήσει	τυραννηθείς

PRESENT	AORIST	PERFECT	PAST PARTICIPLE PASSIVE
τυφλῶ, τυφλώνω, I blind	ἐτύφλωσα	ἔχω τυφλώσει	τυφλωθείς
τυχαίνω, I happen	ἔτυχα	ἔχω τύχει	
	Υ		
ὑβρίζω, I insult	ὕβρισα	ἔχω ὑβρίσει	ὑβρισθείς
ὑγραίνω, I moisten, I wet	ὕγρανα	ἔχω ὑγράνει	ὑγρανθείς
ὑμνῶ (έω), I praise	ὕμνησα	ἔχω ὑμνήσει	ὑμνηθείς
ὑπακούω, I obey	ὑπήκουσα, ὑπάκου-	ἔχω ὑπακούσει	
ὑπανδρεύω, I marry	ὑπάνδρευσα	ἔχω ὑπανδρεύσει	ὑπανδρευθείς
ὑπάρχω, I exist	ὑπῆρξα	ἔχω ὑπάρξει	
ὑπενθυμίζω, I remind	ὑπενθύμισα	ἔχω ὑπενθυμίσει	ὑπενθυμισθείς
ὑπερασπίζω, I defend	ὑπερήσπισα,ὑπερά-	ἔχω ὑπερασπίσει	ὑπερασπισθείς
ὑπερβαίνω, I surpass	ὑπερέβην	ἔχω ὑπερβῆ	(ὑπερβάς)
ὑπηρετῶ (έω), I serve	ὑπηρέτησα	ἔχω ὑπηρετήσει	ὑπηρετηθείς
ὑποβάλλω, I submit	ὑπέβαλον, -λα	ἔχω ὑποβάλει	ὑποβληθείς
ὑπογράφω, I sign	ὑπέγραψα	ἔχω ὑπογράψει	ὑπογραφείς
ὑποθέτω, I suppose	ὑπέθεσα	ἔχω ὑποθέσει	ὑποτεθείς
ὑποκύπτω, I succumb	ὑπέκυψα	ἔχω ὑποκύψει	
ὑπολογίζω, I calculate	ὑπελόγισα	ἔχω ὑπολογίσει	ὑπολογισθείς
ὑπομένω, I endure	ὑπέμεινα	ἔχω ὑπομείνει	
ὑπόσχομαι, I promise	ὑπεσχέθην,ὑποσχέθηκα	» ὑποσχεθῆ	ὑποσχεθείς
ὑποτάσσω, I subdue	ὑπέταξα, ὑπόταξα	ἔχω ὑποτάξει	ὑποταχθείς,-γμένος
ὑποφέρω, I suffer	ὑπέφερα	ἔχω ὑποφέρει	ὑποφερθείς
ὑποχρεῶ, -ώνω, I oblige	ὑπεχρέωσα	ἔχω ὑποχρεώσει	ὑποχρεωθείς
ὑποχωρῶ (έω), I retreat	ὑπεχώρησα	ἔχω ὑποχωρήσει	
ὑφαίνω, I weave	ὕφανα	ἔχω ὑφάνει	ὑφανθείς,ὑφασμένος
ὑφίσταμαι, I exist; I suffer	ὑπέστην	ἔχω ὑποστῆ	(ὑποστάς)
ὑψῶ, ὑψώνω, I lift	ὕψωσα	ἔχω ὑψώσει	ὑψωθείς
	Φ		
φαίνομαι, I appear	ἐφάνην, ἐφάνηκα	ἔχω φανῆ	φανείς
φανερῶ, -ώνω, I reveal	ἐφανέρωσα	ἔχω φανερώσει	φανερωθείς
φαντάζομαι, I imagine	ἐφαντάσθην	ἔχω φαντασθῆ	φαντασθείς
φέγγω, I shine	ἔφεγξα	ἔχω φέγξει	
φείδομαι, I spare	ἐφείσθην	ἔχω φεισθῆ	φεισθείς
φέρω, I bring	ἔφερον, ἔφερα	ἔχω φέρει	φερθείς, φερμένος
φεύγω, I flee, I go away	ἔφυγον, ἔφυγα	ἔχω φύγει	φευχθείς
φθάνω, I reach	ἔφθασα	ἔχω φθάσει	φθασθείς,φθασμένος
φθείρω, I ruin, I wear out	ἔφθειρα	ἔχω φθείρει	φθαρείς,ἐφθαρμένος
φθονῶ (έω), I envy	ἐφθόνησα	ἔχω φθονήσει	φθονηθείς
φιλονεικῶ (έω), I quarrel	ἐφιλονείκησα	ἔχω φιλονεικήσει	φιλονεικηθείς
φιλοξενῶ, I entertain guests	ἐφιλοξένησα	ἔχω φιλοξενήσει	φιλοξενηθείς
φιλῶ (έω), I kiss	ἐφίλησα	ἔχω φιλήσει	φιληθείς
φιμῶ, φιμώνω, I muzzle	ἐφίμωσα	ἔχω φιμώσει	φιμωθείς
φλέγω, I inflame	ἔφλεξα	ἔχω φλέξει	φλεχθείς, -γμένος
φλυαρῶ (έω), I prate	ἐφλυάρησα	ἔχω φλυαρήσει	φλυαρηθείς
φοβίζω, I frighten	ἐφόβισα	ἔχω φοβίσει	φοβισθείς
φοβοῦμαι (έομαι), I fear	ἐφοβήθην, -ηκα	ἔχω φοβηθῆ	φοβηθείς
φοιτῶ (άω), I frequent	ἐφοίτησα	ἔχω φοιτήσει	
φονεύω, I kill	ἐφόνευσα	ἔχω φονεύσει	φονευθείς
φορτώνω, I load	ἐφόρτωσα	ἔχω φορτώσει	φορτωθείς
φορῶ (έω), I wear	ἐφόρεσα	ἔχω φορέσει	φορεθείς
φουσκώνω, I swell	ἐφούσκωσα	ἔχω φουσκώσει	φουσκωθείς
φράσσω, I fence, I block	ἔφραξα	ἔχω φράξει	φραχθείς,-αγμένος
φρίσσω, φρίττω, I shudder	ἔφριξα	ἔχω φρίξει	

PRESENT	AORIST	PERFECT	PAST PARTICIPLE PASSIVE
φροντίζω, I care	ἐφρόντισα	ἔχω φροντίσει	φροντισμένος
φρονῶ (έω), I think	ἐφρόνησα	ἔχω φρονήσει	φρονηθείς
φρουρῶ (έω), I guard	ἐφρούρησα	ἔχω φρουρήσει	φρουρηθείς
φυλακίζω, I imprison	ἐφυλάκισα	ἔχω φυλακίσει	φυλακισθείς
φυλάσσω, -άττω, I guard	ἐφύλαξα	ἔχω φυλάξει	φυλαχθείς,-αγμένος
φυσῶ (άω), I blow	ἐφύσησα	ἔχω φυσήσει	φυσηθείς
φυτεύω, I plant	ἐφύτευσα	ἔχω φυτεύσει	φυτευθείς
φωνάζω, I cry out, I call	ἐφώναξα	ἔχω φωνάξει	φωναχθείς
φωρῶμαι (άο), I am caught	ἐφωράθην	ἔχω φωραθῆ	φωραθείς
φωτίζω, I illuminate	ἐφώτισα	ἔχω φωτίσει	φωτισθείς

X

χαιρετῶ (άω), I greet	ἐχαιρέτησα	ἔχω χαιρετίσει	χαιρετισθείς
χαίρω, **χαίρομαι**, I rejoice	ἐχάρην,ἐχάρηκα	ἔχω χαρῆ	χαρείς
χαλαρῶ, **-ώνω**, I loosen	ἐχαλάρωσα	ἔχω χαλαρώσει	χαλαρωθείς
χαλ(ν)ῶ, **άω**, I ruin, I spoil	ἐχάλασα	ἔχω χαλάσει	χαλασθείς
χαμηλώνω, I lower	ἐχαμήλωσα	ἔχω χαμηλώση	χαμηλωθείς
χάνω, I lose	ἔχασα	ἔχω χάσει	χαθείς, χαμένος
χαράσσω, **-άζω**, I engrave	ἐχάραξα	ἔχω χαράξει	χαραχθείς, -γμένος
χαρίζω, I give as a present	ἐχάρισα	ἔχω χαρίσει	χαρισθείς
χασμῶμαι (άο), I yawn	ἐχασμήσθην	ἔχει χασμηθῆ	χασμηθείς
χάφτω, I eat up	ἔχαψα	ἔχω χάψει	χαφθείς, χαμμένος
χιονίζει, it snows	ἐχιόνισε	ἔχει χιονίσει	χιονισθείς
χορεύω, I dance	ἐχόρευσα	ἔχω χορεύσει	**χορευθείς**
χορταίνω, I satiate, I fill	ἐχόρτασα	ἔχω χορτάσει	χορτασθείς
χρειάζομαι, I need	ἐχρειάσθην, **-θηκα**	ἔχω χρειασθῆ	χρειασθείς
χρεώνω, I charge, I debit	ἐχρέωσα	ἔχω χρεώσει	χρεωθείς
χρεωστῶ (έω,άω), I owe	(imp. ἐχρεώστουν, ἐχρεωστοῦσα)		
χρησιμεύω, I am useful	ἐχρησίμευσα	ἔχω χρησιμεύσει	
χρίω, I anoint	ἔχρισα	ἔχω χρίσει	χρισθείς
χρυσῶ, χρυσώνω, I gild	ἐχρύσωσα	ἔχω χρυσώσει	χρυσωθείς
χρωματίζω, I paint	ἐχρωμάτισα	ἔχω χρωματίσει	χρωματισθείς
χύνω, I pour	ἔχυσα	ἔχω χύσει	χυθείς, (κε)χυμένος
χωνεύω, I digest	ἐχώνευσα	ἔχω χωνεύσει	χωνευθείς
χώνω, I drive or thrust in	ἔχωσα	ἔχω χώσει	χω(σ)θείς,χω(σ)μένος
χωρίζω, I separate	ἐχώρισα	ἔχω χωρίσει	χωρισθείς
χωρῶ (έω), I take in, I hold	ἐχώρεσα,ἐχώρησα	ἔχω χωρέσει,-ήσει	χωρημένος

Ψ

ψάλλω, I sing, I chant	ἔψαλον, ἔψαλα	ἔχω ψάλει	ψαλείς, (ἐ)ψαλμένος
ψαρεύω, I fish	ἐψάρευσα	ἔχω ψαρεύσει	ψαρευθείς
ψάχνω, I search	ἔψαξα	ἔχω ψάξει	ψαχθείς, ψαγμένος
ψεύδομαι, I lie, I tell lies	ἐψεύσθην	ἔχω ψευσθῆ	ψευσθείς
ψήνω, I bake, I roast	ἔψησα	ἔχω ψήσει	ψηθείς, (ἐ)ψημένος
ψηφίζω, I vote	ἐψήφισα	ἔχω ψηφίσει	ψηφισθείς
ψιθυρίζω, I whisper	ἐψιθύρισα	ἔχω ψιθυρίσει	ψιθυρισθείς
ψύχω, I cool, I freeze	ἔψυξα	ἔχω ψύξει	ψυχθείς, (ἐ)ψυγμένος
ψωνίζω, I shop, I buy	ἐψώνισα	ἔχω ψωνίσει	ψωνισθείς

Ω

ὠθῶ (έω), I push	ὤθησα	ἔχω ὠθήσει	ὠθηθείς
ὡριμάζω, I ripen	ὡρίμασα	ἔχω ὡριμάσει	
ὠφελῶ (έω), I benefit	ὠφέλησα	ἔχω ὠφελήσει	ὠφεληθείς
ὠχριῶ (άω), I pale	ὠχρίασα	ἔχω ὠχριάσει	

REVIEW OF LESSONS

LESSON 1

Read aloud and translate in English:

Ποῖος ἔχει τὸ κρέας; — Ὁ πατέρας ἔχει τὸ κρέας·—Ἡ μητέρα ἔχει τὸ τυρί.—Ἡ κόρη ἔχει τὸ τυρὶ καὶ τὸ κρέας.—Ἐγὼ ἔχω τὸ τυρὶ καὶ τὸ ψωμί.—Ἕνα παιδὶ ἔχει τὸ ψωμί.—Σὺ ἔχεις τὸ πιάτο.—Ἡ κόρη ἔχει ἕνα πιάτο κρέας.

Translate and read aloud in Greek:

Who has a plate? — Who has a plate of meat? — The boy has a plate of meat. — The boy has the cheese. — The father has the bread and the cheese. — The mother has a plate of meat. — The girl has bread and cheese. — The child has a plate of cheese.

Read aloud and try to give an answer in Greek:

Ποῖος ἔχει τὸ πιάτο; —Ποῖος ἔχει τὸ τυρί;—Ποῖος ἔχει τὸ κρέας;—Ποῖος ἔχει τὸ ψωμί;—Ἔχεις ψωμὶ καὶ κρέας;—Ἔχεις ἕνα πιάτο κρέας;—Ποῖος ἔχει ἕνα πιάτο κρέας; — Ἔχει ὁ πατέρας κρέας;—Ἔχει ὁ πατέρας τὸ κρέας;

LESSON 2

Read aloud and translate in English:

Σὺ ἔχεις τὸ πιπέρι καὶ τὸ ἁλάτι.—Ἡμεῖς ἔχομεν τὸ ψωμὶ καὶ τὸ κρέας.—Δὲν ἔχομεν τὸ ποτῆρι.—Ἔχετε τὸ γάλα καὶ τὸ βούτυρο;—Ναί, ἔχομεν τὸ γάλα καὶ τὸ βούτυρον.—Ὁ πατέρας καὶ ἡ μητέρα ἔχουν τὸ ἁλάτι.—Δὲν ἔχουν τὸ πιπέρι.—Τὸ παιδὶ καὶ ἡ κόρη ἔχουν τὸ γάλα.

Translate and read aloud in Greek:

The girl has the water and the wine. — Who has the salt and the pepper? — The child has the salt and the pepper. — We have the butter and the milk.—We have not the wine.—Give me the meat, please.—Please give me the wine and the water.—The girl and the boy have the cheese.

Read aloud and try to give an answer in Greek:

Ἔχετε νερό;—Τὸ παιδὶ καὶ ἡ κόρη ἔχουν γάλα; —Ἔχεις ἁλάτι καὶ πιπέρι;—Δὲν ἔχετε τὸ κρέας;—Ὁ πατέρας καὶ ἡ μητέρα ἔχουν βούτυρο; —Ἔχουν ἁλάτι καὶ πιπέρι; — Ἔχετε ἕνα ποτῆρι νερό;—Δὲν ἔχετε ψωμὶ καὶ τυρί;—Ἔχεις τὸ νερὸ καὶ τὸ γάλα;

LESSON 3

Read aloud and translate in English:

Ποῦ εἶνε ὁ καλὸς πατέρας;—Ὁ καλὸς πατέρας εἶνε ἐπάνω.—Ἡ καλὴ μητέρα εἶνε κάτω.—Ποῖος εἶνε μέσα;—Ἡ κακὴ γυναῖκα εἶνε μέσα.—Μία γυναῖκα εἶνε ἐπάνω.—Ἡμεῖς εἴμεθα μέσα.—Σεῖς εἶσθε ἔξω.—Τὸ καλὸ παιδὶ εἶνε ἐδῶ.—Εἶνε καλὸ παιδὶ ἢ κακό;—Εἶναι καλὸ παιδί.—Δὲν εἶναι κακό.

Translate and read aloud in Greek:

Where is the good woman? — The good woman is downstairs. — The good man is upstairs. — The father is downstairs. — He is not downstairs. — He is inside. — The good mother is outside. — The bad boy is not here. — The bad boy is upstairs. — The good girl is here. — She is inside.

Read aloud and try to give an answer in Greek:

Ποῦ εἶνε ὁ πατέρας καὶ ἡ μητέρα; — Ποῦ εἶνε τὸ καλὸ παιδί;—Ποῖος εἶνε ἐπάνω;—Ποῖος εἶνε κάτω;—Ποῦ εἶνε ὁ καλὸς ἄνθρωπος; Ποῖος εἶνε καλὸς καὶ ποῖος εἶνε κακός;—Ποῦ εἶνε ἡ κακὴ κόρη; Εἶνε ὁ κακὸς ἀδελφὸς ἐδῶ;—Ποῖος εἶνε ἔξω καὶ ποῖος εἶνε μέσα; — Ποῦ εἶναι ὁ ἀδελφὸς καὶ ἡ ἀδελφή;

LESSON 4

Read aloud and translate in English:

Γιάννη, ἔλα δῶ.—Πῶς εἶσθε; — Εἶσθε καλά;—Ὄχι. —Δὲν εἶμαι καλά.—Εἶμαι ἄρρωστος.—Ποῖοι εἶνε ἔξω; — Αὐτοὶ οἱ ἄνθρωποι εἶνε ἔξω.—Ποῦ εἶνε αὐταὶ αἱ γυναῖκες;—Αὐτὲς αἱ γυναῖκες εἶνε κάτω.—Ποῦ εἶνε αὐτὰ τὰ παιδιά;—Αὐτὰ τὰ παιδιὰ εἶνε ἔξω.—Αὐτὸ τὸ πρᾶγμα δὲν εἶνε καλόν.

Translate and read aloud in Greek:

Who is sick? — The man is sick. — This woman is well. She is not sick. — How is brother John? — Brother John is very well; thank you. — Come upstairs. Sit here, please. — Is this a good thing? — This is not a good thing. — This is a very bad thing. — Who are these women?

Read aloud and try to give an answer in Greek:

Πῶς εἶσθε;—Πῶς εἶνε ὁ ἀδελφὸς Γιάννης;—Ποῖος εἶνε κάτω;—Ποῖος εἶνε ἐπάνω;—Εἶνε καλὰ ὁ πατέρας;—Εἶνε αὐτὸς ὁ ἄνθρωπος καλός;—Αὐτὴ ἡ γυναῖκα εἶνε καλή;—Εἶσαι ἄρρωστος;—Ποῦ εἶνε αὐτὸ τὸ παιδί;—Ποιὸς εἶνε κάτω;—Τί (what) ἔχετε ἐδῶ μέσα;

LESSON 5

Read aloud and translate in English:

Ἔχετε τὸ γάλα τοῦ ἀνθρώπου;—Δὲν ἔχω τὸ γάλα τοῦ ἀνθρώπου.—Ἔχω μόνον τὸν καφὲ καὶ τὴν ζάχαρη.—Δός μου τὸ τσάϊ παρακαλῶ.—Θέλετε αὐτὰ τὰ χρήματα; —Ναί. Θέλομεν αὐτὰ τὰ χρήματα.—Δόστε μου τὴν μουστάρδα, παρακαλῶ.—Βλέπετε αὐτὸν τὸν ἄνθρωπον;—Δὲν βλέπω αὐτὸν τὸν ἄνθρωπον. — Βλέπω ἕνα ἄνθρωπον καὶ ἕνα σκύλον.

Translate and read aloud in Greek:

Have you the sugar? — We have the sugar and the milk. — Do you want the mustard? — Yes. Give me the mustard and the salt, please.— Who wants the cheese? — This boy wants the cheese. — Give this meat to the dog. — Give the salt to this man. — Who has the man's coffee?— You have the man's coffee. — I have (the) brother's tea.

Read aloud and try to give an answer in Greek:

Ποῖος ἔχει τὸ κρασὶ τοῦ ἀνθρώπου;—Ποῦ εἶνε τὰ χρήματα τοῦ ἀδελφοῦ;—Ἔχετε τὸν καφὲ καὶ τὸ γάλα;—Θέλετε τὴν ζάχαρη, τὸ ἅλατι καὶ τὸ πιπέρι;—Ποῖος θέλει τυρὶ καὶ κρέας;—Βλέπετε αὐτὸν τὸν σκύλον;—Αὐτὸς εἶνε ὁ σκύλος τοῦ ἀδελφοῦ Γιάννη;—Θέλετε ψωμὶ καὶ κρέας;—Βλέπετε ἀνθρώπους ἐδῶ;

LESSON 6

Read aloud and translate in English:

Ποῖος σοῦ δίδει χρήματα;—Αὐτὴ ἡ γυναῖκα μοῦ δίδει χρήματα.—Ἐγὼ σοῦ δίδω κρέας καὶ ψωμί.—Ποιὸς σοῦ δίδει καφέ;—Σὺ μοῦ δίδεις καφὲ καὶ ζάχαρη.—Τί θέλετε κυρία;—Θέλω κάτι.—Θέλω τυρὶ καὶ βούτυρο.—Παίρνετε ὀλίγο κρασί;—Εὐχαριστῶ. Δὲν θέλω κρασί.—Δόστε μου ἕνα ποτῆρι νερὸ μὲ πάγον, παρακαλῶ.

Translate and read aloud in Greek:

Who wants the sugar? — This girl wants the sugar. — She wants the coffee, too. — Who gives you milk? — Brother John gives me milk. — He gives me milk and butter. — What do you want here, sir? — I want a glass of water. — Give me iced water, please. — Who is in the house? — A woman is in the house. — Do you want all the bread? — Yes. Give me all the bread, please.

Read aloud and try to give an answer in Greek:

Τί μοῦ δίδεις;—Τί μοῦ δίδετε;—Θέλετε χρήματα ἢ κρέας;—Θέλετε γάλα ἢ βούτυρον.—Παίρνετε τσάϊ ἢ καφέ;—Ποῖος θέλει ὅλον τὸ ψωμί;—Θέλετε ἕνα ποτῆρι νερὸ μὲ πάγο;—Ποῖος εἶνε εἰς τὸ σπίτι;

LESSON 7

Read aloud and translate in English:

Ἔχετε μία καλὴ πέννα;—Ἔχω μία καλὴ πέννα καὶ ἕνα καλὸ βιβλίο.—Ἐγὼ ἔχω δύο πέννες ἀλλὰ δὲν ἔχω βιβλίο.—Θέλω μία μεγάλη πέννα.—Τὸ μαχαῖρι τοῦ ἀνθρώπου εἶνε μεγάλο.—Τὸ μικρὸ παιδὶ ἔχει τὸ χαρτὶ καὶ τὸ βιβλίο.—Ὁ μικρὸς ἀδελφὸς ἔχει ἕνα μεγάλο σκύλο.—Αὐτὴ ἡ κόρη ἔχει μία μικρὴ γάτα.—Ἡ γάτα αὐτῆς τῆς κόρης εἶνε μεγάλη. Δὲν εἶνε μικρή.

Translate and read aloud in Greek:

Have you a large knife? — I have a small knife. — The woman has a good pen and a small knife. — The woman's knife is large. — It is not small. — The man's dog is small. — The girl's cat is small also. — The little sister has a good book. — The paper of this book is good. — It is very good paper.

Read aloud and try to give an answer in Greek:

Θέλεις ἕνα μαχαῖρι;—Αὐτὸ εἶνε τὸ βιβλίο τοῦ ἀνθρώπου;—Ποῦ εἶνε ἡ γάτα τοῦ Γιάννη;—Εἶνε τὸ χαρτὶ τοῦ βιβλίου σου καλό;—Εἶνε ὁ σκύλος σου μεγάλος;—Ποῦ εἶνε τοῦ πατέρα ὁ φίλος;—Ποῖος εἶνε μέσα μαζὺ μὲ τὴν γυναῖκα;—Ποῦ εἶνε ἡ πέννα τοῦ μικροῦ παιδίου;—Εἶνε ἐδῶ ἡ φίλη τῆς ἀδελφῆς;

LESSON 8

Read aloud and translate in English:

Εἶνε ὁ πατέρας σου καλά; — Ὁ πατέρας μου εἶνε πολὺ καλά.—Ἡ μητέρα μας εἶνε ὀλίγον ἄρρωστη.—Πῶς εἶνε ἡ ἀδελφή σας;—Ἡ ἀδελφή μου δὲν εἶνε πολὺ καλά.—Εἶνε ὀλίγον ἄρρωστη.—Οἱ φίλοι μας εἶνε μέσα.—Εἶνε μαζὺ μὲ τὸν ἀδελφό μου.—Εἶνε καλοὶ ἄνθρωποι;—Εἶνε πολὺ καλοὶ ἄνθρωποι.—Δὲν εἶνε κακοί.—Ἡ μελάνη σας εἶνε καλή.—Ἡ μελάνη τοῦ φίλου μου δὲν εἶνε πολὺ καλή.

Translate and read aloud in Greek:

Who is sick? — My father is ill. — My mother is very well. — Our sister is out with her friend. — Is your brother well? — My brother is very well; thank you. — Who are these men? — These men are my brother's friends. — Are they good men? — They are very good men.— My coffee is very sweet. — Is your sister's ink good or bad? — My sister's ink is very bad.

Read aloud and try to give an answer in Greek:

Πῶς εἶνε ὁ ἀδελφός σου; — Εἶνε καλὰ ἡ μητέρα σας;—Εἶνε αἱ ἀδελφαί σου μέσα;—Εἶνε οἱ φίλοι σου καλοὶ ἄνθρωποι;—Εἶνε ἡ φίλη τῆς ἀδελφῆς σου καλὴ κόρη; —Αὐτὸς εἶνε ὁ σκύλος τοῦ πατέρα σου;—Εἶνε μεγάλος σκύλος ἢ μικρός;—Εἶνε καλὸς σκύλος ἢ κακός;—Ποῖος σκύλος εἶνε ἔξω, ὁ μεγάλος ἢ ὁ μικρός;

LESSON 9

Read aloud and translate in English:

Εἶνε αὐτὸς ὁ σκύλος σου;—Ναί, αὐτὸς εἶνε ὁ σκύλος μου.—Ἐκεῖνος εἶνε ὁ σκύλος τοῦ ἀδελφοῦ μου.—Ἔχετε μαχαῖρι; —Δὲν ἔχω μαχαῖρι. —Ἔχω ἕνα μολύβι, ἀλλὰ δὲν ἔχω πέννα.—Εἶνε ἡ ἀδελφή σας στὸ σπίτι;—Ἡ ἀδελφή μου δὲν εἶνε εἰς τὸ σπίτι.—Εἶνε εἰς τὸν δρόμον.—Τίνος (or ποίου, whose) εἶνε αὐτὸ τὸ πρᾶγμα; —Αὐτὸ τὸ πρᾶγμα εἶνε τοῦ πατέρα μου.

Translate and read aloud in Greek:

Is this your book? — No, sir. This is not my book. — It is my sister's book. — This book is very good. — That book is not so good. — What is on that table? — A book and a knife are on that table. — Who is in the street? — My mother is in the street with my sister. — My father is in the house. — Give me that thing, please.

Read aloud and try to give an answer in Greek:

Ποῖος εἶνε αὐτός;—Αὐτὸς εἶνε ὁ πατέρας σου;—Εἶνε ὁ πατέρας σου στὸ σπίτι; —Ποῦ εἶνε ὁ ἀδελφός σου;—Εἶνε ἄρρωστη ἡ μητέρα σας;—Ποῖος εἶνε ἐπάνω;— Τί εἶνε ἐπάνω στὸ τραπέζι;—Τί ἔχετε μαζύ σας;—Ἔχετε ἕνα μολύβι καὶ ἕνα μαχαῖρι;—Ἔχετε ἁλάτι καὶ πιπέρι;

LESSON 10

Read aloud and translate in English:

Ὁ ἀδελφός μου εἶνε στὸ σπίτι.—Εἶνε ὀλίγον ἄρρωστος.—Αὐτὸ τὸ πρᾶγμα εἶνε καλόν.—Δός μου αὐτὸ τὸ πρᾶγμα, σᾶς παρακαλῶ.—Ἡ φίλη μας ἔχει χρήματα.—Εἶνε πολὺ πλουσία.—Ὁ φίλος σας δὲν ἔχει χρήματα.—Εἶνε πτωχός.—Αὐτὸ τὸ ποτῆρι εἶνε γεμᾶτο μὲ νερό.—Ἐκεῖνο τὸ ποτῆρι εἶνε ἀδειανό.—Δός μας ἕνα ἀδειανὸ ποτῆρι, σᾶς παρακαλῶ.

Translate and read aloud in Greek:

Who is here? — My mother is here. My father is at home. — Our sister is ill. She is not so well. — Is her friend sick, too? — Her friend is very well. — Is she rich? — She is not rich. She is poor. — Where is your knife? — My knife is on the table, in the little room. — My pen is in the room also.

Read aloud and try to give an answer in Greek:

Ποῖος εἶνε ἐδῶ;—Ποῦ εἶνε ὁ πατέρας σας;—Ποῖος εἶνε ἄρρωστος;—Εἶνε καλὰ ἡ μητέρα σας;—Βλέπετε τὴν ἀδελφή τους;—Εἶνε ἡ ἀδελφή τους πλουσία ἢ πτωχή;—Εἶνε τεμπέλης ὁ φίλος του;—Αὐτὸ τὸ πρᾶγμα εἶνε εὐθηνό ἢ ἀκριβό;—Θέλετε ἕνα γεμᾶτο ποτῆρι;—Θέλετε γάλα ἢ καφέ;—Ποῦ εἶνε τὰ βιβλία σας;

LESSON 11

Read aloud and translate in English:

Τί βλέπετε εἰς τὸν δρόμον;—Εἰς τὸν δρόμον βλέπω δύο ἀνθρώπους καὶ ἕνα ἄλογον.—Τί βλέπετε στὸ σπίτι;—Εἰς τὸ σπίτι βλέπω δύο τραπέζια καὶ τέσσαρες καθέκλες.—Ἔχετε τὰ χρήματα τῶν ἀνθρώπων;—Ἐγὼ δὲν ἔχω τὰ χρήματα τῶν ἀνθρώπων.—Ἡ ἀδελφή μου ἔχει τὰ χρήματα τῶν ἐργατῶν.—Ὁ φίλος μου ἔχει πολλὰ χρήματα.—Ὁ πατέρας του εἶνε πολὺ πλούσιος.

Translate and read aloud in Greek:

Who is in the house? — Two men and three women are in the house.— Who is in the street? — Four dogs and two horses are in the street. — Do you see three children in the street? — Yes. We see three children in the street. We see two men also. — Is your father in the house? — No. My father is in the street.

Read aloud and try to give an answer in Greek:

Τί βλέπετε μέσα στὸ σπίτι;—Τί βλέπετε μέσα στὸ δρόμο;—Πόσα παιδιὰ βλέπετε στὸ δρόμο;—Πόσα ἄλογα καὶ πόσα κάρρα βλέπετε;—Πόσες καθέκλες εἶνε στὸ δωμάτιον;—Ποῖος ἔχει περισσότερα λεπτά, σὺ ἢ ὁ ἀδελφός σου;—Ποῦ εἶνε τῶν παιδιῶν τὰ χρήματα;—Βλέπεις τὸ κρεββάτι τοῦ ἀδελφοῦ μου;—Αὐτὰ εἶνε τῆς ἀδελφῆς μου τὰ χρήματα;—Ἐκεῖνα εἶνε τῆς μητέρας σου τὰ βιβλία;—Βλέπετε τὴς πέννες τοῦ φίλου μας;

LESSON 12

Read aloud and translate in English:

Γιάννη, κύτταξε ἐδῶ.—Ποῖος εἶνε μέσα στὴν κουζίνα;—Εἶνε ἕνας μαῦρος σκύλος.—'Αρέσεις αὐτὴν τὴν μαύρην γάταν;—Ναὶ κύριε.—'Αγαπῶ αὐτὴν τὴν μαύρην γάταν.—'Η ἀδελφή μου ἐπίσης ἀγαπᾶ αὐτὴν τὴν γάταν.—Θέλετε καφὲ ἢ τσάϊ;—Θέλομεν πολὺ γάλα εἰς τὸν καφέ μας. —Τὰ παιδιὰ ἀγαποῦν τὸ γάλα. —Τὸ γάλα εἶνε πολὺ καλὸν δι' αὐτά.

Translate and read aloud in Greek:

Come here, my friend. — Do you see anything (τίποτε) in the kitchen?— I see a white cat and a black dog. — It is my sister's cat. — My sister likes her white cat very much. — My brother likes this black dog. — Do you like black coffee? — No. I want coffee with plenty of milk. — Our children like milk very much. — You have four pencils. — Give one pencil to your big brother.

Read aloud and try to give an answer in Greek:

Ποῖος εἶνε στὴ σάλα;—Αὐτὸς ὁ μαῦρος σκύλος εἶνε ἰδικός σας;—'Αρέσεις αὐτὴν τὴν ἄσπρην γάταν; —Τί ἀρέσει ἡ ἀδελφή σου;—'Αγαπᾶτε γάλα ἢ καφέ;—Θέλετε μαῦρον καφέ;—Τί ἀρέσουν οἱ ἀδελφοί σου; —Σεῖς θέλετε ἐπίσης τὸ ἴδιον πρᾶγμα;—Πόσα μολύβια ἔχετε;—Θέλετε αὐτὸ τὸ μικρὸ μολύβι;

LESSON 13

Read aloud and translate in English:

Ποῦ εἶνε τὸ μαῦρο μου καπέλλο;—Φέρε μου τὸ ἄσπρο μου πανταλόνι, παρακαλῶ. —Θέλετε τὸ ἄσπρο σας σακκάκι ἐπίσης;—Θέλω τὸ μαῦρο μου σακκάκι καὶ τὸ ἄσπρο μου γελέκο. — Βάλε τὸ καλό σου ἐπανωφόρι. — 'Εδῶ εἶνε τὰ μαῦρα σας παπούτσια.—Βάλετε αὐτὸ τὸ σακκάκι.—Αὐτὸ τὸ ἐπανωφόρι δὲν ἔχει καλαῖς τσέπες.—Τὸ παληό μου σακκάκι ἔχει τρεῖς καλὲς τσέπαις.—'Αρέσεις τὸ καινούργιο μου καπέλλο;

Translate and read aloud in Greek:

Are these my clothes? — Yes. These are your new clothes. — Do you want to go out? — Yes. I want to go to my sister's house. — Do you want your new coat? — No; I want my old black coat. — This coat has four good pockets. — Put on your other hat and your new shoes. — Which hat do you like better? The new or the old one? — My sister likes her old hat better.

Read aloud and try to give an answer in Greek:

Ποῦ εἶνε τὰ καινούργια μου παπούτσια;—Θέλετε νὰ ὑπάγετε ἔξω;—Ποῦ θέλετε νὰ ὑπάγετε (ἢ Ποῦ θέλετε νὰ πᾶτε);—Θέλετε τὰ καινούργια σας ροῦχα ἢ τὰ παλαιά;—Ποῖον πανταλόνι θέλετε;—Πόσες τσέπες ἔχει τὸ σακκάκι σου;—'Αρέσεις αὐτὸ τὸ ἄσπρο καπέλλο;—Θέλεις νὰ βάλῃς ἕνα καινούργιο καπέλλο;—Τί ἀγαπᾷ ἡ μητέρα σου;—Τί εἶνε ἐπάνω στὸ κρεββάτι;

LESSON 14

Read aloud and translate in English:

Αὐτὸ τὸ ὑποκάμισο εἶνε λερό.—Φέρε μου ἕνα καθαρὸ ὑποκάμισο, σὲ παρακαλῶ. —'Η φίλη μου ἔχει ἕνα παλαιὸ μαῦρο φόρεμα.—'Η μητέρα της ἔχει ἕνα καινούργιο ἐπανωφόρι.—Ἡ μητέρα της δὲν εἶνε πολὺ γραῖα. Εἶνε νέα.—Τῆς ἀδελφῆς σας τὸ φόρεμα εἶνε πολὺ ὡραῖον.—Ὁ πατέρας μας δὲν ἔχει πολλὰ χρήματα.—Ὁ ἀδελφός μας ἔχει πολλὰ χρήματα.—Εἶνε νέος καὶ πλούσιος.—Ἀρέσετε αὐτὴν τὴν νέαν κόρην;—Δὲν ἀρέσω αὐτὴν τὴν κόρην.—Τὸ κεφάλι της εἶνε πολὺ μικρό.—Τὸ πρόσωπό της δὲν εἶνε ὡραῖον.

Translate and read aloud in Greek:

Is this a clean shirt? — Do you want another collar? — Yes; bring me another collar, please. — Is this your sister's dress? — No; this is my mother's old dress. — Is your mother old? — My mother is not so old. She is young. — Your father is old. His hair is white. — Your father is rich; is he not? — You are not right; my father is not rich; he is poor. — His brother is very rich.

Read aloud and try to give an answer in Greek:

Εἶνε αὐτὸ τὸ κολλάρο καθαρό;—Θέλετε ἕνα καθαρὸ ὑποκάμισο;—Ἔχει ἡ ἀδελφή σου καινούριο φόρεμα;—Τὸ φόρεμα τῆς μητέρας σας εἶνε καινούργιο ἢ παλαιό;—Εἶνε πολὺ γραῖα ἡ μητέρα σας;—Ἡ ἀδελφή σας εἶνε ὡραία;—Εἶνε ὡραῖον τὸ φόρεμά της;—Αὐτὰ τὰ ροῦχα εἶνε καινούργια ἢ παλαιά;—Ἔχει πολλὰ χρήματα ὁ πατέρας σας;—Ἀρέσεις αὐτὸν τὸν νέον;—Εἶνε τὸ πρόσωπό του μεγάλο ἢ μικρό;—Ἔχετε δίκαιον ἢ ἄδικον;

LESSON 15

Read aloud and translate in English:

Τί σᾶς ἔδωσε ἡ ἀδελφή μας προχθές;—Προχθὲς ἡ ἀδελφή σας μᾶς ἔδωσε μίαν πένναν.—Ποῦ ἐβάλατε αὐτὴν τὴν πένναν;—Τὴν ἐβάλαμε ἐπάνω στὸ βιβλίο.—Τί ἔκαμε ὁ ἀδελφός σου χθές;—Ὁ ἀδελφός μου δὲν ἔκαμε τίποτε χθές.—Ποῦ ἐπήγατε προχθές;—Προχθὲς ἐπήγαμε στῆς ἀδελφῆς μας τὸ σπίτι.—Τί καλὸ πρᾶγμα ἔκαμες χθές; —Χθὲς ἔδωσα χρήματα σ' ἕνα πτωχὸν ἄνθρωπον.

Translate and read aloud in Greek:

Did you have much money?—I had very little money.—Where have you put my hat?—We have put it on your bed.—Go and bring it here, please.—We have brought it. Here it is.—What do you want now?—We do not want anything now. — Yesterday we wanted money. — Did you want much money?—No. We wanted very little.

Read aloud and try to give an answer in Greek:

Τί σᾶς ἔδωσε ὁ πατέρας σας;—Ἐδίδατε χρήματα ὅταν εἴχατε;—Εἰς ποῖον ἐδώσατε τὸ βιβλίον σας;—Ποῦ ἔβαλε τὸ βιβλίον ὁ ἀδελφός σου;—Ποῦ ἐπήγατε χθές; —Τί ἐκάματε ἐκεῖ;—Τί ἐδώσατε εἰς τὸν πτωχὸν ἄνθρωπον;—Ποῦ ἔχεις βάλει τὰ παπούτσια σου;—Τί μᾶς ἔφερες;—Μᾶς ἔφερες πολλὰ πράγματα;—Τί ἠθέλατε εἰς τὸν δρόμον;

LESSON 16

Read aloud and translate in English:

Ὁ πατέρας μας ἦταν ἐδῶ χθές.—Ἦλθε μαζὺ μὲ τὴν ἀδελφή μας. —Ἦταν ἡ ἀδελφή σας καλά;—Ἡμεῖς δὲν τὴν εἴδαμεν.—Ὁ ἀδελφός μας τὴν εἶδε.—Γνωρίζετε τὸν ἀδελφό μας; —Ἐγὼ δὲν τὸν γνωρίζω.—Ἐγνώριζα τὸν πατέρα σας ὅταν ἦταν νέος.—Ἐπήγαινε στὸ σχολεῖο μαζὺ μὲ τὸν ἀδελφό μου.—Ἔχεις ἴδει τὰ καινούργια μου παπούτσια;—Ναί, Τὰ ἔχω ἴδει, ἀλλὰ δὲν εἶδα τὸ καινούργιο σου ἐπανωφόρι.

Translate and read aloud in Greek:

Whom did you see when you were coming from (the) school?—I saw an old friend in the street.—I saw a horse and a wagon.—I did not see many people in the street.—Did you take coffee or milk yesterday?—Yesterday I took milk and coffee.—Have you taken anything to-day?—To-day I have taken only milk.—I take tea now.—When I was young I used to take coffee with milk always.

Read aloud and try to give an answer in Greek:

Ποῦ εἶνε ὁ ἀδελφός σου;—Ἔφερες τὸν ἀδελφό σου ἐδῶ σήμερα;—Ποῖον ἄλλον ἔφερες ἐδῶ;—Ποῖον εἶδες εἰς τὸν δρόμον;—Ἀπὸ ποῦ ἤρχεσο ὅταν σὲ εἶδα;—Ποῖος ἄλλος ἦτο μαζύ σου;—Ἐγνώριζες τὸν ἀδελφό μου ὅταν ἦτο νέος;—Ποῦ ἤσουν προχθές;—Εἶχες τὴν ἀδελφή σου μαζύ σου;—Διατὶ δὲν τὴν ἔφερες ἐδῶ;—Διατὶ δὲν ἤθελε νὰ ἔλθῃ;

LESSON 17

Read aloud and translate in English:

Ποῦ θὰ ὑπάγῃς αὔριον;—Αὔριον θὰ ὑπάγω εἰς τὴν πόλιν.—Θὰ ὑπάγετε μαζὺ μὲ τὴν ἀδελφήν σας;—Βέβαια. Θὰ ὑπάγω μαζὺ μὲ τὴν ἀδελφήν μου.—Τί θὰ κάμετε σήμερον;—Σήμερον θὰ ὑπάγω νὰ ἴδω τὸν πατέρα μου.—Θὰ πάρετε τὸν ἀδελφόν σας μαζύ σας;—Ὄχι. Δὲν θὰ τὸν πάρω μαζύ μου.—Ὁ ἀδελφός μου θὰ ἔλθῃ αὔριον.—Νομίζετε ὅτι θὰ τὸν ἴδετε;—Νομίζω ὅτι θὰ τὸν ἴδω εἰς τὴν ἐξοχήν.

Translate and read aloud in Greek:

When will you see your father?—We will see him to-morrow.—He will come to the city.—My mother will go with him.—Will you give me your pencil?—Yes. I will give you my pencil.—What will you take now?—Now I will take coffee and milk.—What will your sister take?—I don't know. I think she will take milk.

Read aloud and try to give an answer in Greek:

Ποῦ θὰ ὑπάγετε τώρα; — Ποῖον θὰ πάρετε μαζύ σας; — Τί θὰ κάμετε σήμερον;—Θὰ ἔλθῃ ἡ μητέρα σας ἐδῶ;—Θὰ ἔχετε χρήματα αὔριον;—Τί θὰ δώσετε εἰς τὸν ἀδελφόν σας;—Τί θὰ κάμῃ ὁ ἀδελφός σας μὲ τὰ χρήματα;—Θὰ ὑπάγετε εἰς τὴν ἐξοχὴν ἐφέτος;—Ποῦ ἐπήγατε πέρυσι;—Ποῦ ἔβαλες τὸ καπέλλο σου;—Ποῦ θὰ βάλῃς τὰ παπούτσια σου;

LESSON 18

Read aloud and translate in English:

Πόσα χέρια ἔχομεν;—Ἔχομεν δύο χέρια.—Τί κάμνομεν μὲ τὰ χέρια μας;—Ἐργαζόμεθα μὲ τὰ χέρια μας.—Τί εἰμποροῦμεν νὰ κάμωμεν μὲ τὰ πόδια μας;—Μὲ τὰ πόδια μας εἰμποροῦμεν νὰ περιπατῶμεν. — Τί κάμνομεν μὲ τὸ στόμα μας;—Μὲ τὸ στόμα μας τρώγομεν καὶ πίνομεν.—Μὲ τὴν μύτην μας μυριζόμεθα.—Μὲ τὰ αὐτιά μας ἀκούομεν.— Μὲ τὰ δόντια μας μασσῶμεν (ἢ μασσοῦμεν).

Translate and read aloud in Greek:

What can you do with your eyes?—I can see with my eyes.—Can you hear with your nose?—No; I cannot hear with my nose.—I can hear with my ears.—How many ears have we?—We have two ears and two eyes.—We have one nose and one mouth.—We can smell with our nose.—We can eat with our mouth.—Do you want to eat now?—No; I cannot eat now.

Read aloud and try to give an answer in Greek:

Πόσα πόδια ἔχομεν;—Τί κάμνομεν μὲ τὰ πόδια μας;—Εἰμποροῦμεν νὰ ἐργαζώμεθα μὲ τὰ πόδια μας;—Πόσα χέρια ἔχομεν;—Τί εἰμποροῦμεν νὰ κάμνωμεν μὲ τὰ χέρια μας;—Τί κάμνομεν μὲ τὴν μύτην μας;—Εἰμποροῦμεν νὰ τρώγωμεν μὲ τὴν μύτην μας;—Τί θέλετε νὰ κάμωμεν τώρα;—Θέλετε νὰ φάγωμεν ἢ νὰ περιπατήσωμεν;—Ποῦ θέλετε νὰ ὑπάγωμεν;

LESSON 19

Read aloud and translate in English:

Τί κάμνομεν μὲ τὴν γλῶσσάν μας;—Ὁμιλοῦμεν μὲ τὴν γλῶσσάν μας.—Ποῖος ὁμιλεῖ στὴν σάλαν;—Ὁ ἀδελφός μου ὁμιλεῖ μὲ τὴν ἀδελφήν μου.—Μὲ ποῖον ὡμίλεις (or ὡμιλοῦσες) χθές;—Χθὲς ὡμίλουν (or ὡμιλοῦσα) μὲ τὸν φίλον μου.—Θέλω νὰ ἴδω (or ἰδῶ) τὰ δάκτυλά σου.—Εἶνε τὰ δάκτυλά σου καθαρά;—Τὰ χέρια μου καὶ τὰ δάκτυλά μου εἶνε πολὺ καθαρά.—Νομίζω ὅτι ὁ λαιμός σου δὲν εἶνε πολὺ καθαρός.—Ἔχετε ἄδικον.—Ὁ λαιμός μου εἶνε πολὺ καθαρός.

Translate and read aloud in Greek:

Hello, John. How are you? I am not very well.—I am a little sick.—Are you warm?—No. I am cold.—My hands and my feet are very cold.—Do you want to make a fire?—Yes. Have you coal and wood?—We have some coal, but we have no wood.—Do you want a match?—Here is a box of matches.

Read aloud and try to give an answer in Greek:

Εἶνε τὰ χέρια σου καθαρά;—Εἶνε τὰ πόδια σου ζεστά;—Κρυώνετε;—Θέλετε νὰ κάμετε φωτιά;—Ἔχετε ξύλα;—Θὰ μοῦ δώσετε ἕνα σπίρτο;—Βλέπετε κανένα εἰς τὸ σπίτι;—Πόσους ἀνθρώπους βλέπετε εἰς τὸν δρόμον;—Θέλετε νὰ φάγετε τώρα;—Τί θέλετε νὰ φάγετε;—Ἐφάγατε καλὰ σήμερον;

LESSON 20

Read aloud and translate in English:

Καλησπέρα Γιάννη.—Τί κάνεις.—Πῶς εἶσθε ὅλοι;—Εἴμεθα πολὺ καλά. Εὐχαριστῶ.—Ἐγὼ δὲν εἶμαι τόσον καλά.—Εἶμαι ὀλίγον ἄρρωστος.—Τί ἔχετε;—Δὲν εἰξεύρω.—Ἔχω ἕνα μικρὸν πονοκέφαλον.—Τὰ πόδια μου εἶνε κρύα.—Τὸ κεφάλι μου εἶνε ζεστό.—Νομίζω ἔχω πάρει ἕνα μικρὸν κρυολόγημα.—Δὲν εἶνε τίποτε.

Translate and read aloud in Greek:

Are your feet cold?—My feet are not cold. They are very warm.—Have you a headache?—Yes. I have a little headache.—Where is your father? My father is in the store.—My mother is here.—Do you work now?—Yes. I work all day.—Is your brother working?—No. My brother is not working now.

Read aloud and try to give an answer in Greek:

Πῶς εἶσαι, Γεῶργο;—Εἶσαι καλά;—Ποῖος εἶνε ἄρρωστος;—Τί ἔχει;—Εἶνε πολὺ ἄρρωστος;—Ποῦ εἶνε ἡ ἀδελφή σου;—Τί κάμνει ἡ ἀδελφή σου τώρα;—Ποῦ ἐργάζεται;—Ἐργάζεται τὴν ἡμέρα ἢ τὴν νύκτα; —Ποῖος ἄλλος ἐργάζεται ἐκεῖ; —Τί κάμνουν εἰς αὐτὸ τὸ ἐργοστάσιον;—Κάμνουν ὑποκάμισσα διὰ ἄνδρας (men) ἢ γυναῖκας;—Ἠξεύρεις ποῖος εἶνε μέσα στὸ σπίτι;

LESSON 21

Read aloud and translate in English:

Θέλετε ἕνα κουτὶ γλυκά;—Τί γλυκὰ εἶναι;—Εἶνε σοκαλάτες.—Σᾶς ἀρέσουν;—Ναί, μοῦ ἀρέσουν. — Θέλετε νὰ φάγετε κάτι;—Ναί. Πεινῶ πολύ.—Τί θέλετε νὰ φάγετε;—Δόστε μου ὅ,τι δήποτε.—Καθήσατε παρακαλῶ.—Θέλετε ψητὸ βωδινὸ καὶ σαλάτα;—Ὄχι.—Δόσατέ μου δύο αὐγὰ καὶ ἕνα πιάτο μακαρόνια.

Translate and read aloud in Greek:

What have you for me?—I have a box of chocolates.—Are they good chocolates?—I think they are very good.—Have you anything to eat?—Yes. We have roast meat and potatoes.—Do you want some salad also?—No. I don't want any salad.—Please give me some roast meat.—Will you have some macaroni also?—No, thank you. I don't like macaroni.

Read aloud and try to give an answer in Greek:

Τί θέλετε νὰ φάγετε;—Θέλετε σοῦπα;—Θέλετε ψητὸ βωδινό;—Σᾶς ἀρέσουν ἡ πατάτες;—Θέλετε ὀλίγον χοιρομέρι;—Θέλετε νὰ φάγετε αὐγά;—Ἔχετε κουτάλι καὶ πειροῦνι;—Πόσα μαχαίρια ἔχετε; —Διψᾶτε; Θέλετε νὰ πιῆτε κάτι;—Θὰ πάρετε ἕνα φλυτζάνι καφέ;

LESSON 22

Read aloud and translate in English:

Αὐτὸ εἶνε τὸ σπίτι τοῦ ἰατροῦ;—Ναί.—Τὸ ἄλλο εἶνε τοῦ κρεοπώλου τὸ σπίτι.—Τοῦ ἀδελφοῦ μου τὸ ἐπανωφόρι ἔχει μαῦρο χρῶμα.—Τῆς ἀδελφῆς μου τὸ καπέλλο (or τὸ καπέλλο τῆς ἀδελφῆς μου) ἔχει ἄσπρο χρῶμα.—Ἡ Μαρία φορεῖ ἕνα πράσινο φόρεμα.—Χθὲς ἐφοροῦσε κίτρινο φόρεμα.—Ἡ Ἑλένη ἔχει ἄσπρα παπούτσια.—Τῆς μητέρας μου τὰ παπούτσια εἶνε μαῦρα.—Τοῦ παντοπώλου ἡ κόρη φορεῖ κόκκινο φόρεμα.—Τὸ φόρεμά της δὲν ἦτο κόκκινο.—Ἦτο κίτρινο.

Translate and read aloud in Greek:

Is the grocer's house large or small?—The grocer's house is large.—The butcher's house is small.—Helen is wearing a green dress.—Yesterday she wore a yellow dress.—Her coat has a red color.—The pockets of my coat are large.—What fruit will you have?—Will you have an apple or a banana? —I'll take an orange and a pear.—Here are a green pear, a yellow banana and a red apple.

Read aloud and try to give an answer in Greek:

Αὐτὸ εἶνε τὸ σπίτι τοῦ ἰατροῦ;—Εἶνε μεγάλο ἢ μικρό;—Τὸ φόρεμα τῆς ἀδελφῆς σου εἶνε μαῦρο ἢ ἄσπρο;—Τί ἐφοροῦσε ἡ κόρη τοῦ παντοπώλου χθές;—Πεινᾶτε ἢ διψᾶτε;—Θέλετε νὰ φάγετε ἕνα φροῦτο;—Τί φροῦτα ἔχετε;—Τί χρῶμα ἔχουν αὐτὰ τὰ ἀπίδια;—Τὰ μάτια τῆς ἀδελφῆς σου εἶνε γαλανὰ ἢ καστανά;—Ποιὸς εἶνε στὸν διάδρομο;—Εἶνε αὐτὸ τὸ πρᾶγμα ὅμοιον μὲ ἐκεῖνο;

LESSON 23

Read aloud and translate in English:

Ὁ Γιάννης ἐπῆγε στὸν μπακάλη.—Τί ἐπῆγε νὰ κάμῃ ἐκεῖ;—Ἐπῆγε νὰ ἀγοράσῃ πράγματα.—Τί πράγματα ἐπῆγε νὰ ἀγοράσῃ ὁ Γιάννης;—Ἐπῆγε νὰ ἀγοράσῃ ὅ,τι χρειαζόμεθα·—Θέλομεν μιὰ μποτίλια λάδι, μιὰ σακοῦλα ἀλεῦρι καὶ δύο λίτρες πατάτες.—Θέλομεν νέες πατάτες.—Δὲν θέλομεν παλαιές.—Θέλομεν ἐπίσης μία λίτρα ρύζι καὶ πέντε λεμόνια.—Ὁ Γιάννης θὰ ἀγοράσῃ ὅ,τιδήποτε ἄλλο χρειαζόμεθα.

Translate and read aloud in Greek:

What do you want?—I want to buy things for the house.—Who will go to the grocer's? — John will go. — He went; he opened the door; he closed the door.—What did he say to the grocer?—He said to the grocer: Please, Mr. Polites, give me a pound of butter.—Give me also a bottle of vinegar. We want to make a salad.

Read aloud and try to give an answer in Greek:

Ποῦ ἐπῆγε ὁ Γιάννης;—Διατὶ ὁ Γιάννης ἐπῆγε στοῦ μπακάλη;—Τί ἤθελε νὰ ἀγοράσῃ;—Τί χρειαζόμεθα στὸ σπίτι;—Ποῖος ἄνοιξε τὴν θύραν;—Ποῖος ἔκλεισε τὴν θύραν;—Τί εἶπεν ὁ Γιάννης στὸν μπακάλην ὅταν ἐμπῆκε μέσα;—Τί τοῦ εἶπε ὁ μπακάλης;—Τί ἄλλο ἀγόρασε ὁ Γιάννης ἀπὸ τὸν μπακάλην;—Πόσες λίτρες πατάτες ἀγόρασε ὁ Γιάννης;

LESSON 24

Read aloud and translate in English:

Τί ἐρώτησε ὁ μπακάλης τὸν Γιάννην;—Ὁ μπακάλης ἐρώτησε τὸν Γιάννην ἐὰν ἤθελε τίποτε ἄλλο (anything else).—Τί εἶπε ὁ Γιάννης στὸν μπακάλη;—Τοῦ εἶπε ὅτι ἤθελε ἕνα τενεκὲ τομάτες καὶ μία σακοῦλα ἀλεῦρι.—Ὁ Γιάννης ἀγόρασε ἐπίσης μισὴ λίτρα ρύζι καὶ δέκα αὐγά.—Τί ἄλλο ἐρώτησε ὁ Γιάννης τὸν μπακάλη;—Ὁ Γιάννης ἐρώτησε τὸν μπακάλη ἐὰν εἶχε φροῦτα.—Ἤθελε νὰ ἀγοράσῃ μῆλα καὶ ἀπίδια.—Πόσες λίτρες πατάτες ἀγόρασε ὁ Γιάννης;—Ὁ Γιάννης ἀγόρασε τρεῖς λίτρες μικρὲς πατάτες.

Translate and read aloud in Greek:

What did John say to the grocer?—John said to the grocer: Mr. Polites, have you any fruit?—What did the grocer ask John?—The grocer asked

John: What fruit do you want? — John asked: How much are these red apples?—The grocer said: These red apples are five cents.—Those green apples are two cents.—John bought also three pounds of onions.—The grocer put everything in a big bag.—John asked how much they cost.

Read aloud and try to give an answer in Greek:

Τί ἐρώτησε τὸν Γιάννην ὁ κύριος Πολίτης;—Τί τοῦ εἶπε ὁ Γιάννης;—Τί ἄλλο ἀγόρασε ὁ Γιάννης;—Πόσες λίτρες πατάτες ἀγόρασε;—Ἐπῆρε τίποτε ἄλλο ὁ Γιάννης; — Τί ἄλλο ἐρώτησε ὁ Γιάννης τὸν μπακάλην;—Πόσα μῆλα ἀγόρασε ὁ Γιάννης;—Πόσον ἀξίζουν τὰ μῆλα καὶ πόσον τὰ ἀπίδια;—Πόσα χρήματα ἔδωσε ὁ Γιάννης στὸν μπακάλην;—Πόσα ρέστα ἔδωσε ὁ μπακάλης στὸν Γιάννη;

LESSON 25

Read aloud and translate in English:

Ποιὰ εἶνε αὐτὴ ἡ νέα;—Αὐτὴ ἡ νέα εἶνε θυγατέρα μου.—Ἐκεῖνος ὁ νέος εἶνε υἱός μου.—Ἡ ἀδελφή μου ἔχει ἕνα μετάξινο φόρεμα.—Ἐπίσης ἔχει ἕνα καινούριο ζευγάρι ὑποδήματα.—Αὐτὴ ἡ πέννα εἶνε ἰδική σας;—Αὐτὴ ἡ παλαιὰ πέννα δὲν εἶνε ἰδική μου.—Εἶνε τοῦ ἀδελφοῦ μου. Ἐκείνη ἡ χρυσῆ πέννα εἶνε ἰδική μου. — Αὐτὸ τὸ ἀσημένιο ὡρολόγι εἶνε ἰδικό σας;—Ὄχι.—Ἐκεῖνο τὸ χρυσὸ ὡρολόγι εἶνε ἰδικό μας.—Ἐκεῖνο τὸ πράσινο βαμβακερὸ φόρεμα εἶνε τῆς θυγατέρας μου.

Translate and read aloud in Greek:

Is this young woman your daughter? — This young woman is not my daughter. She is my sister.—That young man is my son.—Your son has a new gold watch.—That watch is not his. It is mine.—My daughter has a new silk dress.—Are these her shoes?—No. These shoes are not hers. They are my sister's.—How do you know they are your sister's?—I know them, because I was with her when she bought them.

Read aloud and try to give an answer in Greek:

Πόσας θυγατέρας ἔχετε;—Αὐτὴ εἶνε ἡ μικρή σας θυγατέρα;—Αὐτὸ τὸ μετάξινο φόρεμα εἶνε ἰδικό της;—Ἐκεῖνο τὸ καινούριο ζευγάρι παπούτσια εἶνε ἰδικό σας;—Εἶνε ἰδικό σας αὐτὸ τὸ χρυσὸ ὡρολόγι;—Τίνος (whose) εἶνε ἐκεῖνο τὸ ἀσημένιο μαχαῖρι;—Πῶς γνωρίζετε ὅτι εἶνε τοῦ ἀδελφοῦ σας;—Τίνος εἶνε ἐκεῖνος ὁ μεγάλος σκύλος;—Ἡ κάλτσες σας εἶνε μετάξινες ἢ βαμβακερές;—Εἶνε ἰδική σας αὐτὴ ἡ μαύρη γάτα;

LESSON 26

Read aloud and translate in English:

Γνωρίζετε αὐτὸν τὸν παπουτσῆν;—Ναί, τὸν γνωρίζω.—Θέλετε νὰ πάρετε ἕνα ζευγάρι παπούτσια;—Τί εἴδους παπούτσια θέλετε;—Θέλω δερμάτινα παπούτσια.—Εἶνε πολὺ ἀκριβὰ αὐτὰ τὰ παπούτσια;—Ὄχι, δὲν εἶνε ἀκριβά.—Εἶνε εὐθηνά.—Ποία εἶνε αὐτὴ ἡ νέα;—Αὐτὴ ἡ νέα εἶνε φίλη μου.—Πότε θὰ ὑπάγετε εἰς τὸν ράπτην;—Θὰ ὑπάγω εἰς τοῦ ράπτου (to the tailor's) μετὰ τὸ φαγητόν.

Translate and read aloud in Greek:

What will you do at the tailor's?—I want him to make a dress for my daughter.—Will you go there after dinner or before supper?—I'll go after dinner.—I'll take the baby with me.—Is this your son?—Yes. He is my son. He is a very good boy.—Will you buy a coat for him?—I'll buy a coat and a pair of shoes for him.—When will you go to work?—I'll go to work after dinner.—Now I'll go and see the doctor.

Read aloud and try to give an answer in Greek:

Ποῖος εἶνε ἐκεῖνος ὁ κύριος;—Τί ἐργασίαν κάμνει;—Κάμνει καλὰ παπούτσια αὐτὸς ὁ παπουτσῆς;—Θέλετε νὰ σᾶς κάμῃ ἕνα ζευγάρι παπούτσια;—Τί εἴδους ἀπίδια εἶνε αὐτά;—Εἶνε πολὺ ἀκριβά;—Ἐκεῖνες αἱ βανάνες εἶνε εὐθηνές;—Τίνος εἶνε αὐτὸ τὸ μωρό; —Εἶνε ἰδικόν σας;—Δὲν νομίζετε ὅτι εἶνε πολὺ εὔμορφον;—Πότε θὰ ὑπάγετε στὴν ἐργασία; —Ποῖος ἄλλος θὰ ὑπάγῃ μαζύ σας;—Τί εἴδους ροῦχα θὰ ἀγοράσετε;

LESSON 27

Read aloud and translate in English:

Ποῦ ἦσο χθές;—Χθὲς ἤμουν εἰς τὴν πόλιν.—Προχθὲς ἤμουν εἰς τὴν ἐξοχήν.—Ἔβρεχε προχθὲς εἰς τὴν ἐξοχήν;—Ὄχι.—Δὲν ἔβρεχε. Ὁ καιρὸς ἦτο πολὺ ὡραῖος.—Ἀγαπᾶτε νὰ μένετε εἰς τὴν ἐξοχήν;—Ναί. Μοῦ ἀρέσει νὰ ζῶ εἰς τὴν ἐξοχήν. —Ἡ μητέρα μας ἐπίσης ἀγαπᾶ τὴν ἐξοχήν.—Ὁ ἀδελφός μου ἀγαπᾶ καλλίτερα νὰ μένῃ εἰς τὴν πόλιν.—Τῆς ἐξοχῆς ὁ ἀέρας εἶνε πολὺ ὑγιεινός.—Ἦσο μόνος εἰς τὴν ἐξοχήν;—Ὄχι.—Ἡ ἀδελφή μου ἦτο ἐκεῖ ἐπίσης.

Translate and read aloud in Greek:

Were you in the country yesterday?—Yes. Yesterday I was in the country.—The day before yesterday I went to the city.—Did you go to your sister's house?—No. I went to a friend's house.—Who else went to the country with you?—My father went with me.—Does he like the country? —Yes. He likes the country very much.—He says that the country air is very healthful.

Read aloud and try to give an answer in Greek:

Ποῦ ἦτο χθὲς ὁ ἀδελφός σας;—Ἦταν καλὸς καιρὸς εἰς τὴν ἐξοχήν;—Ἔβρεχε ὅλην τὴν ἡμέραν;—Ποῖος ἄλλος ἦτο εἰς τὴν ἐξοχήν;—Διατὶ ἔμεινε ἡ ἀδελφή σας εἰς τὴν πόλιν;—Ποῦ θέλετε καλλίτερα νὰ μένετε—στὴν πόλιν ἢ στὴν ἐξοχήν;—Εἴχατε καλὴν διασκέδασιν προχθές;—Ποῦ θὰ πᾶτε (or ὑπάγετε) αὔριον;—Ποῖον θὰ πάρετε μαζύ σας;

LESSON 28

Read aloud and translate in English:

Ὁ καιρὸς εἶνε καλὸς σήμερον.—Χθὲς δὲν ἦτο τόσον καλός.—Χθὲς τὸ πρωῒ ἔβρεχε. —Ἐμείναμεν σπίτι.—Δὲν ἐπήγαμε ἔξω.—Σήμερον ὁ καιρὸς εἶνε ὡραῖος. Θὰ ὑπάγω ἔξω μαζὺ μὲ τὸν φίλον μου.—Εἶνε καλὰ ἡ μητέρα σας;—Ἡ μητέρα μου δὲν εἶνε τόσον καλά.—Εἶνε ἄρρωστη.—Ἔμεινε σπίτι ὅλην τὴν ἑβδομάδα.—Λυποῦμαι πολὺ ποῦ τὸ ἀκούω.—Εἰπέτε της ὅτι θὰ χαρῶ νὰ τὴν ἰδῶ πάλιν καλά.

Translate and read aloud in Greek:

Where were you last week?—Last week I was in the country.—We went there with our friends.—Will you go this week also?—I don't know. We will go if the weather is good.—Did you have a letter from your father?—Yes. We had a letter from him last week.—Is he well?—He is very well. He will be home in a few days.—My mother was ill last week.—What was the matter with her?—She had a little cold.

Read aloud and try to give an answer in Greek:

Ἦτο καλὸς ὁ καιρὸς χθές;—Ἔβρεχε ὅλην τὴν ἡμέραν ἢ τὸ πρωῒ μόνον;—Ἐμείνατε σπίτι ἢ ἐπήγατε ἔξω;—Εἴχατε ὀμπρέλλαν;—Ἦσο ἐδῶ τὴν περασμένην ἑβδομάδα;—Ἦτο ὁ φίλος σου μαζύ σου;—Διατὶ ἦτο εὐτυχὴς ὁ φίλος σου;—Εἶχες ἀρκετὰ χρήματα;—Ὁ φίλος σου εἶνε πτωχὸς ἢ πλούσιος;—Ἦτο ἄρρωστη ἡ μητέρα σας χθές;—Τί εἶχε;—Ἔγινε ἐντελῶς καλὰ τώρα;—Εἴχατε γράμμα ἀπὸ τὸν ἀδελφόν σας;—Πότε θὰ ἔλθῃ εἰς τὴν πόλιν νὰ μᾶς ἴδῃ;

LESSON 29

Read aloud and translate in English:

Πρέπει νὰ φύγωμεν ἀμέσως;—Ναί.—Πρέπει νὰ ὑπάγωμε τώρα.—Δὲν ἔχομεν πολὺν καιρόν.—Εἶνε ἀργά.—Εἰμποροῦμεν νὰ μείνωμεν ὀλίγον ἀκόμη;—Ὄχι.—Εἶνε πολὺ ἀργά.—Κάμετε γρήγορα.—Γιάννη, σήκω.—Κοιμᾶσαι ἀκόμη;—Ἡμεῖς εἴμεθα ἕτοιμοι νὰ φύγωμεν.—Κάμε γρήγορα.—Διατί εἶσαι τόσον ἀργός; (or Διατί ἀργεῖς τόσον);—Δὲν εἰξεύρω ποῦ εἶνε τὸ καπέλλο μου.—Ποῦ τὸ ἔβαλες χθὲς τὸ βράδυ ὅταν ἦλθες σπίτι; — Τὸ ηὗρα. Αὐτὸ εἶνε. — Ἀλλὰ δὲν θὰ φορέσω αὐτὸ τὸ καπέλλο.—Θὰ φορέσω τὸ ἄλλο μου καπέλλο.—Τώρα εἶμαι ἐντελῶς ἕτοιμος.

Translate and read aloud in Greek:

Must we go now?—Yes. We must go immediately (ἀμέσως).—How long (πόσον καιρὸν) can we stay here?—We must not stay here any longer.—What is the matter with you, John?—Are you still sleeping?—You must get up quickly.—We must go immediately.—Where is Helen?—Must she come too?—Helen must come with us also.—She is not here yet. She is very late.

Read aloud and try to give an answer in Greek:

Διατί πρέπει νὰ φύγωμε τώρα;—Εἶνε πολὺ ἀργά;—Εἶνε ὅλοι ἕτοιμοι;—Ποῦ εἶνε ὁ Γιάννης;—Κοιμᾶται ἀκόμη;—Διατί κοιμᾶσαι τόσον πολύ;—Δὲν εἰξεύρεις ὅτι πρέπει νὰ φύγωμεν ἀμέσως; — Διατί εἶσαι τόσον ἀργός (or ἀργεῖς τόσον);—Δὲν γνωρίζεις ποῦ ἔβαλες τὰ παπούτσια σου;—Θὰ κάμῃς γρήγορα;—Πότε πρέπει νὰ φύγωμεν ἀπὸ ἐδῶ;—Ποῖον θὰ ὑπάγωμεν νὰ ἴδωμεν εἰς τὴν πόλιν;—Πρέπει νὰ ἔλθω καὶ ἐγὼ μαζύ σας;

LESSON 30

Read aloud and translate in English:

Εἴμεθα ὅλοι ἕτοιμοι.—Θὰ ὑπάγωμεν πολὺ μακράν;—Ὄχι.—Δὲν εἶνε τόσον μακρὰν ἀπ' ἐδῶ.—Πρέπει νὰ περιμένωμεν τὸ τράμ.—Δὲν εἶνε πολὺ πλησίον.—Τὸ τρὰμ εἶνε ἐδῶ.—Πρέπει νὰ τρέξωμεν διότι δὲν θὰ περιμένῃ πολὺν καιρόν.—Ὁ Γιάννης ἀγαπᾷ καλλίτερα νὰ περιπατῇ.—Καὶ ἐγὼ ἐπίσης ἀγαπῶ νὰ περιπατῶ ὅταν ὁ καιρὸς εἶνε καλός.—Μὴ τρέχεις τόσον γρήγορα.—Στάσου καὶ περίμενέ μας.—Θὰ πᾶμε (or ὑπάγωμεν) ὅλοι μαζύ.

Translate and read aloud in Greek:

Where is Mrs. Helen's house?—It is not far from here.—Mrs. Helen has a beautiful house.—The stairs and the floors are very clean.—There are beautiful pictures on the walls.—Where is Mrs. Helen's husband?—Mrs. Helen says that her husband is not home.—We shall see him if we wait a little.—You must wait. It is early yet.—It is not late. We must not lose much time.—We must go soon.—We live far.—We are not so near.

Read aloud and try to give an answer in Greek:

Εἶσθε ὅλοι ἕτοιμοι;—Θὰ περιμένετε ἐδῶ;—Διατὶ δὲν περιπατεῖτε;—Εἶνε πολὺ μακρὰν ἢ εἶνε πλησίον;—Διατὶ ἐστάθης;—'Εδῶ εἶνε τὸ σπίτι τῆς φίλης σου;—Αὐτὸς εἶνε ὁ Κύριος Παῦλος;—Εἶνε σπίτι ἡ σύζυγός του;—Θὰ μείνωμεν ἢ θὰ φύγωμεν;—Διατὶ τρέχετε τόσον γρήγορα;—Πρέπει νὰ φύγωμεν ἀμέσως;—'Εχάσατε τὸν δρόμον;—Διατὶ δὲν περιμένετε ὀλίγον;

LESSON 31

Read aloud and translate in English:

Εἶδες τὴν ἐξαδέλφην μου;—Ναί. Τὴν εἶδα προχθὲς εἰς τὸ σπίτι μας.—Εἶχεν ἔλθει μόνη της;—Ὄχι. Εἶχεν ἔλθει μὲ τὸν μικρόν μου ἐξάδελφον.—'Ο φίλος μου λέγει ὅτι ἔχασε τὰ χρήματά του.—Τὰ εἶχε στὴν τσέπην του ἢ στὸ πορτοφόλι του;—Δὲν γνωρίζω·—Νομίζω ὅτι τὰ ηὗρε.—Ἦσαν μέσα στὸ πορτοφόλι του, ἐπάνω στὸ τραπέζι τῆς σάλας.—Δύνασθε νὰ μοῦ δώσετε πέντε δολλάρια;—Θέλω νὰ πληρώσω διὰ τὰ ροῦχα ποῦ ἀγόρασα.—Λυποῦμαι πολύ, ἀλλὰ δὲν δύναμαι νὰ σᾶς βοηθήσω.—Σήμερον ἐπλήρωσα διὰ τὰ ἰδικά μου ροῦχα.

Translate and read aloud in Greek:

Have you seen my cousin to-day?—I have not seen her to-day.—I saw her yesterday afternoon.—She was at the doctor's house with her mother.—How much money have you lost?—I have not lost any money.—I lost my pocketbook the day before yesterday, but I found it to-day.—Where was it?—It was under my bed.—How much money did you pay for your shoes?—I paid seven dollars for my shoes.

Read aloud and try to give an answer in Greek:

Ποῖον εἴδατε χθές;—Τὸν εἴδατε στὸν δρόμον ἢ στὸ σπίτι;—Ποῖος ἄλλος ἦτο μαζύ του;—'Εχάσατε πολλὰ χρήματα;—Ποῦ ηὕρατε τὸ πορτοφόλι σας;—Ποῖος τὸ εἶχε βάλει ἐκεῖ;—Τί καλὸ πρᾶγμα ἔκαμες σήμερον;—Εἰς ποῖον ἔδωσες χρήματα;—Πόσον ἐπλήρωσες διὰ τὸ καπέλλο σου;—Ποῖον ἐβοήθησες χθές;—Τί ἀγόρασες μὲ τὰ χρήματα ποῦ σοῦ ἔδωσα;

LESSON 32

Read aloud and translate in English:

Ποῦ θὰ ὑπάγετε (or πᾶτε) τὴν Κυριακήν;—Θὰ πᾶμε στὴν ἐξοχὴν ἂν μᾶς ἀφήσῃ ὁ πατέρας μας.—Ὁ πατέρας εἶπε πῶς δὲν πρέπει νὰ πᾶμε.—Δὲν θέλει νὰ μᾶς ἀφήσῃ μόνους.—Νομίζετε ὅτι θὰ βρέχῃ τὴν Κυριακήν;—Δὲν γνωρίζω.—Νομίζω πῶς θὰ εἶνε καλὸς καιρός.—Ἡμεῖς θὰ ὑπάγωμεν.—Δὲν μᾶς μέλει (we don't care) ἂν θὰ βρέξῃ. — Πόσον καιρὸν θὰ μείνετε εἰς τὴν ἐξοχήν; — Θὰ μείνωμεν ἐκεῖ ὅλην τὴν ἐρχομένην ἑβδομάδα.—Τί θὰ κάμετε τὴν ἐρχομένην Τρίτην;—Τὴν ἐρχομένην Τρίτην θὰ ὑπάγω εἰς τὴν ἐργασίαν.

Translate and read aloud in Greek:

Will you work all this month?—I think I'll work every day this month. —I need the money.—If you work all this month, you will have enough money.—Don't you think so?—Yes; I think so.—Last month I had plenty of (πολλὰ) money.—This month I have very little.—Next month I'll have enough.—Next year we shall be rich.—Where will you go next Wednesday?—Next Wednesday I will go to the butcher's house.

Read aloud and try to give an answer in Greek:

Ποῦ θὰ ὑπάγετε τὴν Δευτέραν;—Μαζὺ μὲ ποῖον θὰ ὑπάγετε;—Θὰ σᾶς ἀφήσῃ ἡ μητέρα σας νὰ ὑπάγετε;—Νομίζετε ὅτι θὰ βρέχῃ τὸ Σάββατον;—Πότε θὰ γυρίσετε ἀπὸ τὴν πόλιν;—Ποῖος ἦτο ἐδῶ τὸν περασμένον μῆνα;—Πότε θὰ ἐπιστρέψετε εἰς τὸ σπίτι;—Θὰ ἐργασθῆτε αὐτὸν τὸν μῆνα;—Τί θὰ κάμετε τὸν ἐρχόμενον μῆνα;—Εἰργάσθης τὴν περασμένην ἑβδομάδα;

LESSON 33

Read aloud and translate in English:

Τί εἴδους ἐργασίαν ζητεῖς;—Θέλω ὁποιανδήποτε ἐργασίαν.—Δὲν ἔχω ἐργασθῆ ἐπὶ (for) τέσσαρας μῆνας.—Τί ἐργασίαν γνωρίζεις;—Εἰμπορῶ νὰ κάμω κάθε εἴδους ἐργασίαν. — Εἰξεύρεις (or γνωρίζεις) νὰ μαγειρεύῃς; — Ναί. Εἰργαζόμην μάγειρος δέκα χρόνους.—Τί ἄλλο εἰμπορεῖς νὰ κάμνῃς καλά;—Εἰμπορῶ νὰ βοηθῶ στὴν κουζίνα.—Τί εἶσαι; —Ἀπὸ ποῦ κατάγεσαι;—Εἶμαι Ἕλλην.—Ἔρχομαι ἀπὸ τὴν Ἑλλάδα.—Εἶμαι Ἀμερικανός.—Ἐγεννήθην ἐδῶ.—Ὁ πατέρας μου καὶ ἡ μητέρα μου ἐγεννήθησαν στὴν Ἑλλάδα.

Translate and read aloud in Greek:

Is your father looking for work?—Yes. He is looking for work.—What work can he do? What is his business?—He is a tailor.—Is he a tailor? What does he make?—He makes clothes for men (δι' ἄνδρας) and women. —Can he do anything else?—I think he can do any kind of work.—Where did he work last month?—Last month he worked in a factory.—Is your father a Greek? — Yes. My father came from Greece. — He came when he was sixteen years old.—Did you come from Greece also?—No. I was born here.

Read aloud and try to give an answer in Greek:

Τί ἐργασίαν ζητεῖς;—Τί ἐργασίαν ἔκαμνες πρίν;—Πῶς ὀνομάζεσαι;—Ποῖον εἶνε τὸ ὄνομά σου;—Ποῦ μένεις—Ποῦ εἶνε τὸ σπίτι σου;—Μένετε πολὺν καιρὸν ἐκεῖ;—Πῶς ὀνομάζεται ὁ πατέρας σου;—Πῶς ὀνομάζεται ἡ μητέρα σου;—Πόσον ἐτῶν εἶσαι;—Ποίαν ἐργασίαν εἰμπορεῖς νὰ κάμῃς;—Εἶσαι Ἀμερικανὸς ἢ Ἕλλην;

—Ποῦ ἐγεννήθης;—Ἐγεννήθης ἐδῶ;—Ποῦ ἐγεννήθησαν ὁ πατέρας σου καὶ ἡ μητέρα σου;—Ὁμιλεῖτε Ἑλληνικά; Ἐννοεῖτε καλὰ Ἀγγλικά;

LESSON 34

Read aloud and translate in English:

Πόσα χρήματα κερδίζεις τὴν ἑβδομάδα;—Τώρα κερδίζω εἴκοσι ὀκτὼ δολλάρια τὴν ἑβδομάδα.—Πρὶν ἐκέρδιζα τριάντα δολλάρια.—Πληρώνετε πολὺ ἐνοίκιον;—Πληρώνομεν σαράντα δολλάρια τὸν μῆνα. — Τὸν περασμένο χρόνο ἐπληρώναμεν μόνον τριάντα πέντε δολλάρια.—Ποῦ μένετε; —Σὲ ποῖον μέρος μένετε;—Μένω εἰς τὸ ἑκατὸν-ἑξῆντα, Νέα Ὁδός.—Πέρυσι ἔμενα στὸν ἀριθμὸν τετρακόσια εἴκοσι, Δυτικὴ Ὁδός.—Ὁ ἀδελφός μου μένει εἰς τὸν ἴδιον δρόμον.

Translate and read aloud in Greek:

Where do you live now?—Now I live at sixty-eight Park Street.—Last year I lived (I used to live) at eighty-four John Street.—Did you live alone or with your father?—I lived (I used to live) alone.—How much do you want to earn a week?—I must make twenty-five dollars a week.—Last year I used to make six dollars a day.—We cannot pay so much here.—We shall pay you twenty-two dollars. You will work only thirty-five hours a week.—I must make more money.—My family cannot live on twenty-two dollars a week.

Read aloud and try to give an answer in Greek:

Ἐργάζεσαι τώρα ἢ ζητεῖς ἐργασίαν;—Πόσα χρήματα κερδίζεις;—Πόσα ἐκέρδιζες πέρυσι;—Μένεις μαζὺ μὲ τὸν πατέρα σου;—Ἔχετε οἰκογένειαν;—Πόσα παιδιὰ ἔχετε;—Ποῦ μένετε ἐφέτος;—Ποῦ ἐμένατε πέρυσι;—Πόσα χρήματα ἐκέρδιζες εἰς τὴν ἄλλην σου θέσιν;—Διατὶ ζητεῖς περισσότερα χρήματα;—Εἶνε πολὺ ἀκριβὰ τὰ πράγματα ἐφέτος;—Πόσον ἔχει τὸ ψωμί; Πόσον τὸ κρέας;

LESSON 35

Read aloud and translate in English:

Γνωρίζετε τί ὥρα εἶνε;—Ἡ ὥρα εἶνε ἕξ καὶ τέταρτον.—Εἶνε ἕξ καὶ δέκα ὀκτὼ λεπτά.—Τὸ ὡρολόγι σας πηγαίνει ἐμπρός.—Τὸ ὡρολόγι μου πηγαίνει ὀπίσω.—Τοῦ ἀδελφοῦ μου τὸ ὡρολόγι κρατεῖ πάντοτε καλὴν ὥραν.—Τώρα εἶνε ἀκριβῶς ἑπτὰ παρὰ εἴκοσι λεπτά.—Νομίζω ὅτι ἔχετε λάθος·—Εἶνε ἑπτὰ παρὰ εἰκοσιπέντε λεπτά.—Δὲν εἶν' ἔτσι;— Αὐτὴ εἶνε ἡ ἀκριβὴς (σωστὴ) ὥρα.—Τὸ τραῖνον θὰ φθάσῃ εἰς τὰς ἑπτὰ ἀκριβῶς.—Θὰ εἶνε ἐδῶ σὲ ὀλίγα λεπτά.—Θὰ μὲ ὑποχρεώσετε ἂν περιμένετε ὀλίγον.

Translate and read aloud in Greek:

What time is it, please?—It is eleven o'clock exactly.—I think it is ten minutes to eleven.—My watch is fast.—Your watch is slow.—That clock on the wall keeps good time always.—Will the train come soon?—I don't know. I think it will arrive in fifteen minutes.—The train will arrive at twenty minutes past eleven.—It is twenty-five past eleven now.—The train is very late. It is half an hour late.

Read aloud and try to give an answer in Greek:

Τί ὥρα εἶνε;—Τί ὥραν ἔχετε;—Ἔχετε τὴν σωστὴν ὥραν;—Τὸ ὡρολόγι σας πηγαίνει καλά;—Πηγαίνει ἐμπρὸς ἢ ὀπίσω;—Πότε θὰ φθάσῃ τὸ τραῖνο;—Θὰ φθάσῃ εἰς τὰς δώδεκα ἀκριβῶς;—Δὲν νομίζετε ὅτι τὸ τραῖνο ἔχει ἀργήσει;—Τί σημαίνει ἕνδεκα καὶ σαράντα-πέντε λεπτά;—Θέλετε νὰ περιμένετε ὀλίγα λεπτά;—Νομίζετε ὅτι θὰ ἔλθῃ τὸ τραῖνο ἐντὸς ὀλίγου;—Θὰ φύγετε τώρα;—Πότε θὰ φθάσετε εἰς τὴν πόλιν;—Ὅταν φθάσετε ἐκεῖ τί ὥρα θὰ εἶνε;

LESSON 36

Read aloud and translate in English:

Ποῖον περιμένετε ἐδῶ;—Περιμένω τὸν κύριον Ἀποστόλου.—Θὰ ἔλθῃ μὲ τὸ τραῖνον ποῦ φθάνει εἰς τὰς δώδεκα καὶ τέταρτον.—Θὰ ἔλθῃ καὶ ἡ κόρη του μαζύ του;—Δὲν γνωρίζω.—Νομίζω ὅτι ἡ κόρη του δὲν θὰ ἔρθῃ τώρα.—Νὰ τὸ τραῖνο, ἔρχεται.—Βλέπετε τοὺς φίλους σας;—Δὲν τοὺς βλέπω ἀκόμη.—Νομίζω ὅτι ὁ φίλος μου εἶνε ὁ πέμπτος κύριος ἀπὸ τὰ δεξιά.—Ναί.—Αὐτὸς εἶνε ὁ Κύριος Ἀποστόλου μαζὺ μὲ τὴν κόρην του.—Ποῖος εἶνε ὁ κύριος ποῦ περιπατεῖ μαζύ των—ὁ ἕκτος εἰς τὴν τρίτην σειράν;—Αὐτὸς εἶνε ὁ ἐξάδελφός των Γεώργιος.

Translate and read aloud in Greek:

The train has not come yet.—It will come in a little while.—Look there. It is coming.—Where are your friends?—I see them. They are looking at us. (Μᾶς κυττάζουν or μᾶς βλέπουν).—The gentleman who comes fourth from the end is Mr. Paul. — The lady who comes seventh on this side is his daughter Mary.—Have you known them very long?—I have known them for sixteen years. — They live at two hundred and twenty East Eighteenth Street.—Last year they lived at six hundred West Ninth Street.

Read aloud and try to give an answer in Greek:

Διατὶ περιμένετε ἐδῶ;—Τί ὥραν θὰ φθάσῃ τὸ τραῖνο ἀπὸ τὴν ἐξοχήν; —Ποίους περιμένετε;—Τοὺς γνωρίζετε πολὺν καιρόν;—Ποῦ μένουν τώρα;—Εἰς ποίαν ὁδὸν καὶ εἰς ποῖον ἀριθμὸν μένουν;—Ποῖος εἶνε ὁ τρίτος κύριος ἀπὸ τὸ τέλος;—Ποῦ μένει αὐτός;—Γνωρίζετε τὸ κατάστημά του;—Εἶνε εἰς τὸ βόρειον ἢ τὸ νότιον μέρος τῆς πόλεως;—Θὰ μείνῃ πολὺν καιρὸν μαζύ σας;—Γνωρίζετε τὸ τηλέφωνόν του;

LESSON 37

Read aloud and translate in English:

Πεινῶ.—Θέλω νὰ φάγω.—Γνωρίζετε κανὲν ξενοδοχεῖον ἐδῶ τριγύρω;—Δὲν ἔχω φάγει ὅλην τὴν ἡμέραν.—Γνωρίζω ἕνα ξενοδοχεῖον εἰς τὸν ἄλλον δρόμον.—Εἶνε καλὸν ξενοδοχεῖον;—Βέβαια.—Εἶνε πολὺ καλὸν ξενοδοχεῖον.—Ἐγὼ καὶ ἡ σύζυγός μου τρώγομεν ἐκεῖ κάθε Κυριακήν.—Ποῦ θέλετε νὰ καθήσωμεν;—Ἂς καθήσωμεν εἰς ἐκείνην τὴν πλευράν.—Ἐδῶ ἔρχεται πολὺς ἀέρας ἀπὸ τὸ παράθυρον.—Φοβεῖσθε μήπως πάρωμεν κρύο;

Translate and read aloud in Greek:

Let us see the bill of fare.—Waiter, will you give us the bill of fare, please?—With pleasure, sir. Here it is.—Is this your napkin?—No, I think it is yours. Will you have some soup?—Yes. I like soup, if it is good.—This soup is too hot. I cannot eat it yet.—It will be cold in a minute.—Please read the bill of fare for me.—I cannot read very well. I forgot my glasses this morning.

Read aloud and try to give an answer in Greek:

Πεινᾶτε;—Θέλετε νὰ φάγετε;—Ἀπὸ πότε ἔχετε νὰ φάγετε;—Γνωρίζετε κανὲν καλὸν μέρος ἐδῶ;—Ποῖον μέρος νομίζετε καλόν;—Ποῖον ξενοδοχεῖον γνωρίζετε εἰς τὸν ἄλλον δρόμον;—Ἐκεῖ τρώγετε πάντοτε;—Φοβεῖσθε τὸν ἀέρα;—Θέλετε νὰ κλείσω τὸ παράθυρο; — Ἔχετε πάρει κρύο;—Θέλετε νὰ σᾶς διαβάσω τὸν κατάλογον φαγητῶν;—Τί φαγητὰ ἔχει ὁ κατάλογος σήμερον;—Σᾶς ἀρέσει ἡ σοῦπα ἢ τὸ ψητό;—Διατὶ δὲν φορεῖτε τὰ γυαλιά σας σήμερα;

LESSON 38

Read aloud and translate in English:

Ἔχετε τίποτε νὰ φάγωμεν;—Μάλιστα (yes).—Ἔχομεν πολλὰ φαγητά.—Κυττάξατε τὸν κατάλογον, παρακαλῶ.—Εἶνε κάτω ἀπὸ τὴν πετσέταν σας.—Ἔχομεν ἀρνάκι ψητό, μοσχάρι μαγειρευμένο καὶ κάθε εἴδους μπριζόλες.—Ἐπίσης ἔχομεν φασόλια φρέσκα (fresh), τηγανητὲς πατάτες, καὶ ψάρια ψητά.—Ἔχετε κοτόπουλο ψητὸ ἢ βραστό;—Ἔχομε κοτόπουλο τῆς σχάρας.—Τί εἴδους σαλάτες ἔχετε;—Ἔχομε κάθε εἴδους σαλάτες.

Translate and read aloud in Greek:

What do you want to eat?—Do you like roast chicken?—Have you beefsteak or boiled potatoes?—We have everything.—Please look at the bill of fare. — I'll have lamb chops well done. — Will you have fried or boiled potatoes?—Give me fried potatoes, please.—I don't like boiled potatoes.—Will you have some sauce with your meat?—Will you have any dessert?—I'll take rice pudding and a cup of tea.

Read aloud and try to give an answer in Greek:

Θὰ φάγετε κάτι;—Τί θὰ φάγετε;—Τί ἀγαπᾶτε;—Ποῦ εἶναι ὁ κατάλογος φαγητῶν;—Τί φαγητὰ ἔχετε;—Ἔχετε ἀρνάκι ψητὸ ἢ κοτόπουλο βραστό;—Θέλετε μιὰ μπριζόλα καλοψημένη;—Ἀγαπᾶτε βραστὲς πατάτες ἢ τηγανητές;—Θέλετε ὀλίγην σάλτσαν;—Τί κρασὶ θὰ πίετε;—Ποῖος ἔχυσε κρασὶ ἐπάνω στὸ τραπεζομάνδηλον;—Θὰ πάρετε ριζόγαλο ἢ φροῦτο;—Θέλετε τὴν ζαχαριέρα νὰ βάλετε ὀλίγη ζάχαρη;—Εἶνε καλὸ αὐτὸ τὸ πεπόνι;—Θέλετε ἐπίσης μιὰ φέτα;

LESSON 39

Read aloud and translate in English:

Αὐτὰ τὰ ἀπίδια εἶνε γλυκά, ἀλλὰ ἐκεῖνα τὰ σταφύλια εἶνε γλυκότερα.—Τὸ μέλι εἶνε τὸ γλυκότερον πρᾶγμα ποῦ γνωρίζω.—Σήμερον εἶνε θερμοτέρα ἡμέρα παρὰ χθές.—Ἡ ἐργασία σου εἶνε δυσκολωτέρα ἢ ἡ ἰδική μου;—Ἡ ἰδική μου ἐργασία εἶνε δυσκολωτέρα.—Ποῖος εἶνε καλλίτερος ἄνθρωπος, ὁ ἰατρὸς ἢ ὁ κρεοπώλης;— Ὁ καλλίτερος ἄνθρωπος ἀπὸ ὅλους εἶνε ὁ ράπτης.—Τὸ πρᾶγμα ποὺ ἔκαμα ἐγὼ εἶνε κακόν, ἀλλὰ ἐκεῖνο ποὺ ἔκαμες σὺ εἶνε ἀκόμη χειρότερον.—Ὁ Γιάννης εἶνε δυνατὸς ἄνθρωπος.—Ὁ Γεώργιος εἶνε δυνατώτερος ἀπὸ τὸν Γιάννην.—Ὁ θεῖός μου εἶνε ὁ δυνατώτερος ἀπὸ ὅλους.

Translate and read aloud in Greek:

This thing is heavy; that thing is heavier.—Your work is easy, but mine is easier.—George's work is the easiest.—Helen is prettier than Mary.—John is more careful than George.—Paul is most careful.—My brother is bad; my sister is worse.—Your cousin is the worst boy in town.—To-day is cold, but yesterday it was colder.—The day before was the coldest day of the year.

Read aloud and try to give an answer in Greek:

Ποῖον πρᾶγμα εἶνε γλυκύτερον, ἡ ζάχαρη ἢ τὰ σταφύλια;—Ποῖος ἔχει περισσότερα χρήματα, ἡ ἀδελφή σου ἢ ἡ θεία σου;—Ποῖον εἶνε βαρύτερον, αὐτὸ τὸ μῆλο ἢ ἐκεῖνο τὸ ἀπίδι;—Ἐσὺ εἶσαι καλύτερος ἢ ὁ ἀδελφός σου;—Ποῖος εἶνε ὁ καλλίτερος ἄνθρωπος ἀπὸ ὅλους;—Ὁ γείτων εἶνε νεώτερος ἢ ἡ γειτόνισσα;—Διατὶ δὲν λέγεις τὴν ἀλήθειαν;—Ποῖος εἶπε ψεύματα, σὺ ἢ ὁ φίλος σου;—Ποῖον εἶνε τὸ βαρύτερον ἀπὸ αὐτὰ τὰ κιβώτια;—Μπορεῖς νὰ σηκώσῃς αὐτὸ τὸ τραπέζι;

LESSON 40

Read aloud and translate in English:

Εἰμπορεῖτε νὰ μοῦ ἀλλάξετε δέκα δολλάρια;—Ναί.—Ἐδῶ εἶνε πέντε δολλάρια, τρία μονά, δύο μισὰ δολλάρια, τρία τέταρτα, μία δεκάρα καὶ τρεῖς πεντάρες.—Τί ηὗρες στὸ πάτωμα;—Ηὗρα αὐτὴν τὴν καρφίτσαν.—Μήπως εἶνε ἰδική σας;—Ναί. Ἔπεσε (it fell) ἀπὸ τὸ φόρεμά μου.—Πόσον ἐπληρώσατε διὰ τὸ νέον σας φόρεμα;—Ἐπλήρωσα τρία δολλάρια μόνον.—Δὲν νομίζετε ὅτι εἶνε ἀρκετὰ εὐθηνά;—Ὅπως γνωρίζετε δὲν ἔχομεν πολλὰ χρήματα διὰ νὰ ἐξοδεύσωμεν.—Ὁ πατέρας εἶνε ἄρρωστος καὶ δὲν δύναται νὰ ἐργασθῇ.—Ὁ ἀδελφός μας εἶνε ἄεργος τρεῖς μῆνας τώρα.

Translate and read aloud in Greek:

Can you change a dollar for me? — I think I can. Do you want two quarters, three dimes and four nickels?—When did you buy this hat?—I bought it last month.—Why are you so happy to-day?—I am happy because I have found work. —I was idle for six months.—Your brother was here wearing (φορῶντας) a new ring.—He came to our house singing. He was very happy. Where did he get (ποῦ ηὗρε) that ring?—The ring is a present from his aunt.

Read aloud and try to give an answer in Greek:

Πόσα χρήματα ἔχετε μαζύ σας;—Μπορεῖτε νὰ ἀλλάξετε ἕν δολλάριον;—Ἠγοράσατε νέον ἐπανωφόρι.—Τί ἐπληρώσατε δι' αὐτό;—Δὲν νομίζετε ὅτι εἶνε εὐθηνά;—Νομίζετε ὅτι ἐξώδευσα πολλά;—Πόσα χρήματα οἰκονομεῖτε κάθε ἑβδομάδα;—Πόσον καιρὸν εἶνε ἄεργος ὁ πατέρας σου;—Ποῦ ἐπῆγες τρέχοντας;—Ποῖος ἦλθε ἐδῶ τραγουδῶντας;—Τίνος (whose) δῶρον εἶνε τὸ δακτυλίδι ποῦ φορεῖ ἡ ἀδελφή σου;—Ποῖος ἔδεσε αὐτὸ τὸ δέμα;—Ἐκτύπησες τὸ κουδοῦνι τῆς Κυρίας Παύλου;

LESSONS 41 — 45

Read aloud and give an answer in Greek:

—Ποῖος ἦτο ὁ Σόλων; — Τί ἦτο ἡ οἰκογένεια τοῦ Σόλωνος; — Πῶς εἶχε ὑπηρετήσει τὴν πατρίδα του ὁ Σόλων; — Τί ἐπίστευε καὶ τί ἔλεγε πάντοτε; — Ποῦ εἶχε ταξειδεύσει καὶ διατί; — Τί ἐγίνετο (was taking place) ἐκεῖνον τὸν καιρὸν εἰς τὰς 'Αθήνας; — Μεταξὺ ποίων ἐγίνοντο φιλονεικίαι; — Τί ἐζήτησαν ἀπὸ τὸν Σόλωνα οἱ 'Αθηναῖοι; — Τί ἔκαμε πρῶτον ὁ Σόλων; — Ποῖα χρέη κατήργησε; — Τί ἀπηγόρευσε; — Ποῖοι πολῖται εἶχον τὸ δικαίωμα νὰ ψηφίζουν; —Διὰ ποῖα ζητήματα ἀπεφάσιζαν ὅλοι οἱ πολῖται μαζύ; — Εἰς ποίου τὰς χεῖρας ἦτο ἡ ἐξουσία;— Τί ἦτο ὁ Ἄρειος Πάγος; — Ποίους ἐτιμώρει; — Τί ἐπέβλεπε; — Διατί ἄλλο ἐφρόντιζε; — Εἰς ποίαν ἡλικίαν ἐπήγαινον τὰ παιδιὰ εἰς τὸ σχολεῖον; — Τί ἐδιδάσκοντο τὰ παιδιὰ εἰς τὰ σχολεῖα; — Τί ὡρκίζοντο οἱ νέοι; — Τί ἔκαμε κατόπιν ὁ Σόλων; — Διατί ἔφυγεν ἀπὸ τὰς 'Αθήνας; — Ποῦ ἐπῆγε πρῶτον; — Ποῦ ἐπῆγε κατόπιν; — Τί ἦτο ἡ Λυδία; — Ποῖος ποταμὸς εὑρίσκετο ἐκεῖ; — Τί εἶχεν ἡ ἄμμος τοῦ ποταμοῦ αὐτοῦ; — Ποῖος ἦτο ὁ βασιλεὺς τῆς Λυδίας; — Ἦτο πολὺ πλούσιος ὁ Κροῖσος; — Τί ἔδειξεν εἰς τὸν Σόλωνα ὅταν ἐπεσκέφθη τὰ ἀνάκτορά του; — Τί ἠρώτησε κατόπιν τὸν Σόλωνα; — Τί ἀπήντησεν ὁ Σόλων; — Τί ἦτο ὁ Τέλλος καὶ πῶς ἀπέθανε; — Ἔμεινεν εὐχαριστημένος ὁ Κροῖσος ἀπὸ τὴν ἀπάντησιν τοῦ Σόλωνος; — Τί ἠρώτησεν ἔπειτα (afterwards) ; — Τί ἔκαμαν ὁ Κλέοβις καὶ ὁ Βίτων; — Ποῦ ἐτράβηξαν τὴν ἅμαξαν μὲ τὴν μητέρα των; — Πῶς ἀπέθανον οἱ δύο καλοὶ ἀδελφοί; — Τί ἠρώτησε κατόπιν ὁ Κροῖσος; — Τί ἀπήντησεν ὁ Σόλων; — Ἤρεσε (was pleasing) ἡ ἀπάντησις τοῦ Σόλωνος εἰς τὸν Κροῖσον; — 'Ελησμόνησε διὰ πολὺν καιρὸν τοὺς λόγους τοῦ Σόλωνος ὁ Κροῖσος; —Εἰς τὸν πόλεμον ἐναντίον τῶν Περσῶν ποῖος ἐνικήθη; — Ποῖος συνελήφθη αἰχμάλωτος; — Ποῦ ἔβαλαν τὸν Κροῖσον καὶ διατί; — Τί ἐνθυμήθη τότε ὁ βασιλεὺς τῆς Λυδίας; — Τί ἐφώναξε; — Τί ἐρώτησε τότε ὁ Κῦρος; — Ποίαν ἱστορίαν διηγήθη ὁ Κροῖσος εἰς τὸν Κῦρον; — Τί ἔκαμε ὁ Κῦρος ἀφοῦ ἤκουσε τὴν ἱστορίαν τοῦ Κροίσου;

GREEK - ENGLISH VOCABULARY

(Numbers Refer to Lessons)

A

ἀγαπῶ, l love, l like, 12.
'Αγγλικά, English, 33.
ἅγιος, holy, saint, 14.
ἀγοράζω, l buy, 23.
ἀγών, struggle, contest, 44.
ἀδειανός, empty, 10.
ἀδελφή, sister, 3.
ἀδελφός, brother, 3.
ἄδικος, wrong, unjust, 14.
ἄεργος, ἀργός, idle, 40.
ἀδύνατος, weak, 39.
ἀέρας, ἀήρ, air, 27.
'Αθηναῖος, Athenian, 41.
ἄθλιος, miserable, 41.
ἀθλιότης, misery, 41.
αἴθουσα, parlor, 22.
αἰχμάλωτος, prisoner, 45.
ἀκάθαρτος, dirty, 14.
ἀκόμη, yet, 29.
ἀκούω, l hear, 18.
ἀκριβός, expensive, dear, 10.
ἀκριβῶς, exactly, 35.
ἅλας, ἁλάτι, salt, 2.
ἀλεποῦ, fox, 22.
ἀλεῦρι, flour, 23.
ἀληθής, true, 39, 45.
ἀλήθεια, truth, 39.
ἀλλά, but, 8.
ἀλλαγή, change, 43.
ἀλλάζω, l change, 40.
ἄλλος, -λη, -λο, other, 14.
ἄλογον, horse, 11.
ἅμαξα, carriage, 44.
ἁμάξι, carriage, 44.
'Αμερικανός, American, 33.
'Αμερική, America, 33.
ἄμμος, sand, 43.
ἄν καί, although, 36.
ἀναγκάζω, l compel, 43.
ἀνάγνωσις, reading, 43.
ἀνακούφισις, relief, 41.
ἀνάκτορον, palace, 43.
ἀνατολή, east, sunrise, 36.
ἀνατολικός, east, eastern, 36.
ἄνευ, without, 44.
ἄνθρωπος, man, 3.
ἄνθρωποι, men, people, 28.
ἀνοίγω, l open, 23.
ἄνω, above, over, 42.
ἀνώτατος, highest, supreme, 42.
ἀξίζει, it costs, 24.
ἀπαγορεύω, l prohibit, 42.
ἀπάντησις, answer, 44.
ἀπαντῶ, l reply, l meet, 44.
ἀπέναντι, opposite, 37.
ἀπίδι, pear, 22.
ἀπό, from, of, 16.
ἀπό, than, 39.
ἀπόγευμα, afternoon, 30.
ἀποθνήσκω, l die, 44.
ἀποφασίζω, l decide, 42.
ἀπόψε, tonight, 32.
ἀργά, late, slowly, 29.
ἀργός, slow, late, 29.
ἄργυρος, silver, 25.
ἀργῶ, l am late, l am slow, 35.
Ἄρειος Πάγος, Areopagus, 42.
ἀρέσω, l like, 12.
ἀριθμοί, numbers (11-22), 33; (30-2000), 34. ordinal, 36.
ἄριστος, best, 41.
ἀρκετός, enough, 28.
ἀρνάκι, lamb, 38.
ἄρρωστος, ill, sick, 4.
ἀρχαῖος, ancient, old, 41.
ἀσῆμι, silver, 25.
ἀσημένιος, of silver, 25.
ἄσπρος, white, 12.
ἄς ὑπάγωμεν, let us go, 30.
ἄτιμος, dishonest, 39.
αὐγό, egg, 21.
αὔριον, tomorrow, 17.
αὐτός, this, 4, 9.
αὐτί, ear, 18.
ἀφήνω, l let, l leave, 32.

B'

βαθύς deep, 39.
βάλλω, βάνω, βάζω, l put, 13.
βαμβακερός, of cotton, 25.
βαμβάκι, cotton, 25.
βανάνα, banana, 22.
βαρύνομαι, l am wearied, 41.
βαρύς, heavy, 39.
βασιλεύς, king, 43, 45.
βασιλικός, royal, 41.
βγάλλω, βγάνω, βγάζω,, l put out, l take off, 13.
βέβαια, certainly, 17.
βιβλίον, book, 7.
βίος, life, 41.
βλάξ, βλάκας, stupid, 14.
βλέπω, l see, 5, 12, 16.
βοηθῶ, l help, 31.
βορρᾶς, north, 36.
βόρειος, north, northern, 36.
βούτυρο, butter, 2.
βράδυ, evening, 20.
βράζω, l boil, 38.
βρέχω, l wet, 27.
βρέχει, it rains, 27.
βροχή, rain, 27.
βῶδι, ox, 44.
βωδινόν, beef, 38.

Γ

γάτα, cat, 7.
γάλα, milk, 2.
γαλανός, blue, 22.
Γάλλος, Frenchman, 33.
γειά σου, hello, 19.
γείτων, γειτόνισσα, neighbor, 39.
γελέκο, vest, 13.
γεμᾶτος, full, 10.
γενναῖος, brave, 43.
γενναίως, bravely, 43.
γεννημένος, born, 33.
γέρων, γέρος, old, old man, 14, 44.

γεῦμα μικρόν, lunch, 37.
Γεώργιος, George, 19.
Γιάννης, John, 4.
γιατρός, doctor, 22.
γίνομαι, I become, 28.
γλυκά, sweets, candies, 21.
γλυκός, sweet, 8.
γλυκύς, γλυκύτερος, γλυκύτατος, sweet, sweeter, sweetest, 39.
γλῶσσα, tongue, 19.
γνωρίζω, I know, 16.
γραῖα, old woman, 14.
γράμμα, letter, 28.
γραφή, writing, 43.
γράφω, I write, 41.
γρηά, old woman, 14.
γρήγορα, quickly, soon, 29.
γρήγορος, quick, fast, 29.
γυαλί, glass, 37.
γυαλιά, glasses, 37.
γυιός, son, 25.
γυμναστική, gymnastics, 43.
γυναῖκα, woman, 3.
γυρίζω, I turn, I return, 32.

Δ

δακτυλίδι, ring, 40.
δάκτυλον, finger, 19.
δεικνύω, δείχνω, I show, 43.
δεῖπνον, supper, 26.
δέκα, ten, 24.
δεκάρα, dime, 40.
δέμα, package, 40.
δὲν εἶνε ἔτσι; isn't it so? 26.
δένω, I tie, 40.
δέρμα, leather, 26.
δερμάτινος, leather, of leather, 26.
δεσποινίς, miss, 6.
Δευτέρα, Monday, 32.
δῆμος, citizens, people, 42.
δημόσιος, public, 42.
διαβάζω, etc., I read, 12, 37.
διάδρομος, corridor, hall, 22.
διασκέδασις, fun, amusement, 27.
διατί, why, 10.
διδάσκω, I teach, 43.
διδάσκομαι, I am taught, 43.
δίδω, etc., I give, 6, 10, 15.
διηγοῦμαι, I narrate, 45.
δίκαιος, right, just, 14.
δικαίωμα, right, 42.
δικαστήριον, court, 42.
διότι, because, 10.
διπλός, double, 40.
διψῶ, etc., I am thirsty, 21.
διώκω, I drive away, 44.
διώχνω, I drive away, 44.
δοκιμάζω, I try, 39.
δόξα, glory, 43.
δολλάριον, dollar, 24.
δόντι, tooth, 18.
δός μου, give me, 2.
δουλειά, work, business, 33.
δουλεία, slavery, 42.
δοῦλος, δούλη, slave, 42.
δρόμος, street, road, 9.
δύναμαι, I can, 18, 31.
δυνατός, strong, 39.
δύο, two, 11.
δυσαρεστῶ, I displease, 43.
δύσις, west, sunset, 36.
δύσκολος, hard, difficult, 39.
δυτικός, west, western, 36.
δωμάτιον, room, 9.
δῶρον, present, gift, 40.

E

ἐάν, if, 6.
ἑβδομάς, ἑβδομάδα, week, 28.
ἐγώ, I, myself, 1.
ἐδῶ, here, 3.
ἔθιμον, custom, habit, 41.
εἶδος, kind, 26. Τί εἴδους, of what kind? 26.
εἰκών, εἰκόνα, picture, 30.
εἶμαι, etc., I am, 3.
εἰμπορῶ, etc., I can, I may, 18.
εἰρήνη, peace, 42.
εἰρηνικά, peacefully, 44.
εἰρηνικός, peaceful, 44.
εἰς, σέ, σ', in, at, to, on, 5.
εἶχα, etc., I had, 15.
ἐκεῖ, there, 3.
ἐκεῖνος, -η, -ο, that, 9.
ἐκκλησία, church, assembly, 42.
ἔλα, ἐλᾶτε, come, 4.
ἐλαφρός, light, 39.
ἐλάχιστος, least, 39.
Ἑλένη, Helen, 22.
ἐλεύθερος, free, 32.
Ἑλλάς, Greece, 33.
Ἕλλην, Greek, 33.
ἐμεῖς (ἡμεῖς), we, 4.
ἐμπρός, forward, fast, 35.
ἕν ἄλλο, another, 14.
ἐναντίον, against, 42.
ἐνάρετος, virtuous, upright, 43.
ἕνας, μία, ἕνα, one, a, 1.
ἕνας ἄλλος, another, 14.
ἐνθυμοῦμαι, I remember, 45.
ἐννέα, nine, 24.
ἐννοῶ, I understand, 33.
ἐνοίκιον, rent, 34.
ἐντελῶς, entirely, fully, 28.
ἐντὸς ὀλίγου, in a little while, 35.
ἐν τούτοις, however, 45.
ἐντύπωσις, impression, 45.
ἐνωρίς, early, 30.
ἕξ, six, 24.
ἐξάδελφος, -φη, cousin, 31.
ἐξοδεύω, I spend, 40.
ἐξουσία, authority, 42.
ἐξοχή, country, 17.
ἔξυπνος, smart, witty, 14.
ἔξω, out, outside, 3.
ἐπάνω, up, on, upstairs, 3.
ἐπάνω, above, over, 42.
ἐπάνω στό, on the, 9.
ἐπανωφόρι, overcoat, 13.
ἐπιβλέπω, I supervise, 42.
ἐπιδόρπιον, dessert, 38.
ἐπίπεδος, level, flat, 40.
ἐπίσης, also, 23.
ἐπισκέπτομαι, I visit, 43.
ἐπιστρέφω, I return, 31.
ἑπόμενος, next, following, 43.
ἑπτά, seven, 24.
ἐργάζομαι, etc., I work, 18, 20, 32.
ἐργασία, work, 20.
ἐργάτης, workman, 11.
ἐργοστάσιον, factory, 20.
ἔρχομαι, etc., I come, 16.
ἐρχόμενος, coming, 32.
ἐρωτῶ, etc., I ask, 24.
ἑσπέρα, evening, 20.
ἐστάθην, I stood, 30.
ἑστιατόριον, restaurant, 37.
ἐσχάρα (σκάρα), grate, 38.
ἕτοιμος, ready, 29.
ἔτος, year, 32.
ἔτσι, so, thus, 26.
εὐθηνός, cheap, 26.
εὔκολος, easy, 39.
εὔμορφος, pretty, 26.
εὑρίσκω, etc. I find, 29.

εὐτυχής, happy, 28.
εὐχαριστημένος, pleased, 27.
εὐχαρίστησις, pleasure, 40.
εὐχαριστῶ, I thank, 40.
ἔφαγα, I ate, 18.
ἐφαρμογή, fitting, 42.
ἐφέτος, this year, 17.
ἔχω, etc., I have, 1, 2.
ἔχω ἄδικον, I am wrong, 14.
ἔχω δίκαιον, I am right, 14.
ἕως, till, until, 28.

Z

ζάχαρι, sugar, 5.
ζαχαριέρα, sugar bowl, 38.
ζεστός, hot, warm, 19, 37, 39.
ζευγάρι, pair, couple, 25.
ζηλεύω, I envy, I am jealous,40.
ζήτημα, matter, question, 42.
ζητῶ, I ask, I look for, 33, 37.
ζῶ, etc., I live, 27.
ζωή, life, 41.
ζωντανός, alive, 45.

H

ἤ, or, 6.
ἤ, than, 39.
ἡλικία, age, 43.
ἦλθον, I came, 16.
ἡμεῖς, ἐμεῖς, 'μεῖς, we, 4.
ἡμέρα, day, 20.
ἤμην, ἦσο, etc., I was, 16.
ἠμπορῶ, I can, I may, 18.
ἠξεύρω, etc., I know, 20.
ἠρχόμην, I was coming, 16.

Θ

θά, (future tense), 17.
θάνατος, death, 44.
θεῖος, uncle, 39.
θεία, aunt, 39.
θέλω, I want, I wish, 5, 15.
θερμός, warm, 37, 39.
θέσις, place, position, 34.
θέτω, I place, 45.
θησαυρός, treasure, 43.
θυγάτηρ,θυγατέρα,daughter,25.
θυμώνω, I get angry, 44.
θυμωμένος,angered, angry, 44.
θύρα, door, 23.

I

ἰατρός, doctor, 22.
ἰδικός, μου, etc., my, mine, 25.
ἰδικός σου, -του, -της, -μας.
ἴδιος, same, 12.
ἰδιωτικός, private, 42.
ἴσιος, straight, 40.
ἱστορία, story, 45.
'Ιταλός, Italian, 33.

K

καθαρός, clean, 14.
κάθε, every, each, 33.
καθέκλα, chair, 11.
κάθημαι, etc., I sit, 21, 37.
κάθησε, καθήσατε, sit down, 4.
καθρέπτης, mirror, 11,
καί, and, 1.
καινούργιος, new, 13.
καίομαι, I am burned, 45.
καιρός, weather; time; 27.
καίω, I burn, 45.
κακός, bad, 3.
κακοῦργος, criminal, 42.
καλά, well, 4.
καλημέρα, good morning, 20.
καληνύκτα, good night, 20.
καλησπέρα, good evening, 20.
κάλλιστος, best, 41.
καλλίτερα, better, 13.
καλλίτερος, better, 13.
καλλίτερος, κάλλιστος, better, best, 39.
καλός, good, 3.
καλοψημένος, well done, 38.
κάλτσα, stocking, sock, 25.
κάμε γρήγορα, hurry, make haste, 29.
καμμία, no one, any one, 8.
κάμνω, etc. I do, I make, 10, 15.
κανείς, nobody, anybody, 8, 22, 37.
κανέν, none, anything, 8.
κανών, rule, 41.
καπέλλο, hat, 13.
κάποιος, someone, 22.
κἄπως, somehow, 40.
καρβέλι, loaf, 24.
κάρβουνα, coal, 19.
κάρρον, wagon, car, 11.
καρφίτσα, pin, 40.
καρφώνω, I nail, I stick, 40.
καστανός, brown, 22.
κατάγομαι, I come from, 33.
κατάλογος φαγητῶν, bill of fare, 37.
καταργῶ, I cancel, 42.
κατάστημα, store, 36.
κάτι, something, 6.
κατόπιν, after, afterwards, 24.
κάτω, down, downstairs, 3.
κάτω ἀπό, under, 37.
καφές, coffee, 5.
κέκι, cake, 38.
κερδίζω, I win, I earn, 34.
κεφαλή, head, 18.
κεφάλι, head, 13.
κιβώτιον, box, 26.
κινοῦμαι, I am moved, I move, 39.
κινῶ, I move, 39.
κίτρινος, yellow, 22.
κλείω, κλείνω, I shut, I close, 23
κοιλάς, valley, 42.
κοιμῶμαι, etc., I sleep, 29, 32.
κόκκινος, red, 22.
κολλάρο, collar, 14.
κολύμβημα, swimming, 43.
κόπτω, etc., I cut, 40.
κόρη, girl, 1.
κόσμος, world, 39.
κοτολέττα, cutlet, 38.
κοτόπουλον, chicken, 38.
κουδοῦνι, bell, 40.
κουζίνα, kitchen, 33.
κουμπί, button, 13.
κουρασμένος, tired, 32.
κουτάλι, spoon, 21.
κουτί, box, 19.
κρασί, wine, 2.
κράτος, state, 42.
κρατῶ, etc., I hold, I keep, 35.
κρέας, meat, 1.
κρεββάτι, bed, 11.
κρεοπώλης, butcher, 22,
κρομμύδι, κρεμμύδι, onion, 24.
κρυολόγημα, cold, 20.
κρύος, cold, 19.
κρυώνω, etc., I feel cold, 19.
κτυπῶ, etc., I hit, I knock, 40.
κυρία, madam, Mrs., 6.
κυρία, lady, 26.
Κυριακή, Sunday, 32.
κύριε, sir, Mr., 6.
κύριος, gentleman, 38.
κυττάζω, etc., I look, 11.
κώδων, bell, 44.